About t

Georgette Heyer novels for
tastes as a teenager. But her
she was given a pile of Mills & Boons to read after she
had had her wisdom teeth extracted! Filled with strong
painkillers, she imagined that she could pen one too.
Many drafts later, Sophia thinks she has the perfect job
writing for Mills & Boon Historical as well as taking art
tours to Europe with her husband, who is a painter.

Regency Rebels

Regency Rebels:

A Convenient Arrangement

SOPHIA JAMES

MILLS & BOON

First Published in Great Britain 2023
By Mills & Boon, an imprint of HarperCollins*Publishers* Ltd,
1 London Bridge Street, London, SE1 9GF

www.harpercollins.co.uk

HarperCollins*Publishers*
Macken House, 39/40 Mayor Street Upper,
Dublin 1, D01 C9W8, Ireland

Regency Rebels: A Convenient Arrangement © 2023
Harlequin Enterprises ULC.

Marriage Made in Money © 2015 Sophia James
Marriage Made in Shame © 2015 Sophia James

ISBN: 978-0-263-32047-3

MARRIAGE MADE
IN MONEY

This book is dedicated to my writing friend, Lizzie Tremayne, who helped me to understand the anatomy of horses and the joy of working with them.

Chapter One

London—June 1810

Amethyst Amelia Cameron's father loved all horses, but he especially loved his matching pair of greys.

'I doubt you will ever see others as fine, Papa, if you do indeed intend to sell them.' Amethyst tried to keep the worry from her voice as the carriage drew to a halt in the narrow lane outside number ten, Grosvenor Place. Things were changing without reason and she didn't like it.

'Well, there's the problem, my dear,' Robert Cameron replied. 'I had the best and now I want for nothing more. Take your mother, for instance. Never found another like her. Would not even have tried to.'

Amethyst smiled. Her parents' marriage had been a love match until the day her mother had died of some undefined and quick illness, seven hours short of her thirty-second birthday. Amethyst had been all of eight and she remembered the day distinctly, the low whispers and the tears; storm clouds sweeping across the Thames.

'I do not think you should part with the pair, Papa. You can easily afford to keep them. You could afford ten times as many; every stallion and mare here in the Tattersall's sales for the next month, should you want.' Looking across the road at the generous roofs of the auction house, she wished her father might order the carriage homewards, where they could talk the matter over at their leisure.

It was not like him to decide on a course of action so quickly and she hoped he might have second thoughts and withdraw his favoured greys before the Monday sales the following week.

Yet as her father hoisted himself from the carriage his breathlessness was obvious, even such a small movement causing him difficulty. The unease Amethyst had felt over the past weeks heightened, though the sight of a man alighting from a conveyance ahead caught her attention.

After the dreadful *débâcle* of her marriage Amethyst had seldom noticed the opposite sex, shame and guilt having the effect of greying out passion. But this man was tall and big with it, the muscles beneath his superfine coat pointing to something other than the more normal indolence the *ton* seemed to excel at. He looked dangerous and untamed.

His dress marked him as an aristocrat, but his wild black hair was longer than most other men wore theirs, falling almost to his collar, the darkness highlighted by white linen. An alarming and savage beauty. She saw others turn as he walked past and wondered what it must be like to be so very visible, so awfully obvious.

'Have Elliott send the carriage back for me around two, my dear, for I am certain that will give me enough time.' Her father's words pulled her from her musing and, dragging her eyes from the stranger, she hoped Robert had not noticed her interest. 'But make sure that you have a restful time of it, too, for you have been looking tired of late.'

Shutting the door, he encouraged the conveyance on before placing his hat on his head. His new coat was not quite fitting across his shoulders where a month ago it had been snug.

Amethyst caught her reflection in the glass as the carriage began to move. She looked older than her twenty-six years and beaten somehow. By life and by concern. Her father's actions had made her tense; after visiting his physician in London a week ago he had taken his horses straight to Tattersall's, claiming that he did not have the time for livestock he once had enjoyed.

A shock of alarm crawled up her arms and into her chest as she saw her father in conversation with the same man she had been watching. Did her father know him? What could they be speaking of? Craning her neck to see more of their engagement, she was about to turn away when the stranger looked up, his glance locking with hers across the distance.

Green. His eyes were pale green and tinged with arrogance. In shock she broke the contact, wondering about the fact that her heart was beating at twice its normal rate.

'Ridiculous,' she muttered and made certain not to look his way again. Tapping her hand hard against the roof, she was also glad when the carriage slowed to its usual speed of just above walking pace.

Lord Daniel Wylde, the sixth Earl of Montcliffe, came to Tattersall's quite regularly just to see what was on offer. Today with the sales about to begin the place was crowded.

'Ye'd be a man who knows his horseflesh, no doubt?' An older man spoke to him as they mounted the steps, no mind for introduction or proper discourse. 'My greys are up and I'd want them to go to someone who would care for their well-being.'

His accent marked him as an East-Ender, the music of the river in his words. A man made rich by the trade of goods and services, perhaps, for his coat was of fine cloth and his boots well fashioned. The well-appointed carriage he had alighted from was beginning to move away, a young woman staring back at them with concern upon her face, but Daniel's interest was snared by the mention of the greys. The superb pair he had seen yesterday belonged to this unlikely fellow? They were the entire reason he was here this morning after all, just to see who might be lucky enough to procure them.

The Repository courtyard at Tattersall's loomed, substantial pillars holding up wide verandas and housing a great number of animals and carriages.

'Your horses aren't on the block today?' Daniel could see no sign of the greys and it was more usual for those lots about to go under the hammer to be on display, especially ones so fine.

'I asked Mr Tattersall for a few days' grace just to think about things,' the other man returned, his cheeks yellowed, but his eyes sharp. 'To give me time, you understand, in case I should change my direction. The prerogative of the elderly,' he added, a wide smile showing off a set of crooked teeth.

Daniel knew he should turn and leave the man, with his roughness of speech and the impossible manners of the trading classes, but something made him stay. The sort of desperation that one perceives in the eyes of a person battling the odds, he was to think later, when all the cards had been stacked up into one long, straight and improbable line. But back then he did not have the facts of the stranger's most singular purpose.

'My name is Mr Robert Cameron. Timber merchant.' No shame or hesitation in the introduction.

'Daniel Wylde.' He could do nothing less than offer his own name, though he did not add the title.

The other man did it for him. 'You are the Earl of Montcliffe? I saw the insignia upon your carriage outside and Mr Tattersall himself pointed your personage out to me here last week as a man who knows his way around a horse.'

'Indeed.' Even with the frosty tone of the reply Cameron seemed unfazed.

'My greys are this way, my lord. Would you do me the honour of looking them over?'

'I am not in the market for a purchase.' Hell and damnation, there was no untruth in that, he thought, his hands fisting in his pockets with the sort of rage he had almost become accustomed to. Noticing others looking his way, Daniel tried to soften his face.

'But you are renowned for your knowledge of a fine buy in horseflesh and it is that I seek to be assured of. I was only hoping for the chance of an expert's opinion.'

They had passed beneath the roof delineating the courtyard now and had wandered down into the stables proper. It was darker here and a lot less busy. When the ground unexpectedly fell away the old man tripped, Daniel's arm steadying him before he lost balance completely.

'Thank you, my lord.' Cameron's voice was quieter and the flesh beneath the finely made coat felt alarmingly thin. Life had honed his instincts and Daniel's were on high alert. This man was not quite as he seemed and he wondered at what was hidden.

'Here they are. Maisey and Mick. After my parents, you understand, though they will not be billed as such here. Names of high distinction fetch more in the way of coinage, I am told, and so Mr Tattersall thinks to call them after ancient Grecian gods.'

The greys were of Arabian descent, their distinctive head shapes and high-tailed carriage unmistakable. The horses were small and refined, and Daniel could have picked their lineage out easily from a thousand others.

'Richard Tattersall is a shrewd operator so perhaps you should listen to what he says if you wish to part with them. I know my brother always paid through the nose here,' Daniel remarked.

Gnarled fingers were held against the jibbah bulge on the horse's forehead, and it was easy to see that there was no lack of love between the animal and its master as the horse nuzzled closer.

'Maisie finds any change difficult.' The catch in his voice suggested he did too.

'Why are you selling them, then? If you bred them, you could turn a tidy profit without too much work in it. A few years and the money could be double what a sale now would garner.'

'Time is a commodity I am a little short on, my lord.' The reply was grave. 'But you sound like my daughter.'

'The woman in the carriage?' Why the hell had he said that? He wished he might take such a question back.

'My beautiful jewel.'

Again Daniel was shocked. In his circle it was not done to talk of progeny in such glowing terms.

'Are you married, my lord?' Another impertinence. Did Mr Robert Cameron always speak without thought?

'No. Too busy saving England.' He knew he should adopt a sterner demeanour, but the man was beguiling in his lack of protocol. The memory of a soldier he had once known came to mind. A man who had served with him and saved his life before losing his own on the high hills of Penasquedo. He shook away ennui. Of late the emotion seemed to have hitched a ride upon his shoulders, crouching over everything he said and did; a result of the problems at Montcliffe Manor probably

and the cursed debts that had piled up in the years between his father's indifference and his brother's high-
stakes gambling.

The other looked relieved at his answer.

'A parent would do almost anything to keep a child
happy, you understand?'

'Indeed, I should imagine such a thing to be so.'

'I would give my horses without a moment's hesitation to a husband who had the wherewithal to make
my girl smile.'

'A generous gift.' Where was this conversation leading? Daniel wondered, as a small seed of worry began
to grow.

'I was married myself for twelve long and happy
years before my wife passed on. Well before her time
too, I should say, and for a while...' He stopped and
brought out a large white kerchief to dab his face with.
'For a while I thought to follow. The world is a lonely
place to be without the love of a good woman and it
was the nights that were the worst.' Shrewdness lurked
above sorrow in Robert Cameron's eyes.

The stallion had now come over for its share of attention and Daniel had seldom seen another of its ilk;
leanly muscled and compact, he was built for endur-
ance, head turned towards him and darkly intelligent
eyes watchful. If he had had the money he would have
placed it down right then and there because he knew
without a doubt that offspring from these two would
soon be worth a small fortune on any market in the
world.

'Where did you get them?'

'In Spain. Near Bilbao. I had heard of them and went over to look. Fell in love at first glance and brought them back three years ago.'

'Don't sell them cheap, then. If you hold out for your price, their worth will be increased,' Daniel advised.

'You wouldn't be interested in purchasing them yourself?'

This was not said with any intention at rudeness. It was just a passing comment, a friendly gesture to a stranger. Of course Cameron would think the Montcliffe coffers full. Everybody still did.

He shook his head. If he could have raised the money, he would have bid for the pair in a trice, but that sort of life was finished and had been for a while now. He noticed a few other patrons drifting down to take a look at the greys. And then more came. However, Robert Cameron did not seem the slightest bit interested in singing the praises of his horseflesh any longer which was surprising, given the hard line he had taken just a moment before.

As the crowds thickened Daniel tipped his hat at the timber merchant and made his way out of the crush.

Three-quarters of an hour later, he was glad to sit down on the comfortable seat of his carriage. His right leg ached today more than it had in months and he knew that the bullet would have to be removed before too much longer. The Montcliffe physician had told him that time and time again, but the worry of being left a cripple was even worse than the pain that racked through him each time he stepped on it.

Throwing his hat on the seat, Daniel leant back into the leather and ran his fingers through his hair. It was too damn long and he would cut it tonight after a bath. His valet had once done the job, but Daniel had let him go, as he had had to do with other staff both at the town house and at Montcliffe.

He cursed Nigel again as he did almost every day now, his brother's lack of care of the family inheritance beyond all comprehension. One should not think ill of the dead, he knew, but it was hard to find generous thought when any new debt now joined the pile of all the others.

A sudden movement caught his attention and he focused on a group in a narrow alleyway off Hyde Park Corner. Four or five men circled around another and it was with a shock that he realised the one in the middle was the timber merchant, Mr Robert Cameron.

Banging on the roof of the conveyance, he threw open the door and alighted quickly as it stopped. Twenty paces had him amidst the ruckus and he saw the old man's nose streamed with blood.

'Let him go.' Raising his cane, he brought it down hard on the hand of the man closest to him as the scoundrel reached inside his coat for something. A howl of pain echoed and a knife dropped harmlessly to the cobbles, spinning on its own axis with the movement.

'Anyone else want a try?' He knew he had the upper hand as the thugs backed off, yelling obscenities at him, but nothing else. They were gone before he counted to ten and there was only silence in the street.

Cameron was leaning over as though in pain, his right arm held to his chest.

'What hurts?'

'My…pride.' As he straightened Daniel saw the grimace on his face.

'Did you know them?'

The older man nodded. 'They have been demanding money from me.'

'Why?'

'My business is lucrative and they want a slice. One of their number also used to work for me in the warehouse until I fired him for stealing and I suspect he holds a grudge.' He dabbed at his nose with his dislodged shirt tails. 'If you had not come…'

'I will take you home if you give me your direction.'

As Cameron was about to argue Daniel called his driver down from the high seat to give a hand and ten minutes later they were pulling up in front of a large town house in Grosvenor Square.

No little fortune here then, Daniel thought, as he helped Cameron out. He noticed blood had left a stain on the leather seat at about the same time as the other did.

'If you wait, I will find coinage to cover the cost of the cleaning.'

'It is of no significance.'

Cameron was now leaning on him heavily and he could feel the shaking of fright beginning to settle. As they came to the front door the sound of running feet was heard.

'Are you hurt?' Worry coated the voice of the

woman who came into view, the same woman he had seen in the carriage, anger on her face creasing it badly. Cameron's daughter by his own admission, though she looked nothing at all like him.

'What on earth happened?' She reached his side and all but pulled her father out of Daniel's grasp, the sharp edge of a fingernail carving skin away from his wrist. If she noticed, she did not show it, merely helping her father backwards to a sofa that was perched to one side of the wide lobby.

'Sit down. You look blue around the mouth.' Her own mouth was a tight line of consternation, her dark eyes flashing up at Daniel in question. 'Who did this?'

'A group of blackguards waylaid him not far from Tattersall's.'

'You did not wait for the carriage, Papa. You said to send it at two, did you not?' As if on cue the big clock in another corner struck the half hour of one-thirty.

'I h-had done all I needed to at the auction house.'

'You sold the horses?' A new tone entered her voice, one of censure and irritation. Lord, the girl was a harpy and with no introduction Daniel was hard pressed to say anything.

Robert Cameron was shaking his head and looking worse by the moment. 'The Earl of Montcliffe here helped me and brought me home. Lord Montcliffe, may I present my daughter, Amethyst Amelia Cameron, to you.'

Amethyst? His jewel? She did not suit such a name at all with her dark eyes and angry mouth. Her hair was a strange lustreless brown pulled back into a bun that was fashioned in the most unflattering of styles.

As if she could read his mind her expression tightened and she barely acknowledged the introduction. The clothes she wore were serviceable homespun without embellishment. The sort of dress one might wear to a dowdy funeral, the cloth of black showing up her skin as sallow and underlining the smudged circles beneath her eyes as dark bruises.

She was not a beauty, but she was not plain either. Beneath the downcast glance he caught a flash of anger, abrupt and sudden.

Tipping his head at her, he was surprised when she flushed a bright beet red, though she looked away, ringing for the butler to fetch a physician immediately.

Efficient and calm now, save for the remaining stain of red on her cheeks which made her look vulnerable. He wanted to lay his hand upon her arm and tell her... what? He shook the thought away and concentrated on her father, whose eyes were glued to his daughter, a speculative glance within them.

'I hope you will recover without any ill effects, sir,' Daniel said. 'If you wish to take such an assault further with the law and need verification of exactly what I saw, you may call on me.'

Extracting his card from a thin leather holder in his pocket, he handed it over.

'Thank you for your help, Lord Montcliffe, I have appreciated it greatly.'

Acknowledging the gratitude, Daniel turned to leave, though the daughter, after fumbling in a drawer to one side of the room, came forth with a wad of bank notes.

'I hope this might help in the way of thanks.' Her voice was no longer shrill, but the insult of payment was all Daniel could think of.

Without another word he turned and walked from the room, the butler hurrying to show him the way out.

'Perhaps I insulted him, Papa, by offering him re-imbursement for his trouble?' Amethyst looked down at the substantial sum in her hands. Every other member of her acquaintance would have taken it and with the thankfulness that was intended, but not the Earl of Montcliffe.

She was irritated with herself for allowing such an awkward meeting, but she had been more than sur-prised to see the man outside the Tattersall's auction rooms right here in their town house. She knew Lord Montcliffe had noticed her embarrassment and she chastised herself for even thinking of giving him re-imbursement for a deed of honour.

Such a reward belittled the act, she supposed, by reducing it to terms of cold hard cash. She had heard that the *ton* rarely even carried money, the tarnish of trade and commerce resting instead with their accom-panying helpers and sycophants.

Traders and merchants. Even with a princely sum made from hard work, good luck and risky ventures, the Camerons would not be accepted into any of the higher echelons of society.

Well, she could not care. No doubt Lord Montcliffe

would be mulling over his encounter with them on the carriage ride home before sharing the story of her clumsy attempt at recompense with his peers at some exclusive 'members only' club in the nicer areas of the city. She was so very glad he was gone.

'You need to inform the constabulary of this assault, Papa. You cannot keep pretending that this matter will simply disappear.'

'You think I should pay them?' For the first time ever Amethyst heard a tone in her father's voice that suggested complete uncertainty and she did not like it at all.

'No, of course not. Pay once and they will haunt us indefinitely. These people need to be cut off at the roots.'

Her father laughed. 'Sometimes, Amethyst, you are so like your mother that it brings tears to my eyes.' He took in a breath. 'But if Susannah were here I think she would be scolding me for involving you so much in the business that you have forgotten about living.' The handkerchief pressed to his nose still showed blood appearing through the thickness of the layers of cotton and Amethyst hoped that the physician might hurry. 'A man like Montcliffe would make you smile again.'

'I am quite happy as I am, Papa, and as Montcliffe must have every single woman's heart in London a-racing he would hardly be interested in mine.'

The strange glint in his eyes was worrying for Amethyst knew her father well enough to know just what that meant.

* * *

She wandered across to the mews behind the house after her father had retired. Robert had bought in this particular area in London because of the proximity of the stables that held enough room to house livestock.

The stablemaster, Ralph Moore, was just finishing brushing down Midnight, a large black stallion her father had acquired in the past year.

'It is a sad day when the cream of our livestock is left to languish in the Tattersall's stable on view for sale, Miss Cameron. I know it is not my place to criticise anything your father does and he has been a kind and mindful master, but with a bit of patience and some good luck the greys could be the start of a line of horses England has not seen the likes of before. I have spoken of it with him, but he does not want to even consider such a proposition any longer.'

Such words made Amethyst wary. Why would her father suddenly not want the pleasure of breeding his Arabian pair, something he had always spoken of with much anticipation and delight?

Tonight she felt restless and uncertain and the dangerous beauty of Lord Montcliffe came to mind. She wished she had not blushed so ridiculously when he had looked across at her or seen the returning humour in his eyes. The heat of shame made her scalp itch and, reaching up, she snatched the offending wig from her head and shook out the short curls beneath it, enjoying the freedom.

It was finally getting longer. Almost six inches now. Curlier than it had ever been and a much lighter colour. Soon she would be able to dispense with the hair-piece altogether.

If she had been at Dunstan, she would have saddled up one of the horses and raced towards the far hills behind the house. Here in London the moon was high and full, tugging at her patience, stretching the limit of her city manners, making her feel housebound and edgy.

A noise had her turning.

'When I could not find you I knew you would be here.'

Her father joined her at the side of Midnight's stall, Ralph Moore's departure a few moments prior to his room upstairs allowing them privacy. Her father's left eye was darkened and his nose swollen.

'I imagined you would have gone up to bed early after such a dreadful day,' she said.

'Slumber is harder to find as the years march on.' His glance rose to her hair. 'It is nice to see you without the ugly wig, my love, for your skin appears a much better colour without it.'

Shaking her head, Amethyst looked down at the limp brown hairpiece in her hands. 'I should have a new one ordered, I suppose, but it seems so frivolous for the small amount of time I still have need of it.'

'Well, it is good to see you happier, my dear. Perhaps the exchange with Lord Montcliffe has given you some vitality? He is a good man and strong. Mr Tattersall spoke of him highly as a lord who can be relied upon.'

'Relied on to do what?'

'To look after you. I shall not be around for ever and...'

His sentiments petered away as she began to laugh out loud. 'I hardly think that was what Mr Tattersall was referring to. Besides, an exalted lord of the realm would have no mind to mingle with a woman from trade.'

'But if he did, my love, would you have the inclination to consider him as a husband?'

'Husband?' Now all humour fled. 'My God, Papa, you cannot be serious for he would never marry me. Not for all the gold in England. Men like Lord Montcliffe marry women exactly like them. Rich. Beautiful. Young. Well connected. Debutantes who have a world of possibilities at their feet.'

Her father shook his head. 'I disagree with you. Your mother taught me that those things are not the most important qualities to ensure the success of a union. She said that a partner with an alert and interested mind is worth much more than one of little thought or originality. Besides, we have accrued enough money to lure even the loftiest of the lords of the *ton*.'

His words seeped into her astonishment. 'Why are you saying these things, Papa? Why would you be even thinking of them? I am a widow and I am almost twenty-seven years old. My chances of such marital bliss are long since passed and I have accepted that they are.'

In the moonlight her father's face looked older and infinitely sadder. As he leant forward to take her hand Amethyst felt her heart lurch in worry, the certainty of what he was about to tell her etched into fright.

Midnight's breath in the moonlight, the call of an

owl far off in the greenness of the park, a carriage wending its way home along Upper Brook Street at the end of another busy night. The sounds of a normal and ordinary late evening, everything in place, settling in and waiting for the dawn, allowing all that had happened through the day to be assimilated by a gentle darkness.

The far edge of happiness is here, Amethyst thought. *Here, before the crack of change opens up to swallow it.* She knew what he would say for she could see it in his eyes.

'I am seriously unwell, my dear. The doctor does not expect my heart to last out the year in the shape it is in. He advised me to settle my affairs and make certain everything is in order.'

Worse than a crack. An abyss unending and deep. Her hands closed about his, the chill in his thin fingers underlying everything. She could not even negate all he said and the reply she was about to give him was driven into silence by fear.

'My one and only prayer is that the Lord Above in His Infinite Wisdom might grant me the promise of knowing you are safe, Amethyst. Safe and married to a man who would not forsake you. Lord Montcliffe is the first man I have seen you look at since Gerald Whitely. He is well regarded by everyone who knows him and it is rumoured that his financial position is somewhat shaky. We could help him.'

Stop, she should have said. Stop all this nonsense now. But in the shafts of light she registered something in her father's eyes that she had not seen in a long, long time. Hope, if she could name it; hope of a future for her, even if he was not in it.

The gift of a place and a family, that was what he was trying to give her. There was no thought of greed or power or station. No inkling of a crazed want to surge up the social ladder, either. It was only his love that fostered such thoughts.

'Would you listen with your intellect to what I have to ask you, my love, and perhaps your heart as well?' he asked.

As much as she wanted to shake her head and tell him to stop, she found herself acquiescing.

'There is only us now, the last of the Camerons, and the world is not an easy place to be left alone. I want you to be guarded and cared for by an honourable man, a man who would ward away danger. I want this more than I have ever wanted anything in my life before, Amethyst. If I knew you were safe, it would mean I could enjoy what is left of my life in peace. If I could go to your mother in Heaven and know that I had done my very best to keep you protected, then I would be a happy man. Susannah instructed me to see you lived well in her last breath of life and if it is the final thing that I can do for her then, by God, I am willing to try.'

Crack. Crack crack. Like ice on a winter lake, Amethyst's heart was breaking piece by piece as he spoke.

Chapter Two

'There is someone to see you, Lord Montcliffe. A tradesman by the name of Mr Robert Cameron and he is most insistent that he be allowed to come inside.'

'Send him in.'

'Through the front door, my lord?' His butler's tone was censorious.

'Indeed.'

'Very well, my lord.'

It had been a couple of weeks since the *contretemps* at Hyde Park Corner and Daniel wondered what on earth Cameron might want from him. The Arabian greys had been pulled from auction the day after they had last spoken and the small bit of investigation he had commissioned on the character of the man had been most informative.

Mr Robert Cameron was a London merchant who was well heeled and wily. He owned most of the shares in a shipping line trading timber between England and the Americas, his move into importing taking place across the past eight or so years, and he was doing more than well.

However, when the door opened again and Cameron came through, Daniel was shocked.

The man of a little over a fortnight ago was thinner and more pallid, the bruising around his eyes darker.

'Thank you for seeing me, Lord Montcliffe.' Cameron waited as the servant departed the room, peering about to see no others lingered in the background of the substantial library. 'Might I speak very frankly to you and in complete confidence, my lord?'

Interest flickered. 'You may, but please take a seat.' He gestured to the leather wingchair nearby for Cameron looked more than unsteady on his feet.

'No. I would rather stand, my lord. There are words I need to say that require fortitude, if you will, and a sitting position may lessen my resolve.'

Daniel nodded and waited as the other collected himself. He could think of no reason whatsoever for the furtive secrecy or the tense manner of the man.

'What I am about to offer, Lord Montcliffe, must not leave the confines of this room, no matter what you might think of it. Will you give me your word as a gentleman on that whether you accept my proposal or not?'

'It isn't outside of the law?'

'No, my lord.'

'Then you have my word.'

'Might I ask for a drink before I begin?'

'Certainly. Brandy?'

'Thank you.'

Pouring two generous glasses, Daniel passed one over, waiting as the older man readied himself to speak.

'My health is not as it was, my lord. In fact, I think it fair to say that I am not long for this world.' He held up his hand as Daniel went to interrupt. 'It is not condolences I am after, my lord. I only tell you this because the lack of months left to me owe a good part to what I propose to relate to you next.'

Taking a deep swallow of his brandy, Cameron wiped his mouth with his hands. Labourers hands with wide calluses and small healed injuries. The hands of someone used to many long hours of manual work.

'I want to bequeath the pair of greys to you, my lord. I know you will love them in the same manner as I do and that they will not be sold on, so to speak, for a quick financial profit. Mick and Maisie need a home that will nurture them and I have no doubts you shall do just that. I would also prefer their names to stay just as they are as the Grecian ones suggested by Mr Tattersall didn't appeal to me at all.'

'I could not accept such an offer, Mr Cameron, and have not the means to buy them from you at this moment. Besides, it is unheard of to give a complete stranger such a valuable thing,' Daniel replied, taken aback.

For the first time Cameron smiled. 'But you see, my lord, I can do just as I will. Great wealth produces a sense of egocentricity and allows a freedom that is undeniable. I can bequeath anything I like to anybody I want and I wish for you to have my greys.'

Daniel tried to ignore the flare of excitement that

started building inside him. With such horses he could begin to slowly recoup a little of the family fortune by running a breeding programme at Montcliffe Manor that would be the envy of society. But he stopped himself. There had to be a catch here somewhere, for by all accounts Cameron was a shrewd businessman and a successful one at that.

'And in return?'

'Your estate is heavily mortgaged and I have it on good authority that a hefty loan your brother took out with the Honourable Mr Reginald Goldsmith will be called in before the end of this month. He had other outstanding loans as well and I have acquired each and every one to do just as I will with them.'

'What is your meaning?' Daniel bit out, forcing himself to stand still.

'Coutts is also worried by your lack of collateral and, given the Regent's flagrant dearth of care with his finances, they are now beating a more conservative pathway in the management of their long-term lending. With only a small investigation I think you might find yourself in trouble.'

'You would ruin me?'

'No, my lord, exactly the opposite. I wish to gift you three sums of twenty-five thousand pounds each year for the next three years and then the lump sum of one-hundred-and-fifty thousand pounds.'

A fortune. Daniel could barely believe the proportions of the offer, such riches unimaginable.

'I would immediately sign over the town house in Grosvenor Square as an incentive for you to honour the terms. Then, whenever Amethyst instructs me to do so, a property I own to the north called Dunstan House, with a good deal of acreage about it, shall be endorsed into your care, as well.'

Stopping, the merchant faced him directly. Sweat had built on his brow and his cheeks were marked with a ruddy glow of much emotion. 'There is one thing, however, that you must do for me in return, my lord. My only daughter Amethyst is now twenty-six, soon to be twenty-seven. She is a clever girl and a sensible one. She has worked alongside me for the last eight years and it is her surefootedness in business that has propelled my profits skywards.'

He waited as Daniel nodded before continuing.

'Amethyst Amelia was educated under the capable tutelage of the Gaskell Street Presbyterian Church School and I paid the teachers handsomely to make sure that she acquired all the skills a woman of the classes above her might need to know. In short, she could fit into any social situation without disgracing herself.'

Daniel suddenly knew just where this conversation was leading to. A dowry. A bribe. The answer to his prayers for the selling of his soul.

'You are single and available, my lord. You have two sisters who are in need of being launched into society, a mother who has fine taste in living and a grandfather who requires much in the way of medical attention. All continuing and long-term expenses. If you marry my daughter by the end of July, none of this will ever be a problem again and you will have the means to right the crumbling estate of Montcliffe once and for all.'

'Get out, you bastard.' Daniel's anger made the words tremble. That a man he was beginning to respect and like should think of coming into his life to blackmail him into marrying his daughter. For that was what this was. Blackmail, even given the enormous amounts mooted.

But Cameron looked to be going nowhere. 'I can understand your wrath and indeed, were I in your boots, I might have had exactly the same reaction. But I would ask you to think about it for at least a week. You have promised me your confidence and I expect that, for if a word of this gets out anywhere my daughter's reputation will be ruined. Hence, as a show of my own gratitude for your discretion, I shall leave you the greys regardless of your final decision.'

'I cannot accept them.'

'Here is a document I have written up for your perusal and I earnestly hope to hear from you presently.'

With that he was gone, his glass emptied on the desk and a fat envelope left beside it. Daniel was in two minds as to what to do: send it back unopened with a curt message containing his lack of interest or open it up and see what was inside.

Curiosity won out.

The sheet before him was witnessed by a city lawyer whose qualifications seemed more than satisfactory. It was also signed by his daughter.

'Damn. Damn. Damn.' He whispered the words beneath his breath. The girl had been told of all this and still wanted the travesty? Finishing his brandy, he poured himself another as he read on, barely believing what was written.

He was to marry Amethyst Amelia Cameron before the month was finished on the condition that he have no relations with any other woman for two years afterwards.

Shocked to the core, he took a good swallow of the brandy. Amethyst Amelia Cameron would allow her father to sell her for the promise of what? Under the law any daughter could inherit money, chattels and un-entailed property from a dying father and he obviously loved her. Besides, she had experience in the business and had turned profits for many a year. Cameron had told him that himself. So what was it that she would gain from such an arrangement? They barely knew each other and, even given she was from the trading classes, an heiress of her calibre could garner any number of titled aristocrats who were down on their purse.

As he was?

'Hell!' Daniel threw the parchment into a drawer and slammed it shut, but the promises festered even unseen, malevolent and beguiling.

How on earth had Cameron known so much about his financial difficulties? Would Goldsmith truly call in his brother's loans against Montcliffe before he was ready for them? If he did that, Daniel would be forced to sell the town house, the manor, the surrounding farms and any chattels that would fetch something. Then the Wyldes would be homeless, moneylenders baying for their blood and all the claws unsheathed.

If it was just him, he might have been able to manage, but Cameron was perfectly correct; his sisters were young, his grandfather was old and his mother had always found her gratification in the position the earldom afforded them in society and had freely spent accordingly.

Standing, he walked to the window and looked out over the gardens, swearing as he saw the two greys tied to a post by the roadside and his butler near them, looking more than bewildered.

He had left them just as he'd said. It was begun already. Daniel turned to the doorway and hurried through it.

'I think he took my proposal very well.' Robert Cameron sipped at the sweet tea Amethyst had brought him and smiled.

'You do?'

'He is a good man with sound moral judgement and a love for his family.'

Amethyst bit into a ginger biscuit, wiping the crumbs away from her lips.

'So he signed his name to the deed?'

'Not quite.'

'He didn't sign it?'

Her father looked up. 'He told me that I was a bastard for even suggesting such a thing and said that I should get out.'

'But you left the greys?'

'I did.'

'And he has as yet not sent them back?'

'He has not.'

'Then it is a good omen.'

Robert frowned. 'I hope so, Amethyst, I really do.'

Amethyst tried her hardest to smile. Papa had become thinner and thinner no matter what she might get their French chef to feed him and he had taken to striding about the house at night...watching. He was scared and those that might harm them for their money were becoming braver. The daylight attack near Tattersall's had made her father paranoiac about any movement in their street, any unknown face around the warehouse. Nay, he was eating himself up with worry and she could allow it no longer.

Papa wanted her to be protected and he desperately wanted her to trust in a man again. With time running out for her father Amethyst had allowed him the choice of her groom. Said like that it sounded abhorrent, but nothing was ever as black and white as one might imagine and right now she wanted her father to smile.

'We shall wait a week. If Lord Montcliffe has not come back to us by then with an answer, we will visit him together.' She injected a jaunty positive note into her words but everything in her felt flat.

Gerald Whitely's face shimmered in her memory. The feel of his anger was still there sometimes, just beyond touch, his angry words and then his endless seething silence. A relationship that had blinded sense and buried reason, one bad decision following another until there was nothing left of any of it.

Cold fingers closed over the cross at her throat. Her father was the one person who had stayed constant in

her life and she would do whatever it took to see that
he was happy. Anything at all.

'Your mother made me promise to see you flourish,
Amy. They were the last words she spoke to me as she
slipped away and I had hoped that you would, but after
Whitely…' He stopped, his voice wavering and fright-
eningly thin. 'Lord Montcliffe will make you remember to laugh again. He loves horses and they love him
back. Any man who can win the trust of an animal is
a good man, an honest man, and I can see that in him
when I look him in the eyes.'

She hoped her smile did not appear false as he held
her hand, the dearness of the gesture so familiar.

'Promise me you will try to give him all your heart,
body and soul, Amethyst. No reservations. It is how
your mama loved me and there is no defence for a man
against a woman like that. Such strength only allows
growth and wonder between a married couple and I
know you have been saddened by love…'

She shook his words away, the reminder of bitterness unwanted. Her choice, cankered before it had even
begun.

'When death claimed Gerald Whitely, my love, I
was not sorry. Sense tells me that you were not either.'

So he knew of that? Another shame. A further deceit that had not remained hidden.

'It was the Cameron fortune Gerald was after, Papa.
Perhaps Lord Montcliffe and he are not so unalike after
all?'

But her father shook his head. 'Whitely fashioned
his own demise. Daniel Wylde is only trying to clean

up after the mistakes of his brother and father and is doing so to protect the family he has left.'

'A saint, then?' She wished that the caustic undertone in her words was not quite so unmistakable.

'Hardly. But he is the first man you have given a second glance to. The first man who has made you blush. Such attraction must account for something because it was the same with Susannah and me.'

Despite everything she smiled. 'I imagine that Lord Montcliffe has that effect upon everybody whoever meets him, Papa. I was not claiming him for myself.'

'Because you do not trust your judgements pertaining to the acquisition of a husband, given the last poor specimen?'

Her father had never before, in the year since his death, spoken of Gerald Whitely in this way. That thought alone lent mortification to her sinking raft of other emotions.

Failure. It ate at certainty like a large rat at a wedding feast. Once she had chosen so unwisely she felt at a loss to ever allow herself such a mandate again. Perhaps that was a part of the reason she did not rally against her father's arguments. That and the yellowing shades of sickness that hung in the whites of his eyes.

Death held a myriad of hues. Gerald's had been a pale and unholy grey when she had seen him laid out in the undertaker's rooms. Her mother's had been red-tinged, a rash of consequence marked into the very fabric of her skin and only fading hours after she had taken her final and hard-fought breath.

Amethyst's nails dug deep into her thighs as she

willed such thoughts aside. A long time ago she had been a happier person and a more optimistic one. Now all she could manage was the pretence of it.

It was easier to allow Papa the hope of joy in his final months, the illusion of better times, of children, of the *'heart and body and soul'* love her father had felt for her mother and which he imagined was some sort of a God-given rite of passage. Once she had believed in such a thing as well, but no longer.

All she could muster now was a horror for anything that held the hint of intimacy.

Blemished. Damaged. Hurt.

Daniel Wylde would understand sooner or later the payment required for the Cameron fortune and she was sure he would feel every bit as cheated as she did. But at least Papa would go to his grave believing that his only daughter was safe and happy, the soldier earl he had chosen for her strong enough to ward off any threats of menace.

She leaned down and picked up a small coin from a collection on a plate, balancing it in her palm before flipping it over. *If it shows heads this marriage will work and if it does not…* When the coin fell to tails she chastised herself for playing such silly games.

When Daniel returned from an outing later in the day his mother was ensconced in the drawing room at the Montcliffe town house, a glass of his finest brandy in her hand and a thoughtful look upon her face.

'Have you been procuring new horseflesh, Daniel?

There is a pair of magnificent greys in your stable and I just wondered…'

'They were a gift, Mother. I did not purchase them.'

'A gift? From whom?' The silk in the gown Janet, Lady Montcliffe, wore matched her eyes exactly, a deep sapphire blue. A new possession, he supposed, thinking of the demand for payment that would come across his desk before much longer.

He could have been truthful, could have simply stated that there was a possibility he would be married and that the greys had been a pre-wedding present, but something made him stop. Anger, he supposed, and shame and the fact that to voice such a thing might make it feel more real and true.

With the Camerons he felt removed from society. In their company the preposterous proposed union made a sort of skewed sense that it didn't here in front of his mother.

When he didn't answer, his mother remarked, 'Charlotte Hughes is back from Scotland. I saw her today at the Bracewells and she asked after you. She is looking a picture of health and wealth and was sporting a necklace with an emerald attached to it the size of a walnut.'

'I am no longer interested in Lady Mackay, Mama.' He stressed her married name.

'Well, she seemed more than interested in your whereabouts. She had heard of the fracas at La Corunna, of course, and was most concerned about the injury to your leg. There were tears in her eyes when I told her of it and such compassion is heartwarming.'

Daniel interrupted her. 'Is that my French brandy

you are drinking?' Crossing to the cabinet, he found the bottle and frowned as he saw there was barely any left. His whole family had been falling apart for years. His mother with her drink, his brother with his gambling and his sisters with their brittle sense of entitlement and whining. Only his grandfather had seemed to hold it together, though his body was letting him down more and more often.

'If you are going to lecture me about the evils of strong drink...'

Daniel shook his head. 'This evening I cannot find the energy to do so. If you wish to kill yourself by small degrees with your misplaced grief for my brother's stupidity...'

'Nigel was a good boy...'

'Who mortgaged the Montcliffe property to the hilt as a payment for his escalating gambling habit.'

'He was trying to save the estate. He was trying to make everything right again,' she insisted.

'If you believe that, Mama, then you are as deluded as he was.'

His mother finished the glass of brandy and stood. 'The military campaign in Spain and Portugal has made you different, Daniel. Harder. A man of distance and callousness and I do not like what you have become.'

The sound of screams on a march from Hell with winter eating up any hope for warmth. Dead soldiers stripped of clothes and boots by others needing cover in the middle of a relentless freeze, and hundreds of miles left to reach the coast and to safety. Aye, distance came easily with such memories.

'In less than six months the Montcliffe properties will be bankrupt.'

He had not meant to say it like this, so baldly, and as his mother paled a compassion he had long since let go of spiked within.

'I have tried to tell you before, Mother. I have tried to make you understand that Nigel finished what our father started, but I can no longer afford to say it kindly. The estate lies precariously on the edge of insolvency.'

'You lie.'

'The bank won't lend the Montcliffe estate another penny and I have been warned that Goldsmith could call in one of Nigel's outstanding loans before the end of this month.'

'But Gwendolyn is to be presented in court and all the invitations to a soirée are written out. Besides, I have also just ordered several ball dresses from Madame Soulier. I cannot possibly curtail. If I do, others shall know of our plight and we shall suffer a very public shaming. Why, I could not even bear such a thing.'

Turning, Daniel held his breath, the guilt of Nigel's death eating at his equanimity. Years ago they had been close and he wondered if his time away from England in the army had left his brother exposed somehow. Lord knew his mother and sisters were unremitting in their demands. If he had been here, would he have been able to bolster Nigel's will and made him stronger, allowing him a sounding board for good sense and bolder decisions in the economic welfare of Montcliffe?

Taking a deep breath, he faced his mother directly. 'There is only one way that I can see of navigating the Montcliffe inheritances out of this conundrum.'

His mother wiped the tears from her eyes and looked up at him. He had never seen her appear quite as old and lined.

'How?'

'I can marry into money.'

'Old money?' Even under duress his mother remained a snob.

'Or money earned from the toil of hard labour and lucky breaks.'

'Trade?' The word was whispered with all the undercurrents of a shout.

'The alternative is bankruptcy,' he reminded her grimly.

'You have someone in mind?'

He could not say it, could not toss Amethyst Amelia Cameron's name into the ring of fire his mother had so effortlessly conjured up, a sneer on her lips and distaste in her blue eyes.

'Your father would be turning in his grave at such a suggestion. Marry one of the Stapleton girls, they would have you in a second, or the oldest Beaumont chit. She has made no secret of setting her cap at you.'

'Enough, Mother.'

'Charlotte Hughes, then, despite her foolish marriage. She has always loved you and you had strong feelings for her once. Besides, she is a lot more flush these days...'

'Enough.' This time he said it louder and she stopped.

'You have no true understanding of the difficulties that face me, Daniel...'

Her words were slightly slurred and he interrupted her. 'Your line in the sand is in danger of being washed away by strong drink, Mother, and it would help if you listened rather than argued. If you made some sacrifice in the family spending and pared down on the number of dresses and bonnets and boots you required, we may have some ready cash to tide us over whilst I try to extricate us from this Godforsaken mess.'

Already she was shaking her head. Sometimes he wondered why he had not just left and taken ship to the Americas, leaving the lot of them to wallow in the cesspool of their own making.

But blood and duty were thicker than both fury and defeat and so he had stayed, juggling what was left of the few assets against what had been lost into the wider world of debt.

If Goldsmith was to foreclose as Cameron had intimated he would? He shook away the dread.

So far he had not needed to sell any of the furniture or paintings in the London town house and so the effect of great wealth remained the illusion it always had been.

The avenues of escape were closing in, however, and he knew without a doubt that it was weeks rather than months for any monies left in the coffers to be gone. Nay, Cameron's option of a marriage of convenience was the only way to avoid complete ruin.

Upending her glass, his mother called her maid, heavily relying on the guiding arm of her servant as she stood.

'I shall speak with you again when you are less unreasonable.' The anger in her voice resonated sharply.

Brandy, arrogance and hopelessness. A familiar cocktail of Wylde living that had taken his father and brother into the afterlife too early.

He wondered if he even had the strength to try to save Montcliffe.

He met Lady Charlotte Mackay four days later as he exited the bank where he had spent an hour with the manager, trying to piece together some sort of rescue plan allowing the family estate a few more months of grace. And failing. His right leg hurt like hell and he had barely slept the night before with the pain of it.

Charlotte looked just as he remembered her, silky blonde curls falling down from an intricate hat placed high on her head. Her eyes widened as she saw it was he. Shock, he thought, or pity. These days he tried not to interpret the reaction of others when they perceived his uneven gait.

'Daniel.' Her voice was musical and laced with an overtone of gladness. 'It has been an age since I have seen you and I was hoping you might come to call upon me. I have been back from Edinburgh for almost a sennight and had the pleasure of meeting your mother a few days ago.'

'She mentioned she had seen you.'

'Oh.'

The conversation stopped for a second, the thousand things unsaid filling in the spaces of awkwardness.

'I wrote to you, of course, but you did not answer.' Her confession made him wary, and as her left hand came up to wipe away an errant curl from her face he saw her fingers were ringless.

He could have said he had not received any missives and, given the vagaries of the postal system, she would have believed him. But he didn't lie.

'Marriage requires a certain sense of loyalty, I have always thought, so perhaps any communication between us was not such a good idea.'

Small shadows dulled the blue of her irises. 'Until a union fails to live up to expectation and the trap of a dreary routine makes one's mind wander.'

Dangerous ground this. He tried to turn the subject. 'I heard your husband was well mourned at his funeral.'

'Death fashions martyrs of us all.' Her glance was measured. 'Widowhood has people behaving with a sort of poignant carefulness that is…unending and a whole year of dark clothes and joylessness has left me numb. I want to be normal again. I am young, after all, and most men find me attractive.'

Was this a proposition? The bright gown she wore was low-cut, generous breasts nestling in their beds of silk with only a minimal constraint. As she leaned forward he could not help but look.

The maleness in him rose like a sail in the wind, full of promise and direction, but he had been down this pathway once before and the wreck of memory was potent. He made himself stand still.

'I have learnt much through the brutal consequences of mistakes, but I am home alone tonight, Daniel. If you came to see me, we might rekindle all that we once had.'

Around them others hurried past, an ordinary morning in London, a slight chill on the air and the calling voices of street vendors.

He felt unbalanced by meeting her, given their last encounter. Betrayal was an emotion that held numerous interpretations and he hadn't cared enough to hear hers then.

But Charlotte Mackay's eyes now held a harder edge of knowledge, something war had also stamped on him. No longer simple. Two people ruined by the circumstances of their lives and struggling to hold on to anything at all. The disenchantment made him tired and wary and he was glad to see her mother hurrying towards them from the shop behind, giving no further chance of confidence.

Lady Wesley had changed almost as much as her daughter, the quick nervous laughter alluding to a nature that was teetering on some sort of a breakdown.

'My lord. I hope your family is all well?'

'Indeed they are, ma'am.'

'As you can see, our Charlotte is back and all in one piece from the wilds of Scotland.'

When he failed to speak she placed her arm across her daughter's. The suspicion that she was trying to transmit some hidden signal was underlined by the whitened skin over her knuckles. Charlotte looked suddenly beaten, the fight and challenge drained away into a vacuous smile of compliance.

Perhaps the Wesley family was as complex and convoluted as his own. Jarring his right foot, he swore to himself as they gave their goodbyes. His balance was worsening with the constant pain and the headache he was often cursed with was a direct result of that.

If the Camerons were to know the extent of his infirmity, would they withdraw their offer? Robert Cameron had told him that his daughter needed a strong husband. A protector. The beat of blood coursing around the bullet in his thigh was more distinct now just as the specialist he had seen last month had predicted it would become. If he left it too much longer, he would be dead.

The choice of the devil.

He had seen men in Spain and Portugal with their limbs severed and their lives shattered. Even now in London the remnants of the ragtag of survivors from the battlements of La Corunna still littered the streets, begging for mercy and succour from those around them.

He couldn't lose his leg. He wouldn't. Pride was one thing but so was the fate of his family. Dysfunctional the Montcliffes might be, but as the possessor of the title he had an obligation to honour.

For just a moment he wished he was back in Spain amongst his regiment as they rode east in the late autumn sunshine along the banks of the Tagus. The rhythm of the tapping drums and a valley filled with wildflowers came to mind, the ground soft underfoot and the cheers of the waving Spanish nationals ringing in his ears. A simple and uncomplicated time. A time before the chaos that was to be La Corunna. Even now when he smelt thyme, sage or lavender, such sights and sounds returned to haunt him.

The London damp encroached into his thoughts: the sound of a carriage, the calls of children in the park opposite. His life seemed to have taken a direction he was not certain of any more; too wounded to re-enlist, too encumbered by his family and its problems to simply disappear. And now a further twist—a marriage proposal that held nothing but compromise within it.

He tried to remember Amethyst Cameron's face exactly and failed in his quest. The dull brown of her hair, the wary anger in her eyes, a voice that was often shrill or scolding. The prospect of marriage to her was not what he had expected from his life, but in the circumstances what else could he do?

His eyes caught the movement of a little girl falling and scuffing her knees. An adult lifted her up and small arms entwined around the woman's neck, trusting, needing. Daniel imagined fatherhood would be something to be enjoyed, though in truth he had seldom been around any children. He turned away when he saw the woman watching him, uncertain perhaps of his intentions.

He was like a shadow, filled in by flesh and blood, but hurt by the empty spaces in his life. He wanted a wholeness again, a certainty, a resolve. He wanted to laugh as though he meant it and be part of something that was more than the shallow sum of his title.

If he did not marry Amethyst Amelia Cameron, the heritage of the Montcliffe name would be all but gone, a footnote in history, only a bleak reminder of avarice and greed. Centuries of lineage lost in the time it took for the bailiffs to eject the Wyldes from their birthright. The very thought of such a travesty made him hail a cabriolet. He needed to go home and read the small print and conditions of the Cameron proposal. He could not dally any longer.

A sort of calmness descended over the panic. His life and happiness would be forfeited, but there might be some redress in the production of a family. Children had no blame in the affairs of their parents and at thirty-three it was well past time that he produce an heir. An heir who would inherit an estate that was viable and in good health. An estate that would not be lost to the excesses of his brother or the indifference of his father.

Such a personal sacrifice must eventually come to mean something and he was damn well going to make certain that it did.

Chapter Three

The note came the seventh day after they had last seen him, a tense and formal missive informing them that Lord Daniel Wylde, the sixth Earl of Montcliffe, would be calling upon them at two in the afternoon.

Amethyst had been watching for him by the large bay window in the downstairs salon and she stiffened as she heard his carriage draw to a stop on the roadway in front of the house. Lord Montcliffe was here. She looked across at her father, his fingers knocking against his side in the particular way he had of showing concern. It did not help at all.

There were tea and biscuits already set out on the table and the finest of brandy in an unopened bottle. Every glass had been meticulously cleaned and snowy-white napkins stood at attention beside the plate of food, well ironed and folded.

'Lord Daniel Wylde, the Earl of Montcliffe, sir.' The butler used his sternest voice and made an effort not to look at anyone. Amethyst had instructed him on the exact art of manners before their guest had arrived.

And then the Earl was there, dressed in dark blue, the white cravat tied at his throat in the style of a man who hadn't put too much care into it. Not a fop or a dandy. She was pleased, at least, for that.

'Sir.' He looked at her father. 'Miss Cameron.' He did not even deign to glance her way, the anger on his brow eminently visible. The folder that Papa had made ready with the documents outlining the terms of their betrothal was in his hands. Each knuckle was stretched white. 'I accept.'

He threw the deeds on the table where they sat between the fine brandy and the fresh biscuits.

I accept.

Two words and she was lost into both method and madness; the Cameron fortune would remain intact and her own fate was sealed. For good or for bad. She felt her heart beating loud and heavy and, placing her hand on her breast, she pressed down, wanting this moment to stop and start again as something else.

But of course it did not.

'You accept?' Her father's voice was businesslike and brisk—a trader whose whole life had consisted of brokering arrangements.

The Earl nodded, but the expression on his face was stony. An agreement dragged from the very depths of his despair and nothing to be done about any of it. He knew as little of her as she did of him; two pawns in a game that was played for stakes higher than just their happiness alone. She had always known that, since the pounds had begun to roll into the Cameron coffers from the lucrative timber trade to and from the Americas. Great fortunes always came with a price.

'You have signed every condition, then?' Her father again. She thought he sounded just as he did when he was clinching a deal for the sale of a thousand yards of expensive American mahogany and she wondered at his calm and composure. She was his only daughter and again and again in her lifetime her father had insisted that she must marry for love.

Love? Unexpectedly she caught the eyes of the Earl. Today the green was darker and distrusting. Still, even with the stark fury of coercion on his face, Daniel Wylde was the most beautiful man she had ever had the pleasure of looking upon.

Such looks would crucify her, for nobody would believe that he might have freely chosen her as his bride. She swallowed and met his glance. No use going to pieces this late in the game when the joy on her father's face was tangible. Papa had not appeared as happy for months.

'This is your choice too, Miss Cameron?'

'It is, my lord.' The floor beneath her began to waver, all the lies eliciting a sort of unreality that made her dizzy.

'You understand the meaning of the documents then?' he pressed.

'I do.' A blush crept up her throat as she thought of the clause stipulating the two years of monogamy. Her father's addition, that proviso, and though she had ar-

gued long and hard with him to remove it, Robert was
not to be shifted.

Montcliffe turned away. The stillness she had noticed outside Tattersall's was magnified here, a man
who knew exactly his place in the world and was seldom surprised by anything.

Save for this marriage of convenience.

'I hope then that the person you placed to look into
my financial affairs can be trusted, Mr Cameron. If
word were to leak out about my straitened circumstances and this unusual betrothal, I doubt I could protect your daughter from the repercussions.'

'Mr Alfred Middlemarch, my lawyer, is a model of
silence, my lord. Nary a stray word shall be uttered.'

Their parlourmaid knocked timidly at the door,
asking if she could come in to pour the tea. The Earl
crossed the room to stand by the fireplace and chose
brandy for his sustenance. When Hilda filled his glass
to a quarter inch from the top Amethyst winced. On
reflection, she thought, perhaps such a task was supposed to belong to the lady of the house and she wished
she had not instructed the maid to return to do it. It
was seldom that they had such lofty visitors and every
small detail of service took on an importance that it
previously never had.

Was this how she would live her life from now on?
she wondered. On the edge of eggshells in case she
were to inadvertently place a clumsy foot wrong? The
tutors at Gaskell Street had tried their best with the
vagaries of manners, but she imagined they had had

about as much practice with the higher echelons of London society as she had.

To give Montcliffe some credit he sipped his tipple carefully from the top before placing the glass down on a green baize circle especially designed for such a purpose. She doubted her father had ever used them before, her eyes catching circles of darkness in the white oak where errant drinks had seeped into the patina of the wood.

Blemished, like them, the outward appearance of Papa and herself reflecting a life that had been lived in trade and service, with little time left for the niceties of cultured living. Amethyst wished she had at least gone out and bought a sumptuous dress for this occasion, something that might lift the colour of her skin into lustre.

She smiled at such a nonsense, catching the Earl's eyes again as she did so. When he looked away she saw that the muscle under his jaw quivered. In distaste? In sympathy? Usually she found people easy to read, but this man was not.

'I will announce our betrothal in *The Times* next week, if that is to your liking, Miss Cameron.'

So few days left?

'Thank you.' She wished her voice sounded stronger.

'I should not want a complicated ceremony given our circumstances.' A slight shame highlighted Daniel Wylde's cheeks after he said this and it heartened her immensely. He was not a man in the habit of being rude to women, then? She clutched at the cross at her throat and felt relieved.

Her father pressed on with his own ideas. 'I was thinking we might hold the ceremony here, my lord, with a minister from our Presbyterian church, of course, and any of your family and friends you care to invite. I would have the first of the money promised transferred into your bank account within the week.'

The give and the take of an agreement. Again Daniel Wylde looked at her as if waiting for her to speak. Did he imagine she might stand up and negate all that her father had so carefully planned? Montcliffe had seen just exactly what those who might hurt her father were capable of. Lord, she brought her hand up and felt the scar just beneath the heavy wig at her nape. It still throbbed sometimes in the cold and the headaches had never quite abated.

'After the nuptials we will repair to my family seat north of Barnet.'

'No!' It was the first real alarm Amethyst had felt. 'I need to be close to Papa and as he is retiring to Dunstan House then this is where I should like us to live…'

'I am certain we can work something out, my dear.' Her father now, placating such an outburst.

Again she shook her head, the pulse of her blood beating fast. 'I want to add a condition that I may live at Dunstan House, though if the Earl wishes to reside at Montcliffe Manor, then he may.'

'Difficult to fulfil the clause of mutual cohabitation for a full two years if that is the case, Miss Cameron.' His voice held a timbre of irony.

The clause her father had insisted upon. She glared

at Robert, but kept her silence and was unexpectedly rescued by the very one she thought she would not be.

'It does not signify. We will reside wherever you wish to.' The Earl's tone was slightly bored. An unwanted wife. An unwelcomed cohabitation. Easier just to take the money and acquiesce.

'Then that is settled.' Her father, on the contrary, looked pleased with himself. The thought that perhaps he had over-exaggerated his own illness came to Amethyst's mind, but she dismissed this in the face of his extreme thinness. 'We shall ask if the children from Gaskell Street can be a part of the choir...'

'A small and simple wedding would be better, Papa.'

'I agree.' Lord Montcliffe spoke again. 'My family, however, are proponents of the High Anglican faith.'

'Then you bring your man of God and the service can be shared.' Papa had hit his stride now and the Earl looked to have no answer to such an unconventional solution. In fact, he looked plainly sick.

'A good solution, I think,' Robert went on to say. 'Then we can all be assured that you will be most properly married.' Standing after such a pronouncement, he walked to the door. 'But now I shall leave you alone for a few moments. I am sure there are things you might wish to say to one another without my presence to inhibit you.'

Amethyst glanced away, her father's words embarrassing and inappropriate. What could the Earl and she possibly have to talk about when there was a palpable distrust in the air? Usually Papa was more astute at reading the feelings of others and seldom acted in a manner that she found disconcerting.

When the door closed behind him, softly pulled shut inch by inch, Lord Montcliffe looked straight at her.

'Why would you agree to this charade, Miss Cameron?'

She asked him another question quickly back. 'Did you love your father, my lord?'

He looked perplexed as he answered, 'No.'

That threw her momentarily, but she made herself continue on. 'Well then, I think you must understand that I truly do love mine. Father, I mean.' Her voice shook. She was making a hash of this. 'Papa is ill and his one and only wish is to see me well protected and cared for. He is so ill that I fear—' She stopped, the words too shocking to say.

'Then why choose me in particular?' The tone of his fury was recognisable.

'You liked horses and you made it your business to save Papa from the attack in the alley when you could have so easily just gone on. I do not wish for a mean husband or an inconsiderate one, you understand. Also the army has made you strong. Another advantage, if you like.'

'A trade-off, then? Like the timber your father imports?'

'Exactly.' This was turning out to be a lot easier than she had hoped.

'Damn.' He swore and reached forward to tip her face up to his own.

'Are you truly as cold-blooded as that, Miss Cameron?' His green eyes narrowed as if he was listening for an answer and Amethyst was simply caught in the unexpected warmth of them. Paralysed. The darker green rim was threaded with gold.

'So there is no more to this agreement than the plain and blunt terms of commerce?' He let her go as she twisted away, uncertain of the words that he was saying and even more uncertain of her own reaction to them.

'If my father had not been ailing, I should not even be thinking of a betrothal, my lord, but he is fearful and fidgety and the doctor had made it clear that unless he relaxes and stops worrying...' She swallowed, her bottom lip wobbling. 'Your estate is falling into pieces about your feet and my father is dying. Our alliance should stave off the consequences of them both, yours for ever, and mine even for just a while. A business proposition, my lord, to suit us both.'

He turned away and walked to the window. No woman had ever spoken to him so plainly before. Usually the opposite sex fawned about him, the wiles of femininity well practised and honed and saying all that they thought he wished to hear.

Miss Amethyst Amelia Cameron seemed to possess none of these qualities and he was at a loss to know how to proceed.

'So I could have been anyone?'

When she did not answer, he added, 'Anyone with a dubious fiscal base and a strong military background?'

She looked over at him then with the directness that was so much part of her, a frown marring her forehead.

'You needed to be unmarried, of course, and not too old.' He was about to speak when she took a breath and carried on further. 'I also sincerely hope that I have not taken you from the arms of someone you love, for if that is the case I should absolve you from all the agreements between us. As a measure of good faith we would throw in the greys as a means to buy your silence on such a sensitive matter.'

He swore again and she flinched. The worth of the greys would not begin to cover the debts of Montcliffe.

'Why did you not choose a man you have some *tendre* for or one you had at least some notion of?' While she was being so brutally frank he thought he might at least discover something of the woman he would be tied to.

Her hand went to brush away the hair from around her face in a feminine and uncertain gesture. Against the window and in the light of a harsh afternoon sun she looked almost beautiful, a strong loveliness that was not much lauded in society these days, but one which caught at him in an unexpected twist of want. Not a woman of the same ilk as his sisters and mother with their constant neediness and fragility.

'There is no one else.' She did not even attempt platitudes.

Daniel had no experience of speaking with a woman who would not be cowed by his title or by him personally and for one unlikely moment he thought he might tell her just that. With an effort he gathered himself together.

'Truth be told, Miss Cameron, I am caught in this ruse as certainly as you are.'

'Then perhaps it would be wise for us both to make the best of it. I would not hound you for much time or for sweet words, my lord, but what I would ask is that around my father you pretend a *tendre*, allowing him the contentment he deserves in what little is left of his life.'

'Would your mother have approved of you being such a martyr?'

A flash of anger came into her eyes, lighting the brown to a clear and brittle velvet. He was surprised by such a quick change. Not quite the demure woman he had imagined, after all. 'I think you forget, my lord, that I am as much a martyr to my family as you are to yours.'

'Touché.' Indeed she was right, the long line of Montcliffe ancestors all looking at him to save the Earldom for posterity. 'And if your father dies sooner rather than later, are the conditions within our marriage null and void?'

Her face crumbled into sheer distress. 'I sincerely pray that Papa should not succumb to his malady so readily, My lord. I should also impress upon you that putting aside a marriage so quickly would need to be most carefully handled.'

He almost laughed, thinking that she had no idea at all as to the whims of the *ton* in their dealings with the protection of large inheritances. Indeed, a hundred marriages that he knew of were conveniently forgotten about in the face of shapely courtesans and willing mistresses. Another thought also worried him. Perhaps in her circle of acquaintances such a truism was not as absolute.

He had never been a flagrant womaniser, but neither was he a man who would want to be bound for years in a union without love or respect.

When Robert Cameron came back into the room Daniel lost his chance to ask exactly what she thought to get from this alliance personally. Her father looked absurdly pleased with himself, a smile from one side of his face to the other.

'I hope you have been able to find out a little about each other. My Amethyst was the cleverest of all the young ladies at her school, my lord, and won the first prize for academic endeavour for her year.'

'I am certain he cannot be interested in such things, Papa, and—'

But Daniel did not allow her to finish. 'Rest assured, Mr Cameron, I am.'

Her father frowned and helped himself to a drink. His bride-to-be stood perfectly still, a statue before the windows, her lustreless hair caught in the shafts of sunlight as she warned her father off saying more. Another darker thought suddenly occurred to him.

'Have you had trouble with those who waylaid you before?'

Cameron looked at his daughter. God, Daniel thought, had Amethyst Cameron been hurt by the thugs too?

'The wheel of a carriage we were in sheared off just under a year ago because it had been cut almost right through,' she answered, the fright in her eyes visible. 'Our conveyance overturned a number of times and Papa and I were caught inside. We were out on business, you see, and those responsible knew we would be travelling on that road on that day.' Daniel did not speak, but waited as she went on. 'Papa was hurt a little and I was hurt a lot.'

'Who are these people?'

'Criminals who prey on those who might afford to pay them. Men who see an opportunity in the threatening of others and who with a great amount of force can intimidate without fear of redress.' Robert gave him this answer.

'So you refused their demands?'

'You pay once and you never get free,' Amethyst answered, her eyes daring him to criticise things that he knew nothing about. 'People have been brought in to protect us since, and this was working well until...' She faltered.

'Until I found your father in the alley a few moments away from having the life being beaten out of him?'

Unexpectedly she smiled. 'They were more afraid of you than any man Papa had employed before. It is one of the reasons we offered you the marriage agreement.'

'I see.' Did these people always have to be so wearingly honest in their truths? Daniel's own jaded understanding of principle had long ago been leached from him and there was a sort of brave virtue in such directness. The *ton* would tear such rectitude to pieces, he thought, and wondered how life could mould people so differently.

'Have those demanding money ever contacted you in the form of a letter?'

Robert took over the discourse now. 'Once they did. More normally they just turn up unannounced at the warehouse door.'

'Do you still have the correspondence?'

'Yes.'

'And yet you have not sought anyone to help you in this matter?'

'Help me?' Robert's voice was puzzled.

'Threaten them back. Make them realise they were playing a game they had no hope of ever winning.'

The Earl's tone was weary, Amethyst thought. The utter nuisance of having to deal with people of the trade who had a raft of bullies chasing after them was more than he wanted to consider. Why, he probably thought such inconvenience was par for the course, just another way to show how base and shabby those below him in rank really were.

She wondered if he would simply turn tail and let himself out of this room full of problems, his beautifully cut tailcoat showing off fine shoulders and the breeches long and tapered legs.

A man of reduced means but of great presence, a man whom women would watch with hope in their hearts. Even she had watched him as he had ascended the stairs with her father outside of Tattersall's and dreamed that she was a different girl with softer hair falling to her hips in luxurious waves as he admired her.

Such nonsense made her smile. She was her father's daughter with trade flowing through her less-than-exalted blood line, the hunt of a good deal or an unexpected profit making her life...whole. Women like her did not marry for love and men like Lord Daniel Wylde invariably chose the beautiful butterflies who were the toast of a society Season.

It was only lack of money that stopped him doing exactly that and thinking otherwise would lead to disappointment. The marriage agreement held as much fear for her as it did for him, but she needed her father protected and she wanted to see him face the last months of his life with hope.

She had visited his doctor alone on her own accord after her father had told her of his ailment. The specialist had reiterated that there was little more the medical fraternity could do, but had been most insistent on the medicinal value of hope. Miracles had arisen from a happy demeanour or a looked-forward-to occasion that the sick one had no intentions of missing. Aye, he had said in tones that bridged no argument, there were miracles in the benefits of laughter that even the greatest brains of the time had not yet figured out. 'Keep him happy, Miss Cameron, and he may live longer. That is the only sage advice I can give you at this point.'

Well, Amethyst decided, she would do everything in her power to advance this theory and her papa would have each second of his life tempered with good humour and possibilities. She swore to the heavens above that this would be so.

A few moments later after a general conversation

with her father on the merits of a horse that had won a recent race at Newmarket, Lord Montcliffe reached for his hat and made for the door, giving only the briefest of goodbyes to her as he left. A man who was being forced into something he plainly did not want and yet, given his circumstances, could not refuse.

They were so much the same, Amethyst thought, as the door shut behind him and the hollow silence that was left only underlined the awful truth of her musing.

Chapter Four

Daniel sat in his library that evening before a fire that was both warm and comforting. Looking up, he frowned at the portrait of his brother lording it over the room. He would have a servant take the painting down on the morrow and he would find a landscape of Spain he knew to be somewhere in the confines of this town house. Nigel's foolishness had brought the Earldom to this pass and he wanted no more of a reminder of his brother's handsome visage smiling down upon his own dire straits.

The cool of early evening moved in about him despite the fire flame in the hearth, his leg still aching with the slightest of movements. Outside a dog called, the plaintive howl answered as he listened and silently counted the hours until the dawn. How often had he sat like this since his return from Europe? Even as he massaged the tight knots in his thigh, others formed in their place, iron-hard against the skin that covered muscle. His leg was getting worse. He knew it was.

Would there come a day when he could not bear weight upon it at all? He swore beneath his breath and resolved not to think about it.

A knock at his door had him returning his leg to the floor and when his man came in with a card showing that Miss Amethyst Cameron was waiting to see him, his eyes glanced at the clock. Half past eight. My God. No time at all for a young and single woman of any station in life to be calling upon a gentleman without the repercussion of ruin. Following his servant to the lobby he found his bride-to-be standing there, no lady's maid at her side and no papa to keep everything above board and proper, either. Glancing around, he was relieved to see a Cameron footman waiting in the shadow of the porch, ready to shepherd her back through the evening.

'I am very sorry to come at such a late hour, but I need to speak with you, my lord.'

Worry marred her brow and she seemed relieved as he gestured her through to the blue salon, the scent of lemon and flowers following her in. Her dull brown hair this evening was pulled back and fastened with a glittery pin. It was the first piece of jewellery he had ever seen her wear.

'Carole, one of the little girls at Gaskell Street, made the fastener for me and presented it to me this evening,' she explained when she realised what had caught his attention. 'A beaker was broken at the school last week and she fashioned the shards of china into a clip.' Her smile broadened and it had the effect of making her eyes look bigger in her face than they usually were.

And much more gold. Perfectly arched dark eyebrows sat above them.

'I have just come from the school concert, my lord.' Even as she said it she removed the clip from her hair and deposited it in a large cloth bag she carried.

'You work there?'

'No, I am a patron, my lord, a small recompense for all that they did for me as a child. We are building a new dormitory that will be ready in a matter of only a few weeks and there is much yet to finish and so—' She stopped abruptly and blushed. 'But you cannot possibly be interested in any of this. Papa said I should only speak of happy things, light topics and suchlike. Orphans and all of their accompanying poverty, I suppose, do not come into that category.'

He had to smile. 'I hope I am not quite so shallow, Miss Cameron. The work sounds useful and interesting.'

'Then you would not stop me being involved? You would allow me the independence that I need after this marriage?'

When he nodded Daniel had the sudden impression that he might have been agreeing to far more than he knew he was, but she soon went on to another topic altogether.

'Papa's insistence on a harmonious union should not be too onerous either, my lord. Nowhere in the marriage document is there any mention of how many days a year we would need to reside together. It need not be a trap.'

'Are you always this forthright, Miss Cameron?'

'Yes.' No qualification. She looked at him as if he had just given her the biggest compliment in the world.

'Clinical.'

'Pragmatic,' she returned and blushed to almost the same shade as a scarlet rug thrown across a nearby sofa.

Such vulnerability lurking amongst brave endeavour was strangely endearing and although he meant not to Daniel caught at her hand. He wanted to protect her from a world that would not quite know what to make of her; his world, where the cut of a cloth was as important as the name of the family and the consideration of others less fortunate in means was best left to the worry of others or to nobody at all.

As he had already noted, she smelt of lemon and flowers, none of the heady heavy aromas the ladies in court seemed to be drawn towards and desire ignited within him, as unexpected as it was unwanted. Abruptly he let her go.

'You must know that it is not done for a lady to visit a gentleman alone, Miss Cameron, under any circumstances.'

'Oh, I am not a lady, my lord.'

'You soon will be.'

Again she shook her head. 'I do not wish to change, Lord Montcliffe. There is just simply too much for me to do. This is why I have come to make certain that you know…' She stopped, and he got the impression she was trying to work out exactly how she might give him her truths.

'Know what?'

'I will marry you, my lord, and my father will in turn nullify the debts of your family. But in exchange I wish for two things.'

She waited as he nodded.

'I want you to make certain no one will ever bother my father again and I want you to promise that when Papa leaves this world...' her voice caught '...you will let me go.'

'Let you go?'

'I will not contest the monies at all, though I will expect a substantial settlement and Dunstan House, of course, and its accompanying lands.'

'My God. You are serious?'

She nodded her head. 'I am a business woman, my lord, and astute enough to know that this marriage is only one of convenience. You would never have chosen me without the enticement of great wealth and I accept that, but I do want civility and fairness.'

Each word she said was more astonishing than the last. He had had all manner of women throwing themselves at him for years and here was one telling him to his face that a marriage between them was purely a matter of business, and finite at that.

'What of your needs in this union, Miss Cameron?'

'I don't have any as such, Lord Montcliffe. I simply want my father to be content in the last months of his life. That is all.'

Daniel was not one to turn away from such a gauntlet.

'And emotion? Where does that fit into this conundrum?'

She shook her head vigorously, the brown tresses marked with no sheen from the lamplight. She had stepped back too, her strange large bag positioned between them like a barrier.

'I do realise that as a titled gentleman you would require the production of heirs and as such this agreement will give you the time to find a woman you would want as the chosen mother of your children. You are not so old, after all, and gentlemen of the *ton* have a marked propensity to choose much younger wives from what I have observed.'

Without meaning to he smiled, such direct honesty so very unfamiliar.

His glance went to her lips, full and defined, and he felt a surge of desire. God, it had been years since his libido had been so fickle and months since he had last bedded a woman.

The world seemed to stand still between them, any logic sucked into pure and utter confusion. Any other female of his acquaintance would have simpered and flushed in such a situation, but she stood there watching him, her glance strong and unwavering.

'I also hope you are of the same opinion concerning this marriage as I am and share the belief that it would require no…no…' She stopped, searching around for what to say and failing.

'Intimacy?' He gave the word in humour, but she paled visibly, reminding him in that moment of a skittish colt, wanting to be reassured on the one hand and ready to bolt on the other.

'I realise, my lord, that there must be a great many

young women in the *ton* who would jump at the chance of being an earl's wife in general and your wife in particular. Even with the imminent financial collapse of the Montcliffe estate I feel certain you would still be a good catch. With the Cameron fortune behind you there would be a far better chance of acquiring exactly the sort of woman you would wish for. I could simply disappear and never be seen again, a former spouse who should not be a problem if I was to be thought of as dead. I would be quite happy with such an outcome if Papa was no longer with me. Indeed, I could go to the Continent and settle under a different name.'

'You are seriously expounding bigamy?'

He began to laugh then, because what she said was becoming more and more outlandish and because he could barely believe that she was saying it.

'Perhaps I am, my lord, though in the very best sense of the word, of course, and mutually agreed. I would also like to add that I wouldn't have acquiesced to a union between us if I had not liked your character. I realised, quite early on, that it was most unlikely you would have ever been attracted to me in the slightest, had we met under other circumstances, and there was a good deal of safety in that.'

A challenge thrown down between them, Daniel thought to himself, and given with such an engaging and disarming frankness.

'Such safety, Miss Cameron, is not the best building block for any marriage and I shall show you exactly why.' Without asking for permission, he dispensed with the bag and brought her into his arms.

* * *

She should have been horrified. She should have fought off his grip and demanded release as his hands brought her in and his lips came down on hers. But her head would not obey her heart as warmth seared into disbelief and the world narrowed to a feeling that began in a place low in her stomach, before exploding everywhere.

His kiss was not gentle or tentative or kind. It was raw and masculine with an edge of anger demanding response. It was deep and unexpected, his tongue finding hers as the angle of the kiss changed, slanting on to another plane, splayed palms guiding her in, the sound of breath, the dissolution of the world around them, the focus of heat and want and need.

Another language that she had had no notion of. The clock in the corner with its heavy beat seemed to stop as she tasted him in return, his strength, his toughness, the sheer and potent force of a man who understood the power he wielded. There was no question of resisting. When her nails traced a runnel in his skin to bring him closer, his lips slid down the sensitive line of her neck. They would mark each other with this moment, she thought, as she tipped her head, the column of her throat exposed to the hard pull of his mouth.

But as his hand wandered to trace the line of her bottom under her billowing skirt she jerked back, the hue on her cheeks rising. This was unlike anything she had imagined. The danger of her response made her feel dizzy.

She needed to be gone, away from this room, away

from the things that she knew must be reflected in her eyes and on her face and in the hard twin buds of desire that pushed against the material in her bodice.

She was pleased both for the coat and for the fact that he had turned to face the window so that she did not need to see his expression. Not yet. With shaking hands she opened the door.

'I am glad we had this…t-talk, my lord, but now I must go.'

Then she was outside, her footman following closely behind down the steps of the Montcliffe town house. As they gained the road the servant gestured to the Cameron conveyance a good hundred yards away to collect them. She had asked the driver to park there, away from the prying eyes of others.

She prayed Daniel Wylde would not follow to demand an answer to all that had transpired between them. Her father was dying and she would do anything at all in her power to make him happy, even marry a man who, she knew in that very second, could only break her heart. Wiping away a tear, she swallowed and took a deep breath, the strength she had always kept a hold on returning.

At least he understood now the parameters of this relationship. Or did he?

'Hell.' Daniel adjusted the fit of his trousers over a growing hardness. She had dumbfounded him with her reaction to his kiss, no tepid chaste reply, but a full-blown taking of everything he had offered, the promise of lust in the way her teeth had come down on his bottom lip, egging on all that he had held restrained.

Like a siren. Like a courtesan. Like a woman of far more experience than she was admitting to.

His plain little intended mouse-to-be was baring her claws and turning into a lioness and all before they had even got up the matrimonial aisle. Nothing made sense any more because the only thing he was thinking about was following her and demanding the completion of an intimacy that had left him reeling.

He was glad that her scent lingered in the room, glad to keep the promise of Amethyst Cameron for a little while longer. The cloth bag she had brought in was still beside the sofa, abandoned in her moment of panic, some item of clothing spilling out on to his thick burgundy Aubusson carpet.

As he hauled the thing upwards, one handle broke and the contents tumbled out. An apron and a tattered Bible were the first things that had fallen at his feet, Amethyst's name printed in the frontispiece of the book and underlined in different colours. He smiled, imagining her doing such a thing. Beneath that was a ragdoll with a torn dress and another toy whose identity he could not determine—a cat perhaps, its paws missing. Incredibly, a diamond ring also sat there amongst the folds of cloth, the carat weight sizeable, and the cut, colour and clarity unmatched. Valuable and forgotten, strands of cotton and dust caught in the clasps of gold.

Any other woman of his acquaintance would have worn the thing on her finger, showing it off, enjoying the admiration of others, but not Amethyst Cameron.

No, to her the dismembered cat probably had more of a value and the Bible a better use.

Stuffing the lot back in the bag, he called to his footman.

'Have this delivered to the Camerons' home in Grosvenor Square immediately.' Daniel did not wish to take the thing himself, an unaccustomed fragility setting his countenance on edge after the last few minutes with his bride-to-be.

He tried not to notice the curiosity in his man's eyes as he handed the bag over.

Her father was still up when she got home and Amethyst's heart sank. Of all the nights he had delayed retiring to his bedchamber, why did it have to be this one?

'Papa.' She tried to keep her voice steady, but knew that she had not succeeded as he stood.

'What has happened? You look…different.'

She almost smiled at that. *Different.* Such a word came nowhere near the heart of all that she felt.

'I went to see Lord Montcliffe.'

'And?'

'I am not certain if he was the right choice after all. I think he might want a lot from me, more than I should be willing to give.'

Her father laughed. 'Your mother said that of me.'

'He kissed me.'

The stillness in his eyes was foreign. 'Did you like it?'

Her heart thudded as she nodded.

'Then he was the right choice, Amy, for although society is disparaging in allowing any intimate contact between intending couples I think that it should be mandatory. As long as it is a consenting thing. He did not force you?'

'No.'

'If your mother was here, she would tell you of the power of feelings between a man and a woman and she would say it better than I. Whitely knew nothing about you, my dear. He did not appreciate the layers in a woman or the complexities.'

Anger rose where only guilt had lingered. Until this moment Amethyst had always thought their broken marriage was her fault, but after Daniel Wylde's kiss she wondered. Gerald had kissed her a few times in the very early days of their courtship, but his pecks were tepid reflections of all she had felt in the heated atmosphere of Lord Montcliffe's library. The breath constricted in her throat and she swallowed back worry. If she could react this way to one of the Earl's kisses, what might happen if things went further? The teachers at Gaskell Street had always drilled her upon the proper and correct reactions a lady might show to the world and she was certain that her response tonight would have been well outside any appropriate boundary.

Decorum and seemliness were the building stones of the aristocracy. The gentler sex was supposed to be exactly that, after all—women devoid of all the more natural vices men were renowned for. She wished her mother was here to give some advice and direction.

Her father, however, seemed, more than ready to supply some.

'Whitely was a conniving liar, that was the problem. He was no more than an acquaintance when you married him and nothing more when he died. I tried to warn you, but you would not listen. If your mother had still been alive, I am certain things would have been different, but it is hard to advise anyone against something they have their very heart set upon.'

His words dug into Amethyst's centre. Her fault. Her mistake. Her deficiency to tumble into a relationship that had been patently wrong from the very start.

With Gerald there had been no true underpinning attraction. With Daniel it was the opposite. She did not know him at all and yet... She shook away the justification. Lust was shaky ground to build a relationship upon and she could not afford another disaster.

Her father's coughing started in a little way at first, a clearing of a throat, a slight impediment. But then his eyes rolled back and he simply dropped, folding in on himself, a slight man with his jacket askew and his spectacles crushed underfoot.

She shouted out as the doorbell rang and the Cameron butler and a stranger rushed into the room, the bag she had left at the Montcliffe town house abandoned at their feet as they both lifted her father to the *chaise longue*. Wilson untied his cravat and loosened his collar, arranging Robert on his side so that his breathing was eased.

Amethyst could not move. She was frozen in fear as the numbness spreading across her chest emptied her of rational thought. Was it his heart? Was this the final moment of which the specialist had spoken?

'Get a doctor.' Their butler seemed to have taken charge and the man she did not know nodded and left the room. A Montcliffe servant, she supposed, returning her bag. Nothing made sense any more. The housekeeper scurried in with a hot towel and a bowl, the maid kneeling with new wood to stoke up the heat of the fire, Wilson trying to awaken her father from the stupor he had fallen into. The moments turned into a good half an hour.

And then Lord Montcliffe was there, his voice calm with authority as he took in the situation, a doctor at his side.

Amethyst's jaw ached from where she held it tightly together, but when he took her arm and led her across to her father, she went.

'Hold his hand and sit beside him. Talk to him so that he knows you are there.'

When Robert's wilted fingers came into her grasp she held on. Cold. Familiar. The scar upon his little finger where he had fallen through glass, a nail pulled out by heavy timber. A working man's hand and the hand of a father who had loved her well. She brought the back of it to her lips, paper-thin skin marred by brown spots, age drawn into years of outside work. Kissing him, she willed him back, willed him to open his eyes and see her. The doctor frowned as he felt for a pulse.

'Is there other family we can call?'

She shook her head.

Just her and just Papa. The horror of loss ran through her like sharpened swords and her teeth had begun to chatter, shock searing into trauma. For a moment the next breath just would not come.

Daniel kneeled down before her, hoping the panic he could see in her eyes might allow her more of an ease of breath. 'Anything that can be done for your father will be, Miss Cameron. MacKenzie, my physician, is the best doctor there is in London. Do you understand?'

Her eyes focused upon him, a tiny flare of hope scrambling over alarm.

'Already with the blankets and the fire he is becoming warmer and the blueness is leaving his lips.'

This time she nodded her head, one slow tear leaking from her left eye and tracing its way down her cheek.

Both of the Camerons looked as pale as the other and as thin. He had not noticed her thinness until this moment, when devoid of her coat in the bright light he could see her arms and her collarbones and the meagreness of her waist.

She did not court fashion, that much was certain. Her boots were sturdy leather and well worn, as though they had covered many a mile, and still had some life left in them. But sitting there in the grip of tragedy, there was a fineness about Amethyst Cameron that was mesmerising. All he wanted to do was to hold her away from the hurt and make things better. To protect her against a world that was often cruel, complex and dishonest. To shield her from pain, duplicity and scorn.

When the doctor gestured him over he stood.

'Mr Cameron will need to be watched, my lord, but I think we have passed the worst of it. All his vital signs are settling and I should well imagine that he will recover from this turn.'

Daniel knew Amethyst had heard the given words even though she was a good distance away. He also knew that if he stayed in the house without a chaperone for any longer then tongues would begin to wag. It was late after all.

'I will leave the doctor with you then, Miss Cameron, and hope your father has a good night.' He met her eyes only briefly and her countenance was one of worry, no glimpse at all alluding to the kiss they had shared less than an hour earlier. He was pleased for it.

'I appreciate your help, Lord Montcliffe.'

So formal and distant, he thought, as she escorted him to the front lobby, one of the servants finding his coat and hat. Her hair looked odd too, the front of it hitched askew in a strange fashion. Nothing about this woman seemed to make sense to him and he was relieved to slip through the door and into the coolness of the night air.

Leaning against the portal and closing her eyes for just a moment Amethyst listened to the Montcliffe carriage pull away. 'One second, two seconds, three seconds,' she counted, holding the world back from all that was crashing in upon her. Her mama had taught her this years before, a small space of time in which to collect one's thoughts or feelings. The feeling of Daniel Wylde's kiss snaked into her consciousness even as she tried to shut it out.

When at length she gathered herself, Amethyst caught her reflection in a mirror opposite and horror and laughter mingled on her face in equal measure.

Her wig had been snagged at some point and was sitting at an angle on her head, the right side dragging the left down and giving her an appearance of someone out of sorts with the world.

With care she readjusted the hairpiece. Had this just happened or had Lord Montcliffe seen it as well? The whole evening had been tumultuous; her father's strange malady counterbalanced against the Earl of Montcliffe's unexpected kiss.

Wiping her forefinger along the lines of her lips, she then held it still, the impression of flesh sending small shards of want into a sense that had long been dormant.

She was known for her composure and her unruffled calm. She seldom let things bother her and always managed people with acumen and honesty.

Unflappable Amethyst. Until Lord Daniel Wylde.

He made her think of possibilities that would not come to pass. She was ruined goods and she was plain. Without the Montcliffe financial problems and the collection by her father of the extensive Goldsmith debts, he would never have given her a second glance.

She could not allow herself to be one of those pathetic women who didn't see the truth of their loveless marriages and held on for year after year for something that was impossible.

Two years was what she could give him. Two years

in which her father would not be sad or worried or unhappy. If he even lived that long, which was doubtful.

The Earl of Montcliffe would not love her and she would not let herself love him. But together they could manage. The kiss had thrown her, that was all, an unexpected chink in the armour she had long pulled about her.

Liar. Liar. Liar. The words ran together as a refrain as she hurried back to her father.

Lucien Howard, Earl of Ross, sat beside Daniel in the card room of White's an hour later. Smoke swirled around in curls and the smell of strong liquor filled any space left as some patrons won a little and others lost a lot.

'I hear you bought those remarkable Arabian greys at Tattersall's?' There was a good measure of curiosity in his friend's query.

'You know enough about my present circumstances, Luce, to know I could never afford them.'

'Then why are they in your care?'

'Have you heard of the trader, Mr Robert Cameron?'

'No. Who is he?'

'A man who sells timber to the world.'

'Lucrative, then?'

'Very. He wants me to marry his daughter.'

Brandy slopped against the side of the glass as Lucien lurched forward. 'You agreed?'

'The matching pair of greys came as a sweetener. Montcliffe Manor is bankrupt and it will only be a matter of months before the rest of the world knows the fact.' He raised his glass and then swallowed a good part of the contents of the bottle he had ordered. 'If I do nothing, it will all be gone.'

Lucien was quiet for a moment, but then he smiled. 'What does the daughter look like?'

'Passable.'

'Your bastard of a father must be laughing in the afterlife then. At least he was a man of his word. I remember him insisting that you wouldn't inherit a farthing of his fortune and he meant it.'

'The curse of the Wyldes?' Daniel's thoughts fell into words.

'How long do you have left, do you think, if you sat it out and did nothing?'

'It will only be a matter of weeks before the first creditors arrive.' Leaning back against soft leather, he ran his hands through his hair. 'I have had word that they are already circling.'

'I'd lend you money if I had any, but my situation is about as dire as your own.'

'Your grandfather wants to disinherit your side of the family again? I heard about it from Francis before he left for Bath.'

'Where he has gone to try to sort out his own financial woes, no doubt. Seems he has a cousin a few times removed there causing him some trouble.'

Daniel smiled. 'The three of us have our problems then, though mine could be solved before the month is up.'

'You will go through with it? This betrothal?'

'Marriage or bankruptcy? I have little choice.'

'It wasn't supposed to be like this. We were all going to travel to the Far East and make our fortunes, remember? God, that sort of innocence seems so long ago.'

'The naivety of youth.'

'Or the hope of it. Marriage is a big step, Daniel. Is this bride-to-be at least intelligent?'

'Undeniably.'

'Does she simper?'

'No.'

'An heiress who has brains and is not prone to whining? Perhaps you have made more of a match than you imagine. What colour is her hair?'

'A dull mouse.'

Lucien began to laugh. 'And her eyes?'

'Brown.'

'Is she fat?'

'Thin.'

'Short?'

'No.'

'Mama was always certain you would marry the moody but beautiful Charlotte Hughes. She is back, you know, from Scotland and without the husband.'

'Spenser Mackay died by all accounts.'

'But in doing so he left her a fortune which she probably needs about as much as you do. The *ton* likes to think you were heartbroken when she left, Daniel.'

'A good tale is often more interesting than a truthful one.'

'Have you told the Countess about your upcoming nuptials?'

'I haven't.'

'But you will?'

'No. The wedding is in a few weeks' time. Mother would need at least a month to get ready for it and even that might not be enough. Would you be the best man, Luce?'

'I would be honoured to.'

'Francis will be the usher, I hope. I sent a message to Bath yesterday telling him of the plans. The announcement will be in *The Times* next week.'

'A few more hours of peace, then. When can I meet your intended?'

'I'm calling on her on Monday. Perhaps you might accompany me?'

A furore at the other end of the room caught their attention and Lord Gabriel Hughes, the fourth Earl of Wesley, strode in, a tall stranger hanging on his shoulder and pushed off with a nonchalance that was surprising.

'London is not as it was, my lords. Nordmeyer insists that I insulted his sister and wants to call me out for it.'

'And did you insult her?'

'She sent me a note arranging a meeting and he found it. I hardly think that was my fault.'

'But you would have met her if the letter had arrived?'

'Undoubtedly.'

Laughter was as good a medicine as any, Daniel thought as Gabe ordered a drink. A few years ago he and Gabriel Hughes had been good friends, but he hadn't seen much of him lately. Charlotte's influence, perhaps. The women in the family had always been surprisingly persuasive.

'I hear you were the one who bought the pair of greys showing at Tattersall's a few weeks back, Montcliffe. Richard Tattersall had designs to procure them himself, but it seems you beat him to it with an irrefusable offer.'

Daniel wondered where this story had originated. Robert Cameron, perhaps, for the man was as wily as he was rich.

'The Montcliffe coffers must be in good shape, then, for they would have not come cheap,' Gabriel remarked. An undercurrent of question lay in the words. 'And speaking of good shape, my sister is home again and had hoped that you might call upon her?'

'I saw her today. In Regent Street.'

'How did she appear to you?' The heavy frown on Gabriel's forehead was worrying.

'In good health. Your mother was with her.'

'She seldom allows Charlotte out of her sight. I think she is worried that grief might get the better of her.'

'Grief for the death of her husband?'

The short bark of laughter was disconcerting. 'She realised that Spenser Mackay was a mistake before she had even come within a cooee of the Borderlands.'

'Another man, then?' Lucien joined in the conversation now.

But as if realising he had said too much, Gabriel Hughes gestured to the waiter and ordered another drink.

'I propose a toast to our bachelorhood, gentlemen,

and long may it last.' As Lucien lifted his glass Daniel caught his eyes and the deep humour obvious in the blue depths was disconcerting.

Chapter Five

Daniel Wylde and she were in bed at Dunstan House, candlelight covering their bodies and her hair to the waist.

'Love me for ever, my beautiful Amethyst,' he said as he brought his lips down upon her own, hard and slanted, desire moulding her body into his, asking for all that she knew he would give her. His fingers framed her face, tilting her into the caress, building the connection. 'Love me as I love you, my darling, never let us be apart.'

And then she was awake in her own chamber at Grosvenor Square, the moon high outside. Alone. The dream of Lord Montcliffe dissolved into a formless want and the need that she had no hope in wishing for dissipated. He would not love her like that, he could not.

Pushing back the covers, she stood and lit a candle before crossing to the bookshelves on one side of the room.

Here behind a row of burgundy leather tomes she found what she had hidden. Her diary. A narrative of

Gerald Whitely and their time together, every emotion she had felt for him penned in black and white. And in red, too, her blood smeared across one page mixed in troth with his. A small cut below the nail of her thumb. Sometimes she felt it with the pad of her opposing finger. He had laughed at the time and told her she was being melodramatic. Then he had stopped laughing altogether. The small book fell open at one of the pages.

I hate him. I hate everything about him. I hate his drunkenness and his anger. I hate it that I was stupid enough to become his wife. I think Papa suspects that there is something wrong between us and I hate that, too.

As she riffled through to the end of the book, there seemed to be a myriad of variations on that theme and she remembered again exactly what hopelessness felt like.

After his death she had not trusted anyone except for her father. After Gerald the world of possibility and expectation had shrunk into a formless mist, her big mistake relegated to that part of her mind which refused to be hurt again, but even thirteen months later the horror had left an indelible mark.

The business of making money had been healing, saving her from the ignominy of venturing back into the pursuit of another mate. Oh, she had gone to Gerald's funeral and attended his grave, placing flowers and small offerings because it was expected. She had also worn her mourning garb for the obligatory year because she could have not borne the questions that might have occurred otherwise. Even in death she had not betrayed him.

A single tear dropped upon the sheet below, blurring the careful writing.

A blemished bride. Then and now. Granted, she came to this next union with a dowry that was substantial and with the means to save a family on the brink of devastation. It must count for something.

But the kiss Daniel Wylde and she had shared was worrying because in it were the seeds of her own destruction.

Not like Gerald Whitely. Not like him at all.

The voyeur inside her who had been watching others for years was threatened, the safe distance she had fostered shattered by a hope she had never known, for when Lord Montcliffe had taken her hand and then her lips something in her had risen and his gold-green eyes had known it had.

Looking back, she could not understand just what had led her into the mistake of marrying Whitely in the first place. Loneliness, perhaps, or the fact that the years were rushing by. Certainly it had not been a blinding love or even a distilled version of affection. No, she had married Gerald because no one else had ever given her a second look and she was starting to feel as if spinsterhood was just around a very close corner.

Her father's respect for his business acumen might have also made a difference. Amythest wanted to marry a man whom Robert would regard with fondness and Gerald had arrived at the warehouse with glowing references and a comforting confidence. A man who at first brought her flowers and pretty hand-kerchiefs and professed that he had never in his whole life seen anyone as beautiful as she was.

When the nasty side of him had surfaced a month or so before their marriage she should have cut her losses and run. Her father would have understood and there was no one else whose opinion she cared much about. Yet still she had persisted in believing that she could calm Gerald's anger and gently soothe all the problems he seemed to have with others.

Marriage had changed that. The admonishments had been verbal at first, just small criticisms of her dress and her hair. Then he had used his fists.

Fear had held her rigid and distant, the shame and the anger at her stupidity buried under a carefully constructed outer mask. She could not believe that she had been so gullible and foolish as to imagine a wonderful life with a man she had barely known. When he had died sixteen months later Amethyst had not seen him for a good handful of weeks before that and her heart-felt relief added to the guilt of everything.

Four mornings after the kiss she had shared with Lord Montcliffe she felt full of anxiety. Her intended was waiting downstairs in the Blue Salon and he had brought a friend with him. To see what trap the Earl had tumbled into, she supposed, the sour taste of trade balanced by a wife who was at least wealthy enough to save Montcliffe.

After nights of poor sleep and lurid dreams Amethyst felt exposed; pinned to a board like a butterfly in some scientific laboratory, wings outstretched and colours fading into dust. No possible defences. No protection against the disdain he surely must be feeling.

At least the wig felt like armour and the dark purple bombazine in her gown was sturdy enough to withstand any amount of derision. As she opened the door of the salon they had been directed to, the smile on her face was tight.

'My lord.' She did not allow Daniel Wylde to take her fingers or to touch her as she inclined her head.

'Miss Cameron.' There was a slight hesitation in his greeting. 'I hope your father has had a few comfortable nights and is feeling better after his fall.'

'He is, my lord, thank you, though he is under strict instructions to stay in bed for a few more days yet. Your doctor was most insistent about that. Perhaps I should have informed you,' she added as an afterthought, suddenly uncertain of the rules around being unchaperoned even in her own house.

'We will not stay long. May I introduce my good friend to you? Lucien Howard, Earl of Ross, this is Miss Amethyst Amelia Cameron, my intended.'

The man who stood by the mantelpiece watched her carefully. With hair as pale as Daniel Wylde's was dark, he held the same sort of stillness and menace. She also thought she saw a hitch of puzzlement in his eyes.

'Montcliffe has told me all about you, Miss Cameron.'

'I should not think there would be much to say, my lord.'

Unexpectedly Lord Ross laughed. 'Actually, I am more surprised by all he didn't.'

Glancing over at Daniel, Amethyst wondered how much honesty he would allow. She decided to test him.

'It is a truism that great wealth holds a loud persuasion. As a good friend of Montcliffe's you must realise this.'

The stance of relaxed grace did not change a whit, but Lord Montcliffe had moved closer and Amethyst felt that same sharp jolt of shock with an ache. She did not look her best today, she knew it. The wig itched unremittingly and the red around her eyes from poor sleep did her no favours whatsoever. She had tried to assuage the damage with some powder she had asked her maid to fetch from the pharmacist yesterday, but the application was difficult and she wondered if instead of hiding the problem she had accentuated it. She wished now that she had simply wiped the powder off before entering the room.

'Miss Cameron runs the books for the Cameron timber company, Luce. According to her father she is irreplaceable in her knowledge of the trade.'

Was the Earl criticising her? His words did not seem slanted with distaste so mayhap this was another example of her not comprehending the ways of the *ton*. His friend's face was carefully schooled to show as little emotion as Montcliffe's did, allowing her no way of understanding the truth.

'I have heard it said that you have a knowledge of

horseflesh too, Miss Cameron? Your father's pair of greys were the talk of the town a few weeks back and, when I went in to look them over, Tattersall mentioned your name on the ownership deeds.'

'Papa and I generally consult on new purchases, my lord. That particular pair was procured on a trip we made to Spain together three years ago.' She stopped, thinking perhaps she sounded boastful.

'I see. Montcliffe raised horses when we were younger too. Before the war took us into Spain and they were lost to him.'

'You were in the army, as well?'

'It is the curse of an estate of great title, but little in the way to support it, Miss Cameron. 'Twas either that or the church and the stipend in religion is miserable.'

As he said the words Lucien Howard turned and the light from the window directly behind him fell across a large swathe of scarring at his neck. Averting her eyes, Amethyst hoped he had not seen just where her interest lay, though when she glanced over at Daniel she knew a momentary consternation. The easy-going lord of the realm seemed replaced by another, hard distance coating his every feature, memory overlaid by anger.

War wounds. She had seen the soldiers from the Peninsular Campaign as they had stumbled up the quayside of all the ports between Falmouth and Dover the previous year in the final days of January. She had been in the south with her father, checking on a new timber delivery, and the filthy, ill and skeletal men had been a shocking sight. Thirty-five thousand men had crossed the Spanish frontier to march against Napoleon and eight thousand had not returned. Lord Montcliffe and his friend Lord Ross had no doubt been amongst those on the crowded transports in the Bay of Biscay storms. She could barely imagine what nightmares such a journey would have brought.

Daniel was a stranger to her, all the pieces of his past unknown and the sum of his whole unchartered. The cold thought clawed into consciousness but she shook such a musing away, colouring as she realised her guests were looking at her as though expecting an answer to a question.

'I am sorry, I did not hear what you asked.'

'Lucien wished to know if you would allow his younger sister to help you get ready on your wedding day.'

'Oh.' Amethyst did not quite know how to answer this. She had always been surrounded by men in the business of trading timber and had seldom had the time to foster any relationship with women.

The Earl of Ross took up the conversation now. 'Christine lost her betrothed in the march up to La Corunna and she is a little depressed. Helping in the preparation for a wedding might be just the distraction she needs.'

'I should imagine your sister would find me most dull.'

'She loves hairstyles and dresses and decorating homes.'

Amethyst's heart sank.

'And she can make an occasion of anything.'

Hard to make an occasion with the two participants

pressed into a union neither wished for. Placing a false smile on her lips, Amethyst nodded.

'Then I would be most thankful for her help.'

Montcliffe appeared as though he was about to laugh, but the arrival of the maid with an assortment of small cakes and lemonade put paid to that expression. Pouring three generous glasses, she handed one to each of them and invited them to sit down.

'The speciality of the house is this lemon syrup. I hope you will enjoy it.' The lemonade was cold and sour, exactly the way she and her father liked it, yet both men looked to be struggling with the taste. Even yesterday she might have been mortified to think that the beverage was not quite right, but today for some reason the fact made her smile.

The control she seldom lost hold of had seemed to slip of late and the small victory was welcomed. She knew, of course, that they would be far more at home with some alcoholic drink, but it was only just midday and the hour seemed too early to be serving something as strong without Papa present.

When Lord Montcliffe stood she was certain that he would be taking his leave, but he walked across to the window instead to observe a view of the park opposite.

'This house is well situated. Do you take exercise there?'

'Sometimes I do, my lord. More normally though I ride my horse in Hyde Park in the late afternoon.'

'Will you be there tomorrow?'

He had not turned, but she felt a palpable tension as he waited for her answer.

'I shall. I take a turn or two around Rotten Row most days.'

'Good.'

At that Lucien Howard also stood and both men gave their leave and were gone within a moment. When the door shut behind them Amethyst remained very still. Had Daniel arranged a meeting between them for tomorrow or not? The two almost-full glasses of lemonade stood on the table and she picked up the one Daniel had used and sipped from it. Ridiculous, she knew, but he made her feel that way: girlish, breathless, terrified.

Her father's bell was ringing. Papa was waiting for an account of the meeting, she supposed, but still she did not move. Would Daniel ride alone tomorrow? Her maid always accompanied her to the park, but stayed on a seat near the gateway. Would this allow them some privacy? Did she want it?

Gerald had been disappointed in her so very quickly. She had held his attention only briefly before he had ventured forth to find other avenues of satisfaction. He had found her gauche and stiff. He had told her that the night he had left for the last time, a wife who was nothing like he had imagined she would be, but she could not dwell on it. 'I deserve to be happy, and so does Papa,' she muttered to herself and caught sight of a small bird on a branch outside.

'If I close my eyes and count to ten and it is still there, then all shall be fine.'

When she opened them the sight of an empty branch

greeted her, the buds of new leaves shivering with the motion of its parting.

Signs. She looked for them everywhere now, good and bad, but the hectic tinkle of her father's bell had her moving from the room and up the wide oaken staircase.

She absolutely had to tell him. Today. Now. This minute. The early evening light sending redness into his raven hair and the green of the oaks all about them.

I have been married before. My husband died in a brothel because he could no longer abide the pretence of me in his marriage bed. It was not a successful union and by the end of it we hated each other.

That was what she should have said. Out loud. With conviction. Let Daniel run before the knots tied them irrevocably together and the blame game began. But she stayed silent as she watched him rein in his steed and move beside her. The time to confess everything about her tawdry past was not quite right and she wanted just for this moment to enjoy his company. Next time. She would definitely tell him of her unfortunate mistake next time they met.

'I did not think you were coming,' he remarked.

'Papa passed a fidgety night and I have spent the day reading to him as it makes him relax. I was not certain you would wait.'

'Then we both have much to learn about the other, Miss Cameron, for I have the patience of a saint.'

He didn't look like anything celestial with his wild black hair caught in an untidy queue and his snowy cravat highlighting the darkness of his skin. Nay, today atop the power of his steed he looked like a soldier who might rule the world and use it in whatever way he wished.

The wickedness of his smile and the dancing pale green in his eyes took her form in, a scorching languid perusal that made her glance away. If she had been braver, she might have laughed into the sudden breeze and used his words as a challenge. She might have even thrown back her own. But the days of her certainty had long gone and the battered ends of the mouse-brown wig flew against her face, making her eyes water.

This is me now, this person, small and damaged and scared. A man like this is not to be played with, not to be taken lightly. The weight of the Cameron fortune was heavy on her shoulders and her father's sickness heavier again as she stayed silent.

'Our marriage notice will be in the paper tomorrow morning. I just thought to warn you of it.'

'Warn me?' She could not quite understand his meaning.

'Society has the habit of being ingratiatingly interested in those who gain a title.'

'Unexpectedly, you mean?'

'A new countess is everybody's business, Miss Cameron. It is the way of the world.'

His focus suddenly centred on a small group of mounted women on the path, the stillness in him magnified as he muttered something under his breath.

'It is probably prudent to say nothing of our upcoming nuptials at this stage.' He stopped his horse and waited and she did the same. 'The *ton* is a small group, but their propensity to gossip is enormous and one wrong word can set them into a frenzy.'

Lady Charlotte Mackay and Lady Astoria Jordan were exactly the pair Daniel had no inclination to meet. Dressed in the finest of riding attire, they looked the picture of well-heeled perfection as they slowed down to chat. Amethyst, on the other hand, seemed to have drawn into herself, lips pursed and eyes dull. The light on her hair did nothing to help her appearance either. For the first time since he had met her he wondered if she wore a wig, ill fashioned and dreary. The thought was surprising.

Charlotte's beauty, on the other hand, seemed to radiate around her, the soft blond of her *coiffure* under the riding cap catching the light and falling in an unbroken line to her ample bosom. A tinkling laugh completed the picture.

'Daniel. I knew it was you.' His name curled from her tongue as an invitation, the intimacy that they had once shared drawn into the words. Her glance took in the woman he was with and his bride-to-be stilled perceptibly.

'Lady Charlotte Mackay, this is Miss Amethyst Cameron.'

'Amethyst. An unusual name, I think.' A frown marred the space between Charlotte's sky-blue eyes as she tried to place the family. 'Are you of the Camerons from Fife in Scotland or those closer?'

'Neither, Lady Mackay.' Amethyst's answer was

quietly given and then she smiled, deep dimples evident in each cheek and a knowing humour across her face.

Strength and honour had its own allure, Daniel thought, watching her deflect the other's interest with such acumen. Out here in the open with the promise of a ride before them and a beautiful summer's evening foretelling a hopeful outlook, Charlotte looked over-dressed and overdone. However, as if realising that she would have little more in the way of conversation from Amethyst, she turned her attention towards him.

'I will be here tomorrow at the same time. Perhaps we might enjoy a ride alone.' Her hand closed over Daniel's sleeve and in her inimitable style she leaned across to him, the riding habit she wore cut as low as it could be. 'For old times' sake. For the world that was before it all turned different. For us,' she whispered closely, the breath of her words across his face daring more.

Once he might have smiled back his assent and followed her to the ends of the earth. But that was then and this was now. Amethyst Cameron had looked away, her eyes on the trees far in the distance as the horse below her shuffled.

Tipping his hat to both ladies he disengaged Charlotte's grasp and made his steed walk on. When they were out of earshot he tried to explain.

'Lady Mackay is lonely and—'

Amethyst interrupted him. 'I don't require an explanation, my lord. I won't be that sort of wife.'

He laughed, but the sound was not humorous. 'Then what sort of wife will you be, Miss Cameron?

She did not answer, but the red flush of anger on her face was telling and what had been a comfortable and easy meeting was suddenly difficult. But he needed to explain to her honestly so that she did not imagine he would be a philandering husband.

'We were lovers for three-and-a-half years between the stints of my army duty.' Now she looked around at him. 'I was twenty-seven when I met Charlotte and thirty when she ran off and married Lord Spenser Mackay. He was an extremely wealthy Scottish landowner, you understand, and I was a second son and a soldier.'

'So she broke your heart?'

His laughter this time was much more genuine. 'At the time perhaps I thought that she had.'

'But now...?'

'Now with the wisdom of distance there is the greatest relief in the realisation that we would never have suited.'

'I got the impression that she thinks exactly the opposite.'

'Then she is wrong.' The distance had returned to his voice. 'Do you have a ball dress?'

'Yes. Why?'

'There is a ball on Saturday night which will be well attended. I hope you might accompany me to it?'

'Would your family be there?'

'No. Mama has a slight cold and my two sisters are still young.' He hesitated for a moment. 'I thought you might have known all my particular familial circumstances when you made me your choice of groom?'

For the first time he heard Amethyst laugh as though

she meant it. She simply tossed her head back and sounded happy. He was mesmerised.

'I left the snooping to my father, my lord.'

'And I passed muster?'

'It was the time you spent with Sir John Moore in La Corunna that sealed it for my father, I think. It was said that you were quite the hero on the heights of Penasquedo and he has always admired those who might lay down their life for crown and country, you see.'

'And what of your choice?'

The good humour vanished in a second.

'I no longer trust myself enough to make wise decisions.'

'Which implies that you have made some foolish ones?'

'People change on you when you least expect it, my lord.' She looked at him directly now, the dark of her eyes marked with a softer gold.

'Aye, that they do. Lady Mackay became a woman I did not recognise, but I wouldn't say her intransigence was my problem.'

The small show of her dimples heartened him. 'The blame was hers, you mean.'

'Entirely.'

'And you moved on without looking back?' she asked curiously.

'I did.'

This conversation was taking a surprising turn. Honesty was something she favoured and Lord Daniel Wylde had not held back about his past or lied about it.

Unlike her.

Such knowledge shrivelled her good mood, though their kiss of the other day still lingered below each glance and word. A scorching and undeniable truth embracing neither logic nor reason.

Passing into a narrower path, he took the reins of her horse and pulled them both to a stop. 'Even given the unusual circumstances of our union, Miss Cameron, I want us to be friends.'

Friends. As she had been at first with Gerald Whitely. She hoped he did not see the consternation on her face because what he was offering was honourable.

'I certainly would not wish for two years of bickering.'

She shook her head. Everything he said made perfect sense and she had come into this betrothal only with the expectation of filling the last months of her father's life with happiness. But the kiss they had shared had skewed things, made them different and she could not help but hope that he might eschew convention and take her in his arms, here in the most public of places. That he might kiss her again, show her it had not been all a figment of her imagination, fill in the empty fears with a warm certainty.

But of course he did not, he merely called his horse on and challenged her.

'You ride well, Miss Cameron. At Montcliffe after we are married I would deem it an honour to pit my horse against your own.'

She gave him a smile, her roan shimmying as she let her attention wander. With Montcliffe beside her and the summer breeze in her face Amythest felt the sort of freedom that she had missed for months now.

'I think for a fair competition you would have to allow me a starting distance. Your mount looks as if he might beat anything he was up against.'

He laughed and the sound was honest and true. 'Deimos here was well blooded in the Peninsular Campaign in Spain.'

'Deimos?' she repeated the name. 'The Grecian spirit of dread and terror?'

He smiled. 'Not many would know that.'

'You took him to the Continent?'

'I rode with the Eighteenth Light Dragoons under Lord Paget.'

'Is that where you hurt your leg?'

'On the last day at La Corunna. The medic couldn't get the bullet out.'

'So it is still in there?' she asked, horrified.

'And hurting like hell.' Unexpectedly he smiled. 'I don't usually talk about the injury and certainly seldom admit to any pain.'

'Why do you not simply have the shot removed then? Here, in London?'

'The surgeon said that it lay near an artery. If they accidentally severed it during the operation, I should lose either my leg or my life, so at this stage the option of doing nothing is the sensible one. Besides, to complete my side of the marriage deal I still need to scare people away from your father, Miss Cameron.'

'I think you could do that anyway, Lord Montcliffe, with one leg or two.'

'Do you?' His demeanour had changed. Now he leant towards her, taking the bridle to hold her mare still. She felt the blood in her cheeks rise as it never had before, so red that her whole face throbbed with the consternation.

'I like it when you blush.'

Daniel Wylde was lethal. With just a few words he could make her forget everything and believe in fairy tales with happy endings against impossible odds.

Better to remember the way Charlotte Mackay had looked at her with that innate snobbery so prevalent in the English upper classes as she had sniffed out the presence of trade like a bloodhound. Tomorrow when the notice of their intention to marry went into the papers Amethyst could hardly bear to think of what the repercussions would be. But the very worst of it was that she wanted this man before her, wanted his kisses, his smiles and his compliments, no matter what.

'The ball you speak of, would it be very formal?' she asked apprehensively.

'It would indeed. Did they ever teach you how to dance at your Gaskell Street Presbyterian Church School.'

'They taught me what they knew, though there were times when I wondered just how much that actually was.'

'Did you learn how to waltz?'

'No.'

'A pity, for they call it the dance of love.' Now his amusement was easily seen. 'If you like, I would be most happy to teach you the steps.'

* * *

He loved the way she was so easily flustered, this woman of commerce and business and brusqueness, though his attention was caught by a series of heavy pins around the line of her hair that had been dislodged by the movement of the ride.

'Do you wear a wig?'

Her fingers instantly came up to where it was he looked, pushing the dull brown hair forward in one easy swipe.

'I do.' Her hand shook as she tried to secure the loosened clips.

'Why?' Surprise at her admission had him frowning.

'The accident in the carriage that we told you of. I had my head shaved so that the surgeon could drill into my scalp to release the pressure on my brain.'

My God. No simple accident, then, but an operation that could have so easily killed her. He tried to hide his concern and concentrated on the fact that she had survived. 'What colour is the hair beneath?'

'Not this shade.' The lowering sun radiated on her face, altering the plain sallowness of her complexion. 'It is lighter. And curlier. I did not think it would take this long to grow back, though, so I retrieved this old hairpiece from my mother's things. Now I regret it. But on saying so I do not wish you to think I am vain, it's just that....' She stopped, her teeth worrying her bottom lip and confusion sending her eyes away from his.

Sometimes she looked so unexpectedly beautiful that for the first time since he had met her he allowed himself to imagine something finer between them, his sex swelling with the promise. Amethyst Amelia Cameron was honest to a fault and forthright and direct. She did not simper or lie or pretend. He was so very sick of the deceit of women, that was the trouble. Charlotte Mackay had for ever cured him of liars and his sisters and mother had done the rest with their duplicity and falsities.

He wished they were somewhere else, somewhere quiet and private, some place that he might bring her up against him and reassure her that he did not think she was vain, but the pathways of the park were filling with more riders and the crease on her forehead told him that she was as astonished as he by their candour.

'We should go back.'

She glanced away from him and nodded, her fingers tense on the leather reins and every nail bitten to the quick. He wondered why she did not wear the riding gloves he could so plainly see tucked into the fold of her belt.

The dream came again that night of the carriage turning over, the scream of the horses and the cold of the day. Her hand had been caught by her thick woollen glove against a seat that had come loose and she could not free herself and jump to safety as her father had done.

Over and over and over, in the slow motion of fear. She had not lost consciousness when her head slammed against the roof or lapsed into a faint as her wrist had broken. No, she had lain there as the dust settled, the bright stream of blood turning the day to red and listening to the last dying breaths of one of the horses.

Her father had reached her first and by his expression she knew things must have been bad. 'My broken doll,' he had whispered, words so unlike his usual diction she had thought she must already be dead.

But the pain came later, as did the fear of heavy gloves, and carriage speed and long-distance travelling. Unreasonable, she knew, but nevertheless there. She had seen Daniel look at her bare hands and wonder.

Her fingers went up to feel her hair. It was finally growing, a good amount of curl now covering the pink baldness of her scalp. She could have almost dispensed with the wig altogether, but it had become a sort of disguise that she liked in the time since she had put it on and now she was loathe to simply do away with it. People did not notice her as they once had. She blended in more, the colour of the hairpiece picking up some tone in her skin that kept her hidden. She could walk amongst a crowd and barely feel a glance.

Her tresses had once been her crowning glory. Gerald Whitely told her that time and time again before she had married him. Afterwards he had barely mentioned it, the long silences between them hurtful and unending.

A light tap on her door had her pulling the neck of her nightgown up.

'Come in.'

Her father walked forward, the silver cane the only vestige of his fall the other evening, though he leant on it with quite some force.

'I saw the light under your door.'

'You could not sleep either?'

He shook his head. 'You seem out of sorts lately and I keep wondering whether this marriage agreement is the cause of it? Lord Montcliffe is after all quite forceful and if you should wish to nullify—'

'No, Papa.' She cut across his words and watched his face light up. 'I am quite happy with things as they are.'

'It is just the marriage notice will be in the paper tomorrow and I should imagine after that things might change a little.'

'Lord Montcliffe said the same this afternoon when we were riding. He asked me to a ball on Saturday evening, a formal occasion with much of society in attendance.'

'And you agreed?'

'He made it difficult to refuse.'

Her father sat down on the chair opposite and wiped his brow. 'I am uncertain of the ways of all this. Perhaps we should employ a chaperone for you, Amethyst, so that we don't get things wrong.'

'I do not think it will be necessary, Papa. We will repair to Dunstan House as soon as we are married and then we need not worry at all.'

'Montcliffe is amenable to that?'

'He once told us that he would be. Besides, a friend of his, the Earl of Ross, asked if his sister might be able to assist in the preparation for the wedding. Perhaps I could also ask her for a little assistance with the ball as well. It seems she is most creative with these things and

I have a few gowns that could be altered to make them more fashionable without too much trouble.'

The smile on her father's face was bright with relief. He looked happier than he had been in a long while.

'If we had some notion of how many people would attend your marriage ceremony, that would also be of a help. The contract stated the marriage would take place before the end of July and the weeks will run away if we do not get it all in hand.'

'It will be a small group, Papa. No more than twenty.'

'But the Montcliffe family will be there?'

'I am not sure, Papa. They all seem distant from one another.

'A shame that, for family is all you have to rely on in the world when it comes down to it.'

'I am uncertain Lord Montcliffe would agree as he seldom speaks of his.'

'Well, I shall send them invites, nonetheless, for it is only good manners.'

A sense of dread began to play in Amethyst's mind. Would the Montcliffes be difficult? Would they accept her? Would they come? Only a few weeks until her wedding and she still had not procured a dress. Tomorrow she would send a note to Lady Christine Howard to see if she might consent to help her.

'You are marrying whom?' His mother's voice was shrill and disbelieving.

Both his sisters sat very still at the dinner table, their eating utensils poised to listen.

'Miss Amethyst Amelia Cameron.'

'And you say her father is a man of trade?'

'Mr Robert Cameron is a successful timber merchant and is far wealthier than the Montcliffes have any hope of ever being.'

He hated that he should have to qualify his choice of bride in monetary value, but it seemed such an explanation was all Janet Montcliffe understood. She looked furious.

'Amethyst? What sort of name is that?'

'Hers.' Daniel was tired of being careful and polite. His mother's frown deepened.

'We will be the laughing stock of the *ton.*'

'I doubt that sincerely, Mother.'

'Do you love her, then?' This question came from his oldest sister Gwen, the sort of light shining in her eyes that could only belong to a naive and unworldly girl.

'Of course he does not.' His mother answered for him. 'The interloper has simply tipped her cap at the title and managed to do what a hundred well-brought-up daughters of society have not been able to. She has brought your brother to heel and he will regret it, mark my words. You are marrying well beneath your station in life, Daniel, but any remorse afterwards will be useless. You will be tied to the upstart for life.'

'I am taking it that you will not be attending the wedding ceremony then, Mother?'

'None of us will be. I could not bear to look on Miss Amethyst Cameron's face and see the gleam of victory within it. The girls should not be allowed anywhere near such...*tradespeople* either.' She almost spat the word out. 'As for your grandfather, he is sick and hasn't the energy for all this nonsense so you are alone in your foolish choice of bride. I had such high hopes for you, too.'

Daniel stood as the resulting silence lengthened. 'Then I shall bid you goodnight.'

With that he simply walked to the door and left.

He found himself lingering in the confines of Grosvenor Square. The Cameron house was dark save for a light on the second floor where the curtains had been drawn. The shadow of a woman caught in candlelight moved in a way that made him frown. His wife-to-be was dancing alone in her room and the outline showed no sign of the shape of her wig. A waltz, he determined by the beat of steps she took, a practice of the dance of love.

The tension he felt began to lessen and lighting a cheroot he leant back and watched. Janet Montcliffe and her bitterness had been a constant in his life, the anger and the rancour almost normal.

Amethyst Cameron, unlike his mother, was a logical and reasonable woman and one who held to the tenet of wording differences of opinion in a sane and sensible way. She did not whine or moan or berate. He liked her smile and her dimples and the low timbre of her voice. Her clothes might be shapeless and ill-formed but when the wind had caught her riding attire and pressed the material against her body he saw that there was a surprisingly shapely form beneath. He was intrigued by the description of her hair. Light and curly. Velvet-brown eyes would complement such a shade admirably.

After the scene at the dinner table tonight he wished he was anywhere but in London town. A different life was one he had been dreaming of for quite a while now. He smiled as the shadow drifted closer to the window and hoped she might pull the curtain back to look down and see him.

He liked talking to her. He liked her blushes and the quiet way she had dealt with the snobbery of Lady Charlotte Mackay. He liked her father.

Breathing out heavily, he wondered what all this meant.

He had always felt homeless, but Amethyst Cameron had had the effect of anchoring him. His father had been a man who was melancholic and weak and as his bitterness grew he had sworn that no offspring from his unhappy marriage would ever see a penny of the family money. An unhappy coupling that had brought out the worst in both of them, Daniel suddenly reasoned, and the thought made him drop his cigar beneath his boot and stomp out the embers. Nigel and he had been caught in the crossfire of their parents' shortcomings. The spending of great sums of money and long holidays apart had dammed up the resentments for a while, but even that had not altered their basic dislike of each other. When his father had fallen from his horse after a long drinking binge his mother had buried him with a smile on her face.

Daniel did not look back as he strode into Upper Brook Street and hailed a passing cabriolet.

Chapter Six

'No, this is a far better colour on you, Amethyst. See how the gold brings out the shade in your eyes.' Lady Christine Howard smiled as she wound a darker gold band about the neckline. 'With just a bit of manoeuvring we can lower the bodice and attach it. If I fashion it carefully, it will fold like this to show off your curves.'

Lord Ross's sister was like a small whirlwind, her clever fingers pushing the fabric into a shape that was indeed flattering.

'You do not think it a little daring?'

'Absolutely not. Compared to some of the other gowns on display you will look like a novice newly released from a French convent.' Christine laughed loudly and Amethyst joined in. Nowhere at all lingered the depression or sadness that her brother had spoken of, though the large ruby ring she wore on her marriage finger alluded to a lost betrothed.

'The trick of it is to believe you are the most beautiful woman in the room and act like it.'

Amethyst's face fell. Such a thing sounded impossibly difficult.

'Your hair will need to be done differently, of course, to have any hope of pulling it off. The wig must go.'

'You knew I wore one?'

'Does not everybody? You could look so much prettier than you do now with it gone and I love the art of dressing hair.'

Like a shop dress form, Amethyst was pulled this way and that and the strangest thing of it all was that she was beginning to actually enjoy the unfamiliar pampering and the rapid conversation.

'Your husband-to-be has most of the women of the *ton* panting after him and why would he not, for he is beautiful.'

'Too beautiful for me.'

The words were out before she realised she had said them, but Christine appeared completely unfazed.

'You hide what you have, that is the trouble, but it is time to come out from the shadows. More importantly you have a fortune and is that not what all of the men of the *ton* need these days? I know Lucien does. It is a great pity you do not have a sister for then he could marry her and we would be related and no longer poor. I do hate how money, or rather the lack of it, defines one.'

'In my circle of acquaintances it doesn't, really.'

'That is why you are such a refreshing find, Amethyst, and why I like being here to help you.'

Christine reached into the case she had brought with her for another piece of fabric, this time the lightest shade of red and held it to Amy's face. 'Next time you buy a gown, choose this shade. See how it suits your skin? What colour is your real hair, by the way, or do you have none?'

Because there was no artifice or malice in the question Amy undid the pins and lifted the dull brown wig away, fluffing out her curls beneath.

'There was a carriage accident,' she explained as Christine stood in silence. 'It has only just begun to grow back properly again.'

'I did not expect you to be so blonde,' the other woman finally said. 'Has Montcliffe seen you without your wig?'

'No.'

The resulting laughter worried her. 'Then we will be able to greatly surprise him come Saturday and I for one cannot wait to see the look on Lady Charlotte Mackay's face when she understands what she is up against.'

'I have met her already.'

'Where?'

'In the park riding the other day. She barely talked to me.'

'That is because she is formidable and scary and so are all her friends. So be warned, while she is undeniably beautiful, she also finds people's weaknesses and uses them to her full advantage. Word has it she wants Lord Montcliffe back and will do anything to achieve her goal, so don't be fooled. Beneath her pale and refined appearance lies a character of pure steel.'

'She would not have been pleased to see our marriage notice in the paper, then?'

'Indeed. It is a wonder Lady Mackay has not been around here already saying all that she imagines you would want to hear whilst searching around for the secrets that you don't want revealed.'

Gerald Whitely.

The thought struck Amethyst with a blinding ferocity. How easy would it be for her to find out about him? A cloud of worry descended, though when Christine brought forth a folded cloth threaded with glass-headed pins, she decided not to think about her many problems.

Gerald belonged in the past and that is where she wished for him to stay. Nobody in the *ton* had the slightest idea of who the Camerons were and where they had come from. She would tell Daniel, of course, about her first husband and a few of her reasons for being most grateful when he had died, but that was all.

Perhaps she could have a conversation with him about it all at the ball on Saturday. If she asked the Earl to take her home afterwards that might give her a moment of privacy to try to make him understand the nature of her past.

When Christine indicated that she had finished attaching the band of cloth to her gown Amy turned to the mirror and was astonished. The gold in the silken cloth brought out the colour in her eyes and her hair and made her complexion appear almost flawless.

'I cannot believe that this is me.'

'It will be even better on Saturday,' her new friend returned, 'because I will put your hair up like this and fashion it with flowers.'

Clever fingers arranged the curls in a way that gave the impression of far more hair than she had and Amethyst smiled.

'See,' Christine exclaimed. 'With a simple smile everything comes together in exactly the way that it should.'

On the evening of the Herringworth ball Daniel Wylde and Lucien Howard waited in the salon downstairs with Robert Cameron.

'My daughter will be down presently. Your sister, Lord Ross, is helping her to dress as we speak and I have been banned from going anywhere near the upstairs bed chambers.'

Looking at a clock on the opposite wall, Daniel nodded. It was still considered early in society terms and so they had all the time in the world to wait. Besides the brandy that Robert had plied them with upon their arrival was both smooth and rich.

He wondered as he took the first sip whether he should have asked his sister Gwen to help Christine with Amethyst's preparation for the ball, but dismissed the thought as most unworkable. Perhaps after the wedding he could make certain that both Gwen and Caroline spent more time with them at either Montcliffe Manor or Dunstan House in the hope that his mother's influence over the young girls might lessen. He envied Lucien for the smooth ease of the Howard family dynamics, in spite of Lucien's contrary grandfather.

'I have not known Amethyst to take quite this much trouble with her appearance before.' Robert Cameron was peering at the clock.

'It will be the influence of my sister, Mr Cameron, for she is meticulous in her observation of detail. Your daughter will not have a chance to take breath once Christine hits her stride.'

'Well, people and things have been coming and going all day, my lords. Let us pray she won't be disappointed with the outcome for her hair is still so...' He stopped and fidgeted with the brandy bottle, seeming uncertain in the present company as to whether he should go on or not.

'Short.' Daniel finished the sentence off. 'She told me of it whilst we were riding in the park the other day.'

Robert Cameron smiled and leant back in his chair. He was still far too thin, but he looked healthier and more relaxed. 'Then that is a relief to hear, for I doubt my daughter has confided in anybody else and sometimes I wish she would.'

'You have no other relatives at all?'

'None. I was an only child and so was Susannah.'

Daniel thought for a moment how freeing that must be in the light of all the difficulties with his mother. Lucien's frown had deepened, though. The Howards had generally always been a close-knit family and he was probably wondering at how the Camerons could have been so isolated. Robert, however, was expounding on their aloneness in a voice that sounded worried.

'The business has taken much of our time, you see, but in the past week I have sold a great deal of it off to a competitor who has always expressed an interest in buying it. I hope now that Dunstan House might be my principal place of residence, a quieter life with the horses, you understand. A home where we might become part of a community.'

Their conversation was interrupted by a butler who appeared at the door. 'Miss Cameron and Lady Christine have instructed me to tell you that they are ready, sir.'

The rustle of silk was followed by small steps on the marble floor and then his wife-to-be was before him. Daniel could barely recognise her.

Gone was the dull brown lustreless wig, replaced by light blonde curls tucked up into a band of small yellow roses, the honey, straw and gold of her tresses making her dark eyes and eyebrows stand out in a way they had not before. In the light of the candles her skin looked transparent, the previously sallow tone of her skin transformed now into almost alabaster.

Daniel found himself on his feet, speechless at the transformation. Her golden gown clung too, displaying the curves only hinted at in the shapeless clothes she normally favoured. She filled out the bodice of her dress admirably though her waist was tiny. When she saw where he looked she began to speak immediately.

'Christine assures me that this neckline is most tasteful and not at all racy and that other women wear far more revealing outfits.' Her fingers tugged at the darker shade of material that swathed the bodice.

Gloves, the lightest of gossamer lace, barely covered the glow of her skin.

'You look...different.' He hardly recognised his own voice as the dimples marking her cheeks deepened, her bones elegant and sculpted in the light. Her lips were painted with a quiet pink and it emphasised the fullness of them. He could barely breathe properly with the transformation.

Palms open, she gestured to the dress. 'This is the result of hours and hours of work on Christine's behalf, I am afraid, my lord. Tomorrow I shall be just as I was.'

But for Daniel time seemed to stand still, caught in astonishment and trepidation. Before Amethyst Cameron might have been largely invisible in a society ballroom, but now...now the knives could be out and sharper than they might otherwise have been.

When he glanced across he could see the same sort of astonishment on Lucien's face that must have been evident upon his own. Christine simply looked as though she might laugh out loud.

God, he wished they did not have to go out at all, society and its expectations bearing down upon them with all its infatuation with beauty and grace. Her father was watching him too, eyes keen and his smile broad, giving Daniel the impression that he had known all along how truly lovely his daughter was.

'I think we should ask Lady Christine to help again in the preparation for the wedding day, my dear. You have not looked so pretty in an age and I want a full report tomorrow on all the happenings at the ball,' Robert said.

Only pretty? Daniel swallowed the words back and looked over at Lucien. There was a definite challenge in his green eyes.

'I am more than certain tonight shall prove a most interesting experience, Mr Cameron.' Lucien's drawl was slow and languid.

'Lord Montcliffe, Miss Amethyst Cameron, Lord Ross and Lady Christine Howard.'

As their names rang out across the ballroom the conversations filling the generous space quietened and heads turned their way.

This was exactly what Amethyst had been dreading, this exposure coupled with a public knowledge that she was from the lowly echelons of trade. She held in her breath and wondered if she might ever release it.

'I always pretend there is a field of grass before me at this moment,' Christine trilled, 'and that the colourful gowns are flowers. And I never look anyone in the eye.'

Despite her trepidation Amethyst smiled and the awful horror of being so very visible faded into something she was more able to cope with. Daniel did not look even vaguely nonplussed by all the attention. Rather he seemed almost bored, an Earl who had graced countless ballrooms and endless society functions just like this.

His world, Amethyst thought. His heritage. Today he wore a large ring on the first finger of his left hand. She had not noticed him sport any jewellery before and this one was substantial— the crest impaled with a lion in red on one half and a series of white crosses in gold on the other. The family badges of a noble birth passed down from father to son. Just another small token of an exalted lineage and a further example of how unsuitably matched they were.

She had decided in the end not to wear any jewellery at all, letting the golden gown speak for itself with its intricate folds and detailing, but in this room with all the glamour of the *ton* she wondered if such lack was a mistake. Here, she felt out of place, the lessons from Gaskell Street leaving her totally unprepared for such opulence. She wanted to take Daniel's hand and hold it close, an anchor in a world that was foreign and a man who could easily overcome any difficulties. But she did not, of course, for he had moved away slightly, making no attempt to claim her.

As they came to the group of people standing at the bottom of the steps she smiled politely and waited for Daniel to speak.

'When did you get back, Francis?' he asked one of the men.

'This afternoon.'

'And your cousin?'

'Was long gone and had left no word of her return.' His eyes flicked towards Amethyst, the startling depths of hazel guarded and questioning. 'The *ton* is abuzz with your news, Montcliffe. Rather hasty, I might add, given that when I saw you last week you made no mention of a would-be wife.'

Lucien laughed. 'The call of rich and beautiful is a

strong one, Francis, as I am sure you must appreciate. Were you not on exactly the same mission in Bath?'

The words were both familiar and strange to Amethyst. Lord Ross could hardly think her beautiful, but she was rich. And was this Francis trying to find his own wealthy intended?

Of a sudden the hazel eyes of the stranger softened and he bowed his head towards her.

A mark of war lashed the newcomer's left cheek in one cruel and unbroken line, leaving her to wonder at the pain that such a wound must have inflicted. If he noticed her looking, he made no reaction to show that he cared.

'We were all at school together and followed each other to the battlefields,' Daniel explained. 'Overfamiliarity sometimes breeds a contempt of manners, but I am certain my friend will remember his soon.'

This time a true smile creased the ruined face. 'I beg your pardon for my rudeness, Miss Cameron. My name is Lord Francis St Cartmail, Earl of Douglas, and I am more than interested to know if you have sisters?'

'I have already explored that avenue, Francis,' Christine quickly informed him. 'For my brother, you understand. But sadly she is an only child.'

'Then we still have to find our own fortunes, Luce.'

Laughter ensued, mirth that was neither embarrassed nor apologetic. The sort of laughter that told Amethyst these were friends who were in it for the long haul, thick or thin, good or bad. And it seemed that each warrior before her was also facing financial ruin.

The war, she wondered, or the war wounds? It cannot have been easy for them to come back into the glittering perfection of the *ton* from the hell of a Peninsular Campaign. Who would understand what they had been through and what they had seen, save for those who had returned with them. Forging bonds, closing the ranks. There was an ease in shared sorrow.

Compared to these three, the other men here looked effeminate and affected. She also saw the interest of many of the ladies in the assembly stray in their direction, some glances hopeful and shy whilst others were more bold and direct. When Daniel's arm unexpectedly touched hers she looked down, his large fingers encased in a glove, the fabric of his jacket contrasting against her shimmering gown. A connection, amidst all the movement and chatter, the spark of a vibrating energy running into her fingers. Almost burning.

He must have felt it too because he pulled away, the contact lost, but not before she saw shock in his eyes.

A waltz began to be played by a string quartet stationed at the head of the room. A Viennese waltz played quickly. She had danced to this in her room in Mayfair as a practice. Back-two-three. Back-two-three. Her heart raced even faster when Daniel turned and asked her to dance.

Daniel found it difficult to know exactly what to make of Miss Amethyst Cameron as she came into his arms, her wheat-gold curls piled beneath yellow rosebuds and the gown of a darker hue sending the shade of her eyes to a burnished velvet.

She did not look as if she belonged here amidst the

ton and the ballroom and the vacuous pursuits of those with little else save social soirées to occupy their time. She was so much more than that—an interloper who would bide here for a while just to watch it all.

It was the strength in her that made the others look weaker, he decided, for women who needed men to survive had a certain brittle incompetence that was shown up by Amethyst's independence. His arms tightened about her.

'Thank you for coming.'

'You thought I might not?'

He smiled and led her into the dance. 'I watched you practising the waltz the other night from the street. Your shadow had fallen against the curtain.'

Her breath stilled, puzzlement making her pull back a little. 'Why were you there?'

'I was walking. I walk sometimes when I cannot sleep and when the sense of life is questionable. My wanderings brought me to Grosvenor Square.'

'Then, given our unusual marriage contract, you must have found yourself exercising a lot of late, my lord. I might add that practice does not make one perfect so I hope my lack of prowess as a dancer doesn't disappoint you.'

The imbalance was back, clawing into reason, her eyes full of laughter tonight and as close as they had been when he'd kissed her. He wanted to again. God, how he wanted to.

'This marriage is not all about the money, Miss Cameron. Your father's offer was unexpected and generous, but...' He stopped and looked away.

'You did not have to take it?'

Shaking his head, he brought her closer, but wrapped together in the arms of a crowded room there was so little space to be honest.

He liked the way she smelt and felt, he liked how her head fitted just beneath his chin and how the warmth of her skin came through the gossamer lace of her gloves.

Perfect.

Hell, he was turning into a man he did not recognise, the soldier in him submerged beneath another force. He could feel her breath against his throat, too, and the small intimacy held him in thrall.

'Your hair looks nice.' He could have phrased it better, he supposed, could have talked of the colour or the curl or the way it matched her skin, could have used the flowery words that women were supposed to like. But she answered before he could dredge up more.

'Christine hid the shortness in the flowers.' Her eyes met his own. 'It must be exhausting to be a constant part of an assembly such as this, my lord? So much attention upon us and so much expectation.'

'It hasn't always been so. In the army I was largely free of it. My older brother was the one in the public eye and I left him to it.'

'When did he die?'

'Almost eighteen months ago now in an accident whilst out hunting at Montcliffe.'

'Perhaps he was not as happy as you thought him to be, for the dubious habits of gambling and fast living don't point to a man at peace with himself.'

Daniel hoped his laughter did not sound too unkind. 'The duty of an Earldom rules out many of those personal luxuries. He was supposed to be protecting the Montcliffe name, not gambling it away to anyone who would meet him at the card table. When he lost, Montcliff Manor lost as well.'

'It was sold?'

'No, I have largely closed the place up for now. Most of the servants were given their notice, but I have kept on a very small staff.' He had hated taking livelihoods away from people who had worked at Montcliffe Manor for years and whose great-great-grandfathers and grandmothers had toiled at the same job in other centuries.

'Your brother wasn't a champion of family heritage, then. My father has tried to inject tradition at Dunstan House even though the history is not our own.'

'What's it like?'

'Beautiful. It is made of honey-coloured stone and sits behind a lake. My father wrote a poem about it when we first went there and I had it framed.'

'Only one?'

She laughed. 'He never took to the pen again in such a descriptive way. *"The rooks swarming and the swallows skimming and the oak trees reflecting in the lake."* My mother would have loved it.'

'But she had died by then?'

'Yes. When I was eight.'

'So it was always just the two of you?'

'It was. Just us, and that is why Papa…' She stopped, a line of worry etched into her brow.

'Why he is so important to you? Why you wish for him to be happy?'

The music swirled about them, the notes of the violinists to one end of the room plaintive. Amethyst had never heard such music played before, but everything about tonight had been like a dream and Daniel's hand across her gossamer-silk gloves made her feel different.

Even with his injured leg he danced well, the quiet push of his body against hers as he led her around the floor. If his brother Nigel had been weak and fickle, Daniel was strong and solid and good, a man who would protect his family with all that he had, a soldier who had fought for crown and country and had spilled his blood in doing so. A husband as unlike Gerald in every way that it was possible to be.

The thought made the breath in her throat shallow. Here in the midst of society in the bosom of a group who could so easily revile her, she felt safe and protected in Daniel's arms. But she needed to tell him of her first marriage before much longer, needed to make him understand that such a mistake sometimes left you floundering for the right words and the proper explanations. A further reflection made her stiffen. Gerald's business deals had taken him into the world of the *ton*. Perhaps some here had even met him. The room felt suddenly warm.

'Your friend Lucien mentioned that you once bred

horses?' she asked, trying to push her anxiety aside for now.

'I did indeed, at Montcliffe, before I sold most of them and bought a commission into the army. Deimos was the only one left of that line.'

'You will like the stable at Dunstan House, then. Papa has not held back in buying the best of livestock, although lately he has lost interest in the project because of his health. The Arabian greys were a part of his big plan.'

'Yet he looked more robust tonight.'

The sentiment made her smile. 'I think it is your influence, my lord, and I thank you for it.'

His fingers tightened on her own. 'I need to find you a ring. Is there any stone you might favour?'

She shook her head. 'I seldom wear jewellery.'

'There was a large diamond ring at the bottom of the bag you left at my town house. When I lifted it the contents fell out.'

Gerald's ring. The one he had given her when he had pledged eternal love and loyalty in the chapel at Gaskell Street. He had won it at cards, she was to find out later, from a man who had stolen it from his sister in order to stay at the tables. A symbol as broken as its promise. She had forgotten she had even thrown it into her cloth bag where it had lain forgotten until the night Daniel had kissed her.

'I dislike diamonds.' She tried to keep the anger from her voice.

'Then you must be the only woman in the entire room who does.'

'And I prefer my hands bare of any adornment.'

So nothing can catch. So that the gloves she wore in public could easily slip off at the end of an event.

'Because of the scars on your wrist?'

He had noticed? She thought that even through the sheer silk and lace they had been hidden. The skin above muscle torn away from bone was healed now, but there were other scars that would never mend.

Missing a step, she fell against Montcliffe, his strength gathering her in and holding her steady.

'Everyone harbours secrets, Amethyst.'

She liked the way he said her Christian name, with that precise accent of privilege. She also liked the way his breath fell against her scalp, the soft whisper of her freed curls so different from the heavy cloying feeling of the wig.

She noticed others watching them, some covertly and others more directly. If she could, she would have closed her eyes and only felt Daniel's arms about her, the steady beat of his heart, the smell of strength and maleness and honour. She wished her father might have been here to watch the pageantry and the beauty, the chandeliers above, the violinists in the leafy grotto, the women dancing, bedecked in every colour of the rainbow, jewels sparkling in the flame.

A different life and so very far removed from ledgers and order books and the brisk trading of timber. So very different from Gerald, too, with his heavy fists and his angry ranting, all the faults in the world everyone else's save his own.

Her father would have loved to have seen her enjoying a night like this, being a part of society in a way he had never imagined she would.

Here in this room it was beauty that was most remarkable, the old lines of tradition and the mark of history holding its own kind of thrall. Swallowing back a growing delight she let Lord Montcliffe guide her around the floor.

As he caught his sore leg on an intricate step Daniel was pleased when the music ceased. He needed a drink badly, the back of his throat dry and a dread in his stomach that he remembered from the battlefields.

No control. No damn certainty. Amethyst was his bride of convenience and yet here he was, falling under her spell. Like a green boy. Unmistakably stupid. Two years she had made him promise until they could end it all. Just a union of utility to benefit her father and his family. How much plainer could she state it?

Francis handed him a drink when they were once again back within the group. A fine smooth brandy that did away with the foolishness. He made certain that he did not stand next to his wife-to-be, slipping into the space between his two best friends instead. His leg ached and throbbed, but there were other parts of his body too that were bursting into a life long since deadened.

He wanted Miss Amethyst Amelia Cameron. He did. He wanted to lie down with her in their marriage bed for all the hours of all the nights of his life and listen to her heartbeat. She was honest and real and true. A woman who did not lie or simper or deceive.

God, what would it be like to live with a woman who did not use every waking hour to plan the next gown or soirée as his sisters and mother were prone to, their constant gossip and ever-present fits of displeasure marring this day and then the next one.

Simple. Uncomplicated. Truthful.

When Gabriel Hughes came towards them with his sister and mother in tow, Daniel frowned. Charlotte looked as beautiful as ever, but she no longer held any sway over him. Tonight he could not even see what her attraction must have been.

'We meet again, Lord Montcliffe. It is becoming a habit, though of course your marriage notice in the paper was a decided surprise. To a lot of people, I expect, your mother included. I can't imagine she was pleased.' Her voice was hard, an edge of anger upon it and another thing that he could not name.

Amethyst was listening, as was Christine, though Lucien was trying to make a decent fist of a conversation with them to give him some privacy.

With her blue eyes flashing Charlotte Mackay used her words like swords, the sharp point of meaning aimed true. She knew Janet Montcliffe had always favoured an alliance between them, two pre-eminent families of the *ton* melded into an ordained partnership. Any association with the world of trade was as offensive to Charlotte as it was to his mother and she made no attempt whatsoever to conceal her feelings.

Gabe and Lady Wesley looked less sure as to the purpose of such an outburst. Indeed, her mother was trying to pull Charlotte away, her teeth set in a rigid smile of fluster, but her daughter was having none of it.

'I should like to ask Miss Cameron a question if I may, my lord.' The silky tone of her words signalled danger and the group around them fell into silence. 'I would like to ask her if she knew a man called Mr Whitely?'

The bottom fell out of Amethyst's world, a single terrible thump of something breaking into a thousand shards of shame and all the more dreadful because it was so unexpected and public.

'Mr Gerald Whitely?' She hated the way her voice sounded as she echoed the words back, but she needed to give herself a moment to think.

'Your husband, Miss Cameron, or should I say Mrs Whitely. The man you married. Surely you remember him?'

'Oh, you have it very wrong, Lady Hughes, for she is not spoken for. Miss Cameron is about to be married in the next few weeks to Lord Montcliffe and I think…' Christine's sentiments broke across the growing silence, petering out as she realised with amazement that the accusations could actually be true.

'Gerald Whitely? The name is familiar.' Lord Ross's voice came through the fog. 'Was he not the one who set up a company early last year to swindle wealthy investors out of their funds?'

'Amethyst?' Daniel spoke now, the timbre in his voice drawn, and when she looked up his pale eyes were icy.

'It...is a...mistake.' She could barely get the words out.

'Then perhaps the *ton* would like to hear why a married woman should insist on using her maiden name when her true one might elicit howls of derision.' Charlotte's tone rang with victory though it hollowed as her brother bundled her up and pulled her away, his mouth grimly set.

'You have said your piece, Charlotte. It is now time to leave.'

Christine had stepped back too, the distance between the Howards, Francis St Cartmail, Daniel and her widening by the second. Further away others began to take note of the emotion and the exchanges, a whisper of question circling the room.

'Could I t-talk with you...alone?' Amethyst needed to get away from here, to get outside. Her breathing was strange and the world was beginning to waver. Shock, she thought, and guilt. Every single part of her felt torn.

But Daniel did not move. Two seconds and then three. Both Lucien and Francis on either side of him looked at her strangely, an immobile trio of disbelief mixed with disdain.

'I n-need to explain.' The lies. The omissions. She swallowed and thought she might be sick, here in the grand ballroom of the *ton*, all over her golden foolish dress. 'Please.'

Daniel finally stepped towards her, but he said nothing as he took her arm, a passage of empty space opening as they made their way to the staircase and then down it. Amethyst tried her best not to meet one single person's glance as they went, though she could hear the undercurrents of disparagement all around.

'Trade, of course.' 'Blood will always tell.' 'To think she imagined to hide a husband.'

It was over. Everything. She should have explained to him before now. Lies upon lies upon lies and this is where it got you. Here. The complete disintegration of her name and her character and the derision of the *ton*.

Taking their cloaks and hats from the butler, Daniel strode out to hail his carriage. Any contact had long since gone and he made no effort at all to meet her eyes or to talk.

'There are th-things you need to…'

'Wait until we are alone.' The quiet cold indifference in his voice was far worse than any anger.

A minute later his horses were moving, much faster than she liked, racing towards Grosvenor Square, careening around the corners of the dark London streets.

'Now perhaps you might tell me the truth. Were Lady Mackay's accusations about your marriage to Whitely false or not?'

'It was not as you think…and it was never…' Her attention was caught by the speed the carriage was gaining, fast, much faster than she was comfortable with. The old fear came at her out of nowhere, robbing breath and sense as she lunged for the door handle, peeling her gloves off and keening.

'God.' The Earl's voice came through a melted screen of light. 'What the hell is wrong with you now?'

His discarded cane was in her hand without conscious thought, smooth and warm as she belted the roof as hard as she could, once and then twice before he snatched it away.

'Are you crazy?'

'Too…fast.' Mouthed now as she could not even whisper the words. The carriage would turn over as it had before, she could feel the wheels leaving the ground and lurching sideways. Her heartbeat made her head ache and the old sweat of fear broke out all over her. Then all she knew was a spiralling fog, like snow at night and cold, tunnelling in. She did not try to fight the darkness.

Chapter Seven

They were at Dunstan House and the curtains across the French doors of her room were billowing wide. Like the sails of the Cameron ships on the wind as they raced for the Americas, cargos laden and a blue horizon seen in every direction.

Her father sat in a chair reading, his glasses perched on his nose and a bright floral cushion on his lap. Amethyst's mind searched for an answer as to why they were here and why she was in bed at this time of the day, half a dozen vials of medicine lined up on the table beside her.

Of a sudden the room spun in small and rapid circles, making her blink. Squinting, she reached out, hoping to find balance. Something was not right just beyond thought, the time, the place or the company.

'Papa.' The word was thick in the dryness of her mouth, but her movements had alerted him and, dropping the book on the floor, he reached over to take her hand.

'How do you feel?'

Daniel. He was gone. The ball. Gerald. The wild ride in the carriage home. Too fast.

'How long…since the ball?'

'Three days. This is the first time you have known me.'

'Only…you…here?' Her eyes perused the corners of her chamber, searching. When her father nodded Amethyst allowed the heaviness of her lids to close and she slept.

She knew she was calling his name in the dark and through the night. But Daniel Wylde, the sixth Earl of Montcliffe, would not come because he no longer trusted her, no longer cared.

A cold compress was pressed to her forehead and she touched her father's hand.

'Tired.' She could barely keep her eyes open. 'I feel so tired.'

'Then I will stay with you until you sleep and when you wake up again I shall still be beside you.'

His words were quietly spoken, yet were so very genuine. She could not remember a time when her father had let her down or failed her. 'I love you, Papa. You have always been here.'

'And I always will be, my jewel. Don't worry. Everything will turn out just exactly as it should, I swear that it will.'

The dizziness was back, hovering at a distance, but closing in. She needed him to know something, but it was hard to think what it was now.

'Daniel?'

'Shush.'

'He makes me…happy.'

The tears fell of their own accord, welling in her eyes and running warm across her cheeks.

'And now…I have lost…him.'

'No.' All the reassurance in the world in that one simple word and as she fell back into sleep she smiled.

The next time she awoke it was dark and two candles on the mantelpiece laid a circle of light across the bed, the white of the counterpane so bright it hurt her eyes to look at. Holding up a hand to dim it, she was surprised by a small cut on her wrist, the blood around the wound dried and powdered. Her father was still beside her, in different clothes now and without the book.

'They bled you. The doctors. I asked them if it was truly necessary but the humours are tricky things, they said, and the melancholy needed to be released from your body.'

Her father looked both exhausted and worried.

'Lord Montcliffe?'

'He left as soon as he brought you home from the Herringworth ball and I haven't heard from him since.'

'Did he tell you…anything?'

He shook his head. 'Maisie and Mick were delivered the next morning and I brought you here the day after that.'

'I see.' And she did. Charlotte Mackay's accusations played on her memory as did the speed of the carriage as Daniel had taken her home. She had acted appallingly, but high emotion, guilt, shame, shock and fright had played their parts, too.

'The doctor administered laudanum to calm you down, my dear, but I do not think it agreed with you. I stopped the dosage the day before yesterday.'

That was why she felt nauseous then and slightly removed from the world. Her mouth was so parched she could barely swallow but all she could think about was the sense of betrayal in Daniel's pale green eyes.

And the hurt.

The sick feeling in her stomach worsened. He must think her mad and deceitful, a woman who held no regard for honesty or manners; the wife of a man at the centre of a scandal that had rocked all of London. The kiss they had shared came back with full force: a moment in her life she would never forget, a gift of what it might be like to be with a man whom you truly loved.

She turned her face into the pillow and sobbed.

Daniel knew what the lawyer would say. He knew it before the legal retainer even opened his mouth and began to speak.

'I am acting on behalf of the Honourable Reginald Goldsmith. He has instructed me to call in the loan your brother took out against your family estate and he would like the sum paid back in full by the end of this month.'

'I see.'

Smythe shook his head and lifted a yellowing page. 'I am afraid you do not, my lord. The sum is enormous.' Turning the document so that it could be read with more ease, Daniel was stunned.

Five thousand pounds. A king's ransom. So much more than he'd imagined Nigel to have gambled; a fortune that he had no way of getting his hands upon now that Amethyst Cameron had disappeared into the countryside with her father.

'Is there any way I could stretch out the payments?'

'Perhaps for a few months if you were lucky.'

'But no more?'

The lawyer shook his head. 'My client is taking ship to the Americas in twelve weeks because his only daughter has settled in Boston. He wants a clean break and he is more than hopeful that the debts should be discharged before he goes. *Completely discharged,*' he emphasised the words again and wiped his brow. 'Is there a problem with this, Lord Montcliffe?'

'No.' The glint in Smythe's eyes was full of conjecture.

'Your marriage to Miss Cameron should help. I have heard that the family is extremely wealthy. Timber, is it not?'

Daniel stood. He did not wish to hear any conjecture on his own personal life from a man for whom the words 'appropriate' or 'confidential' appeared to mean nothing. Taking his leave, he was glad Smythe did not engage in further conversation.

He walked along the river in a light rain, the water winding along with him, full of the noise and movement of commerce. Perhaps one of the Cameron ships was docking at this moment, ready to be discharged of its heavy cargo.

Amethyst Cameron.

He no longer knew what to make of her, the shifts of emotion exhausting. He had deposited her at home with her father after the ball and left immediately, her behaviour in the carriage so very deranged and Charlotte's truths still ringing in his ears. The next morning he had sent back the greys. Even to save Montcliffe he could not be for ever tied to a mad and lying wife.

Gerald Whitely, at least, was dead. He had found out that through an investigator he had employed to make sense of it all. But still the whole ending had been maudlin and awkward.

Swearing, he conjured up her face on the night of the ball, her lightened hair showing up the velvet gold in her eyes. Beautiful and crazy. He had not heard a word from the Camerons since and on enquiry found that they had packed up the London town house and headed for their country estate of Dunstan House somewhere up north.

Good riddance, he should have thought, the whole episode so public and brutal. A lucky escape from a woman who was both deceitful and unstable. Yet underneath other thoughts lingered. Amethyst's thinness. The way she smiled. The dimples that dented her cheeks and the careful diction of her words.

He had not made a public statement about anything though the *ton* was, of course, abuzz with the happenings. His mother had caught him in the breakfast room that very morning and made her opinions quite clear.

'From what I have heard you are well shot of Mrs Whitely, Daniel, and you can now concentrate on the search for a far more suitable match. The Earl of Denbeigh's wife, Lady Denbeigh, has been most direct with her wishes for her daughter's future. From all accounts the young lady appears to be a well brought-up, softly spoken girl with an admirable fashion sense. Trade needs to marry trade and those from the *ton* should find a partner within the same ranks. It is these unwritten laws of society that keeps it all working, you see, and if you seek to change it for whatever reason there are always complications and sordid ones at that.'

She twirled the end of a light-brown curl around her finger. 'Your man said you no longer have the greys stabled here in London. Are they at Montcliffe?'

'No. I sent them back to the Camerons. They were part of the wedding settlement.'

'But I had heard that they were worth a fortune.'

'They are.'

'Then I should have kept them if I were you. It would have been some payment for all the humiliation we have suffered since.'

The loud shout of a street pedlar brought Daniel back into the moment, an unkempt fellow playing a wooden flute and touting for a few pennies as he finished. Digging into his pocket, he dropped in an offering.

How the hell could he rescue Montcliffe? The edges of his world were flattening out and he was in danger of falling off the end of it unless he could come up with something.

A pawnshop sign opposite caught his attention and, checking to see that no conveyance was bearing down upon him, he walked across the road towards it, pulling off the heavy gold signet ring from his little finger as he went.

'I think you should send back the greys, Papa. Lord Montcliffe can't wish for the agreements to continue as they were, not after...what has happened, but we do need to ensure his discretion.'

Amethyst finally felt better today and had dressed to come down to the dinner table with her father, who watched her with a growing frown upon his face.

'You won't fight for your reputation, then, or for Lord Montcliffe?'

'He was never mine to fight for, Papa. Surely you can see that?'

'The first man who has made you live again and smile again and you give him up on a sigh? Your mother would have been disappointed in you.'

'Why? Because I can understand that in the distaste of the *ton* lies a way to complete devastation? Daniel Wylde wanted me as little as Whitely did. The pair of greys arrived from him before a new day had dawned properly. Even Gerald gave me a few months.'

'A few months of hell.' Robert stood, his voice louder than she had ever heard it, 'and the scars to prove it. The worst thing about it all was that I could do nothing as Whitely systematically wore you down into a daughter I didn't recognise any more. After him you looked over your shoulder with a fear of life, love and happiness.'

He held up his hand as she went to speak. 'Montcliffe gave you back something whether you admit it or not, Amethyst. For the first time in a long while you have seemed...happy. You took risks, you lived.'

She began to laugh because anything else was too awful to contemplate. 'I agreed to the terms because I thought that was what you wanted, Papa. The doctor said you needed to be relaxed and rested if you were to survive your failing health and you have looked more robust since.'

'I do not think your agreement to marry him was all about me, my dear. You called for Daniel Wylde when you were sick, again and again, and you begged for him to come back.'

'It was the laudanum.'

'No, it was the truth.'

'What are you trying to say, Papa?'

'That the Earl was the best thing that has happened to you in a long time and if you don't do anything to make him understand the situation as you know it you will never be accepted into polite society again. That really would kill me.'

A gathering dread made her feel cold.

'We will introduce better conditions.' Her father's voice held no question as he continued on.

'Conditions?'

'A year of marriage and fifteen thousand pounds every four weeks and then a lump sum at the end.'

She shook her head. 'No more, Papa. We'll simply

stay here at Dunstan House. I never need to return to London again.'

'Hiding, then? Like your hands in the gloves and your hair beneath the wig. You're twenty-six, Amethyst, soon to be twenty-seven, and there are not too many of the good years to go. Child-bearing years, the chance of a family and of happiness is dwindling with each and every successive month you tarry. Even now—'

She stopped him. 'I am not an old maid yet.'

'But you might be if you are not careful. Then what would Susannah have to say? Flourishing, she instructed. Make our daughter flourish, were the last words she ever said to me. If you have your way of things there will be no chance of that.'

'So you are saying?'

'That the marriage between you and Daniel Wylde, the Earl of Montcliffe, goes ahead.'

'No.'

'The marriage goes ahead and you show Montcliffe exactly who you are. You tell him the truth about Whitely and the way he used you and hurt you.'

'No, I can't do that.'

'Then I will call in each and every debt his estate owes and ruin him. Is that what you want?'

'I don't believe you are saying these things, Papa.' Horror stripped her words back to a whisper.

'If you tell me you have absolutely no feelings for Lord Daniel Wylde, I will stop. All of this. We will simply leave England and head…anywhere. But you must also remember that there is every good chance according to the best of London's specialists that you will soon be completely alone and without my support.'

She was silent. She tried to speak, she did, from the well of sense and logic and reason she knew was inside her, but the words just would not come.

Relief passed into the lines of her father's face. 'Very well. I shall send Montcliffe a message tomorrow outlining the new conditions, Amethyst. If I have not heard back from him by the end of the week, I will go down to London myself and visit him. I do not think he is a person who would break his word on keeping the silence of our demands and I also know that Goldsmith will be calling in his own debts, too.'

'My God.'

'Are we in agreement, then?'

She could imagine Daniel receiving both her father's and Goldsmith's demands all in the same month. Pale green eyes rose in memory, the golden shards warm with humour at the ball and then icy with distaste in the carriage.

Once he had admired her, she could tell that he had. Once he had trusted her and lauded her honesty and truth. Once he had kissed her, sensuously, expertly, so that the blood in her temple had pounded in an unending and heavy din. More. More. More.

That was the worst of it. She had pressed her body back against his own as they had danced and known the hard outline of his sex. She had felt his breath mingle with hers, life-giving and wonderful, his lips so close, his smile just for her, the light of the chandeliers falling in quiet patterns across them, magical and bliss filled.

Oh, how he must be laughing now.

Crazy, deceitful Amethyst Cameron, trading her way into a betrothal that he did not wish for and refusing to let him go.

If she had any sense left, she would instruct her father not to take things further, then simply accept what had happened and move on.

To what? To where?

The quandary bewildered her. Without the Camerons' money Daniel would have to sell Montcliffe Manor and she knew him well enough to understand that would be something he would hate to do. Marriage, then, to another heiress, another woman who might sweeten the pot with gold and property. And a hasty one at that given the timings.

Nay, she might still be the best of all evils if she threw down her cards in the right order and gave him space to play it out. Marriage was like business, after all, and both parties had to feel they had made a good deal or things quickly went sour.

'I will agree to try again, Papa, but this time I will write my own conditions.'

'Very well.' The smile in his eyes was bountiful.

Taking a sheet of paper from an armoire on one side of the room, she proceeded to do just that.

Daniel could not believe what he was reading. The Camerons' lawyer, Alfred Middlemarch, on the other side of the table sat very still, no expression on his face, a man used to the strange and fickle ways of the very rich.

'And they want me to sign this today?'

'They do, my lord, and most generous Mr Robert Cameron has been, there is no doubt on that. I do not think he wishes to draw out the procedure, so to speak, but wants a quick and expeditious process so that all concerned might move on in the right direction with their lives.'

The right direction?

Goldsmith's lawyer had been to see him again yesterday with his own amended set of demands. Four weeks now and no longer the stated twelve to repay the debt. A coincidence? Daniel thought not. Other debtors, too, had foreclosed as word had spread of the poor financial status of the Wyldes. He could barely keep up with the sums mooted or the spiralling escalation of debt.

'There is also a page of further conditions that Miss Cameron herself has penned. She asked me to give them to you under strict confidence and made me promise to reiterate that you were not to let anyone else know of them. Including myself. She has made me promise that I shall burn the paper as soon as you leave unless you wish to take it with you.'

The missive was sealed, the red wax engraved with the letter 'C', two yellow ribbons splayed out beneath it.

Pulling on the tabs Daniel brought the sheet into the light. The hand was neat and small, flourishes of fancy every so often at the end of a sentence.

If you are reading this I want you to know how sorry I am for all that has happened. It was not meant to be this way.

*Your family's well-being is as important to you
as my father's happiness is to me, so if this marriage is to go ahead I propose that:*

*You can build up a stable of breeding horses
at the Dunstan stables that would be unlike anything else seen in England.*

You have carte blanche *on buying the livestock.*

*We will have as little to do with each other's
daily lives as you wish for.*

*My personal fortune will be at your disposal
to ensure the future of the Montcliffe lineage and
property as well as that of Dunstan House.*
Yours sincerely
Amethyst Amelia Cameron

'Damn.' He muttered the word beneath his breath
and the man opposite looked up.

'I hope it is to your liking, my lord.' The expression-
less face of Middlemarch neither softened nor hardened. 'Will you take it with you or shall I burn it?'

'I will keep it.'

'Very well. I do not wish to hurry you along, Lord
Montcliffe, but...'

'You are a busy man.'

'Exactly. The Camerons have always been good clients and honest people. Their payments are regular and
prompt and in all my years of working with Mr Robert
Cameron I have seldom heard one bad word against
him, professionally or personally.'

The Montcliffe family lawyer chose that point to

turn from the window. Mr Athol Bailey was of the old school of law, but had allowed the Cameron's legal representative to outline the terms of the agreement mooted in his office. For his own benefit Daniel thought, but also as a means to an end. The Montcliffe fortune was in danger of collapsing completely and the severity of the problem was not going to just go away. Bailey spoke now as he rounded the desk to sit in a leather chair to one side of it.

'The word about town, Lord Montcliffe, is that other parties hold several loans against the Montcliffe estate and they are interested in settling them quickly. Lord Greyton's representative, for example, is a colleague of mine and, whilst I hope I do not speak out of turn, I would say that the general opinion is that you are on the verge of bankruptcy. As your family retainer, my lord, and given the expenses that your mother incurs in her daily and general life, I would advise you to reflect very carefully about an offer that could only be conducive to the financial well-being of the Wyldes from now on and into the future.'

'I see.'

For the first time that morning Bailey smiled and, looking over at the Cameron's lawyer, Daniel spoke. 'Will you take a message back for me? I would require an answer as soon as possible.'

'Of course.'

'Could you tell the Camerons that I agree to their proposals, but the small wedding will be held at Montcliffe Manor. I want only my bride and her father to be in attendance. No one else.'

'Certainly, my lord.'

'Could you also tell Miss Cameron that I shall be sending her a bill for the damage incurred to the roof of my carriage whilst she was under the influence of her fit of madness.'

'Indeed, my lord.' Middlemarch's countenance did not falter as he handed over one of his inked quills. 'Just here, if you may.' He waited until the deed was signed before flipping over to another. 'And here.'

Finally the old lawyer stood, depositing the documents into a well-worn leather briefcase. 'I consider my business done and I would like to thank you both for allowing me the time and place to present this agreement. I hope you are as happy with the outcome as I know my clients shall be, Lord Montcliffe, and I wish you the very best for the future.'

Ten minutes later Daniel was back on the street and his mood was as black as the clouds he could see amassing over to the west. He had been played like a fish on the line, the bait of his own demise as imminent as the Camerons would know it to be. Until this past week he had not had one single debt of his brother's presented to him. Did Robert Cameron have some dealings there as well to force his hand and hurry things up?

But why would he do so? Surely a dozen other down-on-their-luck lords could be cajoled into a union with Miss Amethyst Cameron and with far more ease, even given the scandalous nature of her first husband's business.

His mind went back to the carriage ride home. She

had acted like a crazed woman, with little sense or reasonableness, her shrill cries still ringing in his ears. He had never met another like her, that was the trouble, one part innocent and the other part as deceptive as hell. She was her father's daughter on the one hand and her own particular mix of madness on the other.

Yet he had signed on the dotted line. For his mother and his sisters and a grandfather who barely knew the time of day.

'More fool me,' he muttered, pleased to see his town house materialise before him and also the possibility of a stiff drink. His lineage would stay safe and Montcliffe Manor would not need to be sold. Such protections would have to be enough. The dull ache in his thigh mirrored the pain in his head.

Charlotte Mackay arrived on his doorstep just as he did and this time there was no mother or brother anywhere in sight.

'Might I come in just for a moment, Daniel? I realise that I am hardly the person you wish to see, but I would appreciate at least a moment or two of your time.'

Today she was dressed in a woollen cloak with the buttons done up tightly to her neck. With a quick nod he showed her through to his library, but he did not sit down as he waited for an explanation as to why she had come.

'I am more than sorry for the scene at the Herringworth ball. I have been trying to get up the courage to allow explanation, but it has been hard.' Swallowing she looked at him.

'The allotted period of mourning society deems

appropriate for a bereaved widow has been most...
difficult and it is only in the past month that I have
been allowed to enjoy my life again. As a result of everything I have come to the conclusion that a year of
black clothes and dour conversation shows not only
the nonsense of marriage but also my unsuitability to
such a state.'

'In what way?' For the life of him he could not understand why she should be telling him this.

Her right forefinger tucked an errant golden curl
up into the folds of her hat as she gave him answer. 'I
am committed to enjoying every single moment I have
left to me, Daniel. After Spenser I saw that sometimes
bad things can happen.' Shaking her head, she went
on, drawing herself up a little. 'Your finances are in
a poor state. I have heard that from many people and
your brother's problems at the card table are no longer
a secret. As my own bank accounts are most healthy
I thought perhaps as a friend I could offer you a way
out of the mess you now find yourself in.'

He knew what was coming and he tried to stop her
by holding up his hand, but she took little notice of
the gesture.

'I will pay off some of your debts in exchange for
you and I becoming lovers again. I have missed you
and I made a huge mistake when Spenser offered for
my hand. But now there is an opportunity for us...'

'No.' He could say it in no other way than that.

'No?'

'Thank you, but I cannot take you up on the offer,
Charlotte.'

'Because you are angry at me for ruining your chances with Mrs Whitely?'

At that he laughed. 'Hardly.'

'Then why?'

He took his time in answering. 'Spenser was an only child and the last of his family line. I have heard it said that his parents want you to reside with them in Scotland in return for the large sums of money they have bestowed upon you and which you accepted on your husband's death. It seems Spenser Mackay's mother thinks of you as a daughter?'

'You sound like my mother, Daniel, and I do not want to hear this.' Moving closer, she brought her fingers along the line of his cheek. 'Scotland is full of sad memories for me and I want to feel again what I did, with you, in your arms, before it all went wrong.'

Once he might have been flattered by the offer she had just made him, but now all he could think about was the chaos of their past. 'I think, Charlotte, that the time for us has gone.'

'Kiss me then and tell me that afterwards.'

She did not wait for him to move, but pressed herself up against him, her lips brushing along his own, warm and full and remembered. The same smell of gardenias and the same feel of softness.

Shaking his head, he placed both hands on her shoulders and moved her away. Carefully. The clock in the corner boomed out the hour of three and apart from the sound of its heavy ticking there was silence in the room.

'You won't allow me in because of your brother?

Nigel was a…dalliance. I knew as soon as we had slept together it was a mistake.'

He tried to smother the anger that he could feel building. 'If it was not Nigel, then it would have been someone else, Charlotte, and by then I did not care enough anyway.'

'You are refusing me?'

'I am.'

'But I love you, Daniel. I have always loved you.' She was crying now, the tears running down her cheeks. 'You were distant at the end of…us. If you had been more attentive, none of this would ever have happened. But we can change it and with only a little effort we could again be—'

'Stop. The time for regrets is past and you have duties now to Spenser Mackay's family and to your own.'

Rather than placating her, this line of argument made her wail louder. 'Then both of us have lost and all for nothing, and you will regret this, I know that you will.'

Gathering up her reticule, she opened the door, his man coming forward immediately to show her out. When she was gone Daniel crossed to his desk and sat down. The letter he had received at his lawyer's today rustled and he brought the sheet from his pocket. Amethyst's demands juxtaposed against those of Charlotte's made him feel his life was taking a less-than-salutary course.

Lucien's voice in the corridor had him flicking the missive into a drawer as he waited for his friend to come into the room.

'Tell me that was not Lady Charlotte Mackay in the carriage I just saw pulling away, Daniel, for I thought that affair was long since over.' As he dropped into the leather chair nearest the desk he reached out for the decanter, upturning a clean glass and pouring a generous libation.

'It isn't what you think. We are friends.' As he said it he wondered if Charlotte and he were even that.

'She's poison, damn it. She betrayed you with Nigel and she could so easily do so again.'

'I know.'

'Do you?'

'Lady Mackay will be returning to Scotland to live. She just came to say goodbye.'

'She still loves you. You can see it in her eyes. My guess is that she came to beg forgiveness as she tried to inveigle her way back into your bed with money and sex. The cloak she wore was a surprise though, but-toned as it was to the neck. Not her usual style.'

Daniel finished his drink before he spoke. 'Let it go, Luce. There is no purpose in flogging the past.'

'Maybe not, but your present difficulties can be laid squarely at the feet of Lady Mackay and rumour has it that Goldsmith is calling in his loan. Can you pay him?'

Daniel shook his head, helping himself to more of the same smooth wine. 'There are others as well. Nigel was busier than I had thought.'

'Pity Amethyst Cameron turned out to be such a du-plicitous liar. I liked her before that. Francis told me to tell you that you should follow him to America. By his accounts there is a fortune to be made there.'

'I don't have enough time left to find it.'

'Your mother?'

'Is finally terrified. In the past few days and for the first time ever she is cursing Nigel to a most uncomfortable afterlife.'

'At least she is recognising he is the architect of much of the Montcliffe misfortune. I could sell Cosgrove Hall. It is mine outright to do as I want with and it should fetch something even in its dilapidated state. At least the land around is arable.'

Daniel smiled. 'I thank you for that, Luce, but it would hardly cover the first loan that was presented.'

'Marry a girl whose family is flush, then, a young debutante who'd fall in love with you in a second. That would do the trick.'

'I think any chaperone would be hurrying such prospects away from me. There is a big difference in thinking a family on the verge of ruin and the knowing of it. Besides, I am too jaded to be tiptoeing around such innocence.'

And he was, Daniel thought in surprise. Even the idea of such a bride made him feel...nervous. He was thirty-four next birthday and he felt older than that again. He didn't want a woman he could hardly speak to or one who would be running home to her mother every time the going got tough. Which it would. His leg was aching tonight and he knew very soon he'd need to get a surgeon to look at it properly.

'Did you find out anything more of Gerald Whitely then? You mentioned that you were looking into it the last time we met.'

Daniel nodded. 'He died in the bed of a prostitute, it seems. Two shots to the head and no one ever held accountable. His crooked schemes of business were apparently funded by the Camerons' money.'

Lucien swore. One of the riper expressions remembered from army life.

'My thoughts exactly.'

'I can't see Miss Cameron being enamoured with someone of that ilk even after all that has happened and I am sure she could not have condoned his scandalous get-rich deals, either. As an impartial viewer I would also like to say that for the first time in a long while you seemed happy when you were with her.'

The words rang in Daniel's head like a death knell as he struggled to change the subject to something lighter. He hadn't been happy in so long, that was the problem. He couldn't remember a time when he had truly laughed or enjoyed something just for the fun of it.

A band of yellow roses in golden curls came to mind, and lips that turned up at each end even when she did not smile. After Nigel and Charlotte, honesty was the yardstick he had measured people by and Amethyst Cameron had failed that test miserably in the end.

If the Camerons sent back an agreement to his terms, would he still go through with it, knowing all that he did? Was Montcliffe Manor worth such a sacrifice?

Charlotte's presence today had unsettled him, but so had his mother's constant tears. The carrot of building up his own breeding stable also sat at the back of his mind. With luck and good management he could begin to prosper and in a couple of years he might be able to pay back much of the debt. Amethyst had come to him stipulating her own terms, after all, so she would not be clinging on to something unsustainable either.

A marriage of convenience and with many of the terms in his favour? He could build up his breeding stock and begin again. A new life with the freedom of money and time. But even that prospect failed to allow him any renewed hopefulness and his shattered right thigh hurt like hell.

Chapter Eight

She would be married in an hour. Again. In a house she had no notion of and in a dress hurriedly made, with little interest on her part for the end result.

She looked terrible, that much she could see, her eyes red and swollen and the eczema that had a tendency to appear when she was stressed staining her cheeks and the soft skin beneath her mouth.

A blemished bride.

An unwanted bride.

A second-hand bride.

A bride who would stand at the altar only because of a series of conditions that would allow her husband a separate life apart from hers. Montcliffe had signed such stipulations in haste, hadn't he, the avenues of finding a solution to his own problems closing in.

Unlocking the golden cross that she wore around her neck, she laid it down on the bedside table.

'I do not want you to be a part of this charade, Mama.' Her neck seemed empty without the chain, though today her mother felt close.

Susannah Cameron had been a redhead, with a freckled skin and a verve for life that was uncompromising. She had risked the small loan her father had bequeathed to her when he had died as a down payment for the first of Robert's boats. The best spend of my life, she had said to Robert again and again as Amethyst had grown, the love her parents shared a constant and joyous source of wonderment.

So different from this marriage, the ghost of Gerald Whitely surfacing in threat. 'Daniel Wylde will turn out just like me,' some spectral voice whispered. 'The very same, you just wait, for you are cursed and marked.'

Swallowing, she turned away from the mirror. Her maid had helped her to dress, but had gone now to let those downstairs know that she was ready. Amethyst thought her hair looked nothing like it had when Lady Christine had threaded it with roses. Rather it was spiked and ill shaped, the golden band of her mother's she had insisted on wearing seeming as out of kilter as her dress.

Pure white. She wondered if she should have worn the colour, but the seamstress had already begun on it when the thought occurred and so she had taken the path of least resistance and left it as it was. At least the veil would hide some of her defects. With care she pulled the gauze across her face and smiled, glad of the opaqueness and privacy.

A few moments later she entered the downstairs salon at Montcliffe, a room of huge proportion and elegance, though sparsely furnished.

Lord Daniel Wylde was there, of course, and her father. Beside them stood the minister and an older woman.

Four people; two of whom she did not know. The conditions he had insisted upon. A small marriage. Uncelebrated. Forgettable.

'We shall repair to the chapel for the ceremony.' Daniel's voice, but he neither took her hand nor looked at her directly, leaving it to her father to accompany her. The room appeared otherworldly through the gauze.

'You look lovely, my dear,' Robert said beneath his breath, and for the first time that day she smiled.

'I think even you know that that is a lie, Papa.'

The house had been a revelation when she had first seen it the day before. It was huge for one thing and sombre for another. Not a house one would feel at home in, she had thought, and wondered at what sort of a childhood the manor might have provided for a young Daniel. Everything looked old and the faded spaces on the walls alluded to another long-ago time when Montcliffe Manor must have been magnificent.

The Earl had met them briefly here yesterday, outlining the planned ceremony in formal tones and then leaving. The same butler she remembered from the London town house had shown them to their rooms on the first storey and the dark furniture in each was as Spartan as the rest of the place.

She had not seen him since. Today he looked taller and as forbidding as his house. She wondered if she had truly ever known him, a stranger with whom she had shared a kiss.

The minister stood at the pulpit and gestured for them to come before him.

'Who gives this woman in marriage?' he asked gravely.

'I do.' Robert's voice was guarded, as if he too wondered if they had not made an enormous mistake.

And then her arm was threaded with that of Daniel's, superfine beneath her fingers and the outline of heavy muscle under the fabric.

Delivered.

Into a union that neither of them looked forward to and married under the solemn words of promise. Little words that meant both everything and nothing.

A ring was slipped on to the third finger of her left hand, the huge diamond glinting in the light and pulling at her skin.

'I now pronounce you man and wife.'

And it was over, the older lady signing beneath their names, a legal witness along with her father to the nuptials.

Her husband's full name was Daniel George Alexander Wylde. Something else she had not known about him.

Robert took her hand as she stepped back, his glance warm when he looked at the ring. 'A substantial diamond,' he said, and she knew that there were things he did not know about her either. The day was threaded with strangeness and juxtaposition. When Amethyst glanced up she saw Daniel watching her, his pale eyes hooded.

The wedding breakfast was set up in the blue salon to one end of the house and, once they were all seated, an awkwardness overcame everything. At least the minister was talking, his words running into each other in a never-ending stream. Otherwise there might have been silence as each player in this travesty sought their place within it.

A headache burned into her temples, the laudanum still in her system somewhere and making itself felt. Her father looked worried and thin, none of the certainty that had been there in the days leading up to this moment evident. She had no clue at all about Daniel's frame of mind because an implacable mask crossed his face and his eyes were a flat distant green.

The food was lovely, a light soup and then chicken and beef with an array of sauces and roasted vegetables. A cake was presented, too, and it sat on the end of the table couched in a feigned joviality, two figures carved in icing upon it, their arms entwined around each other.

Amethyst drank deeply from her wine glass, something she seldom did, but the velvet-smooth red banished some of her worries. Then her groom stood to propose a toast.

'To my bride. May this union be kind to us both.'

The hollow thud of her heart made her feel sick and, as she lifted her hand to push back a falling curl, the diamond ring sliced a scratch right across her cheek. Her father used a snowy-white napkin to wipe away the blood.

* * *

How he hated this.

His new wife looked scared and lost, but he was too angry to understand anything other than retribution. Symbols. The blood, the diamond, the cake with its ridiculous illusion of happiness and joy. He felt none of it. Too few people at the table, too many lies left unsaid.

This wedding was a parody and the guest list reflected the fact. He had not told Lucien or Francis that he was getting married and his own family thought he had gone to Montcliffe Manor to recover from the events at the Herringworth ball. Recover? Like he had after La Corunna? In their ignorance he saw just how little they knew about him.

Robert Cameron was looking disappointed rather than furious and that annoyed him further. He had been coerced into this whole situation by a master. The timber merchant could not expect him to enjoy it.

The huge diamond on his wife's finger was patently wrong and he saw now that part of the gold clasp had worn free from the stone it held. It had hurt her.

Yesterday he might have smiled at such a travesty, but today the short spikiness of her hair pulled at him somehow. She had threaded a gold headband through the curls in an effort to emulate what Christine Howard had once done, but it only added a poignant awkwardness and the scars on her wrist above the gaudy diamond were reddened. Like her face.

When he had raised the veil after the vows all he saw was skin that was rough and raw, her dark eyes taking in the fact that he was seeing her at her very worst.

But even like that she looked beautiful to him. He ground his teeth in rage.

Her father was speaking now to the small and mismatched group around the table, thin lines of sickness etched into his face.

'I have always called Amethyst "my jewel" and I hope in the coming years you might see the truth in these words for yourself, Lord Montcliffe.' He raised his glass and toasted. 'To Lord and Lady Montcliffe. May their union be blessed with love and laughter.'

At least he had not intimated heirs. Breathing out, Daniel looked at the fob at his waist. Another few minutes and this would all be over.

Her groom kept checking the time, five minutes and then ten. The food was tasty and the conversation around the table increasingly more congenial, but he did not join in the talk and neither did she, the minister and her father doing most of it.

Unexpectedly the older woman next to her leant over and squeezed her hand. 'I am Julia McBeth and when I was married I wondered what I was doing, but my Henry was the sweetest man a bride could want. Daniel Wylde is like that too, underneath. He is kind and good.'

She spoke quietly, but in her eyes there was a genuine concern.

'I was the Earl's governess when he was young. His mother was not the sort of woman who took to children easily, you understand, so the two boys became like the sons I could never have myself. I am a distant cousin from a branch of the family that invested unwisely, so the position here was a godsend at the time, and the boys made everything bearable. I left Montcliffe Manor when Nigel and Daniel were sent up to school, but kept in good contact with the boys afterwards.'

'You must miss Nigel, then?'

'Oh, I do, but he always needed his younger brother to keep him…stable. When Daniel went off to the Peninsular Campaign with General Moore I think Nigel lost his direction and could not get it back.

'So he died before my husband returned?'

'Just a day or so after, actually.' The frown across her forehead alluded to something more, but Amethyst did not wish to ask about it. 'My husband passed away three years ago and although I had been away from Montcliffe for a very long time Lord Montcliffe asked me back to stay. A goodness, that, for I had nowhere else to go and I think he knew it.'

'Do his mother and sisters ever come here?'

'The Countess is a city woman. I doubt she has ever enjoyed the place and only a small handful of staff has been kept on which would not suit her at all. Certainly even as a young mother Lady Montcliffe left for London at the drop of a hat and for very long periods of time.'

'Then it is most appropriate that you are here today, Mrs McBeth.'

'Julia. Everyone calls me that and if you have need of an ear you know where to find me.'

'Thank you.' A slight happiness came through all the strange uncertainty as she was given a glimpse of the younger Daniel. A leader and kind with it. The sort of man that Gerald had never been.

When the meal finally came to an end the Earl of Montcliffe stood.

'Might I have a word with you in private in the library, my lady?' My lady? She was that to him now? So formal. So very polite.

'Of course.'

She followed him down a dark corridor that opened up into a large and light room, a garden off to one side with double doors for access. Books lined each end, all leather-bound and well ordered.

Here was another thing then that she had discovered about him. He read.

'Your lawyer gave me your handwritten note outlining the demands of this marriage. A marriage in name only, I am presuming, given your edict for separate lives.'

Did he want more? Looking up, she saw he did not.

'For appearances' sake would you be happy to inhabit the adjoining chamber to my own whilst here at Montcliffe Manor? It might stop any gossip that I would not wish to engender. The door between us would remain locked, the key on your side.'

She nodded.

'Did your father read the conditions you wrote?'

'He didn't.'

'His seemed to contradict your own.'

'I think he hopes for much more than each of us would wish to give, my lord.'

'Indeed?'

His hand reached out towards her and he tipped her chin up into the light, peering at her injured cheek. 'That should not have happened.' Colouring profusely, she felt the heat of his words roll across her face. 'Did you love Gerald Whitely, Amethyst?'

'No.'

For the only time in that whole day he smiled like he meant it, as he let her go. 'We will stay here at Mont-cliffe until the day after tomorrow. Then we shall travel to Dunstan House. Your father will accompany us.'

'You have spoken to him of it?'

'Yes.'

He turned then to the cabinet behind him and, using a key, unlocked a safe that held a long leather box. She saw a profusion of small boxes within, but stayed quiet whilst he opened one container and then the next. Finally he found what he sought and came to stand beside her.

'Give me your left hand.' With trepidation she did so, watching as he carefully removed the ugly diamond ring and replaced it with a delicate deep purple amethyst set in ornately wrought rose gold.

'The clasp on this one won't hurt you.'

Smooth and beautiful, the underlying colours of red and blue glinted in the light of the room. No small worth.

'It is my birthstone.'

'I know.'

She was surprised at this. 'What stone is yours?'

'A diamond for April.'

Without meaning to she laughed and the humour was not lost on him.

'The hardest substance on earth.' He waited for a moment before carrying on. 'Imbued in the folktale is the belief that diamonds promote eternal love.'

A new awareness filled the space around them.

'We barely know each other, but the circumstances that have thrown us together require at least some effort of knowledge. Perhaps if we start here.'

'Here?'

'My parents loathed each other from the moment they married and I do not wish to be the same. Is politeness beyond us, do you think?'

She shook her head.

Her hand was still in his, the warmth of skin comforting and sensual, though after a quick shake he allowed her distance.

'Would you come for a ride with me around the Montcliffe estate this afternoon?'

'In your carriage?'

'I thought after our last jaunt together that you might prefer horseback. The stables here are not quite empty yet.'

When she nodded he leant down to ring the bell and a servant she hadn't seen before appeared immediately.

'Could you show Lady Montcliffe back to her room?' He consulted the same watch she had seen him glance at before. 'Would an hour be enough time for you to be ready?'

'Yes.'

'Then I will see you at the stables at four.'

A slight gesture to his man had him turning. He did not look back as he opened a further door to one end of the library and disappeared from view.

He walked into his brother's chamber after their conversation and sat in the chair before the desk in the untouched room. Nigel was everywhere, in the models of ships that might ply the Atlantic much like Cameron's fleet and in the books of maps that he had treasured in a wayward pile next to his bed. He had barely been in here since his brother's death, but this was a room he had often enjoyed as a youth.

Daniel could not decide which emotion he felt more, love or anger, but they were both closely aligned to the guilt he had never let go of.

He should have been able to save Nigel as he had in their childhood when his brother would ride too fast or lean out too far. Daniel had been younger by eighteen months, but he had always felt older, more in control, and the Earldom had not suited his sibling's temperament.

Responsibility worried Nigel and he began to drink heavily. A week before Daniel left for Europe he had found Charlotte Hughes *déshabillée* in the attic of the stables entwined in the arms of his brother, an identical look of shame and shock on both their faces.

His former lover was no loss whatsoever, but Nigel's betrayal was. Daniel had not sought him out when he left England with his regiment, an action he regretted when a bullet went through his leg in Penasquedo as he tried to shelter Moore from the battle, and regretted again when the fever took him into the realm of pain, heat and hopelessness on the transports home.

Charlotte had long gone north with her rich Scottish beau by the time he returned and his brother had been drawn into the company of a group of men who had forgotten what was good and true and sound about life.

Sometimes Daniel thought he had forgotten, too, but he was fighting to cling on and Amethyst Cameron was a part of that, despite the lies about her dead husband.

After he had begun to recover from the wound to his thigh from La Corunna he had gone to recuperate at the London town house. His mother and sisters had left to stay with an aunt in Coventry, the sudden shock of the death of Nigel affecting his mother in a way that had made her even more unstable. Hence, when Daniel arrived home from the hospital and in no fit state to travel, his grandfather was the only person left in residence in town.

Harold Heatley-Ward had been a man of few words all of his life, but in the time they were thrown unexpectedly together, he had begun to talk more and Daniel would hobble each night to his grandfather's sitting room.

'Your mother was never an easy woman, Daniel. I blame my wife for spoiling her and allowing her every wish. Sometimes disappointment and frustration can help to build a character's resilience. Janet never had a chance to nurture hers and as an only child was wont to get whatever she favoured.'

He'd produced a large bottle of whisky after the

confession, taking the top off it with a sort of quiet excitement.

'The stuff of legend,' he had said. 'Brandy hasn't a heart compared to the best of what Scotland can offer and whilst we are alone with no one to sanction our taste we should enjoy it.'

And they had until well into the following morning.

'Your brother left you a letter, by the way,' his grandfather had confessed at around three o'clock, words slurred. His movements were clumsy, too, as he went to retrieve the missive from a drawer next to his bed. From the drink or from the creeping arthritis, there was no true way to tell.

'Nigel made me swear that I would not give this to you until we were alone. Unseen if you like. From such instructions I have taken it that he did not wish for your mother to read the thing.'

'Have you? Read it, I mean?'

'No. It is sealed.' He handed over the note. 'From Nigel's state of mind when he gave it to me I think I have a fair idea about what it might contain.'

Daniel hadn't known whether to open it up then and there or leave it until later. But, cognisant of his grandfather's worry, he broke the wax.

Daniel,

You always knew what to say and do. You should have been the Earl because I have made an awful hash of it and I don't know which way to turn any more. Now that you are home in Eng-

land again the Montcliffe estate may have found its saviour.

Seeing you yesterday in London has confirmed my belief that if I wasn't in the world things would be easier for everyone. However, I am sorry for ending it the way that I hope to. A shot to the temple is quick, but unlike you I have always been a coward. I also sincerely hope that any debt I have incurred will die with me. I pray and hope history will record my demise as an accident.

Grandfather has promised to deliver this letter to you when a moment arises where he has you alone. I think he understands me better than anyone. Tomorrow I leave for Montcliffe Manor and I don't mean to come back.

The letter was signed with an N., embellished with two long flicks and underlined.

Closing his eyes against the tilting world, Daniel screwed the paper up in a tight ball and tried to hold in the utter sadness.

'His servant was adamant that the gun went off by mistake as he jumped a fence?' The question in his grandfather's tone was brittle and Daniel passed the missive over and waited until Harold had read it.

'It is not a surprise,' the old man finally said, tears welling in his eyes. 'Nigel took the world too seriously until he started to gamble, then he forgot to think about anything else at all. Your father was afflicted with the same sort of sickness.'

Anger claimed reason at the ease of such an excuse as Daniel stood, trying to control his fury. 'When I was in Spain I saw men fight for their country and die for liberty and loyalty. This sort of death is...wasteful.'

But his grandfather shook his head. 'Be pleased that the same melancholy that took over your brother's mind was not inherent in your own.'

'A coward simply lets go. A braver man might fight.'

'You were the only one of the Wyldes who ever knew how to do that. You escaped, can't you see, with your friends and your school and your unwillingness to belong here in a household that did not understand the importance of family or loyalty or lineage.'

He had never belonged. The thought came quick and true. But neither had Nigel, in the cutthroat tug of war between his parents and the quieter but equally brutal boarding school that they were both finally sent to.

There Daniel had met Lucien and Francis, but Nigel had drifted on the edges of friendships, never quite establishing himself in any particular group.

'Janet would most likely be even more heartbroken if she knew the truth. If we could keep this from her...?'

Harold left the option as a question, and Daniel found himself nodding as he took the confession over to the hearth, struck a tinder and watched the flame catch. Indeed, an accident whilst out hunting was a lot more palatable to explain.

The smoke rose in small curls from the missive, there was a slight flare of flame and then it was gone.

Scuffing the ashes with his boot to make sure the damning truth was lost, he turned to his grandfather.

'I am glad Nigel felt he could at least trust you in the end.'

The old man merely nodded his head and bent to watch the last puffs of grey smoke, tears still rolling down both his cheeks.

Montcliffe was a beautiful property, Amethyst thought, the house sitting on a lake and surrounded by sloping meadows and falling to a river that wound through a valley. Everything was green.

'My father and Nigel never really understood the history here at Montcliffe or the beauty of it.'

On top of the same large black stallion he had ridden in London her husband looked…unmatched. Amethyst smiled at the word and his eyebrows rose.

'But you love this place.'

He nodded. 'It's the peace of the country, I suppose, and the silence, though I have not spent as much time here as I would have liked to.'

Each word made her pleased. He was not a man who over-enjoyed the party life, then. Like Gerald.

'And your family?'

'This was my father's heritage. My mother seldom ventures far from the social scene in Brighton in summer or London over the winter. I doubt she enjoyed it here right from the time she and my father married and my sisters have not either.'

'You are lucky to have so many close relatives.'

When he laughed she wondered if he felt the same,

but the sun was on her face and it felt so good to be riding. Here and now, the strained events leading up to their wedding were further afield.

'Did your first husband like horses?'

The bubble popped completely, but she made herself answer.

'I think he felt daunted by any outdoor pursuit.'

'What did he like then?'

Not me.

She wondered what would happen if she just said it, blurted the truth out about how in the end he hated every single thing she stood for. But that honesty was too brutal even for her, and there were things that she would never tell another soul. Staying silent, she did not add all of the sordid, degenerate and shameful facts and there were so very many of them.

'The mistakes of others are not our own,' he said quietly.

She smiled, liking his sentiment, but the tears that sat at the back of her eyes felt close.

'My father has a habit of saying the same.'

'Then it is time you believed it.'

'Papa insists that people come upon the destiny they deserve, but I always thought that was a bit harsh.'

'Why?'

'Sometimes destiny just falls on our heads and squashes us flat.'

He began to laugh. 'If you are referring to yourself, you have never seemed squashed to me.'

Delight ran through her at the compliment and just like that the ache in her body was explained.

She was falling in love with the Earl of Montcliffe. She was. She was allowing herself to believe the fairy tale and ignore all the conditions of what, to him, would be simply a way out of bankruptcy.

He was innately kind—had not Mrs McBeth told her so?—and he was a gentleman reared in the art of manners and comportment. He had asked for civility and she had agreed, so her ridiculous want for more could only embarrass them both.

Already he was looking away, waving to a man who worked in the fields. The late sun gave the Earl's hair dark red lights and when his horse reared to one side he easily controlled it, gentling the stallion with a few well-chosen words.

She had never before been around someone who was as effortlessly certain, the smile on his face breaking the skin around his eyes into lines. Perhaps he was also a man who laughed a lot. She hoped so.

'Your father's pallor seems better here than in the city?'

'That is because his favourite places are the countryside and the ocean, and he thinks the land is beautiful around here.'

'Did you ever go with him to the Americas?'

'When I was younger I did. But then…' She stopped.

'Then?' He looked at her carefully, a slight puzzlement in his eyes.

'I became a different person. I would like to say that the display of histrionics in the carriage was not my finest hour, my lord. The accident that resulted in the loss of my hair came when travelling too fast and now whenever I am inside a conveyance that goes at more than a walking pace, I panic. Normally I am innately sensible and very correct. I like order and regularity and control and seldom let my emotions rule me. My temperament is usually far less emotional and far more calm, if you are able to believe it. After the Herringworth ball the shock of everything made me…unreasonable and I am sorry for my behaviour.'

A shout had them both turning and a man on a horse was coming across the field towards them.

'Smithson is one of the cottars and he wants a word with me. We will have to finish this conversation later, but thank you for the explanation.'

Nodding, she jammed her shaking hands into the divided skirt of her riding attire and hoped Daniel had not seen the racing pulse at her throat.

Chapter Nine

They had an early dinner and it was a simple affair, the leftover meats from the wedding breakfast and a bowl of fruit in season. Mrs Orchard, the housekeeper, had cut up the cake and arranged the pieces carefully on a plate. The same figurines from the wedding now twirled in the middle on their own revolving pedestal. An eternal embrace.

Her father was in a good mood, his appetite the best Amethyst had seen it for months as he helped himself to the food.

'Your man showed me around the stables, Lord Montcliffe, and impressive it was, too. Who built them?' The lilt in his voice was audible.

'My great-grandfather. He was a firm believer in the philosophy that horses need a view to thrive so every stall looks across the lake.'

Robert began to laugh. 'You will find Dunstan House to be nowhere near as attractive, though we can rebuild everything to imitate the style here if that is your wish.'

The conditions of their union came to the table with them, Amethyst thought, all present and accounted for, each one a reminder of the absence of what should have been. She wished her father might just leave it at that, but as he went on with the discussion any hopes sank.

'The greys are to be brought up next week from London for I was certain you would want them back. Mr Tattersall has been at me for another chance to market them, but I said that he would have to wait in line for the progeny. He was most interested to know that you would be involved in a breeding programme, my lord, although I did tell him we would not be changing their names.'

'Here's to Maisie and Mick, then.' Daniel raised his glass and laughed. 'But don't give them to me, give them to my wife.'

A strike of excitement flared inside Amethyst.

'Very well, but on the condition that you will teach my daughter what you know about horses, my lord. She has always been an avid rider, but we have never had the time for more.'

He turned to her. 'Is this something you wish for?'

'It is.' She hoped her father would not notice the expression that she was sure would be in her eyes as she helped herself to a slice of cake.

Indifference was getting harder. The ring glinted against the light, its purple depths lending a richness to the gold and the wine she'd had was making her relax.

Her husband's voice was soft as her father spoke with Julia McBeth on the other side of the table. 'You would like to try your hand with the horses, then? Be warned, though, for the work can be hard.'

He gestured for a servant to refill her glass.

'I have a few mounts of my own in London which I will have brought up. Nowhere near as many as I used to have, but still...'

'Enough to start.'

He smiled and looked at her and the feeling that was hidden in her heart swelled to bursting, though loud footsteps just outside the chamber took their attention.

When a young girl hurried in Daniel stood and the newcomer threw herself into his arms, her long dark hair loose and her eyes overflowing with tears.

'Andrew Howard...is hurt and...I have...lost Caroline completely.' Her breath was ragged and fast as though she had been running for a long while.

Daniel looked more than taken aback. 'What are you doing here, Gwen? Where is Mama?'

Gwen. His sister? His arms were still about her, though she grabbed his hand now and began to pull him from the room.

'Andrew is outside...I think your man is helping him from the carriage, but Caroline...is at an inn about five miles back.'

'A shabby sort of two-storey building with a large fireplace outside?' When she nodded he asked a further question. 'Why were you there?'

'We were coming to see you as we were worried about you,' the girl wailed. 'Mama forbade us to make the journey to Montcliffe, but Andrew managed to procure a carriage and we came anyway. Caroline needed to stop for…' She left the rest unsaid as she carried on. 'Andrew said he would be our guard…and now he is hurt. Badly I think, because there is a lot of blood and it is all our fault.'

Daniel was already striding outside and everyone followed him. Lucien's younger brother lay on the ground with a blanket over his shoulders, the butler kneeling across him.

'He is in need of a doctor, my lord.' The servant looked worried. His sister simply tipped her head back and wailed, a loud and awful noise that filled all the space around her.

'Stop it.' Daniel gave her no quarter and surprise made her cease. Already he was lifting the boy in his arms and bringing him inside, shouting orders for one of his staff to ride to find the doctor and to another to make ready a bed. Blood dripped across his dress jacket and soaked the bright white fabric of his shirt.

Once the boy was lying on a sofa, Daniel took a blanket from the chair and ripped it into long bandages, fastening them tightly above the injury. The rate of bleeding slowed as he ordered his butler to exert pressure on the offending thigh.

Mrs Orchard had brought through hot water and towels and another pile of quilts, one of which she proceeded to wrap Daniel's crying sister in. Gwendolyn's continued sobbing was obviously getting on everyone's nerves, so Amethyst led the girl to a chair and sat her down.

'When did you last see your sister?'

She could tell Daniel was listening though his attention was still on the injured boy.

'An…hour back. But there…were people there and they were drunk and I could not find her. Andrew was in a fight. The man hit him with a metal pole, I think, and there was so much blood. I knew Montcliffe was close so I helped him into the carriage and brought him here.'

She had begun to shake quite badly, the shock of it all settling in.

'You did well and he already looks better.'

The paleness of Andrew's face was alarming, but he had begun to shiver less violently and accept small sips of sweet hot tea. Daniel moved away.

'Keep them both warm, Mrs Orchard, and give them each some brandy. I am going to find Caroline.'

Amethyst stood. 'I would like to come, too. I am a good rider and you might need a woman to help with your sister.'

Uncertainty flickered across his face, but the situation was too dire to lose any more time in trying to persuade her to stay back.

'Very well. Meet me in the stables in ten minutes. I won't wait longer.'

They rode through the growing dusk at speed, the sound of his horse's hooves matching the beat of hers. He was astonished at her prowess.

If his sister was hurt in any way… He shook away the thought and drew in his reins, waiting as Amethyst

Cameron came in beside him. Nay, Amethyst Montcliffe now.

'That is the roof of the inn there.' He tipped his
head to listen, music coming from the same direction.

'It's a good sign, I think. If they were hurting your
sister, they wouldn't sing.'

He almost smiled, but didn't. Rape followed few
rules. My God, he had seen that time and time again in
Spain when the whole campaign had fallen to pieces,
and the baser nature of men had come to the fore.

'Stay here and mind the horses. If anyone comes,
scream as loud as you can and I will hear you.'

'No.' A knife was in her hand, wicked, sharp and
ready. 'I can help you.'

'You know how to use it?'

'With proficiency.'

The look in her eyes didn't brook argument. Taking
the reins of both horses, he fastened them to a branch.
'Stay behind me, then, and if I say run, you run. Understand?'

Gesturing her assent, she stepped back, the darkness of the riding clothes she had changed into blend-
ing with the shadow and reminding him of some of the
women in Spain who had marched to the call of the
drum and followed their men into battle. Brave and
surprising. He liked having her there, a point of refer-
ence in the darkness and another pair of watchful eyes.

If anyone had hurt his sister, he would deal with
them without a backward glance, he swore that he
would. The anger in him shivered over disbelief.

The singing men were outside, gathered around

a table and drinking. One was old enough to be his grandfather and the other two looked to be so drunk they would be no threat to anyone save themselves. Motioning to Amethyst, he skirted around a line of trees which brought them up to the front door of the inn. A few patrons were drinking at the bar, but there was no sign of any problem. When a faint noise from above caught his attention, he surged up the stairs and into a room at one end of the passageway.

Caroline was in a corner, crouched down with a broken bottle held out in front of her and her dress ripped down one arm. Three young men were trying to coax her out, their method of doing so bringing a shout from Daniel's throat and filling the room with fury.

A poker sat in one of their hands, the ashes from a fire scattered about their feet. When he looked at his sister again he saw the angry mark of a burn on the bare skin of her upper arm.

The perfect certainty he had always felt in battle suddenly claimed him and he moved forward.

Daniel exploded into action without warning. In less than a minute three men lay at his feet, with barely a noise, hardly a movement. Amethyst had never seen someone fight like that before, the grace of his fury unwinding into a lethal force, the strength of his fists and body simply obliterating any resistance.

Tenderness took over as he brought his sister into his arms, checking her for other injuries and holding her as she shook violently without making a sound.

'You are safe, Caroline. We are here to take you home. Did they hurt you elsewhere?'

'No. They asked me to have a drink with them. I know I should not have said yes, but I couldn't find Gwen or Andrew and so I agreed. They brought me upstairs and I knew then...' She couldn't go on and her brother bent to lift her into his arms.

'Tell me if anyone so much as looks at us, Amethyst.' He made no effort to keep his voice down as he retraced his steps.

Finally they walked out through the front door and into the evening, the soldier in her husband so very clearly seen. No one spoke. No one touched them. No one moved in the stillness of the oncoming night, save them.

Then the horses were before them, whickering at their presence. Amethyst held her knife ready until they were mounted. Daniel threw his cloak around his sister and wrapped her in tight.

'Get on your horse, Amethyst.'

She did it in one quick movement and he tipped his head, gesturing a direction as he spoke.

'They won't follow.' The strength in the Earl's voice was comforting. His hair in the oncoming darkness had fallen loose and lay across his shoulders and he had collected a bruise on his cheek from one flying fist. He had never looked more beautiful to her or more distant.

Much later Daniel called her to his library. Each of the injured young people had been seen to by the doctor and sent to bed and all were expected to have made a good recovery by the morning. Her father had long since retired, but Amethyst had stayed in the downstairs salon reading just to make sure that there was no more trouble.

The Earl was standing at the window as she walked in. He had changed his clothes and now wore a shirt and a loose cravat. His jacket was draped across a chair nearby and he held a drink in his hand.

'Can I offer you something?'

Amethyst shook her head.

'Will you sit for a moment?'

He motioned to two chairs positioned before the fireplace. The grate held the warmth of low embers.

'Caroline was lucky. The doctor said the burn on her arm was superficial and he has dressed and wrapped it. Her fearfulness may take a little longer to recover from, of course, and I doubt she will be venturing anywhere on her own in the foreseeable future. But there is nothing…that she can't recover from.'

'What about Andrew Howard? How is he faring?'

'A little worse. He has a substantial wound on his leg and a large bruise on the back of his head. I have sent word to Lucien who will come to look him over, no doubt.'

'And your mother?'

'Has been informed of the happenings. Unfortunately, I suppose she will also descend upon us.' Drawing a hand through his hair, he continued speaking after a few seconds of silence. 'She is a woman whom life has disappointed and as such goes to great pains to make sure others feel the same way.'

'So she won't like me?'

'Probably not.' He didn't mince the words and for that she was grateful. 'But she does not like me much, either, so we should be about even.'

Shocked, Amethyst looked straight at him. 'But you are her son.'

'She hated my father with a vengeance and I suppose I remind her of him.'

'And Nigel didn't.'

'He was more persuadable and usually did exactly as she wanted. I was less biddable, but families are complicated things and I have long since ceased trying to understand mine.'

Amethyst waited as he took a drink. The bruise on his cheek had swollen and was threatening to close up his right eye.

'Where did you learn to wield a knife?'

Shocked by his directness, she was mute.

'Every other woman of my acquaintance would not know how a blade fits within their fist. But you do. Why?'

She wanted to tell him, she did. She wanted to spit out all the horror of her first marriage in one unbroken line of thought, but this was neither the time nor the place. Not yet. She needed to get to know him better first.

'The docks are dangerous and I was often there at night.'

She didn't know if he believed her or not as he leant forward.

'You surprised me, Amethyst, and that is something

not many people have managed to do before. Do you carry your blade now?'

'Yes.'

'Could I see it?'

With only a little hesitation she brought the leather sheath from a deep pocket and laid it on the table between them. To keep a knife on her person in the safety of his home must alert him to some of the things she would rather keep hidden. She also knew that she no longer wished to lie to him.

Picking up the scabbard, he extracted the knife, the multiple grooves on the handle which allowed a better grip taking his attention.

'A double-edged stiletto blade and well balanced, too. Does your father know you carry it?'

She shook her head. 'It would only worry him.'

At that he laughed. 'I am your husband and it worries me. But for now we will leave it at that. I have a request that you might be able to help me with over the next few days. Both of my sisters are...in need of some backbone, for they whine too much and they think too little. Their journey up to Montcliffe today surprised me, however, and made me think there still is a chance to rescue them from my mother's influence, if you like. The thing is, Amethyst, I want them to be more like you.'

'Like me?'

'Stronger. More certain. They have taken on my mother's propensity to complain about nothing and it is wearisome and unattractive. Perhaps with a little coaching and some hours spent in your company they might see the value in pursuing a different path, a braver direction.'

'Should I take this as a compliment, my lord?' Amazement gave Amethyst's words a quiet lilt. 'Most gentlemen of the *ton* want docile wives who think only of the things your sisters are probably fond of.'

'Which is why most marriages in high society are shams.'

Despite everything she laughed. My God, she could never have had this conversation with Gerald, not in a million years.

'And what exactly is our marriage then, my lord, if not a sham?'

The gleam in his pale eyes strengthened. 'You tell me, Lady Montcliffe.' Finishing the last of his drink, he placed it on the table before standing and drawing her up to him, only the smallest of spaces left between them. 'I would also like to thank you for your help today.'

'Thank me?' Every part of her body was squeezed into a breathless waiting.

'It is our wedding night, after all, and even a marriage of convenience should mark the occasion in some way.'

His fingers stroked the sensitive skin on the back of her neck as he looked at her, the gold threads in his eyes easy to see at such a close distance. 'There are secrets on your face that you might one day tell me and I have my own as well. But right now, here, in this room, there is only the vestige of a difficult evening behind us and the hope of a better day before us. Perhaps we could find it in us to celebrate at least that?'

'How?' She was wary.

'Like this.'

His lips came down across her own with care. He did not force or cajole, he merely waited to see what it was she would do.

A choice, melded with words of thanks and gratitude, a dark night outside and a warmth within. If he had demanded more she might have left, but he did not. The touch of his tongue against her mouth, only asking, and his hand resting lightly against the small of her back.

She did not know what happened between them when they touched, but the same feelings as before rose within her, a longing, an affinity, the woman in her whom Gerald had never discovered pressing forward into the hard edge of his passion, two people melded together in a raw and utter need.

How long had she waited for just this thrall, no rational thought or logic. Her hands went on their own accord to rest on the muscles of his shoulders. Hers. To hold and have. For ever.

But he could not love her back.

The pain of loss rose unexpectedly, spilling into her like ruined wine and making her draw away. She saw need flint in his eyes before distance covered it, the lover swallowed by the soldier as he let her go.

One foot, then two, and although the silence between them screamed with questions she was not brave enough to answer. Yet.

* * *

She looked broken and small. He had noticed this thinness from time to time, but tonight it worried him more, her eyes huge in her face, the shadows beneath them dark.

There was something she was not telling him, the shape of it lingering in fear, her breath forcing panic down to a place where she could manage it. If anyone could understand such things, it was him. He tried to set her at ease.

'I like kissing you.'

Her blush was expected, but her tears were not. He had never seen a woman cry on a compliment before. She wiped them away with the back of her sleeve, hurriedly, as if she had no time for such emotion.

'My father has had the first of the money transferred into your account, Lord Wylde. It should go some way in helping with...' She stopped and breathed out hard, as if she had said too much and did not wish for what would come next.

'With the agreements. Just that?'

She nodded and he felt something shift inside him. Amethyst had been hurt and badly. By Whitely in all likelihood, the husband she had been married to for sixteen months. If she couldn't talk about it, he would ask Robert Cameron privately about the man tomorrow.

A log dropped in the fire and a shower of sparks lit the grate. Home and hearth.

'I want you to know that I would not have married you just for the money.' He dredged up the rest. 'I married you because I liked you.'

This time her smile was real, no pretence in it or anger.

'And perhaps I like you back, Lord Montcliffe.'

'A good start then?'

She nodded and in her eyes was the swell of decision. 'Gerald Whitely was not the man I thought him to be and my mistakes have made me wary.'

He could see what this admission had cost her by the quickened blood pulsing at her throat.

'He came to us as a clerk who was recommended by a friend of my father's. Papa liked him at first, but then he tried to dissuade me from taking the relationship further. I wanted love in a marriage and permanence.'

'But you did not get it?'

'No.' The violent loss in her eyes darkened them, so that they were almost black in the shadows of the room. There could be no mistaking the hatred lurking at the edges, either.

What the hell had Whitely done to her?

'At La Corunna I realised fate could be cheated because I should have died there with a bullet through my thigh and the blood running out of me in a stream, but I didn't. Ever since I have been of the opinion that we each have the choice to worry about what has come before or to forget it.'

A frown marred her brow. 'What of the pain in your leg—does that allow you to forget?'

Her intent told him the question was important and so he took his time in answering.

'Sometimes it does not. In the cold of winter, on the dance floor, after a ride of some distance, at these times I remember. But here with you, in a warm room and on my wedding night, it ceases to demand a constant attention and so the ache itself is lessened.' He stopped for a moment, considering his words. 'You are safe here, Amethyst. I would not ask from you anything you did not wish to give. At least be assured of that.'

Her half-smile wound about the corners of his heart. 'Gerald said that to me, too, and I was foolish enough to believe it.'

And then she was gone, turning for the door and running, the skirt of her riding outfit swishing as she went.

She sat as still as she could and listened. To her heartbeat, to her breathing, to the small sound of her hand as it moved against the silk counterpane.

For so long she had felt...sad. Her father had known of it, but he didn't understand the truth of why. Nobody did. Yet tonight with Daniel Wylde in a room of books and honesty something had changed, some hard part of guilt, leaving room instead for the fluid movement of truth.

She had told him some of it. Just a little, but enough. He could make of it what he would. She knew he had seen the hatred for Gerald in her eyes that could not be hidden, though she wondered about the shame. Had that remained concealed? She hoped so.

Standing, Amethyst walked across to the full-length mirror and simply looked at herself. Against the dark riding clothes her hair caught the light from the candle in a way that surprised her. She almost looked pretty.

She had not thought that of herself before, but tonight she did. Perhaps that came from Daniel's kiss. For so long she had been this other woman, frightened by life and lost in her work.

Joyless. Her father had said that about her when he had insisted on this marriage and all its agreements. 'You used to be happier, Amy. You used to know how to laugh. Now you seem only joyless.'

'Gerald.'

She whispered the name into the night. He had taken that part of her that believed in love and possibility and twisted all she had been into who she was now. Daniel had told her the past was gone and could not creep into the present unless you let it. She liked that about him.

'I am enough,' she said, suddenly surprised by how fervently she meant it. 'And my husband enjoys kissing me.'

A power, that, given without the knowledge of what had been taken from her. She held on to his words with hope.

A noise in the room next to hers alerted her to the fact that he had come up to bed and she crossed to the doorway so that she might better hear his movements.

Her eyes went to the key on her side of the portal. If she turned it so that it was unlocked, would he take that as an invitation and come in so that they might talk more? Clasping her fingers tightly together in case she should actually go ahead and do it, Amethyst waited till any noise stilled and then she crept most quietly to her own bed.

* * *

The early part of the next morning brought Daniel's sister Gwendolyn into her room, the girl's face uncertain and contrite.

'I hope this is not an intrusion, Lady Montcliffe, but I was wondering if you might have a moment to speak with me?'

Amethyst put down the book she was reading and gestured to a chair beside her. Gwendolyn's dress had been cleaned and pressed, a small tear in the fullness of her skirt artfully repaired.

'I have come to say thank you for your help yesterday in recovering Caroline.'

'You are most welcome.' Amethyst knew there was more to come by the look of intrigue on the younger girl's face.

'Caro said that you wielded a knife. She said that you knew how to use it, too. She told me I was not to tell anyone at all about such a fact and especially not our mother, but...' She stopped and looked uncertain about how to proceed.

'You have questions?'

'Mama is always telling us that we should be docile and sweet and that embroidery and tapestry and reading are the kind of things a husband will be looking for in a marriage. But our brother has been pursued by women for years and years and he did not choose someone like that at all...' The rambling came to a stop as the girl realised what she was saying.

Amethyst picked her words carefully. 'Our marriage might have been a little different from others, Gwendolyn, but I would say to you to be honest to yourself. Be the person you wish to become and follow the interests you want to pursue. Only then will you find a husband who will truly suit you.'

'I love riding and horses and if I could I would live in the country. Mama and Caroline are more interested in gowns and boots and bonnets.' She hesitated before carrying on. 'Are things like fashion and hairstyles important to you, Lady Montcliffe?'

Despite herself Amethyst laughed. 'Not especially. I have only ever had a few gowns at a time and my hair is much too short to do a lot with. From what I can see society seems to dedicate a great amount of time to what one looks like, but I was always too busy helping my father balance books and sourcing timber to care.'

'But you are rich? Richer than anyone else we know?' Gwen's blue eyes flashed fiercely. 'Mama says you come from trade, but it seems to me that you know a lot more than I ever will. You are free to learn things, different things, and in the end you still get to marry an Earl.'

Amethyst did not know whether to tell her of the nature of their union, but then decided against it, choosing to let Daniel's sister see the possibilities before her and not the problems.

'If you would like to come up to Montcliffe Manor to stay with us for a while, you would be most welcome. We could ride together and you could show me the places you liked as a girl when you were here.'

A heavy frown settled across the young brow.

'We did not come here much because Mama never

enjoyed it and after Papa died in a riding accident my mother never wanted to stay at Montcliffe Manor.'

'Then we will find new memories, Gwendolyn.'

'Gwen. All my true friends call me Gwen.'

Amethyst smiled. My God, could it be just this easy to fit in? Could the women of the *ton* be exactly like those from the other parts of society; some difficult, some judgemental and others only searching for their way in life? Like Gwen was.

The pathway into the future suddenly did not look so impossible. Amethyst liked Christine Howard and now she understood Daniel's younger sister better, too. How many friends did one truly need?

Reaching over, she took the girl's hand in her own. 'You will find all the things that you need to, Gwen, I promise, and if there is anything that Daniel and I could help you with you have only to ask.'

'Could you teach me how to wield a knife?' The query came back quickly.

'Absolutely.' There were no qualms at all in her answer.

Lucien Howard was at the lunch table when Amethyst came down, as was Daniel, her father and Julia McBeth. Today her husband wore all black, the darkness of his clothes making him look even more dangerous than he normally did.

'I hear felicitations are in order, Lady Montcliffe. Pity I was not invited.' Lucien's voice held a good deal of humour within it.

Daniel's didn't. 'Lucien has come to pick up his brother.'

'I see. How does Andrew fare this morning?'

Lord Ross shrugged. 'He should be down joining us any second. From his recounting of the tale he was the hero of the hour.'

The subject of their musings arrived just as he finished the sentence.

'Who are you saying was the hero of the hour, Luce?' Today a black bruise on Andrew's chin had darkened and he used a crutch to walk.

'You are, Drew.'

Daniel supplied that and his tone sounded grateful. 'If you had not insisted on accompanying my sisters on their foolish journey from London, God knows what else could have happened.'

Charmingly the boy blushed and Amethyst looked away at her father who was in conversation with Julia. The widow brought out the best in Robert and she was glad to see his plate piled high. A new sort of contentment began to fill the empty corners of the past and she caught Daniel's eyes upon her before looking away. The right one had swelled up even further in the night, making him look dissolute.

She wanted to kiss him again, she wanted him to hold her against his warmth and never let go. Her ridiculous heart was beating faster than it normally did just on that one small glance and when she lifted her fork she saw her hand shake.

'You seem flustered this morning, my dear. Perhaps

it is the lingering effects of yesterday's adventure?' Robert remarked.

'Perhaps.' When her father smiled in that particular way her heart sank. She had never been a good liar, that was the trouble. She had never been one of those people who could conceal everything behind an implacable mask.

Like her husband.

'It seems we will be at Montcliffe longer than we had anticipated, but I must say that the area is growing on me. The rolling hills and the greenness and the peace of it all.' Papa was effusive in his praise and Julia laughed.

'Everybody says that after a few days' residence. I could never understand why the Lady Wylde did not come here more often. If it were mine, I should never leave it.'

'But you live here now, do you not?' Papa sounded more than interested.

'Only for another few weeks. I will be travelling north to stay with my sister after that.'

Again Amethyst saw a look on her father's face that made her puzzled, but she could dwell on it no longer as the door opened and a well-dressed woman she had never seen before stood before Daniel, a look of utter disdain upon her beautiful face.

'I have come to take your sisters home, Daniel,' she said, her voice imperious and harsh. 'I also presume that this woman's presence here means that this foolish alliance of yours has already taken place much against my wishes.' Her disdainful glance swept over Amethyst without the slightest degree of interest.

'Indeed it has, Mother,' the Earl replied frostily as he stood. 'This is my wife, Lady Amethyst Montcliffe, and her father, Mr Robert Cameron. I think you know all of the rest.'

'I do.' Lady Montcliffe made no attempt at niceties whatsoever.

'If you would wait in the library, I will come to you directly, Mother, for there are a few things I need to tell you. Gwendolyn and Caroline shall be readied to leave presently.'

But the newcomer was going nowhere. 'Is that you, Andrew Howard? Was it you who put this nonsense into the girls' heads and led them on to a merry goose trail that could have ended in such tragedy?'

The bravado on Andrew's face wilted, though it seemed Lord Montcliffe had had enough of his mother's poor manners as he took her by the arm and shepherded her from the room.

'Daniel's mother was always a difficult woman,' Lucien offered into the silence. 'And his father was little better. Daniel would come and stay with my family most holidays and, looking back, I cannot even remember one where he went home. Nigel came too, sometimes, but he was melancholic and nervous.'

'When he died I didn't feel surprised, really.' Andrew spoke up now. 'Mama used to say that he was not long for this world, remember?'

Lucien took up the tale now. 'Well, Daniel looked after him as best he could, but sometimes even he lost his patience and that's saying something. Nigel was in London when he got home from La Corunna. Daniel had a fever and a leg that looked like it might be septic and he'd lost so much weight from dysentery that the doctors thought he wouldn't make it, yet Nigel only talked incessantly about his own problems. Daniel yelled at him to go away and come back when he was in a better mood, but Nigel was killed in a hunting accident two days later here at Montcliffe.'

'And Daniel blamed himself?'

Her words fell into the silence and Lucien looked at her quizzically.

'I think he did. He seldom spoke of his brother afterwards.'

Glancing around at Julia, Amethyst saw her worried blue eyes were swimming in tears.

Lucien walked into the library late in the afternoon as Daniel was tidying up the deeds from the minister and filing them into the family bible. A marriage of convenience this might be, but it would be recorded in posterity as real. Daniel was glad for that. After yesterday he understood his bride was not the trembling sort of girl that was so predominant in society. No, Amethyst Amelia knew how to wield a knife and ride a horse with the best of them.

Lucien looked more than concerned. 'Could I speak to you, Daniel, in confidence?

The serious tone of his oldest friend alerted him to the fact that something was wrong. 'Of course. Is Andrew—?'

He didn't finish as Lucien broke in. 'After the fracas at the Herringworth ball I took it upon myself to look further into the death of Mr Gerald Whitely and there are things I think you should know.'

Closing the cover of the family bible, Daniel sat down.

'What things?'

'He spent an inordinate amount of time at the Grey Street brothel and word has it that he...he liked to play rough.'

'Damn.'

'My thoughts exactly.'

'Define rough.'

'He gave several of the women there black eyes and split lips. Worse if anyone ever mentioned his...affliction.'

'Affliction?'

'He had had some sort of accident to the groin as a child. I don't know what damage it caused.'

Lord. Had Amethyst ever been hurt by him? he wondered.

Lucien wasn't finished. 'Perhaps Miss Cameron failed to tell you of the relationship between them because it was so terrible. Not lying exactly, just a bending of the truth. She never kept the bastard's surname because...' He tailed off.

'Because he was a bully. Because she was glad he was dead.' Daniel finished the thought for him.

Amethyst with her knife in hand and the ability to use it well. Had she learnt because she had had to?

Because she'd had a husband who had taken his anger out on her?

His eyes went to the clock. Too late to try and find out the truth tonight. Yet would she want him to confront her with it tomorrow? His wife was proud, independent and capable and her marriage to Gerald Whitely must be something she would have liked to have forgotten about altogether. He needed her to tell him of it, on her own terms and in her own time.

As a confidant, not an interrogator.

If he picked his moment and had patience she would come to understand that she could trust him.

Finishing his drink, Daniel poured himself another and indicated to Lucien to join him.

Chapter Ten

The next morning began with a fire in one of the cottages and so Daniel was called down to deal with that until well into the afternoon.

When he got back John, the old stablemaster, was waiting for him on the front steps of Montcliffe.

'There has been a mishap, my lord, with Deimos. I took him out into the fields after lunch and he got frisky with a few of the mares. Before I knew it he had taken the fence and gone over into the next paddock, but as he came back one of the younger fillies got in his way and there was a tumble. The long and the short of it, my lord, is that your stallion has a gash on his left fetlock. I knew ye'd want to be dealing with it yourself, so I came up here to find you.'

'How bad is it?'

'Bad enough, I think.'

Daniel's heart sank at the implications. Deimos had been with him in the gruelling Peninsular Campaign and the big black stallion had won over his heart.

Turning for the stables, he was surprised to see his wife waiting for him around the first corner of the building. He was glad that she had dispensed with the brown hairpiece altogether and he wished he might have been able to simply grab her hand and lead her off somewhere to talk. But with Deimos injured his priority lay in the stables. Still, he liked the way she smiled at him, her short golden curls making her look like a beautiful woodland sprite.

'I heard about the accident.'

Her voice was concerned as she stepped into the space beside him. John behind them kept up a low monologue of the way things had transpired all the way to the stables.

'Stay here,' Daniel ordered when they reached Deimos's stall, positioning Amethyst on the other side of the half-door and closing it behind him. Inside Deimos stood, head hanging near the ground and the air of injury about him tangible.

Moving slowly, Daniel went to the steed's head, allowing the stallion the knowledge of him being there, as he turned his hand against the big muzzle and let him sniffle.

'What's happened?' he crooned. 'I leave you for but a moment and you're hurt. And no war either. Just fillies,' he added, clicking his tongue as the horse raised its head to look straight at him. 'They're always trouble, lad, and it's a fine wonder you have not figured that one out yet.'

Worry sat in the quiet words and the love between them was obvious. By his own admission Amethyst knew that Deimos had carried him through months of chaos in Spain and that they had come home together on the lighters through the winter storms in the Bay of Biscay. What sort of bonds would something like that forge? The tone of his admonishment softened into a whisper as strong fingers slid across a dark topline to the left-hand flank and settled on the leg beneath.

As he knelt, Amethyst balanced on the stall door in order to see better, though when the stallion's tail began to twitch she was suddenly afraid he might kick out.

'Careful.' She tried to keep her voice low, but the anxiety within had both of them looking up at her in surprise.

'He won't hurt me. He is as steady as a rock, are you not, Deimos, and we have been in far worse scrapes than this one.'

As if the stallion understood he simply turned his head away and stayed still. The stoic lines of the beautiful animal made Amethyst's eyes moisten.

'Is it bad?' When Daniel lifted the injured leg from the ground she held her breath as the blood dripped beneath. If he had sliced open a vein...?

'It's a tear from the knee to the fetlock, but by the looks of it it's missed all the major tendons and arteries,' Daniel answered as he placed the leg down again.

A jagged diagonal wound came into her view, the skin pulled back to reveal the muscle beneath. She noticed he didn't touch it with his fingers, but skirted around the outside as though feeling for something.

'He'll recover,' he said finally. 'With a little luck and

some hard work he will be fine again. I'll get the supplies I need now and stay down here with him tonight.'

The light was falling and the dusk burnished Daniel's hair as he stood. Pulled into a loose queue at his nape, the leather ties were fraying at each end. His beauty never ceased to startle Amethyst. Daniel Wylde's was not a pretty sort of beauty, but a dangerous menacing magnificence that eclipsed all other men. Like the sun in the daytime sky or the full moon hanging low on a summer's eve, one could not remain unaware of his presence. Christine Howard had expressed it well when she had helped her in the preparations for the ball.

'Montcliffe is the man all the girls of the ton *want to take home, but I think he would eat them up before they ever had the chance to tame him.'*

Smiling at such folly Amethyst looked about her. Once the Montcliffe stables must have been magnificent, she mused, for even now in its faded glory the marbled manger and decorative filigree walls caught her attention. Craftsmen had laboured here long and hard on wood and metal and glass. Beneath her feet the floor was inlaid with small stones fitted into patterns that would be easy on horny hooves.

The head groomsman had returned to stand beside her. 'It were a strange accident, my lord, and I am sorry for it. One moment I had his head and the next...'

'I don't hold you at fault, John, but if you could find some empty pails and clean cloths I'd be grateful. I'll get what else I need from the kitchens.'

'Ye'll do the mending yourself then, my lord?'

'I will.'

Daniel had slipped through the door to rejoin her, his mind on the tinctures and ointments he would need, she supposed, a man who would not easily let others do something he could manage himself. Her heart swelled with a kind of aching want; to reassure him, to hold him close against all disappointment, to make this injury disappear and see Deimos well again.

'I would like to help.'

His glance ran across her gown and he smiled, the lines around his eyes deep in the twilight.

'I'll find something else more appropriate to wear,' she added, trying to keep the pleading from her query.

'Very well. It will take me a good half-hour to rustle up the things I need from Mrs Orchard in the kitchen. If you meet me there...'

Walking briskly down the aisle of stones for the doorway, she was glad to go before he had the chance to change his mind.

His wife had not only swapped her clothes, but she had been transformed into a lad, complete with breeches and a shirt. No small metamorphosis either, her legs well defined in the tight pantaloons and the shirt buttons undone around the neck. The most surprising thing was that the outfit looked as though it had been made for her.

'Papa and I travelled in Spain together a few years back. It was easier as father and son at times. I always wore a substantial hat,' she added as his scowl deepened, 'and a coat in public. A long one and well buttoned.'

He wanted to tell her to go and find a jacket now, but the hour was advancing and Deimos needed attention. He hoped John, the old stablemaster, had retired for the night.

Amythest's bottom before him as they traversed the path was round and curvy, little hidden in the cut of cloth or the line of her legs. His wife was tying him in knots and enjoying it for he could see the jaunty lilt in her walk as she turned into the doorway of the stables.

The evening had fallen and although the light was still reasonable he knew he needed more as he followed her in. Striking a lamp, he found an exposed nail and turned it to hold the wire handle. Deimos looked up at him, brown eyes full of liquid hurt.

'Nearly there, lad,' he murmured and lifted the two baskets of supplies into the stall along with a bucket of hot water and cloths. Steam rose in plumes from the pail and the smell of the gathered herbs was pungent.

In Portugal and Spain he had tended to many horses and as his mind centred on what he must do here he bade Amethyst to come in and join him. Another pair of hands would be a godsend and he was glad it was her behind him. Above all the other odours, lemon and lavender wafted.

'I'll bathe the wound first and then make a poultice. These bowls will be for the chamomile and thyme steeped in water for cleaning. If you strip off the leaves, we can make a paste and then add water to it. Warm water, not too hot or too cold.

'All right, Dei?' he asked from his place behind the stallion. In response the horse turned, the rope tied to the ring on the stable wall pulling tightly. When he had seen what he needed to he breathed in deep, wrinkled his brow and turned his head away as Daniel began to touch the wound softly, rubbing it downwards. The dirt he could determine embedded in the flesh would come out easily, but from experience it was the tiny particles that you could not see that made a horse sick.

With effort he pushed such a thought away. He would not allow anything to happen to Deimos, he swore it, no matter how long it took to make him better.

A few moments later Amethyst passed him the paste of leaves and he mixed it with water and salt, letting it dribble down the fetlock and seep into the straw. Chamomile stopped inflammation and thyme seemed to hold away the sickness. An old woman in the village here had shown him these remedies as well as others as a youth and he had never forgotten them.

The Montcliffe housekeeper arrived at the stable half an hour later, a pail of boiling water in one hand and numerous rolled bandages in the other.

'If ye'd be needing more, send up word and I'll bring it down.'

'I think this will do, Mrs Orchard. It's just a case of putting in the time and hoping now.'

When her eyes caught sight of what Amethyst had on they widened and she drew back. 'Well, I will be leaving you to it then, my lord.'

'Thank you.'

As she left he smiled. 'It seems she was as shocked as I was by the sight of you.'

'Well, we are married.'

'Indeed. Though in all honesty she probably knows we sleep in separate beds.'

Now it was Amethyst's turn to look horrified and he could not help but laugh as she blushed.

He took pity on her. 'Here, hold this.' The china bowl was exactly what he needed for the poultice and with measures of bran, linseed and beeswax he fashioned a thick paste. Adding a generous dab of fresh honey, he formed a shape in his palm, carefully patting it about the six-inch gash on his horse's leg.

'Give me your hand.'

'Pardon?'

'Your hand. Is it clean?'

She nodded. 'I have had it in the warm water and leaves.'

'Good.'

Depositing the whole concoction in her waiting palm, he guided her to the wound. 'Press like this.' Her skin was warm against his as he crouched down with her between his knees and his mind wandered to a more pleasant imagining. When Deimos whickered, his attention came back and he made himself stand.

'Keep it there while I prepare the wadding. I don't want it to drop off.'

A moment later linen covered the broken skin and she pulled her fingers away in time for the next layer.

Then, placing more salt in the boiling water, Daniel added the rolls of cloth, airing each of them for a few seconds before slapping them on to Deimos's leg and winding them around the fetlock. Amethyst moved to one side to allow him access whilst still holding the bran paste in place, her fingers in spaces he would not have been able to manage had he been alone.

Finally it was finished and, tying the lot off with a series of firm knots, he straightened. The sharp pain in his right leg took a moment to subside.

Amethyst felt Daniel's arm against hers as she stood and so she waited.

For what?

The feel of his body next to her own was familiar and here in the quiet of a windless night she did not want to pull away.

His shirt was wet with the thyme and chamomile tincture, as was hers, the hours of doctoring taking its toll. Realising that both palms were stinging from the heat of the bandages, she opened them to the night air and enjoyed the coolness, fingers splayed.

'Thank you.'

A gratitude that came from his heart. She could hear the tone of it in his voice and see it in his eyes as he watched her.

'I've never seen anyone else manage a wound as skilfully as you did.'

'Then you know nothing of the army. If a soldier can't doctor his own steed, he is in trouble.'

'Even officers?'

He laughed. 'There was not much distinction of ranks towards the end of 1808 as we marched north through Spain through the winter snow. It was each man to his own to simply survive.'

'But you did—survive, I mean.'

'Barely.' Now the laughter was gone.

'I'd heard of it, of course, through the papers and from the tales around London. I even saw some of the soldiers coming off the ships on the south coast. So many men lost and so much blame.'

'You speak of General Moore, I think, but he was a good man who garnered the respect of those about him. Napoleon had upwards of three hundred thousand men at his disposal and we had gone into Lisbon with only thirty-five so to get as many men back to England on the sea transports as the general did was some kind of a miracle.'

Amethyst smiled. Daniel was not a man to blame or whine and moan about things. He just got on with trying his best and fixing it up. Gerald had never stopped in his constant barrage of the wrongdoings of others. She remembered that about him so very clearly it was as if he had only died yesterday.

'I will sleep in the empty stall next to this one tonight just to make certain Deimos does nothing to undo all our good work.'

As the stallion moved Daniel unlatched the half-door and helped Amethyst out, loosening the rope that tethered his horse before joining her.

'Such a night's labour deserves a celebration.' He brought a hip flask from his pocket and undid the cap, offering it to her. When she took it she saw his initials had been placed in the silver, a crest pictured above them.

'It was a present from Lucien a few years back. He

bought it in a marketplace in Lisbon and had it engraved there, but the second initial was drawn wrongly.

DCAW.

Daniel George Alexander Wylde.

Remembering his names from the wedding registry, she smiled, though as she took a sip she was not prepared for the strength of the draught.

'Whisky,' he explained, 'and straight from the stills of northern Scotland. It will put hair on anyone's chest.'

Laughing, she handed it back. The top buttons on his shirt had been loosened and the hard lines beneath were easily seen. A man's chest, muscle sculpted and browned. On his right forearm a thick opaque scar trailed from the wrist upwards, disappearing beneath the fabric at his elbow. She wondered how much further it went.

Outside the quiet had settled and the lantern at their feet made the night sky darker. In the ring of flame it was only them, the deep silence punctuated by the snuffling of horses in their various stalls. She made no effort to step back.

As if she had willed it, his finger traced a path from her cheek to her bottom lip. She could taste the salt as she leaned forward, but neither of them spoke as his other hand followed the bones of her neck.

'I want you.'

He was not offering love, but his confession held something more honest because she felt it too, this pull of flesh and bone.

Perhaps lust was exactly what she did need, with chamomile and thyme still in the air and the warmth of healing close. She felt different; on an equal footing in their dirty clothing from the shared task of helping with Deimos, the gap of birth and blood lost amidst more important things.

She wanted more. She did. She wanted the heart, body and soul love her father spoke of and her parents had known. She wanted honesty and strength of purpose.

His lips came across hers slowly, as if to give her the chance to pull back, and in his eyes she saw a question. Then she thought of nothing as his mouth opened upon hers asking for things she had no knowledge of. A force of breath, the feel of his hands, his body pressed tight as he showed her what it was that could exist between a man and a woman.

No small quiet demand either, but in the breaking of a caution she had always kept a hold of, a freedom surged. He would allow her his body without restraint and to do with it as she willed? Nipping at his bottom lip, she felt an answering push, and claimed the response. His gift of acquiescence reflected in the pale green and gold of his eyes.

'You are so very lovely,' he whispered and she felt it, even with her shortened hair and dirty clothes.

'Only with you.' The boldness in her was foreign, unchartered, but when his hand strayed to the buttons on her shirt a new danger surfaced.

Feeling her stiffen, Daniel changed his ploy. He did not want her scared or threatened in any way. Behind them Deimos had moved to the manger and was taking great mouthfuls of the hay stacked in marble. A good sign that, the return of appetite. He smiled into the soft skin at Amethyst's throat and tipped her head to one side so that he might place his mouth across the trembling beat of blood.

'Here,' he said softly as he bore down upon the spot, suckling in a gentle rhythm, 'and here,' he said again as his mouth moved upwards, the red whorl of his first tasting marked into the white of her skin.

His.

'You are mine,' he said and saw the flutter of her eyelashes, long and silky, the velvet brown of her irises lost in darkness. To have. To hold. To need. No woman ever before had made him feel quite like this. Possessive. Overprotective. Obsessed.

His wife by rule of law and God.

Pushing back the fabric of her shirt, he found soft white lawn and lace beneath, the swell of her womanhood exposed through the open weft. When one finger ran across the proud hard nipple, a cry was wrenched from her throat, pulse racing and breath shallowed.

She did not stop him. Rather she arched into his grasp as though wordlessly asking for what came next. His hand slipped beneath the scalloped edge of lace and cupped one breast. The abundance surprised him, no little bounty here despite her slenderness, and his thumb traced again across a budded nipple.

Dark eyes flew open.

'What is this?' she asked, licking dry lips with her tongue as she did so, but holding him there, her hand placed across his, the layer of fabric between them.

'Loving, Amethyst, between a man and his wife. No wrongness in it.' His own sex was rock hard and he knew she could feel him, pushing into the space between. Leaning down, he brought his mouth to her breast.

She couldn't think, that was the problem, couldn't place one thought next to another as his mouth did things to her insides she had never thought possible.

This was what she had read about, heard about, wondered of, this connection which did not hold to the bounds of logic. The pull from his suckling speared down into her stomach and lower, every part of her quivering with the touch, balanced on a precipice which she did not want to fall from as she stretched into acceptance.

Nothing else existed here save for them, melded into each other like iron filings in an ancient forge and heated beyond melting point. Shapeless entities save for desire and a knowledge that could not be stopped.

Even without the words of love she wanted him, her breath fogged in the lamplight and rising upwards.

When she simply surrendered he stilled, her whole being borne to a place that shattered into feeling, waves of release rolling through the tightness, her nails clasped about him like talons in the skin. No time frame or true certainty.

And then a shaking. Of sadness, she was to think later, and of regret. Of missing this for ever and of all the wasted years. Gerald Whitely had made her believe in abstinence and frigidity, her birthmark only sealing in the ugliness, drawn as it was across her top left-hand thigh in a single swathe of red.

His hands moved downwards and into the folds of her breeches. He had lost the struggle to be gentle many minutes ago and his avidity was worrying. In war he was always calm, but here in love a wildness ruled.

The crunch of feet on the gravel a few feet off had him pushing her behind him, though he relaxed as the face of John, the stablemaster, peered through the dark.

'Mrs Orchard sent me down to see if I could escort Lady Montcliffe back up to the house, my lord. She said there is a hot bath waiting and some supper. She'll send food down for you, too, if you are ready.'

He made himself take a deep breath and stepped away from his wife, who was fumbling with the undone buttons on her shirt front. With an effort he tried to find in the interruption some measure of calm as he passed three china bowls across to John.

'If you will take these up with you, Mrs Orchard is wanting them back. Ask her to send down some more water and herbs, if you would, and an apple or two if she has them.'

Amethyst was looking at him, a wobbly uncertain smile on her face, and then she was gone, following the stablemaster up towards the kitchens. Daniel watched her until shadow replaced form and then turned to lean against the wall behind.

He had wanted to take her on the filthy floor of a working stable. The full flush of need left him reeling and he knew he had marked Amethyst with his mouth and that the red whorls of bruising would be even more noticeable on the morrow.

She made him into a man he did not recognise, the more usual temperance replaced instead by a desperate carnal greed. She was his wife, for God's sake, and Gerald Whitely had probably hurt her more times than Daniel could possibly imagine. If he had been allowed the free rein of his desire, could he have done the same? Even now with all these thoughts his rod was stiff and ready, a haze of need making his head buzz and his eyesight blur. A man no better than those soldiers he had seen in the last weeks of the march, any woman young or old a target for their violent ardour.

He had always been in control and had been raised to treat a woman with respect. Until Amethyst. Until the smell and feel of her had burnt into reason and left him crazy.

The ache in his groin intensified and he turned to slam his fist hard into the solid wall behind him, once and then twice more.

Even then the pain did not entirely negate his desperate need and as he swore Deimos lifted his head across the half-wall to watch him.

'We are both of us made damn fools by women,' he said quietly, cradling his bloodied hand as he prayed to God for strength.

Amethyst got up as soon as the first light of dawn crossed the eastern sky and dressed in a sprigged muslin gown with a half-cape to match.

The stables looked deserted as she reached them and, walking down the aisle, she found Daniel tucked into a bed of straw. In sleep he looked younger than he did awake, the lines of responsibility drawn in the daytime upon him lessened in slumber.

'Deimos was restless all night, my lady.'

John had come up to stand beside her, a bunch of fresh straw in his arms.

'His lordship bathed the leg twice more in the early hours and applied fresh poultices. Honey and garlic, I think he used this time, though it's the heat that does it.'

'A difficult night, then?'

'Indeed.' The old man's eyes took in more than she might have wanted, his glance crossing over her colourful gown and carefully brushed hair.

She wished she might stay there and watch over her husband, but she imagined the busy routine of a stables was not one to be easily interrupted and she did not want to be in the way.

'How long will he sleep for?'

'A few hours yet, I'd say, my lady. Deimos reared up at one point when the Earl took him outside and a hoof connected with his bad thigh. Whisky seems to have allowed him some slumber, though it's a two-sided relief. He will have a headache when he comes round and the mood to match it.'

Her eyes took in the top of his right leg where the blanket had fallen away. A smear of old blood had soaked through the fabric of his breeches, darkening the beige into a dirty brown. She also saw his silver flask lying on the straw in a way that pointed to the fact that there was nothing left in the bottle. When she had sipped at it last night the level had been almost to the top.

Unshaved and dishevelled, Daniel looked somehow vulnerable. She wished she could have pulled the blanket up against the chill and covered him, but the stable was quickening into work for the day so she moved back.

'I'll let his lordship know you were here, then, Lady Montcliffe. He'd be pleased no doubt that you came to see how Deimos fared.'

'Thank you.'

'I wouldn't expect him up at the big house for a few more hours yet, mind. That's a fair bit of alcohol he's consumed.'

His laughter followed her outside, though as she got to the top of the path she saw her father and Mrs McBeth standing together. When she joined them Robert smiled.

'Julia wanted to show me the wildlife in the pond at the front of the house. She also says kingfishers, jackdaws and pipistrelle bats are common around here, so I'm looking forward to seeing those, too.' He frowned as he looked at her more closely. 'You look tired.'

'Lord Montcliffe's stallion was injured and we spent the night in the stables tending to him.'

'All night?'

'No. I returned to the house around one o'clock, but the Earl is still there.'

'Working on Deimos?' The question came quickly from Julia.

'No. He is sleeping.'

When Amethyst caught the light blue eyes she saw worry, understanding and acceptance. Daniel had been her charge for many years, but now she was leaving his well-being to a young wife and trusting her to see him safe. The connection between her and Julia Mc-Beth was unexpected but strong and she saw her father had felt the same sort of affinity for the older woman.

A new beginning for them all then and in a landscape that was both beautiful and peaceful. Even Dunstan House paled against the countryside here and the magnificence of Montcliffe Manor.

Bidding her father and Julia goodbye, she watched them walk together, talking all the way until they were lost from sight.

Today she needed to speak with her husband and be honest about her relationship with Gerald. She needed to tell him things and explain. She also wanted him to kiss her again and hold her in the same way he had yesterday, passion filling every single part of her body.

Snatching at a daisy flower in the grass, she peeled away the petals and chanted an old ditty from her childhood.

He loves me, he loves me not.

The chant continued until a small pile of plucked white was scattered about her.

He loves me...

The last petal. She smiled as she walked towards the house.

Chapter Eleven

The Earl was present for neither lunch nor dinner and when Amethyst asked Mrs Orchard of the whereabouts of her husband, the housekeeper was vague and unhelpful.

Lucien and Andrew Howard had left for London earlier in the day and Gwen had opted to travel with them on the promise that she could return and spend some time with her brother and his new wife the following week. Daniel's mother and her youngest daughter had departed the day before. So it was just her father and Mrs McBeth who were left in the parlour after the night-time meal and both of them looked exhausted.

'Would you mind if we retired early, my love? Julia has planned another morning ramble for me to enjoy tomorrow and I don't want to miss it.'

Amethyst was amazed. Her pale, thin and ill father seemed here to have been given another lease on life. Even his clothes seemed to sit on him better.

'Of course not, Papa. I was about to go up myself.'

Her eyes glanced at the ornate timepiece on the mantel. Eight o'clock. Perhaps she could find a book in the Montcliffe library before she went upstairs. The thought cheered her.

A few minutes later she stood in front of the bookcase and perused the contents. All manner of tomes graced the shelves, from the weighty pens of the ancient Greek philosophers to the lighter one of Maria Edgeworth's *Tales of Fashionable Life*. She smiled. She could not in a million years imagine Daniel Wylde reading that.

Where was he? she thought. Was he in his chamber or had he been called away? She had caught sight of John earlier and asked after Deimos. By his account the stallion was on the road to recovery and the Earl had left the stables after the midday lunch.

Back in her room, she crossed to their shared doorway and stood to listen. No noise or movement could be heard on the other side, which led her to the conclusion that he was not there. Another thought surfaced. Had he regretted their marriage already and journeyed back to London? Perhaps Andrew had worsened or Caroline? She could not believe the Earl wouldn't at least have informed her of something so terrible and pushed the notion away. She wished it was last night again and that they were in the stall with his stallion. She wanted to feel his mouth on her breast and find the love marks on her body as she had this morning when she had taken off her nightgown.

Surprising. Drawn in passion. Treasured. All the

feelings that Gerald had never been able to give her with his accusations and his anger. Her fault, he had said, but increasingly she was beginning to understand that the problem had been his own and that in her innocence she had not comprehended such a falsehood.

In the stall last night Daniel's manhood had pressed against her in a way she had never felt Gerald's do. Oh, he had kissed her nicely at first and at least with some modicum of need, but she had not seen any outward sign of masculine lust.

With Daniel it was entirely different and it was addictive to think that she, the plain and boring Miss Amethyst Cameron of her first husband's angry tirades, might affect the one man whom every lady, young and old, of the *ton* coveted.

Lord Montcliffe liked her. He liked kissing her and he liked her blushes and if John the stablemaster had not interrupted them she was sure her husband would have asked for…more.

She fanned her face with her hand and crossed the room to look at herself in the mirror. The whorls of red still showed in the crease of her neck and across the swell of her bosom. Thrilling reminders as she flicked her thumb across her nipple in the same motion as he had and a sharp pain of want pierced thinly. Changing. Quickening. For so long she had been afraid of everything and now she wasn't.

Tears sprang to her eyes, the hope in her reflection obvious. Would Daniel want her as much as she wanted him? Would he allow her to make the first move or was it proper to wait for a man to initiate intimacy?

Another worry then surfaced. Would the birthmark on the top of her left thigh be as much of a problem for him as it had been for Gerald? He had hated the mark and on the few occasions when they were first married and he had tried to take her to his bed he had been unable to remain there. She had not known much of what should have happened between a man and a woman, but she knew enough to understand his deep loathing of her own inadequacies.

'You are ugly,' he had railed, 'and you make no attempt at all to entice me. Ugly, thin and marked.'

The embarrassment of such words still lingered, anger and shame there in the mix, but also puzzlement. She could not imagine Daniel shelving his masculine passion for such a thing.

The small fire in the grate sparked and a handful of red embers glowed against the back of the chimney. If they stayed there whilst she counted to five everything would be all right, but if they faded...

Closing her eyes, she chanted the numbers quickly, pleased to see the sparks still lived against the dark and sooty framework when she opened them again.

The signs were changing, she thought, and for the better. The petals the other day and now the sparks. Perhaps things would be all right, after all, and the hopes and dreams she had of this marriage would come to pass. Threading her hands together, she knelt beside her bed and prayed her very hardest that the sort of love her parents had enjoyed might be transferred to their lives as well.

* * *

Breakfast the next day was a strained affair. Amethyst had been married for nearly four days and yet she had seen her husband for less than twelve hours during all that time.

Her father ate quietly next to her as she picked at the scrambled eggs she had on her plate. Julia on the other side of Robert looked worried as well.

'I was certain Mrs Orchard would know something of the movements of the Earl, though she swore that she did not when I asked her this morning.'

'Is it normal for Montcliffe to simply just disappear like this?' Her father asked that question.

The older lady shook her head. 'No, I imagine it is most unusual unless he has been called away to London, which could be the case.'

'He said nothing to you at all, my love?'

'We were busy with the stallion, Papa. The next morning I went down to see how the Earl had fared, but he was asleep. The horse had been restless by all accounts in the night and the old stablemaster told me that Lord Montcliffe had tended to it.'

'How is Deimos now?' Julia's question held concern.

'I'll go down to see John after breakfast and ask. I had not imagined Lord Montcliffe to just leave Montcliffe Manor given the stallion's accident and that is what is so strange.'

She did not add that from her point of view his disappearance was also surprising. Their last meeting had been full of the promise of more intimacy and to find herself left without an explanation was odd.

'Julia and I are off to look at various houses in the area today. Perhaps you would like to come and join us? We could pack a picnic and have it by the river for the weather is mild and no rain is predicted.'

Amethyst shook her head. A whole day away from Montcliffe Manor and the hope of seeing Daniel was not a prospect she looked forward to.

'Thank you for asking me, Papa, but I think I will visit Deimos this morning and take him some fruit.'

An hour later she hung on the half-door and watched the enormous stallion. Today he was ready to greet her and far more interested in his surroundings. The left fetlock still held a bandage, but he did not favour the leg as he once had.

'Hello, beautiful.' She held out an apple brought from the kitchen and the horse took it from her, crunching down the fruit in seconds. 'I see you are a lot better. Your master will be most pleased.'

'Oh, indeed he is,' John said from behind her. 'He asks morning and night about Deimos's progress.'

Amethyst's heart began to beat faster. Morning and night? He was here somewhere, then? Her eyes took in all the corners of the stables and saw nothing.

'You have been speaking to my husband?'

The old man frowned. 'Of course.'

'Where is he?'

'In the annexe, Lady Montcliffe. It's Mrs Orchard's hope that the fever will be breaking soon, though from what I can see…'

Fever? The annexe? What on earth had happened?

'Where exactly is the annexe, John?' Amethyst tried to keep her voice even, but the pitch had risen considerably and for the first time in their conversation the old stablemaster looked uncomfortable.

''Tis behind the main house, my lady, through the kitchen gardens and out the back. It used to be the quarters of the Earl's grandfather, so it is well furnished and comfortable. If you get lost, ask any of the servants and they will give you direction.'

'Thank you.' She walked away at a pace that she hoped would not draw attention, but every part of her wanted to break into a run. Daniel was here and he was sick and she had not been told anything of it at all. The anger in her mounted as she strode around the corner to the kitchen.

A serving maid walked down the path with a tray of untouched food as she approached the door, her face paling as their glances met.

'My lady…I think Mrs Orchard would like to see you before…'

'Oh, I am more than certain that she would,' Amethyst returned, her tone cutting. Continuing on, she gave the girl no more attention and was glad the servant seemed to have decided reinforcements were needed, her retreating footsteps becoming fainter and fainter.

The room was dark when she opened the door, and hot, a good ten degrees warmer than the summer's morning outside and it took a moment for her eyes to acclimatise from sun to shadow. Then she took in breath. Nothing made any sense here, the dying stalks of reeds in vases and the ancient carcase of an animal on the table strung out with pins and beads. The air around her was filled with the smell of pitch and sulphur.

A crunch beneath her feet made her look down. Eggshells, crumbled into pieces and mixed with what looked to be apple and bread. On the table in the middle of the room old bottles were arranged in a long line with bags of canvas above, the brown sediment dripping from each corner collected in a large brass pail. A jar of honey and several dishes of dried spices sat next to them with pills in brown paper twists, all opened to show a good many had already been administered.

A groan of pain took her attention.

'Daniel?'

The noise stopped.

She was in the smaller rear chamber in a second and there in a bed of blankets her husband lay, woollen fabric wrapped around his head and his face crimson with the heat. When he saw her recognition flinted and his hand came up.

'Go…away…'

But she had already seen what he was trying to hide. His naked right leg was swollen to three times its normal size and the flesh of his thigh was purple and mottled.

'My God.' She was across the room in a second, the flat of her palm against his skin on his forehead. Heat radiated out, the dryness of it more worrying than anything else. Pale eyes watched her, grimacing as he failed to sit up.

'Stay still,' she ordered and began to strip away the

heavy bedding before crossing to the windows and opening them. The air came rushing in, a draught that dispensed somewhat with the awful smell of sulphur and pitch and rustled the lawn curtains. Returning to his side, she snatched the wool from his head and threw the thing right out of the window. It sailed past the astonished presence of Mrs Orchard.

'What do you think you are doing?' The housekeeper's voice was furious. 'His lordship has expressly told me that you were not to know of this, ma'am. He wants to handle it in his own way, he does, and if he could talk I am certain he would be asking you to leave.'

'Get...out...now.' Amethyst did not even try to moderate her anger. 'And send John the old stablemaster in to me immediately.'

The woman looked as though she might argue, her face crimson with anger, but thinking better of it she turned on her heels and left. Daniel simply allowed his head to fall back against the pillows, all energy spent.

Her palms touched his thigh and he let out a cry. 'It serves you right that this hurts so much.' She pressed harder, determining the flesh was swollen but not putrid. 'You spent all of one night and the next day tending to your horse and yet you did not think to help yourself. The village doctor will be sent for immediately.'

His right hand snaked out and caught her arm. 'No... not...doctor.' His voice was rough and his lips were dry. A small smear of honey would fix that, but it was the entreaty in his eyes that made her hesitate.

'Why would you not call a doctor?'

'My…physician…wants…it off.'

Then she remembered. He had told her of this fear once before and it explained everything. The strange and quackish medicine of Mrs Orchard, the hidden annexe and the secrecy. My God, he truly believed he would lose his leg and this was his method to try to save it?

She removed the blanket and looked down. Mrs Orchard had cut the trousers away almost to the groin and the flesh pushed hard against fabric.

A series of bottles next to his bed also caught her notice. *Emetic. Purgative. Clyster.* The labels were carefully drawn in a hand that was precise and bold. Gathering all three together, she walked to the window and calmly hurled them after the strange woollen hat. There was a smashing of glass and then silence.

His pale eyes contained just a hint of humour as she rejoined him. 'Now that we have got rid of those we can start to get you better. Certainly you will never recover if this quackery is all you receive.'

His lips turned up slightly, heartening her. Surely there could be no humour left in someone who was dying?

'And while we are at it I'd like to say that being married means just that. Someone by your side. Someone who will fight for you. Someone that cannot be pushed away when things get difficult. I should expect that from you if I were sick and so whether you like it or not you are going to get just the same from me.'

A slight cough behind her made her turn.

'Ahhh, John. I am glad that you are here because

I wish for you to fetch chamomile and thyme, honey, bran, linseed, hot water and bandages. And beeswax, wasn't it? All the things we used on Deimos's fetlock. And a good wad of linen.'

His smile told her that he would comply. 'Oh, and tell Mrs Orchard to leave the pails of boiling water at the door when she brings them, for I do not wish to see her.'

Through the haze of pain Daniel realised Amethyst was ordering everyone around and that the fit of temper made her eyes more golden and her cheeks a flushed pink.

Damn it, why did she not leave him to his fever and his suffering? He did not want to be poked and probed and made ready to have his leg severed. He just wanted to die here, whole and complete, the life in him flowing out by degrees.

He didn't want her to see his leg either, the ugly hugeness of it or the scars. He wanted to turn away on the bed and have her gone, disappeared, only the purgatives left, and the medicines that made him so sick he forgot everything else.

His brother had cheated this sort of death with a quick bullet to his temple, but he had not been brave enough to do the same. If his leg went, Amethyst would be saddled with a cripple for the rest of her days and the things they had planned to do together like riding would be lost. He didn't even want to contemplate what an amputation might do to any prowess in the matrimonial bed. He would be bloody useless and because she was kind she would pretend he wasn't. God, help me he thought, as his wife's small hand came into his own and his fingers closed about them.

Holding on.

The tears on his cheeks surprised him, but he could not even turn his head away.

She felt his plea and knew his pain, but she made herself staunch. A wife who went to pieces was not what he needed now at all and she was damn well going to chase him to the afterlife and back to make certain that he did not die.

'I love you.'

There, she had said it out loud into the room, with all its clutter and its debris and the tears on her husband's face. 'I have loved you since the first moment I saw you on the steps of Tattersall's because you are strong and beautiful and good. If you die, I will too, I swear it, from a broken heart and a broken life. So if you have any decency at all you will fight to survive this and you will fight hard.' His glassy eyes watched her, the fever marking spots of red into the white, and barely blinking. 'I will love you for ever, damn you, Daniel Wylde. Do you hear that? It's for ever with me.'

She could not make it plainer, but already he looked to be slipping into sleep. If she shook him awake again, would it be better or worse for him? With no other experience in healing save that with the stallion she simply stood and watched, making certain his chest rose and fell, and was pleased when the old stablemaster came back with the supplies they needed.

'The village doctor has been sent for, ma'am, but Mrs Orchard asked me to tell you that Dr Phillips is at least two hours away at a difficult birthing for the maid in the parlour has a sister who works for him.'

'Then we will start without him. The fever needs to be brought down and the wound to his leg has to be dressed. I had thought to treat it in the same way the Earl treated Deimos.'

Unexpectedly the older man smiled. ''Tis not much difference between the wounds of a man or a horse, to my way of thinking, ma'am, and if Mrs Orchard's home remedies have brought the master to this bad pass then I'd say it's time to try something else.'

'You think it will work?'

'It did a treat with the stallion, though it took a few days. The wound has the same sort of look to it and there is no worse damage to the flesh that I can see.'

'You'll help me then?'

In reply he rolled up his shirtsleeves and set to stripping the leaves of chamomile and thyme into the warm water before adding a lump of salt to the brew.

Amethyst cut away the last of the breeches with her knife, pleased for the long shirt the Earl wore to cover his modesty. Still, her cheeks flared with the endeavour and she hoped when a nightgown had been sent down from the house and they dressed him later, he would not ask who had cut away the last of his trousers.

The chamomile-and-salt paste obviously stung him even in his unconscious state, for he rolled from side to side trying to get away from their ministrations. It took her a long time to brush the wound out with the linen until it looked a healthier pink.

As John readied the poultice she saw he had added his own mix of ingredients, which differed a little from those Daniel had applied to Deimos. Comfrey, angelica and feverfew were just a few of the herbs she recognised, but he had also peeled many cloves of garlic and crushed them into the paste. When he applied it to the wound the balm seemed to hold its shape with ease and she asked him about it.

'It's the stickiness of comfrey that does it, my lady. My mam used it all her life on us and I never forgot. Once Da lost three toes in an accident with an axel and she had him walking in weeks. Didn't turn bad, neither.'

The linen wadding and hot bandages came next and when the last of it was applied John positioned the Earl's wounded leg on a high stack of cushions.

'Can't do this with the horses, ma'am, but I would if I could. It does wonders for the drainage.' He stood back. 'Now with a good amount of thin chicken broth in him and the windows open he has the chance to get well.'

Amethyst reached for his hand, both their palms reddened from the heat and dried with white lines from the salt. 'I will never forget this, John.'

He smiled. 'You've the way with his lordship that he needs, I think, ma'am. It's been a rough few years with the army and his brother so a bit of peaceful rest will do him good. I will tell Mrs Orchard to send one of the maids over with that broth. Make sure you have some, too.'

When he left Amethyst used the time to clean up all the basins and pails and twigs that were left around the floor. The village doctor had finally arrived, but on seeing what she had done had informed her that he could not have managed better and then left. The birthing he had been attending was a difficult one and he needed to get back, though he promised to return to Montcliffe in the morning.

Drawing out a thin clean sheet from a large linen cupboard Amethyst arranged it across her husband, tucking in the top around his chin. Later she would find lavender for the room and perhaps a scented candle, but for now a tiredness descended upon her. Pulling a chair up to the bed, she dropped into it, glad to be off her feet.

It was dark and late and the pain that bloomed at the edges of his mind pulled him awake so quickly he felt the thumping of his heart in his chest.

Daniel's glance fell downwards and he saw his leg propped up with pillows and bandaged from groin to knee. As he wriggled his toes the relief that swamped him was enormous. It hadn't gone, then, and he still retained the feeling.

The days of being sick ran into each other, though he remembered Amethyst shouting something at him, anger in her eyes. He remembered John here, shadowed through the heat of a steamy room. He thought Dr MacKenzie from London had been by the bed at some point too, prodding at him and opening his eyes. But now there was only a dark silence.

He was alive and the breath he took no longer hurt in each and every part of his body. The room was clean, with cool, fresh linen arranged across him and the awful smell of sulphur gone.

He tried to lift his arm to wipe his dry lips, but the energy needed defeated him. Instead he turned his head and saw his wife on the leather chair and fast asleep. In stillness he watched, her small breaths rhythmic and deep, and the silky lashes on her cheeks long in repose.

Parts of the past days came back through the ether. The heat of the bandages, the smell of garlic, a cold flannel gently wiped across his forehead, water dribbled between dry lips.

I love you.

He stiffened, trying to catch the cadence of the words.

Had she said it or had he?

Tiredness swamped him and even the light of a candle burning on the mantel seemed too bright. He groaned.

'You are awake?' Her voice was soft as she came from slumber, but he could only watch her, the wheat-and-gold curls held back with a band of dark blue cloth.

'You have been ill. John and I have been tending to you and the fever broke this afternoon.'

Leaning over, she applied honey to his lips. He could not even lick away the sweetness. 'I will find you a drink for I am sure you must be thirsty.'

Standing, she went from his sight, but her footsteps

were close. Then she was back, one hand cradling his head and bringing him up. The fresh water was sweet and cold, though she allowed him only little sips.

'Too much will make you vomit again.'

Again.

'Your physician was called from London and he said to give you only tiny amounts until your stomach can manage it. He says it will be a few days until the sickness subsides.'

'MacKenzie was here, then?' Nausea rolled through his body in slow and undulating waves.

'Is here. Mrs Orchard has put him up in the house. He is pleased with your progress, too, because the swelling on your leg has gone down and the colour is better. There was a blockage and he removed it.'

A blockage? The bullet?

Daniel tried to ask her about it, but he could not. The skin beneath his wife's eyes was bruised purple and the scratch from the ring on her cheek had scabbed. Exhausted. Because of him. Where was Mrs Orchard? Why were the servants not here helping her?

Swallowing, he spoke, though the words came out as a whisper.

'Thank...you.'

Tears welled in her eyes before she wiped them away with a quick and embarrassed dash. He saw that her hands were blistered and with a huge effort reached out for the one that was nearest.

'Sorry.'

He was asleep again before she could even answer, his fingers limp and warm. Sorry I have been sick? Sorry I cannot love you?

Had he heard? Would he guess? Did he remember what she had told him in the quiet watches of his illness? And now that he was getting better, how did she hide what she truly felt?

She couldn't and the danger of it all spiralled.

Bringing his fingers to her lips, she kissed each one, strong fingers with war imbued within them, no pampered and indolent lord, but a man who had lived through battle as well as peace and who had defended himself and his country.

A knock on the door took her attention and, laying his hand down on the counterpane of the bed, she crossed to see who was there.

Her father stood on the top step, question on his face. 'I wondered if you were coming back up to the house this evening. It is late?'

She shook her head. 'I think I will remain here tonight, Papa. Lord Montcliffe is restless and may need me.'

'Every man needs his wife, my jewel, especially one who has been so sick.'

'I love him, Papa.'

'I know.'

'I am not certain if he loves me back.'

A small frown crossed his face and then a smile. 'Your mother would have said listen for things other than the words, Amy, and she would have told you to be patient. Love comes in many forms,' he added and reached forward to lift up the gold cross at her neck. 'It is here in your mother's gift and there in your blistered hands. Look for it in Daniel Wylde, Amethyst, but do not be greedy. Men can sometimes be afraid of love.'

'Were you?'

'When I first met your mother I was. And now...'
He stopped himself before saying more, but she saw
secrets in his eyes.

'It is Julia?' Her question held no regrets.

Without hesitation he nodded.

'I have seen a house not far from here for sale. It
has a garden that runs from the steps at the front to a
lake beyond it.'

As he spoke he beamed in a way she had not seen
him do for so very long.

'If you are to live at Montcliffe Manor I would like
to be close. Julia has expressed an interest in living
around Barnet as well for she has no fixed abode to
call her own. I know my heart is weak and there may
not be many months left for me, but still...?'

And then Amethyst knew. The truth as it must have
been for all the days of their visit. Her father was enamoured with Julia McBeth, with her light brown
and curling hair and her gentle pale blue eyes. A kind
woman, a good woman. A woman who might see him
comfortable and looked after for these last months or
hopefully even years of his life.

'Susannah said to make you flourish, Amethyst,
and I think you will here, but I also need a life. Do
you approve?'

She flung herself into her father's arms and showed
him with every ounce of love just how delighted she
was with his choice of both companion and of abode.

'You know that I do. Anything to make you happy

and relaxed were what the doctor ordered and this seems exactly that.'

When he had gone Amethyst sat again at Daniel's side. She felt safe finally. Indeed, if she had her way she would stay well out of the way of society and cocooned in the green heart of the countryside for ever.

Chapter Twelve

She was there watching him when he awoke again.

'I cannot be...good company.' The words were easier to say now. 'If you wish to go...'

'I don't.'

'It is late?'

She nodded and he looked across at the window. The curtains were not drawn and the light of a full moon fell into the room. After one o'clock, at least, and more like nearly two from the slant of shadow.

'Dr MacKenzie has had to go back to London, but he insists that you are being left in able hands.'

'Yours?' He smiled and moved his foot, bending his knee so that he could see the bandage and reassure himself that his leg was still there. Pain shot into his thigh, but it was bearable now, a lesser hurt. 'It looks a lot like Deimos's fetlock.'

'John helped me.'

The lines from his eyes crinkled with humour. 'What did MacKenzie say?'

'He said he thought he should be using the poultice in his own practice and he left something for you. He was certain you would be pleased.'

Leaning over to the small cupboard beside the bed, she took out a dish and picked up a bud of hard metal.

'This bullet came from your thigh.'

Relief rushed through him, making the blood beat in his ears. 'He got it out, then?'

'Dr MacKenzie said that the swelling dislodged it from the bone. He has never seen that happen before. He also said that I was to get you up walking as soon as I could.'

Daniel couldn't believe the elation of knowing he hadn't died or been left badly crippled by an amputation. He wanted suddenly to go outside into the light of the moon and feel the cold air upon his face, to put weight upon the bone and feel it strong and usable and real.

Shimmying up on the pillows, he moved his legs around to the side of the bed. His thigh throbbed, but he made himself wait until his body became accustomed again to the new position.

'I hope it was not you who had to dress me?' His nightshirt was long and bulky. There was nothing underneath it save his skin.

When she coloured he muttered something softly under his breath.

'John fashioned this for you.' Amethyst handed him a stick carved from hard wood. Its handle had been made into the head of a stallion, the rippled seams of dark knots giving the illusion of a mane. The cane felt good in his hand and sturdy as he stood, imbalance keeping him still until the world righted again.

Limping outside, Daniel sat by the front door on a chair Amethyst had placed there, the herbs from the kitchen garden pungent. He was relieved to be away from the bed.

'Nigel and I used to play here when we were young. Julia would bring us treats from the kitchen.'

'She is a good woman.'

He nodded.

'My father is most enamoured of her.'

Daniel smiled and for a moment they stayed quiet, nothing between them but silence, though his mind raced with all the other questions he needed answers for now that he felt stronger.

'Did Whitely ever hurt you, Amethyst?'

Even at a distance he could tell that she stiffened. 'Why do you ask?'

'Lucien said the man had a reputation for striking out with his fists in the heady dens of London's most expensive brothels.'

She breathed out hard before answering. 'He had a sickness, I think, that he could not control.'

'Did he hurt you?' The anger in his voice was obvious, but even with effort he failed to soften it.

'He was a man prone to high emotion that he had no way of controlling, you understand, and on top of that he liked to drink. More and more as our marriage progressed and he realised that our union had been a terrible mistake. It was probably my fault, too, because by that time I knew I could not abide him anywhere near me and I said so. The night-times were the worst because he was not able to...' She stopped and took a deep breath, reasoning Daniel would hardly wish to hear about their more intimate problems. 'He lashed out with words at first and then with his fists. A month after our nuptials he lost control and punched me in the stomach, as hard as he could. He told me that he could ruin my father's reputation completely with some of the things he knew and I believed him.'

'What happened next?'

'I was sick all over his boots.'

'God.'

'So he left and did not come back again for nearly a fortnight afterwards. By then I had arranged a tutor in the art of self-defence, using the same knife that you saw me with the other day. He never touched me again.'

'Never?'

'He had discovered other women who were more than pleased to accommodate him. He had our money behind him and was in the process of setting up his own dubious business schemes, which we knew nothing of until it was too late. Besides, I was more in the way than anything and he made certain to tell me I was ugly every time he saw me.' She took a deep breath and went on. 'I have a birthmark on the top of my left thigh, the kiss of the fairies my mother used to tell me it was, but to Gerald it was the stamp of the devil.'

'And to you...what is it to you?'

She turned away, but not before he had seen her tears. 'It was my shame.'

The shame of her own feebleness and paralysis. The

shame of allowing another governance over sense and strength. The shame of not telling her father all that was happening and yet failing to deal with it well by herself.

She could tell Daniel wanted to say something by the anger that flicked across his brow, but he didn't. Rather he took her hand in his and they sat there, just the two of them, her perched on the top step and him on the dainty inside chair, watching the sky and the stars and the large full moon above them.

Finally he spoke. 'Marks on the body show the journey of life, Amethyst. Were we to survive every year unblemished I doubt we would have truly lived.'

He lifted the sleeve of his nightgown and she saw the same wound she had once before noticed, this time uncovered. 'It is not pretty, I know, but if I touch this I think of how lucky I was to survive.'

'What happened?'

'My brother pushed me into a grain machine when I was nine.' He smiled then, his white teeth easy to see in the moonlight. 'Nigel got the fright of his life, but the scar turned out to be a godsend. Every time he played roughly after that I made sure he got a glimpse of it and he usually stopped.'

His thumb stroked her wrist and he looked across at her. 'This is the same sort of badge. You prefer carriages moving at the slowest of paces and who can blame you for that? Look at Whitely as another lesson, but know that one foolish marriage doesn't mean you have made another.'

She couldn't help but frown at his logic. 'But I did

not decide to marry you for any other reason than to make my father happy in the last months of his life. A reason that was foolish to the extreme in any way you might look at it.'

'Then it's lucky I am nothing like your first husband...' he returned and laughed out loud, the sound ringing in the empty chambers of her heart and filling them with gladness.

My goodness, how she loved him. She wanted to say it out here with the night-time masking her shyness, but she couldn't. He was still weak from all he had been through and he needed to be back in bed. Besides, if he did not feel what she did everything would change and she could not risk such disappointment. Better to leave it as it was, the hope of something, the taste of possibility. When he recovered there would be plenty of time to talk.

He awoke to her there in the morning curled upon the bed beside him and for the first time in days his body seemed free of heat and sickness. She lay in a full day gown on top of the counterpane, a pillow carefully positioned between them. Her hair was loose from the band she wore and the curls jostled wildly in short lengths of gold and blonde.

Beautiful. More beautiful than any other woman he had ever known, inside and out.

The revelation was startling. He had not married an *ingénue* who would take fright at things out of the ordinary. He had not married a society princess either, with a constant want for the very best and the most expensive. Amethyst Amelia was brave and true and real, a woman who would walk by his side and watch over him as he would her. A partner. A friend. A lover, too, if he could ever get his strength back.

Gerald Whitely by her own admission had been a brute of a husband. The stakes had heightened. He needed to woo his unusual bride and court her and make her understand that without him life was... unliveable. He smiled at such melodrama, but inside he knew he had finally met the woman who completed him and so very unexpectedly.

Firstly, however, he needed to get better.

'You are certain you do not need my help?' She finished fussing with the things on his bedside table just to make sure that he had all he needed and close by.

He had moved back into his room at Montcliffe this morning and much to his surprise Robert Cameron had hired a good many extra hands from London to make certain that he was well cared for.

'No, all is in order, Amethyst,' he said from his place in the wingchair by the fire. He had dressed this morning in his own clothes and his hair had been trimmed.

'You can do something for me before you go, however. Could you send your father to see me?'

'Now?'

'If it is possible.'

'Of course.'

Daniel saw the puzzlement and question in her eyes, though she said nothing as she gave him her goodnight and let herself out of his chamber.

The formality between them since leaving the annexe broke his heart, but there were things he needed to do first to make this marriage right. For her sake and for his.

Robert arrived a few moments later. He looked far healthier than he had in London, and happier. The influence of Julia McBeth, Daniel supposed, and gestured for his father-in-law to take a seat near him by the fire.

'Thank you for coming so quickly.'

'Amethyst said it was important.'

'It is, although I did not enlighten her as to what it was I needed to say to you.'

'I see.' A heavy frown covered the brow of the other and he fidgeted with a handkerchief he took from his pocket.

'Can I offer you a drink?

'No, thank you, my lord. The hour is late and I would not sleep well if—' He stopped abruptly. 'I am an old man now, Lord Montcliffe, and age leads me to say things that I could not have as a youngster.' He took breath. 'My daughter is a good honest woman and if you think she is not quite the wife you want I would urge you to give it more time because—'

He didn't finish because Daniel interrupted him.

'I want to ask for Amethyst's hand in marriage, Mr Cameron, but properly this time.'

Astonishment made the other's eyes wider. 'But you are already married, my lord.'

'I need the conditions and amendments gone. No limits anywhere. A true marriage.'

Robert suddenly seemed to get the gist of what he was asking, for his cheeks reddened with emotion. 'You want for ever?'

'I do.'

He cleared his throat. 'Then I would be most honoured to revoke any conditions and give you my whole-hearted blessing.' With intent, he thrust out his hand and the Earl took it. A handshake to nullify convenience. 'I have dreamed of this, of course, and hoped it might come to pass, for Amy has been happier here than I have ever seen her.'

'Then that brings me to another matter altogether.' Daniel's voice was measured. 'That of Gerald Whitely.'

Robert paled at the name.

'I am surprised that as a doting father you did not realise the man's true nature and deal with him.'

'True nature?'

'On Amethyst's own admission he hurt her physically. Then he proceeded to break down any belief in herself.'

'I know.'

'Pardon?' The anger in the word was harsh.

'I made it my business to find out all that I could about Whitely after Amy married him, Lord Montcliffe. A friend of mine had sent him to me with a high recommendation, but as a father I could see how unhappy he was making her. The discoveries I made were not comforting. Each fact I found out seemed worse than the last one, for he had confounded us into believing he was something he most definitely wasn't.'

'Which was a fraudster with violent tendencies?'

'I see you, too, have done your homework. But he was all that and worse. It was he who tried to murder us in the carriage accident on the way to Leicester. If we were both to die, all the Cameron money would be in his hands and since niceties between us had long since broken down I could not trust that he wouldn't try it again when we survived. I had him followed one night in London by a chap called Black John Lionel who was known in the docklands as a fixer, a man who might scare others off their chosen course of action, you understand.

'He found Whitely alone in a brothel he frequented in Grey Street with two shots through the head. A youngish gentleman had pushed past him in a hurry to leave as he had walked up the stairs and he imagined that the man was the one who had dispatched Whitely a few moments earlier. When Lionel came back to Grosvenor Square and reported what he had found out I paid him some more to be quiet about it and Amethyst stayed safe. The constabulary never made an arrest for the crime, but I did not want our family pulled through a long and gruelling investigation. Whitely had damaged us enough already.'

Daniel could not believe what he was hearing. 'Does anyone else know of this?'

'Black John Lionel, of course, but other than him, no one save the fellow who killed Whitely, I suppose, but he would hardly be speaking. I can tell you, though, that I hold absolutely no regrets for keeping quiet...'

'Good. I'd have done the same.'

'You would?'

He nodded. 'Without compunction, though I'd have probably shot him myself.'

Robert smiled, but sadness marked his eyes. 'Amy thinks it was the men from the docklands demanding money who tampered with the carriage. I let her believe that because it was easier than the truth and I even encouraged it. From the moment she found out Whitely was dead she began to live again. She knows nothing at all about my involvement with Black John Lionel and I sincerely hope that she never will. I haven't many months to live, so if you could find it in yourself to put my shocking confession aside until then I would be most grateful.'

Pouring out a large brandy, Daniel saw Robert's hand was shaking as he took it. 'In life there are things that have to be done.'

'Thank you.' The older man smiled, relief making him talk. 'It was my fault Amy ever met Whitely right from the beginning when he came to me as a clerk. At first he lived up to the promise of being meticulous and scrupulous, but it was not long before I began to think things were not as they should have been. His work began to suffer and then he made it his business to court Amethyst with all the stealth of a man who could see the acquisition of an easy fortune. There was no love in him, but he was clever in his concealing of it. When I understood that this was going to lead exactly where I didn't want it to go I offered him passage to the Americas and money to set up there as long as he never came within a hundred miles of us again. He married my daughter a week later. A week after that he stole the first thousand pounds and began his schemes to fleece the gentlemen of the *ton* out of their hard-earned cash.'

'Did Amethyst know what he was doing?'

'She was clever enough to recognise that the books were not adding up and that his "work" was dragging money out of our accounts. She got sadder daily and more removed from living and he had made it his mission by then to make certain she knew what he thought of her.'

'She didn't fight back?'

He shook his head. 'He was blackmailing me at that time and he had reason. I'd unwittingly taken up a contract that was a suspect cargo and it turned out to be stolen goods. On hindsight I think he also used the information to keep Amethyst biddable and she was trying to protect my reputation by remaining so. That is the worst of it.'

'My God. The bastard deserved a far slower death than the one he got, but after tonight we forget it. Move on and live.'

'I agree. There is one thing I would like to ask of you, though. In the light of what I have told you, would you be averse to me buying land in the area? I have seen a house not too far from here that I like the look of, though of course I would understand it if you felt uncertain about my presence here.'

'I have no reservations whatsoever and I know Amethyst will be pleased with the news.'

If Robert lived in Barnet, then Amethyst would want to stay at Montcliffe. To be back here for good was something Daniel had not expected, but the thought of his children here and their children marching down through the ages made a wonderful sense. He knew this place, these hills, the sound of the land and the timings of the seasons. He understood the cottars and the farm cycles and the birdsong and the plants in the wood. He had run free here for years of his life with his brother beside him and he had loved it. The realisation that Montcliffe Manor had always been in his blood whether he had known it or not gave him a new sense of belonging.

The man opposite was also a part of that. A friend, a confidant, a father who had taken the brave step of protecting his daughter in the only way he knew how.

'Before we left London, Robert, I had it put around in the docklands that I would not countenance any more attacks on Cameron personage or property. I have employed a couple of old soldiers that I trust to make certain that those who assaulted you near Hyde Park Corner will never threaten you again.'

'Then that has ended, too, and all we have now are new beginnings.' The lines of worry on Robert's face looked softer. 'I think my Susannah must be looking down on me to have made all this possible. Amethyst is very like her, you know. Loyal and fierce. Julia is the same.'

Lifting his glass of brandy Daniel offered up a toast. 'To our women then. May they long keep us safe.'

Her husband knocked at the door that was shared between the rooms as she sat at the dressing table in her night rail, brushing out the short length of her curls. Pulling on a wrap, she moved to turn the key placed on her side of the lock. When the portal opened Daniel stood dressed down in his breeches and an open shirt. He wore no cravat at all.

'Could we talk, Amethyst? In my chamber?'

'Of course.' She noticed he reached for the key and transferred it to his side of the door as they passed through.

The four-poster bed wrapped in dark brocade drew her eyes in a way it had not done earlier and she looked away quickly.

'Would you like a glass of wine?'

'I am not sure…'

'Just a little one? For bravery.'

The word brought a smile to her lips. 'Are you implying I might need it, my lord.'

He moved forward and took her hand in his own. 'Undoubtedly. But then, so will I, my lady, and in equal measure.'

Tonight he seemed different, lighter, less intimidating.

'I am starting to remember more from when I was sick.' He looked at her directly now, the green in his eyes full of question. 'And I am beginning to understand the meaning of some of the things you told me.'

I love you.

She had shouted it at him more than once when she had thought he might not live.

'I remember you saying something about for ever as you urged me to fight. Without you I might have given up and let the darkness claim me, but you shook me awake and gave me your words. So now my question is this: is our marriage only one of convenience, Amethyst, or could we find more within it?'

Not the proclamation she had hoped for and dressed in a lacy nightgown with a large bed a few feet away the language of lust must be taken into account. How much more did he want from her? She swallowed. With only a mention of love she would allow him everything.

'More?'

'Between us,' he answered. 'Like this.'

His fingers crept to the ties of her wrap and as he undid the ribbons she felt the swish of satin pool about her feet in a single and quiet sigh. Now she only wore her thin and sheer silk-and-lace nightgown, sleeveless and cut low, the lace hiding nothing. She made herself stand still, in the warmth of his room and under his gaze.

'You are the most beautiful woman I have ever seen, sweetheart.' One finger traced the outline of her right breast and stopped at the nipple. She took in a breath and waited, the thick ache of her want almost a physical thing.

The magic in his touch and words was like tinder to dry kindling. Fire flame, with the burn of a need that consumed her. Her, Amethyst Amelia with her failed first marriage and her ugly port-wine birthmark. Her, the daughter of trade and of commerce, an unchosen bride who had instigated a marriage of convenience with an aristocrat that had left him no other choice but to sign.

Yet he still thought her beautiful.

'I love you.' She could no longer find it in herself to pretend or to be cautious. 'I love you with all of my heart, Daniel.'

His smile came quickly. 'Ahhh, my Amethyst. I dreamed you had said it and now I know.'

His thumb began to move across her nipple and she could not stop the arching want or her shaky breath or the way her hand fell on top of his, keeping him there at his ministrations, urging response. She could not stop the surge of joy either that swept away sense and left her reeling. For him. For her husband. For a lord who had set her free.

Tears rolled down her cheeks.

'Love me, back,' she whispered.

'I do,' he returned and, lifting her into his arms, took her to his bed.

He laid her down carefully, the long lines of her legs against his counterpane, the fairness of her skin and the heavy bounty of her breasts.

Waiting.

And then it hit him, hard in the place about his heart, that she was his. His bride. His for ever. And she loved him. Another thought came at about the same time as that one. The chaos of her first marriage with Whitely pointed to a lack of true intimacy. Would she allow him all that he wanted or would she be fearful?

Her hand came across his and he could feel the shaking. 'Whitely never...' She did not finish.

'Bedded you?' He suddenly knew that was what she

was saying to him, the shocking truth of it immediate as he recalled Lucien telling him of Whitely's groin accident as a child.

'I think he was...incapable.'

'He has not touched you as a husband?'

The curls shook as she moved her head slowly.

Relief flooded in, but he had never lain with an innocent before and the blood that pounded was not conducive to the patience he would need. No, not at all. His rod was stiff straight as he wiped his hair back and took a breath.

She must have seen his consternation, for she began to speak again. 'But I have seen the animals at the farm at Dunstan House and we have always kept horses, so I know the way of mating and all that it includes.'

'Are you trying to reassure me?' He couldn't strip the amazement from his words. Could she think him untutored in the art of lovemaking?

'I will be twenty-seven next February, and so I am hardly a girl, but if it is reassurance you need...'

He stopped her by leaning forward and laying his mouth against her own, hard and unyielding by way of reply. The lemon scent of her so familiar and her curls were short in his hands. Unlike any other woman, strong and honest and his.

Slanting his kiss, he brought her in closer, his breath ragged, his want untrammelled and the need for possession desperate.

'I do not think you quite understand how it is, my love,' he said softly when he raised his head and looked at her. 'But I promise that you soon will.'

* * *

She felt his other hand lift away the thin-and-nothing barrier of her lacy gown. Naked. Exposed. His eyes met hers before wandering into places no one else had ever seen.

And then he knelt and brought his mouth to the mark at her thigh, the wet warmth of his tongue tracing her shame as if it was beautiful, too; as if the redness was indeed the kiss of the fairies of which her mother had spoken. No quick exploration, either, but a generous lengthy loving that took away all worry and replaced it with only hope.

But other things were happening, his hand against her thigh, the throb inside her between her legs, the longing for a touch she had no notion of, there at the centre of her being.

He stood and doffed his shirt and the brown hardness of him took her breath away.

'I want you, Amethyst.'

'Why?' The word was whispered, brave against the gaze of pale green.

'Because I love you.' Simple. Quiet. He did not drop his glance or qualify the truth with other lesser things and her heart swelled with joy.

His trousers were unbuttoned and his boots untied and then he was naked, too, the candlelight in the room flickering over them both, sculpting contours in flame. Dark against light, hard against soft. His body held masculine grace tempered with the scars of battles that had long since been fought. Touching a knotted line on the sharp bone of his hip, she traced it down.

Then his mouth came across hers. Skin against skin and bone against bone. She caught a dark desire inside him as his tongue tasted, the strength and the fear.

'I should not wish to hurt you.' Whispered close through breath and heartbeat.

'You won't.'

The tension in him was coiled like a spring, the soldier who had always taken action now stymied by something he had not expected. ''Tis a first for me as well, this.'

She only smiled.

'I haven't been a saint, but I have not deflowered a woman before either.'

Deflowered? God, he was making a hash of this, talking like a schoolboy in the moments he should have just shut up and got on with it. But there was something in the gentleness of her gift and words that made him...nervous.

This was the first time she had lain with a man and from all he had ever heard women needed it to be special.

Special when all he could think about was pushing deep inside of her and claiming her in that one momentous final moment of elation that made a man weep with the beauty of it.

The velvet-brown in her eyes was soft, understanding, almost gold under the candlelight.

'Love me, Daniel.'

'For ever, my love.'

And then it was simple, the tight lines of their bodies together, his hand cupping her bottom and bringing her over the hard rod of his need. An opening slick with wetness and a quiet push within.

He heard her gasp and stopped, slowly, slowly, but for ever onwards until the hilt of him was buried in the warmth of her flesh and against the edge of her womb.

'Mine.' He said the word in wonder and watched her take it in, saw the flickering pain on her face change into surprise and then into fire. Felt the waves of her own ecstasy against him, claiming and clenching until he could not know where he ended and Amethyst began, the melded aching orgasm taking them both above thought and reason to a place where nothing existed, save for them.

Suspended there. Without time. Without surroundings. Clinging to desire until the very last tiny echoes had subsided and the world crashed once again into reality.

'Thank you.' He could not remember ever saying that to a woman after making love, but all he could feel was gratitude, his seed holding them together and the hollow beat of his heart finally quieting.

Usually he got up straight away, the feeling of intimacy threatening somehow and empty. But here, now, his hand fell against her back and he held her close, her warmth of skin and her legs straddling his.

More. He wanted her again. Wanted to slip in and stay there for ever. His member rose and nudged her thigh and she simply opened her legs and let him enter.

This time it was slower, the slickness allowing an

easy entrance, the rise and fall of her breasts against his hands as he took her. His tempo quickened just with the thought.

She was rushing again to that place she had had no notion of, the high breathless plane of wanton relief. She could feel herself reaching, tipping into him, his shaft within her deep.

She heard herself cry out, guttural and primal, noises that she had never thought to make before, sounds from the very soul of her need.

Again. And again. Boneless and formless. And this time when the final pulses came she dug her nails into his skin and marked him with the loving, long runnels of redness against the brown.

Afterwards she could not move, but lay there across him, still joined, still feeling the heaviness of him within her, and then she slept.

Birdsong woke him, the twelve-hour candles burned towards the end of their usefulness, the drips of wax across the holders opaquely white and twisted.

Daniel breathed out and watched the last of the night turn into dawn, streaked with the pink of a new day. The sounds of the house were quiet. The swish of an early maid's skirts as she walked the passageway, the creak of timber shedding off the cold of night, the creeping plant outside his window, its greened tendrils knocking against the glass.

All the sounds he had heard for all of the years of

his life. And now there was a new one. Amethyst's quiet breathing, her eyelashes long against her cheeks.

His bride. His wife. His lover now, her body claimed as his own.

Would there be a child? Would this night bring the fruit of conception and the promise of another generation of Wyldes born into the lineage of Montcliffe?

If it was a boy, they could call him Nigel and this time he would get it right. If it was a girl, he hoped that they might find a name of a gemstone as Robert and Susannah had and then he could also call his daughter 'my jewel'.

'What are you thinking?' Amethyst's voice was soft with the morning.

'Of you and of us and our future. I'd like children…'

She pushed herself up at that and her hand went beneath the covers, across his chest and then his stomach to the budding hardness of his flesh.

'So would I.'

'Now?' He could see in her face the languid hope of sex.

Turning over, he brought her beneath him, covering her smallness with his body and finding the very centre of her with his fingers before once again entering in.

When she awoke next he was not there, the day without showing a full sun and a cloudless sky.

Her eyes went to the clock on the mantel. Almost one o'clock. Looking around, she saw piles of books and an old piano she had not noticed yesterday. A globe and guns stacked on small shelves completed the tableau beside it.

A man's room, nothing feminine within it, save for her tangled in the sheets and naked, her thighs tight with his seed and her nipples tender from his kissing.

Like a child she had held him there, his hair dark against the white of her skin. Her hand fell across her thigh and inwards, the throb of delight still present under a different ache. She smiled. Not like the animals in the barnyard after all. The slight tip of her hips brought the feeling back and she reached for a momentary echo, pushing down on the bone of her groin, guided by some ancient knowledge.

Daniel Wylde had healed her and made her whole. He had taken all the doubts and turned them into certainty; the sureness of being loved and of loving back as well.

A gift of place and of beauty, the heart and body and soul kind of love her parents had known and of which the great stories told.

Her story now. No longer blinded by shame. Her fingers traced the mark on her thigh and she remembered his mouth there. Not ugly. Not unsightly.

But beautiful.

He had called her that so many times over so many hours and in the sunshine of a new day she finally felt it.

She came downstairs much later, having bathed and washed her hair and tidied up the scramble of sheets upon the master bed. She felt different, the soreness in her private places only adding to the illusion. She felt wanton too, her mind going to the hours between now and when they could again be in each other, feeling the heat of their loving.

Only the Earl was in attendance at the table.

'Your father and Julia have been journeying around the countryside all day and have sent word that they will be down in an hour or so. Perhaps we might look over the garden before we eat as it will be a while before it is served.'

Hope soared. 'I would like that.'

Outside the courtyard was empty. Leading her around a corner under the overhang of stone, he found a position that shielded them from any unsuspecting servant who might be walking the paths.

He was kissing her before she even turned, hard desperate kisses that spoke of all the frenzy she herself felt, and when they came up for breath he held her closely against him.

'Will there ever be a time when I see you without wanting you?'

She laughed. 'I hope not.' Her finger traced the line of his lips.

'If you keep doing that we won't be having any dinner.' The smile in his words was as obvious as the need in his eyes. 'Would you like to see how Deimos is faring? John has been asking after you, too. I think you have earned his respect as a healer, Amethyst, which, believe me, is a hard thing to do.'

'He has been here at Montcliffe for a long time, then?' she asked him as they walked.

'Since I was a boy. It was John who taught me a lot of the tricks of the trade. His own father was the stablemaster at Montcliffe before him and his father's father before that.'

'History,' she said quietly. 'That is what I love about this place. I have never been so much a part of what has come before.'

'Or after,' he said and brought her fingers to his lips. 'I'd like lots of children to see Montcliffe prosper.'

'Then let us try again for the first after dinner,' she whispered and laughed as he turned towards the stables.

Her father and Julia were both waiting in the small salon next to the dining room when they returned and it seemed to Amethyst that her world had rolled over into something different. Papa looked the happiest she had ever seen him and her own heart sang with the promise of life. The doctor had been right after all: hope was the best medicine for any ailment. She knew he was not cured, but he was definitely happy.

'We have some wonderful news to give you—' Robert's voice was light '—and I have had wine sent up from London to celebrate it with.' He gestured to the bottles in front of him with the four fluted glasses standing beside them. 'Julia has done me the honour of agreeing to become my wife and I have signed the deeds today on a house not far from here in which we intend to live.'

'I hope you will give us your blessing, Amethyst? I realise it might seem a sudden thing, but sometimes one just knows.' Julia's voice was soft. 'I swear I shall make it my goal in life to keep your father healthy.'

Sometimes one just knows.

Reaching for Daniel's hand, Amethyst understood exactly what Julia was referring to as his fingers tightened about her own.

'I would be delighted to welcome you to the family, Julia, as I haven't seen Papa smile so much in years.'

As the wine was poured Robert handed them all a glass. 'I would like to make a toast, then, to for ever. For us all.'

Much later they lay together in the main chamber, the time well after one in the morning.

'I love you more than life itself, my Amethyst,' Daniel said into the darkness and the sound of it curled into his heart. 'And I am glad that you waited for me.'

She smiled. 'Gerald finally did me a favour.' Her words were soft against his chest. 'If he had been a better man, I might not have met you.'

'He is dead. He will never hurt us again.'

'And the others. The ones who tampered with our carriage on the road to Leicester?'

'They will not harm us either, I promise.' He tried to keep the anger from the edge of his words.

'Papa was right to choose you as our saviour. He would not have managed to scare them away all by himself.'

'Your father is an amazing man. I think he would do almost anything for love and he's a lot stronger than he looks.'

'Perhaps with Julia's care he can confound all the doctors, though there will come a day when...' She did not go on.

'If we have a boy first, let's name him Robert.' Nigel could wait, Daniel thought, but for Amethyst's father time was fading and the sheer bravery of the older man had never ceased to amaze him. He hoped he could be half the father to his own children as the old timber merchant had been to Amethyst.

'Perhaps when Gwen comes to visit us we might have my grandfather here as well. A change in scenery would do him good and a time away from my mother might be just the thing he needs,' he suggested.

'I'd like that. We could take him to visit my father and show him the horses and...'

She stopped talking when he kissed her.

He had no wish at all to return to society, but resolved to make his life here, amongst the green hills and valleys of Montcliffe. Tracing a pattern across the freckles on his wife's shoulders, Daniel began to tell her of Nigel.

The last secrets were almost the hardest, but he had to let her know of the man his brother had been and of the death that he had chosen.

'He left a note for me with my grandfather and it was not at all what I was expecting. I think he was depressed.'

The night closed about them as he spoke and the shame of suicide lessened under her quiet and gentle acceptance.

Epilogue

Daniel sat with Robert and Lucien in the small sitting chamber off the main bedroom, his eyes glancing at the clock every few minutes.

'We should have gone to London for the birth.' He had told Amethyst this again and again, but she would not listen. Standing, he walked to the window and looked outside.

Oh, God, please let my wife and child be safe.

The refrain had been his mantra for weeks and weeks, words that rolled around in his mind first thing in the morning and last thing at night. He had tried to keep his fear from showing, but he had been sleeping badly for months now and the dreams he did have, if he was lucky to slumber, seemed to mirror his every anxiety. If anything happened to Amethyst, he would want to be dead too. If she died, then he would want to follow, in his heart and his soul and his body

'Susannah used to say that giving birth was a woman's glory and her triumph for being feminine.'

At this moment Robert's sentiments were the last things Daniel wanted to hear. Glory. Triumph. There were so many other words more apt to use as the cries of his labouring wife had fallen down into whimpers.

This was when they died. When their energy was spent and their blood was thin and the will to live waned under constant pain. God, how much practice had he had in that on the battlefields?

But he was a man and strong and fit while she...

A single shout had him at the door before anyone could stop him and he was through into the master chamber, ignoring the protests of Julia, Christine Howard and the midwife.

Amethyst's forehead was slick with sweat when he reached her and the red blush of blood on the sheets beneath was telling.

'Dr MacKenzie will be here soon, my love.'

She gripped his hand.

'I cannot do this without you, Daniel. Please, I want you here...'

He looked around the room, the pale face of Julia and the flushed one of Christine. Only the midwife looked unconcerned.

The midwife had all the herbs and candles his wife had instructed her to bring, but still it did not seem to be enough. Fear rushed in like the enemy and he made himself breathe through it.

For so many battles and for so many years he had found in himself the strength to forsake dread and fight, yet in the end this was the most important battle of them all.

He turned to his wife and smiled, hoping that the glory and triumph of which Robert had spoken just a few moments past was there on his face to see.

'This baby needs to come, my darling, and together we can help it arrive.'

Her fingers entwined around his own and she nodded. 'It won't be long,' she said quietly and then stiffened, her hand squeezing his in a grip that was surprising.

An hour and a half later Amethyst sat changed and washed, her hair arranged in two short thick plaits by Christine, and the swaddled baby at her breast.

'You did it, Amethyst,' Lucien's sister gushed. 'Sapphire is the most beautiful child I have ever seen.'

With a fuzz of blonde covering her head and pale brown eyes Daniel could not help but agree. Her grandfather had his own way of showing relief as he wiped the tears from his eyes.

'Sapphire Susannah Wylde. Your mother would have been pleased.' Robert's voice quivered with the poignancy of memory.

Lucien stood back from the frivolity, the birthing room and a small baby well out of his realm of comfort, but he took a box from his pocket and presented it to Amethyst.

'This comes from my own estate. A moonstone for June and new beginnings. Appropriate, I think.'

The bracelet was entwined in white gold and pearls, an expensive treasure that Daniel knew Lucien could ill afford to give, but his wife's smile when she saw it was priceless.

'Sapphire's second piece of jewellery,' she said and held the gemstone up to the light, 'for Daniel found a tiny bejewelled cap this morning amongst the Montcliffe treasures.' The crystalline structures within the moonstone made it shimmer with every shade of the rainbow, prisms of light filling the room.

And for Daniel the moonstone was exactly what his life now reminded him of. Full, joyous, colourful and rich.

Rich in people and in structure, and in laughter and memories. Rich in place and belonging and happiness. The true riches, he thought, are the ones never imagined.

When Amethyst took his hand in her own he looked down and smiled.

He was home, at last, and at peace with his two most precious jewels. Home in the belonging of family.

* * * * *

MARRIAGE MADE
IN SHAME

Chapter One

London—1812

The familiar sense of nothingness engulfed Gabriel Hughes, the fourth Earl of Wesley, taking all breath and warmth with it as he sat with a glass of fine brandy and a half-smoked cheroot.

Willing women dressed as sprites, nymphs and naiads lounged around him, the white of their scanty togas falling away from generous and naked breasts. A dozen other men had already chosen their succour for the night and had gone one by one to the chambers fanning out from the central courtyard. But here the lights were dimmed and the smoke from dying candles curled up towards the ceiling. The Temple of Aphrodite was a place of consenting lust and well-paid liaisons. It was also filled to the brim.

'I should very much like to show you my charms in bed, *monsieur*,' the beautiful blonde next to him whispered in a French accent overlaid with a heavy, east London twang. 'I have heard your name mentioned many times before and it is said that you have a great prowess in that department.'

Had... The word echoed in Gabriel's mind and reverberated as a shot would around a steel chamber. Downing the last of the brandy, he hoped strong alcohol might coax out feelings he had long since forgotten. Memory. How he hated it. His heartbeat quickened as he swallowed down disquiet, the hollow ache of expectation not something he wanted to feel.

'I am Athena, my lord.'

'The sister of Dionysus?'

She looked puzzled by his words as she flicked the straps from milky white shoulders and the warm bounty of her bosom nudged against his arm as she leant forward. 'I do not know this sister of Diana, my lord, but I can be yours tonight. I can pleasure you well if this be your favour.'

He hadn't expected her to know anything of the Greek gods, but still disappointment bloomed— a woman of beauty and little else. Her tongue ran around pouting lips, wetting them and urging response, dilated pupils alluding to some opiate, a whore without shame or limit and one whom life had probably disappointed. Feeling some sense of kinship, Gabriel smiled.

'You are generous, Athena, but I cannot take you up on your offer.'

Already the demons were arching, coming closer, and when her fingers darted out to cup his groin, he almost jumped. 'And why is that, *monsieur*? The

Temple of Aphrodite is the place where dreams are realised.'

Or nightmares, he thought, the past rushing in through the ether.

Screams as the fire had taken hold; the stinging surprise of burning flesh and then darkness numbing pain. The last time he had felt whole.

Gabriel hated it when these flashbacks came, unbidden, terrifying. So sudden that he had no defence against them. Standing, he hoped that Athena did not see the tremble in his fingers as he replaced his empty glass on the low-slung table. Run, his body urged even as he walked slowly across the room, past the excesses of sex, passion and craving. He hated the way he could not quite ingest the cold night air once outside as the roiling nausea in his stomach quickened and rose.

He nearly bumped into the Honourable Frank Barnsley and another man as Gabriel strode out into the gardens and he looked away, the sweat on his upper lip building. He knew he had only a matter of minutes to hide all that would come next.

There were trees to his left, thick and green, and he made for them with as much decorum as he could manage. Then he was hidden, bending, no longer quite there. It was getting worse. He was falling apart by degrees, the smell of heavy perfumes, the full and naked flesh, the tug of sex and punch of lust. All equated with another time, another place. Intense guilt surfaced, panic on the edges. His heart thumped and fear surged, the sensation of falling so great he simply sat down and placed his arms around the solid trunk of a young sapling. A touchstone. The only stable thing in his moving dizzy world.

Leaning over to one side, he threw up once and then twice more, gulping in air and trying to understand.

His life. His shame.

Coming tonight to the Temple of Aphrodite and expecting a healing had been a monumental mistake. He needed to lie down in dark and quiet. Aloneness cloaked dread as tears began to well.

'I do not wish to marry anyone, Uncle.' Miss Adelaide Ashfield thought her voice sounded shrill, even to her own ears, and tried to moderate the tone. 'I am more than happy here at Northbridge and the largesse that is my inheritance can be evenly divided between your children, or their children when I die.'

Alec Ashfield, the fifth Viscount of Penbury, merely laughed. 'You are young, my dear, and that is no way to be talking. Besides, my offspring have as much as they are ever likely to need and if your father and mother were still in the land of the living, bless their poor departed souls, they would be castigating me for your belated entry into proper society.'

Adelaide shook her head. 'It was not your fault that Aunt Jean died the month before I was supposed to be presented in London for my first Season or that Aunt Eloise took ill the following summer just before the second.'

'But your insistence on an overly long mourning

period was something I should have discouraged. You have reached the grand old age of three and twenty without ever having stepped a foot into civil society. You are, as such, beyond the age of a great match given that you no longer bear the full flush of youth. If we wait any longer, my love, you will be on the shelf. On the shelf and staying there. A spinster like your beloved great-aunts, watching in on the life of others for ever.'

'Jean and Eloise were happy, Uncle Alec. They enjoyed their independence.'

'They were bluestockings, my dear, without any hope of a favoured union. One had only to look at them to understand that.'

For the first time in an hour Adelaide smiled. Perhaps her aunts had been overly plain, but their brains had been quick and their lives seldom dull.

'They travelled, Uncle, and they read. They knew things about the body and healing that no other physician did. Books gave them a world far removed from the drudge of responsibility that a married woman is encumbered by.'

'Drudges like children, like love, like laughter. You cannot know what seventy years in your own company might feel like and loneliness has no balm, I can tell you that right now.'

She looked away. Uncle Alec's wife, Josephine, had been an invalid for decades, secreted away in her chamber and stitching things for people who had long since lost the need for them.

'One Season is all I ask of you, Adelaide. One Season to help you understand everything you would be missing should you simply bury yourself here in the backwaters of rural Sherborne.'

Adelaide frowned. Now this was new. He would stipulate a limited time. 'You would not harry me into a further Season if this one is a failure?'

Alec shook his head. 'If you have no one offering for you, no one of your choice, that is, then I will feel as if my duty to your parents is done and you can come home. Even if you agree to stay half of the Season I would be happy.'

'From April till June. Only that?'

'Early April to late June.' There was a tone of steel in her uncle's voice.

'Very well. Three months. Twelve weeks. Eighty-four days.'

Alec laughed. 'And not one less. You have to promise me.'

Walking to the window, Adelaide looked out over the lands of Northbridge. She did not want to leave this place. She didn't want to be out in the glare of a society she had little interest in. She wanted to stay in her gardens and her clinic, helping those about Northbridge with the many and varied complaints of the body. Her world, ordered and understood; the tinctures and ointments, the drying herbs and forest roots. Safe.

'As I would need gowns and a place to live and a chaperon, it seems like a lot of bother for nothing.'

'I have thought of all of these things and a relative of mine, Lady Imelda Harcourt, will accompany you.'

As she went to interrupt Alec stopped her. 'I realise she is a little dour and sometimes more than trying, but she is also a respectable widow with undeniably good contacts amongst the *ton*. I, too, will endeavour to visit London as much as I am able whilst you are there. Bertram will want to have some hand in it as well, as he has assured me his gambling habits are now well under control.'

Her heart sank further. Not only Lady Harcourt but her cousin, too? What else could go wrong?

However, Uncle Alec was not quite finished. 'I wasn't going to mention this, but now seems like the perfect time to bring it up. Mr Richard Williams from Bishop's Grove has approached me with the hopes that he might be an escort whom you would look favourably upon during your time in town. A further arrow to our bow, so to speak, for we do not want you to be bereft of suitors. One day I am sure you will be thankful for such prudence. Here you are well known, Adelaide, but in London it can be difficult to meet others and a first impression has importance.'

Adelaide was simply struck dumb. She was being saddled with three people who would hardly be good company and her uncle expected her to thank him? It was all she could do to stay in the room and hear him out.

'Men will know you have a fortune and there are some out there who could be unscrupulous in their promises. Great wealth comes with its own problems, my dear, and you will need to be most careful in your judgement. Pick a suitor who is strong in his own right, a man whose fortune might equal your own. A good man. A solid man. A man of wealth and sense. Stay well away from those who only require a rich wife to allow them back into the gambling halls, or ones whose family estates have been falling around their feet for years.'

'I am certain I shall know exactly whom to stay away from, Uncle.' Privately she hoped that every single male of the *ton* would want to keep their distance from her and after this she would never have to be beleaguered by such ridiculous frippery again.

The doctor's rooms were in a discreet and well-heeled part of Wigmore Street and Gabriel had had it on good authority from the books he had acquired over the past months that Dr Maxwell Harding was the foremost expert on illnesses pertaining to problems in men of a more personal nature.

He almost had not come, but the desperation and despondency caused by his condition had led him to arrive for the earliest appointment at noon.

No other people graced the waiting area and the man behind a wide desk gave the impression of disinterest. For that at least Gabriel was glad. He did toy with the thought of simply giving a false name and was about to when the door behind him opened and an older man walked out.

'It is Lord Wesley, is it not? I am Dr Maxwell Harding. I have heard your name about town, of course, but have not had the pleasure of meeting you. In my line of work you are the one many of my patients would aspire to emulate, if you take my meaning, so this is indeed a surprise.' His handshake was clammy and he brought a handkerchief from his pocket afterwards to wipe his brow in a nervous gesture. 'Please, follow me.'

For Gabriel the whole world had just turned at an alarming rate. He did not wish for this doctor to know his name or his reputation. He certainly did not want to be told of a plethora of patients with their own sexual illnesses and hardships who all earmarked him as some sort of a solution.

He suddenly felt almost as sick as he had a week ago outside the Temple of Aphrodite, but as the door behind him closed he took hold of himself. Harding was a doctor, for God's sake, pledged under the Hippocratic Oath to the welfare of each of his patients. It would be fine. The doctor had walked across to a cupboard now and was taking a decanter and two glasses from a shelf and filling them to the brim.

'I know why you are here, my lord,' Harding finally stated as he placed one in Gabriel's hands.

'You do?' With trepidation he took a deep swallow of the surprisingly good brandy and waited. Was it marked on his face somehow, his difficulty, or in the worry of his eyes? Was there some sort of a shared stance or particular gait in those who came through this door for help? Hopelessness, perhaps, or fear?

'You are here about the Honourable Frank Barnsley, aren't you? He said you had looked at him strangely when he met you the other day. As if you knew. He implied that you might come and talk with me. He said his father was a good friend of yours.'

'Barnsley?' Gabriel could not understand exactly where this conversation was going though he vowed to himself that after he finished the drink he would leave. This was neither the time nor the place to be baring his soul and the doctor was sweating alarmingly.

'His predilection for…men,' Harding went on. 'He said you had seen him and Andrew Carrington embracing one another in the garden at some well-heeled brothel and wondered if you might begin making enquiries…'

Anger had Gabriel placing his glass carefully down upon a nearby table. Harding was not only a gossip, but a medic with no sense of confidentiality or professionalism. Before the outburst he had had no inkling of the sexual persuasions of either man and it was none of his business anyway. He could also just imagine the hushed tones of Harding describing Gabriel's own problems to all and sundry should he have decided to trust in the doctor's honour. He was damned thankful that he had not.

He'd buy Barnsley and Carrington a drink when he saw them next in his club as a silent measure of gratitude. But for now he had one final job to do.

'Mr Frank Barnsley is a decent and honourable man. If I hear you mention any of this, to anyone at all, ever again, I will be back and I promise that afterwards no one will hear your voice again. Do I make myself clear?'

A short and frantic nod was apparent and at that Gabriel simply opened the door and walked out of the building, into the sunshine and the breeze, a feeling of escaping the gallows surging over him, one part pure relief, though the other echoed despair.

He could never tell anybody. Ever. He would have to deal with his problem alone and in privacy. He would either get better or he would not and the thought of years and years of sadness rushed in upon him with an awful truth.

His reality. His punishment. His retribution.

But today had been like a reprieve, too, a genuine and awkward evasion of what might have come to pass. He was known across the *ton* for his expertise with the opposite sex and if the scale of his prowess had grown with the mounting rumour he had not stopped that, either, his downfall sharpened on lies.

This is what he had come to, here and now, walking along the road to his carriage parked a good two hundred yards from the doctor's rooms to secure privacy and wishing things could be different; he could be different, his life, his secrets, his sense of honour and morality and grace.

Once he had believed in all the glorious ideals the British Service had shoved down his throat. Integrity. Loyalty. Virtue. Principle. But no more. That dream had long gone in the face of the truth.

He was alone in everything he did, clinging to the

edge of life like a moth might to a flame and being burned to a cinder. There was nowhere else, or no one else. This was it.

He had always been alone and he always would be.

Chapter Two

Two weeks in the London Season had already seemed like a month and this was the fourth ball Adelaide had been to in as many nights. The same grandeur, the same people, the same boring chatter concerned only with marriage prospects, one's appearance and the size of a suitor's purse.

She was tired of it, though tonight the crowd was thicker and those attending did not all have the rarefied look of the *ton*. A less lofty gathering, she decided, and hence more interesting. Lady Harcourt beside her did not look pleased.

'Lord and Lady Bradford are rumoured to be enamoured by the changing tides of fortune and one can see that in some of the guests present—a lot of wealth but no true class. Perhaps we should not have come at all, Penbury?'

Her uncle only laughed and finished his drink. 'Adelaide isn't a green girl, Imelda, and I am certain she can discern whom to speak with and whom to avoid. In truth, even those with genuine titles seem to be rougher these days, less worried by the way a fortune is made or lost.' His eyes fixed on a group of men in the corner.

At that very moment the tallest of them raised his glass and said something that made the others laugh. Adelaide noticed he wore a thick band of silver around one of his fingers and that the cuff on his shirt was intricately embroidered in bronze thread. He was everything she had never liked in a man, a fop and a dandy, handsome to the point of beautiful and knowing it. Nearly every woman in the salon looked his way.

From her place to one side of a wide plastered pillar she watched him, too. Out of a pure and misplaced appreciation, she supposed, the length of his hair as extraordinary as every other feature upon him.

'The Earl of Wesley is the most handsome man in the King's court, would you not say, Miss Ashfield?' Miss Lucy Carrigan's voice rose above the chatter, breathless and adoring. 'It is understood that his London town house has mirrors on every wall so that he might look at himself from all possible angles.'

'And he would boast of this?' The frown that never left the forehead of Lucy Carrigan deepened.

'Well, if you were that beautiful, Miss Ashfield, should you not wish to look upon your form, too?'

Adelaide could only laugh at such a thought. My goodness, the girl was serious. She struggled to school in her mirth and find kindness.

'Perhaps it would be so.'

'My cousin Matilda said Lord Wesley kissed her

once when she was much younger and she has never forgotten the feelings his expertise engendered. Indeed, she is long married and yet she still brings up the subject every few months.'

'And her husband is happy to hear this?'

'Oh, Norman can hardly object. It was Lord Wesley himself who introduced them to each other and steered them on to the pathway of Holy Matrimony.'

'Which he believes in?'

'Pardon?'

'The earl? Is he married?'

Peals of laughter were the only answer. 'Oh, dear me, no. A man like that is hardly going to be tied down to one female, is he, though word has it he did come close.'

'Close?'

'To Mrs Henrietta Clements. Some dreadful accident took her life a few months back, but the whole thing was hushed up quickly because she had left her wedded husband for Wesley. A scandal it was and the main topic of conversation for weeks after.'

Normally Adelaide stayed clear of such gossip, but fourteen days of society living had broken down her scruples somewhat and Lucy Carrigan for all her small talk was proving most informative.

'And so the earl was heartbroken?'

'Ahhh, quite the opposite. For a while nobody saw him at all, but then he began to spend far more time in the vicinity of fast women with questionable morals.'

'You speak of London's brothels?' Adelaide could not quite work out what she meant.

The other reddened considerably and dropped her voice. 'No lady of any repute should ever admit to knowing about such things, Miss Ashfield, even amongst friends.' Lucy Carrigan's eyes again perused the figure of the one they spoke about and Adelaide regarded him, too.

The Earl of Wesley was tall and broad with it, the foppish clothes out of character with his build. But the arrogance was not to be mistaken and nor was the intricately tied cravat that stood up under his chin and echoed the style of the day. The Mathematical, she had heard it called, with its three demanding and precise creases, one horizontal and two diagonal.

He stood with his back to the wall. Even as others came to join the group he was within, he still made certain that he faced any newcomer. And he watched. Everyone. Even her. She looked quickly away as bleached golden eyes fell by chance upon her face.

Lady Harcourt beside her was fussing about the heat in the room and the noise of the band. Tired of listening to her constant stream of complaints, Adelaide signalled to her chaperon that she wished to use the ladies' retiring room and quietly moved away, glad when Imelda did not insist on accompanying her.

A moment later a small bench to one side of the salon caught her attention, a row of flowering plants placed before it allowing a temporary shelter. Glancing around to see that no one observed her, she pushed the greenery aside and slipped through, sitting down to stretch her legs. A row of windows before her over-looked a garden.

She had escaped, if momentarily, from the inane and preposterous world of being presented to society and she planned to enjoy every fleeting second of it.

'Ten more weeks,' she enunciated with feeling. 'Ten more damned weeks.'

A slight noise to one side had her turning and with shock she registered a man standing there. Not just any man, either, but the foppish and conceited Earl of Wesley.

Without being surrounded by admirers and sycophants he looked more menacing and dangerous. Almost a different person from the one she had been watching a few moments earlier if she were honest. The pale gold of his eyes was startling as he looked towards her.

'Ten more damned weeks, until…what?'

A dimple in his right cheek caught the light of a small flickering lamp a few feet away, sending shadows across the face of an angel. A hardened angel, she amended, for there was something in his expression that spoke of distance and darkness.

'Until I can return home, my lord. Until this dreadful society Season of mine is at last over.' The honesty of her response surprised her. She usually found strangers hard to talk to. Especially men who held all of the *ton* in thrall as this one did.

'You do not enjoy the glamour and intrigue of high courtly living, Miss…?'

'Miss Adelaide Ashfield from Northbridge Manor.'

When question crossed into his eyes she continued. 'It is in Sherborne, my lord, in Dorset. I am the niece of the Viscount of Penbury.'

'Ahhh.' The one dimple deepened. 'You are rich, then, and well connected?'

'Excuse me?' She could not believe he would mention such a thing. Was that not just the very height of rudeness?

'My guess is that you are a great heiress who has come to the city on the lookout for a husband?'

'No.' The word came harshly and with little hidden.

He turned. Up close he was even more beautiful than he was from afar. If she could have conjured up a man from imagination personifying masculine grace and strength, it would have been him. The thought made her smile.

'You find society and its pursuit for sterling marriages amusing?' A bleak humour seemed to materialise on his face.

'I do not, sir. I find it degrading and most humiliating. The only true virtue in my list of attributes is wealth, you see, and as such I am…an easy target for those with dubious financial backgrounds.'

The returned laughter did not seem false. 'Such a description of desperation might include half the lords of the *ton* then, Miss Ashfield. Myself included.'

'You are…penniless?' She could not believe he would be so candid.'

'Not quite, but heading that way.'

'Then I am sorry for it.'

The mirth disappeared completely. 'Do not be so. There is a freedom in such a state that is beguiling.'

Again Adelaide was perplexed. His words were not those of a vacuous and dandified lord. Indeed, this was the very first conversation that she had actually enjoyed since leaving Dorset.

He glanced around. 'Where is your chaperon, Miss Ashfield? I could hardly think she would be pleased to see you alone in my company.'

'Oh, Lady Harcourt is back amongst the crowd, complaining of the crush and the noise. I am supposed to be in the retiring room, you see, but I slipped off here instead.'

'A decision you might regret.'

'In what way, my lord?'

Now only ice filled the gold of his eyes. 'A reputation is easily lost amongst the doyens of the *ton*, no matter how little you do to deserve it.'

'I don't understand.'

He smiled. 'Stay close to your chaperon, Miss Ashfield, or one day you surely will.'

With that he was gone, a slight bow and then gone, only the vague scent of sandalwood remaining.

Adelaide breathed out deeply and pushed back the shrubbery, aware that others were now moving in her direction. Suddenly the room seemed larger and more forbidding than it had done before, an undercurrent of something she could not fathom, a quiet whisper of warning.

She had seen these weeks in the *ton* as both a game and a trial, but perhaps it was not quite either. To be roped into marriage on a mistake would be disastrous and life changing. Without pause she hurried back to Lady Harcourt.

She should not have been alone, Gabriel thought, watching as the unusual Miss Adelaide Ashfield rushed past him and back towards safety. She was so far from the usual run of those new to society he had barely believed she was one. Older for a start and much more…beguiling. Yes, that was the word. She did not seem to harbour the cunning and duplicity of almost every other débutante he had met. She was tall, too, her head rising to his chin, and at six foot four that was something that seldom happened. She was not blonde, either, her hair a mix of sable and dark chestnut and her eyes the colour of a winter stream running over limestone. Deep clear blue with shadows of hurt. He doubted the spectacles she wore were for any reason other than a way of making her appear more studious, less attractive. He could not remember seeing another woman ever wear spectacles to a ball. A further oddness that was intriguing.

Men who came for the Season with the hope of finding a docile and curvy blonde would not be interested in Miss Adelaide Ashfield from Sherborne.

'God,' he swore, but his eyes still followed her, pushing past other patrons, barely pausing.

He had frightened her. A good thing that. If one's reason for being in London for the Season was truly not marriage then she should be glued to the side of the harridan she had finally reached. Another man came to join her and Gabriel recognised him as the hapless Bertram Ashfield, no doubt newly come from the card rooms on one end of the salon. He looked defeated and luckless.

A taller man had also joined the party, his sallow face wreathed in smiles. He was talking to Miss Ashfield in the way of one whose words portrayed more than just the pure sounds. A suitor. Observing the way she leaned away from him, Gabriel gained the impression that any tender thoughts were not returned.

Perhaps she did not lie. Perhaps indeed she was here under duress. The scene became even more interesting when Frederick Lovelace, the Earl of Berrick, joined the small group in the company of the Viscount of Penbury himself. The baby-faced earl had the same look of hope in his expression as the other taller man had.

Gabriel smiled. Could Miss Ashfield be a siren perhaps with the penchant to attract men despite her wishing not to?

Look at her damned effect on him!

He rarely spoke with the new débutantes of the Season and certainly never for so long. Even now he wished he might find her again somewhere isolated so that they could converse further, the low and calm voice that did not hold back feelings placating somehow and sensible.

When the music began to play Gabriel knew it was a waltz and he watched as Berrick took Miss Ashfield's arm and led her on to the floor. All débutantes needed permission to dance the waltz and he

wondered which of Almack's patronesses had allowed it.

The trouble was she did not seem to know the
steps, tripping over her feet more times than he
thought possible. Berrick held her closer and tighter
so that she might follow him with a greater ease.

Hell. Why did the chaperon not intervene? Or the
uncle? Did not others see how very inappropriate such
closeness was? He glanced around, but no face was
turned towards the couple in censure.

Perhaps Frederick Lovelace was further down the
pathway of his courtship than Miss Ashfield had let
on? With a curse Gabriel turned for the door. An
early night would do him good for once. If only he
could sleep.

Adelaide saw Lord Wesley leave the room, the sure
steps of his exit and the quiet observation of others.
For one long and ridiculous moment she had imagined that he still watched her and that he might ask
her to dance.

Instead the Earl of Berrick held her to the steps,
his arms too tight and his body too close. The waltz
must soon be finished, surely, and then pleading a
headache she could leave, too. She was at that moment glad of such an elderly chaperon and one who
would be more than happy for an early night.

Her uncle might not be so pleased, of course, but
even he had begun to flag beneath the ludicrous
constant social graces and late-night soirées of the
ton. Bertie would stay, no doubt, locked into the card

rooms in the hope of a win that never seemed to materialise.

'I should like to call upon you on the morrow if I may, Miss Ashfield.'

He looked as serious as she had ever seen another look. Would he be showing his hand as a suitor? Pray God, she hoped not, but when he squeezed her fingers and looked intently at her she knew that such a wish was false.

'You are a sensible girl, well endowed with a brain and the ability to use it.'

She smiled, hating her pasted-on joviality with an ache. She could never before remember playing people so false than here in London.

'My mother, the countess, would like you.'

The music stopped just as she thought she might burst into laughter and Lord Berrick could do nothing but escort her back to her chaperon.

For once the frowns of Lady Harcourt were reassuring and Adelaide took her hand.

'You are tired, Aunt. Perhaps we might leave?'

The older lady failed to hide the relief that flooded into her eyes as she leant upon her charge and they threaded through the crowded room to the exit.

Gabriel dreamed that night of colourful dresses and tuneful waltzes, and of a woman in his arms on the dance floor smelling of lemon and hope. Her dark hair was loose and her eyes mirrored the hue of the flowers the greenery around them was bedecked with.

But something was wrong. The ease of the dream

turned into worry. He must not kiss her. She would
know otherwise. He needed to find some distance
from the softness of her touch, a way of leaving without causing question. But she was stuck to him like
a spider's web, clinging and cold, and the only way
to be rid of her was to push her down and down until
she lay still beneath the marbled font of the destroyed
wooden chapel, the smell of sulphur on the glowing
fabric of her gown and her feet bare.

Henrietta Clements morphed from Adelaide Ashfield, the blonde of her hair pinked with blood.

He tried to shout, but no words came, tried to run,
too, but his feet could not move and the burning ache
on his upper right thigh pulled him from sleep into
the cold and grey light of dawn.

He could barely breathe, his whole body stiffened
in fright and the anger that hung quiet in the daytime
now full blooded and red.

Henrietta had come to him out of fear, he knew
that. Her husband was purportedly involved in helping to fund Napoleon's push into Europe and Gabriel
had been tailing Randolph Clements for a month or
so in an effort to find out more. The Service had had
word of the man's close connections with others in
London who held radical views and they wanted to
see just whom he associated with.

A simple target. An easy mark. But the small notice he had allowed Henrietta Clements had changed
into something else, something he should have recognised as dangerous from the very start.

He laughed, but the sound held no humour whatsoever. Since the fire Randolph Clements had gone to ground, hiding in the wilds of the northern borders, he supposed, or perhaps he had taken ship to France. It didn't matter much any more. If Clements wanted to exact revenge for the death of his wife, Gabriel would have almost welcomed it, an ending to the sorry saga that his life had now become.

The fire at Ravenshill had ruined him, completely, any intimacy and want for feminine company crouched now amongst pain and fury and sacrifice.

He'd broken hearts and promises for years whilst cutting a swathe through the capricious wants of unhappily married wives. Information to protect a country at war could be gathered in more ways than one might imagine and he done his patriotic duty without complaint.

The rumours that circled around about him had helped as he gathered intelligence whilst a sated paramour lay asleep. It was easy to sift his way through the contents of a husband's desk or safe or sabretache without prying eyes, and the danger of stepping into the lair of the enemy had been a great part of the enjoyment.

Until Henrietta Clements.

As he perceived his hand stroking the damaged skin on his right thigh he stopped and touched the silver-and-gold ring he had bought three months ago from the jewellers, Rundell and Bridges, in Ludgate Hill.

'The symbol engraved upon the circle is Christian, my lord, and of course the word engraved is Latin.

Fortuna. Lady luck, and who cannot do with a piece of that.'

The salesman was an earnest young man Gabriel had not seen in the shop before and seemed to have a bent for explaining the spiritual. 'Luck is, of course, received from the faith a believer entrusts in it, for a talisman is only strong when there is that sense of conviction. We have other clients who swear by the advantages they have received. The safe birth of a babe. The curing of a badly broken arm. A cough that is finally cured after months of sleepless nights.'

The ability to make love again?

Did he believe? Gabriel thought. Could he afford not to? Once he would have laughed at such nonsense, but for now he was catching at rainbows and hope with all the fervour of the newly converted. He had paid a fortune for the questionable assistance and had worn it ever since. He wondered momentarily if he should not just snatch the trinket from his finger and throw it into the Thames, for twelve weeks with no sign at all of any inherent powers was probably a fairly conclusive sign of its lack of potency.

Yet hope held him to the wearing of it, even though his own condition had not changed one whit for the better.

It was a week later, despite all his attempts at desiring otherwise, that Gabriel Hughes finally accepted the fact that he was impotent.

He looked down at his flagging member in the darkened room off Grey Street and thought that this was where life had brought him. An ironic twist. An unwanted mockery of fate.

The woman in the bed was beautiful, bountiful and sweet—a country girl with the combination of dewy sensibleness and a sultry sensuality burning to be ignited. She sat there watching him, a clean and embroidered chemise the only thing covering her, a quiet smile on unpainted lips.

'I thought my first customer might be old and ugly, sir. I had wondered if I should even be able to do what my aunt has bidden me to, but I can see that this job is likely to be a lot less difficult than my old one. I worked in a weaving mill, you see, but it closed down. It was me and a hundred other girls and the light hurt my eyes and we were never allowed to just stop. Not like this, sir. Never like this. Never on our backs in the warmth and with a glass of good wine for the drinking.'

'You are a virgin, then?' His heart sank at all such a state would imply.

She shook her head. 'Mary said I was to say I was 'cos the coinage is better that way, but I go to church on Sundays, sir, and could not abide by the lie.'

Gabriel was glad for this fact at least. The first time should be special for every woman. He believed that absolutely.

'My Jack went and died on me before we were married. He got sick one day and was taken the next. It was just lucky that I did not catch the worst of it though I was ill for a good many weeks after.'

The barrage of information ran into the room with

an ease that held him still and listening. For the first time in a long while Gabriel did not wish to be away from the company of a half-naked woman with such desperation. Even the roiling nausea seemed to settle with her words, the information comforting somehow.

'Mam said I should come to London to her sister, who was doing more than well.' She shook her brown curls and laughed. 'I don't think she realises exactly what it is Aunt Mary is up to, but, with little other in the way of paying work back home, I agreed to come in and try it. We haven't yet though, have we?' And, with colourful language, she went on to say just what it was they hadn't yet done.

Gabriel turned towards the window. The phrases she used were coarse, but the talk was relaxing him. Perhaps such candour was what kept the blood from his ears and his breath even. Small steps in the right direction. Tiny increments back to a healing. If he could only stop thinking and do the deed once…

Reality brought his attention to the problem before him as he looked down. Flaccid. Unmoving. The scar tissue on his right thigh and groin in the light from the window was brutal and he pulled his breeches up.

But she was off the bed in a flash, one warm hand clutching his arm. 'Can you stay for a while, sir? Only a little while so that…' She stopped as though trying to formulate what she wanted to say next.

'So your aunt will think you at least earned your keep?'

'Exactly that, sir, and it is nice here talking with you. You smell good, too.'

He laughed at this and removed her hand. Sitting here was not the agony he had imagined after the fiasco in the Temple of Aphrodite and he gestured to her to pour more wine, which she did, handing it to him with a smile. His beaker was chipped on one side so he turned it around.

'Jack used to say we would be married with a dozen children before we knew it and look what happened to him. Life is like a game of chess, I'd be thinking. One moment you are winning everything and the next you are wiped off the board.'

'You play chess?'

'I do, sir. My father taught me when I were little. He was a mill worker, too, you understand, but a gent once taught him the rudiments of the game in a tavern out of Styal in Cheshire and he never forgot it. I have my board and pieces with me. We could play if you like? To waste a bit of time?'

The wine was cheap, but the room was warm and as the girl brought her robe off of a hook and wrapped it around herself, Gabriel breathed out.

Little steps, he reiterated to himself. Little tiny steps. And this was the first.

An hour later after a close game Gabriel extracted a golden guinea from his pocket and gave it to her. 'For your service, Sarah, and for your kindness.'

Bringing the coin between perfectly white teeth, she bit down upon it. Still young enough not to have lost them, still innocent enough to imagine that gold might be a cure for the dissolution of morality. A trade-off that at this point in her life still came down on the black side of credit. *God*, he muttered to himself as he grabbed his jacket.

Henrietta Clements had been the same once. Hopeful and blindly trusting.

He brought out his card from a pocket and laid it down on the lumpy straw mattress. 'Can you read?'

She shook her head.

'If you ever want to escape this place, find someone who can, then, and send word to me for help. I could find you more...respectable work.'

She was off of the bed in a moment, the scent of her skin pungent and sharp as she threaded her arms about his neck.

'If you lay down, I'd do all the work, sir. Like a gift to you seeing as you have been so nice and everything.'

Full lips closed over his and Gabriel could feel an earnest innocence. The pain of memory lanced over manners as he pushed her back.

'No.' A harsher sound than he meant, with things less hidden.

'You won't be calling again?' Sarah made no attempt at hiding her disappointment. 'Not even for another game of chess?'

'I'm afraid I won't.' The words were stretched and quick, but as manners laced through reason he added others. 'But thank you. For everything.'

Chapter Three

The stone was cold, rubbed smooth with the echoes of time. He had tried to reach her, through the tapestries of Christ under thorns, but the choking smoke had stopped him, the only sound in his ears the one of a ghastly silence.

His dagger was in his fist, wrapped around anger, the Holy Water knocked from its place on the pulpit and falling on to marble pocked with time. The spectre of death had him, even as he reached for Henrietta, the trickle of red running down his fingers and her eyes lifeless.

Gabriel woke with the beat of his heart loud in his ears and his hands gripping the sheets beneath him.

The same bloody dream, never in time, never quick enough to save her. He cursed into fingers cradled across his mouth, hard harsh words with more than a trace of bitterness within as his eyes went to the timepiece on the mantel.

Six o'clock. An hour's sleep at least. Better than some nights, worse than others. Already the first birds were calling and the working city moved into action. The street vendors with their words and their incantations. 'Milk maids below.' 'Four for sixpence, mackerel.' The heavier sound of a passing carriage drowned them out.

Unexpectedly the image of the water-blue eyes of Miss Adelaide Ashfield came to mind, searing through manners and propriety on the seat at the edge of the Bradfords' ballroom as she cursed about her ten more weeks.

Where did she reside in London? he wondered. With her uncle in his town house on Grosvenor Square or in the home of Lady Harcourt? Did she frequent many of the *ton*'s soirées or was she choosy in her outings?

Swearing under his breath, he rose. He had no business to be thinking of her; she would be well counselled to stay away from him and as soon as he had caught those who were helping Clements in his quest for Napoleon's ascendency he, too, would be gone.

The society mamas were more circumspect with him now, the failing family fortune common knowledge and the burned-out shell of the Wesley seat of Ravenshill Manor unattended. His father had squandered most of what had been left to them after his grandfather's poor management, and Gabriel had been trying to consolidate the Wesley assets ever since. The bankers no longer courted him, neither did the businessmen wanting the backing of old family money to allow them an easy access to ideas. It would only be a matter of time before society turned its back altogether.

But he'd liked talking with Adelaide Ashfield from Dorset. This truth came from nowhere and he smiled. God, the unusual and prickly débutante was stealing his thoughts and he did not even want to stop and wonder why.

She reminded him of a time in his life when things had been easier, he supposed, when conflict could be settled with the use of his fists and when he had gone to bed at midnight and slept until well past the dawn.

What would happen after the allotted ten weeks? Would her uncle allow her to simply slip back into the country with her fortune intact, unmarried and free?

His eyes rested upon the gold locket draped on the edge of an armoire to one side of the window.

The bauble had been Henrietta's. She had left it here the last time she had come to see him and he had kept it after her death. For safekeeping or a warning— the reminder of love in lost places and frozen seconds? For the memory of why a close relationship would never again be something that he might consider? He had tried to remember how the fire in the chapel had begun, but every time he did so there was a sense of something missing.

For a while he imagined it might have been he who had started it, but subsequently he had the impression of other hands busy with that very purpose. Hers? Her husband's? The men they associated with? The only thing Gabriel was certain of was the hurt and the stab of betrayal that had never left him.

But perhaps he and Miss Adelaide Ashfield were more alike than he thought? Perhaps she had been hurt, too, by someone, by falsity, by promise. It was not often, after all, that a young and beautiful girl held such an aversion to marriage and stated it so absolutely.

He would like to meet her again just to understand what it was that she wanted. The Harveys were holding a ball this very evening and perhaps the Penbury party had the intention of going? He had heard that Randolph Clements's cousin George Friar might be in attendance and wanted to get a measure of the man. Wealthy in his own right, the American had been staying with the Clements for a good while now, but some said he was a man who held his own concealments and darkness.

The inlaid gold on his ring glinted in the light and Gabriel frowned as he recited the Anglican prayer of resurrection beneath his breath. Turning the circle of gold and silver against his skin, he positioned it so that the inlaid cross faced upwards.

Fortuna.

He suddenly felt that he had lost the hope of such a thing a very long time ago.

Arriving at the Harveys' ball later than he meant to, the first person Gabriel met was his friend Daniel Wylde, the Earl of Montcliffe, with Lucien Howard, the Earl of Ross, at his side.

'I am only down from Montcliffe for a few days, Gabe, trying to complete a deal on the progeny of a particularly fine pair of greys I own.'

Gabriel's interest was piqued. 'The Arabian beauties that were standing at Tattersall's a year or so back? The ones that caused a stir before they were pulled from auction.'

'The very same. Perhaps you might be interested in a foal for the Ravenshill stables?' Lucien Howard's voice was threaded with an undercurrent of question.

'My means are about as shaky as your own are rumoured to be, Luce. I doubt I could afford to feed another horse, let alone buy one.'

Daniel Wylde laughed heartily before any more could be said. 'Find a wife, then, who is both beautiful and rich. That's your answer.'

'Like you did?'

'Well, in all truth, she found me...'

The small and round Miss Greene and her younger sister chose that moment to walk past and gaze in Gabriel's direction. He had stood up with her in a dance earlier in the Season as a favour to their bountifully blessed aunt and the girls had seemed to search him out at each ensuing function.

A plethora of other ladies milled around behind them, each one seemingly younger than the next. And then to one corner he noticed Miss Adelaide Ashfield. Tonight she was adorned in gold silk, the rich shade making her hair look darker and her skin lighter.

She was laughing at something the girl beside her had said though at that very moment she looked up and caught Gabriel's glance. From this distance he could see something in her eyes that drew out much more in his expression than he wanted to show. With shock he broke the contact, his heart hammering.

Not sexual, but an emotion far more risky. He almost swore, but a footman chose that exact moment to pass by with an assortment of drinks on a silver tray.

The liquor slid across panic and soothed it. He saw the question that passed between Montcliffe and Ross, but he turned away, the card room as good a place as any to drown his sorrows.

'If you will excuse me, I might try my hand at a game of whist.'

'But a waltz is about to begin, Gabe, and the girl in gold in that corner looks as though she would welcome a dance.'

He left saying nothing though the sound of their laughter followed him for a good many yards.

George Friar was not yet here. He'd hoped to have a word with him, not to warn him off exactly, but to allow the colonial to understand the danger of becoming involved in political intrigues against England. Still, Gabriel was prepared to wait, and it was early.

A hundred pounds later Gabriel acknowledged his mind was not on the game and cashed in his chips.

'Thank you, gentlemen, but that is me out for the evening.'

Francis St Cartmail pulled his substantial winnings

over in front of him. 'Are you sure you will not stay, Gabriel? I could do with as much as you can lose.'

For the first time that evening Gabriel smiled as if he meant it. 'Daniel and Luce are out there somewhere. Get them to sit down with you.'

The other shook his head. 'Ross is skint and Montcliffe is a responsible married man. He spends his extra on the horses he sees with potential and, by God, he is doing well with it, too.'

'You can't get in on the game?'

'Never really interested, I am afraid. But I am off to the Americas in a month or so on the search for gold.'

'You think you will find some?' A fresh spurt of interest surged.

'I do. Come with me. I'd be happy to have you along.'

The invitation was both sincere and unexpected and Gabriel thought that if he had not been consumed in his revenge for Henrietta's death he might have even taken him up on it.

'I met a man a few months back who told me to look for gold in North Carolina, Francis. He said the town of Concord was the place I should journey to and his brother-in-law, Samuel Huie, was the man who would show me where to look. He said Huie had found a nugget as big as his fist while he was out fishing one day. As he did not seem like a man who often embellished the truth, I believed the yarn.'

'Well, I will keep the information in mind and if

I find it in the place you mention, I will keep bring some back for you.'

'Then I wish you all the luck in the world.'

'Thank you for the dance, Miss Ashfield.' Mr George Friar's words were laced with a slight American accent as he drew Adelaide to one side of the room. 'Are you enjoying your time here in London?'

'Indeed, sir.' This was a complete lie, but she knew if she had said otherwise she would have a complicated explanation in front of her.

'I saw you speaking with Lord Wesley the other night at the Bradfords' ball. Is he a particular friend of yours?'

Unexpectedly the blood rushed to her face and Adelaide cursed her reaction, especially when she saw the man's obvious curiosity.

'I am newly come to London, Mr Friar. I barely know the earl.'

'But you have heard the stories, no doubt? He is not to be trusted and it would be wise for any woman to keep her distance.'

Such a confidence made Adelaide shiver.

'A strong opinion, sir. Is he an acquaintance of yours?'

The man shook his head. 'No, but he led the wife of my cousin astray and it cost her her life, an ending she did not in any way deserve.'

'You are implying then some sense of blame on the part of Lord Wesley, sir?' She had made a point of asking Lucy and her other acquaintances here about the chequered past of Gabriel Hughes since meeting him, partly out of interest, but mostly out of the feeling he was somehow being wrongly dealt to. She could not explain her connection with a man who appeared to be everything she had always abhorred and yet... 'From the stories I have heard it was your cousin's wife who had absconded with her lover in the first place?'

This time Friar laughed out loud. 'A woman who is not afraid to voice all that she thinks is a rare jewel in the London court. Why are you not married ten times over already, Miss Ashfield? Can these English lords not recognise a veritable treasure when they see one?'

She brushed off his nonsense though a part of her was pleased at such praise. 'A woman's need for a husband is overrated in my opinion, though my uncle is not to be persuaded otherwise.'

For a moment his visage was one of shock before he managed to drag his expression back.

'Well, Miss Ashfield, I have always applauded honesty in a woman. Would you take a walk with me, perchance, so that I might tell you a story?'

Adelaide looked around. She could see Lord Berrick making his way towards her and wanted to avoid him.

'Perhaps a turn on the terrace for privacy might be in order.' Friar said this as he saw where she looked.

She did not wish to be alone with Mr Friar, she thought, remembering Lord Wesley's warning, but glancing through the glass she observed others lingering there and enjoying the unusual balminess of the evening.

It could not hurt for five minutes to listen to what he had to say, surely, and with the growing warmth in the room she would appreciate a little fresh air.

Once outside Adelaide could tell Mr Friar was trying to think up what words to give her next as he looked over the small balustrade leading into the garden. Finally he spoke.

'There are some who would say that the Earl of Wesley is not the fop he pretends to be. My cousin, for example, was completely crushed by the loss of his precious wife. He does not believe her demise was an accident at all.'

'What does he believe, then?'

'If I could speak plainly, I would say he thinks Wesley killed her for he had become tired of her neediness as his lover and wanted her gone.'

Shock ran through Adelaide at the bitterness in his words and also that such an accusation should be levelled at Gabriel Hughes. 'Presumably the courts thought otherwise, Mr Friar, as I heard there was a case of law to be answered for it.' The thought did cross her mind as to why she should be such a stalwart in her defence of a man whose reputation was hardly pristine, given everything she knew of Lord Wesley had come through gossip.

'Indeed they did, Miss Ashfield, but justice and money walk hand in hand and the Wesley title holds its own sway in such decisions.'

'Such are the words of those who perceive their

case lost by some unfair disadvantage that they can never prove. Better to move on and make your life over than look back and wreak havoc with all that is left.'

'You are not the more normal sort of débutante, Miss Ashfield, with your strong opinions.'

'I will take that as a compliment, Mr Friar, for I am older and a lot wiser. Wise enough to know that people can say anything of anyone and yet the saying of it does not make it true.'

He laughed, but the sound was not pleasant. 'Have you ever been to the Americas?'

When she shook her head he continued.

'I own a large property in Baltimore, in Coles Harbor on the west side of the Jones Falls River. I have come to England to find a partner who might enjoy the place with me, neither a timid bride, Miss Ashfield, nor a young one. I need a woman who would cope with the rigours of the New World and one with enough of a fortune to help me build my own legacy.'

'I see.' And Adelaide suddenly did. She had left the relative safety of the frying pan that was Lord Berrick and jumped into a fire.

It was how the business of marriage worked in London, after all, brides were only a commodity and an article of trade. Men put their collateral on the table and a prudent woman weighed up her options and accepted the most favourable. For life. For ever. It was exactly as Aunt Eloise had said it would be, was it not? Women sold their souls for marriage and regretted it until the end of time.

The thought of it all held her mute, but George

Friar seemed to have taken her silence as acquiescence, for he leaned forward and took her fingers in his own before his lips came down hard upon the back of them.

Cold, wet and grasping. She could not believe he would dare to touch her like this out here amongst others, but as she broke away and looked around she realised everybody on this end of the terrace had left to go inside.

Mr Friar hadn't released her, either, his fingers still entwined in hers and allowing no means of escape, the expression on his face ardent as he breathed out rapidly.

'Oh, come now, Miss Ashfield, I am certain we could do better than that. You look like a woman with a great deal of sensuality about you and, if I say so myself, I am considered something of a catch by the unmarried women of Baltimore. A new life, an adventure and the opportunity to use your considerable fortune in a way that could double it again. Take the chance of it whilst you can. Caution can be most stultifying.'

Adelaide thought quickly. She needed to diffuse this situation and get back inside without causing even more of a scene. 'I am sure you are as you say, sir, a veritable catch, but believe me when I tell you that I have no want for a husband despite my presence here.' This explanation solved nothing, however, for his grip tightened as he pulled her towards him. 'I will ask you one more time to please let me go, sir.' She hated the slight shiver in her words as he met her glance directly and lifted his brows. A game? He thought it such?

'One kiss, then, to convince you. Surely that would not be amiss?'

The sharp slap of fingers on his cheek and his legs caught on the edge of a pot plant tipping him off balance. Even as she reached forward to stop him tumbling he was gone, falling over the balustrade in an ungainly surprise and lying prone and motionless on the path below.

My God, had she killed him? Forgetting about convention and her own safety, she scrambled down after him and saw in relief that he still breathed.

She could hardly just leave him here, but to do otherwise would involve her in discussions she would rather not be a part of. A movement from above surprised her, but she knew who it was immediately.

Chapter Four

'We meet again, Miss Ashfield.'

'In circumstances even more trying than the last time, I am afraid, Lord Wesley. Mr Friar is newly come from the Americas and seems to have a poor understanding of the word "no". His ability to pretend to be something he is not must be the only thing allowing him entrance here for he has few other redeeming features.' She knew she was babbling, but couldn't seem to stop. Surprise and relief at the earl's presence obliterated her more normal reason and fright had made her shake.

As he joined her, Gabriel Hughes placed two fingers across the pulse on George Friar's neck. 'A trifle fast, but given the circumstances…'

Today he looked tired, the darkened skin beneath both eyes alluding to a lack of sleep. His glance had also taken in the telltale mark on the unconscious man's cheek.

'His dress sense is appalling, would you not say?'

At that she smiled. There was a certain sangfroid

apparent in the comment. Indeed, he did not look even the least perturbed about what had happened.

'I didn't push him. He fell across that potted plant and down into the garden.'

'After you slapped him?'

She felt her own blood rise. 'I had asked him to remove his hand from my person, Lord Wesley, and he did not.'

He looked up quickly. 'He didn't hurt you?' His gold eyes were darker tonight, though when she shook her head the anger in them softened.

'Perhaps then it would be better if you were gone when he awakes?'

Taking that as a hint, she turned.

'Miss Ashfield?'

She turned back. 'Yes?'

'If you say nothing of this to anyone, I will make certain that he never does, either.'

'How?' The question tumbled out in horror.

'A firm threat is what I was thinking, but if you want him dead…?'

Could he possibly mean what she thought he did? Friar's explanation of how Wesley had killed Henrietta tumbled in her mind to be dismissed as the upturn of his lips held her spellbound. He was teasing, but already she could hear the voices of others coming closer and knew she needed to be gone. Still she could not quite leave it at that.

'Sometimes I am not certain about just exactly who you are, my lord. Amongst the pomp and splendour of your clothes and the artful tie of your cravat I detect a man who is not quite the one that he appears.'

But Gabriel Hughes shook his head. 'It would be much safer for you to view me exactly as the rest of the world does, Miss Ashfield; a dissolute and licentious earl without a care for anything save the folds in his most complicated cravat.'

No humour lingered now, the hard planes of his face intractable, and as George Friar groaned Adelaide fled. She could not fathom the Earl of Wesley at all and that was the trouble. He was nothing like any man she had met before. Even when he laughed the danger in him was observable and clear. But the colour of his eyes in this light was that of the gilded hawks she'd seen as a young girl in a travelling menagerie that had visited Sherborne, the quiet strength in them hidden under humour.

Lady Harcourt looked up as she came to her side. 'You are always disappearing, my dear. I am certain that is not a trait to be greatly encouraged. If your uncle were here and he asked me of your whereabouts, I would not know, you see, and so it would be far better if...'

Her words petered off as a shout at one end of the salon had them turning and Adelaide saw Mr Friar burst into the room using a large white handkerchief to wipe off his bleeding nose. She was glad he was heading straight for the exit even as she stepped back into the shadow of her chaperon.

Gabriel Hughes came into view behind him, accompanied by Lord Montcliffe, and the Earl of Wesley's left hand was buried deep in his pocket. Walking together, the two men were of a similar height and build and every feminine eye of the *ton* was trained towards them as well as a good many of the masculine ones.

'Goodness me. What is society coming to these days?' Lady Harcourt lifted her lorgnette to her face to get a better view. 'A fist fight in the middle of a crowded ball? Who is that short man, Bertram, with Lord Wesley and Lord Montcliffe?'

Adelaide's heart began to beat fast and then faster. Would there be a scene? Would she be revealed as the perpetrator of the American's questionable condition?

'Mr George Friar is an arrogant cheat,' her cousin drawled. 'Perhaps the Earl of Wesley has finally done what many of the others here have not been able to.'

'What?' Imelda's voice was censorious. 'Broken his nose?'

'Nay, Aunt. Shut him up.'

The Earl of Berrick, standing beside them, frowned. 'I have my doubts that Lord Wesley would put himself out for such a one unless it suited his purpose.'

Bertie nodded in agreement. 'He'd be far more likely to be in the card room or cavorting with the numerous women of the *ton* who are unhappy in their marriages.'

Lady Harcourt gave her grand-nephew a stern look. 'You are in the company of a young girl in her first Season, Bertram. Please mind your tongue.'

'Pardon me, Aunt, and I am sorry, Addie.'

Her cousin gave her one of the smiles that Adelaide could never ever resist.

'Make it up to me, then.'

'How.'

'Come with me as my chaperon to the Royal Botanic Gardens at Kew. There is a physic garden there that I have always wanted to see.'

'You look like hell, Gabe.' Daniel Wylde did not mince his words as they left the Harveys' ball. 'You need some beauty sleep.'

Gabriel heard the concern behind the words. 'I'll live.'

'Who was he, to you? Mr Friar back there?'

'No one. He'd tripped over the balustrade and had fallen. I was the first to find him.'

'I doubt that.' Montcliffe's words were low. 'Unless you have taken to slapping strange men I would say there was a woman involved. Besides, you would hardly take a hard swipe at an injured man unless you had some gripe with him?'

Gabriel swore, but didn't answer.

'Your sister, Charlotte, was unkind, Gabriel, but you were always nicer.'

'It's been a while. People change. I'd be the first to admit that I have.'

'Why?'

One word biting at his guts, so easy just to spill the worries and feel better. Even easier to not. Still it might not hurt to sound Montcliffe out on a little of it.

'What do you know of Randolph Clements?'

'His wife, Henrietta, died in the fire at Ravenshill Chapel. It was rumoured you had something to do with that, but it was never proven.'

'I think Clements killed his wife.'

'And walked away?'

'Unconvicted. Mr Friar here is one of his American cousins.'

'You think he was involved, too?'

'Odds are that he is here in London for a reason.'

'He is single and wealthy. He wants a wife. Many might say that is enough of a reason. Who slapped him before you turned up?'

'Miss Adelaide Ashfield.'

'And she is…?'

Gabriel swallowed hard. 'Penbury's niece and one of this Season's débutantes.'

'The woman in gold?' Montcliffe began to smile. 'God, you have an interest in this lady.'

'No.' He made the word sound as definite as he could.

'Yet you just avenged her for an insult, I am presuming? Such an action indicates more than mere indifference.'

Gabriel had forgotten about Daniel Wylde's quick mind. He could also see the wheels of curiosity turning in sharp eyes.

'You never told me about happened in the bloody chapel? Some say it was you who lit the fire.'

'No, I can't even remember how it started. I know I did try to save her, but then…' He stopped, searching for a glimpse into recall and failing.

'You couldn't?'

'I didn't love Henrietta Clements in the way she wanted me to.'

There was silence, the guilt of it all howling around the edges of Gabriel's sanity like a cold wind blowing relentlessly from the north. He had had liaisons with women all of his adult life, unrequited political connections, and this was the result. His penance. His atonement. The resulting impotence was only deserved and proper. A God-given punishment so very close to the cause of all his destruction—he could not deny it.

If he had been alone he might have hit something, but he wasn't. As it was he held his hands into the side of his thighs in tight fists. The nail on his right forefinger broke into the skin of his thumb.

'Perhaps I hurt your sister in the same way?' Daniel offered the explanation.

'Pardon?' With all his other thoughts Gabriel could not quite work out exactly what was meant.

'Charlotte. I didn't love her enough, either, and we ruined each other. Same thing you are talking of, isn't it?'

The minutes of quiet multiplied.

'But then Amethyst taught me about the honesty of love.'

God, Gabriel thought, *and what I would not give for a wife like that.* Empty loneliness curled into the corners of hope. He had never felt close to anyone and now it would never again be possible.

For a second he almost hated the other's joy. It was

what happened when you were down on your luck. You became surrounded by those who were not. Even his sister, for all her poor choices in life, had written to say that she had met a wealthy and cultured man in Edinburgh with whom she could see a future.

'Come to Montcliffe, Gabe. Some country air might be just what you need. Amethyst is almost eight months along in her pregnancy so she does not come to London any more, preferring the quiet of Mont-cliffe.' Daniel Wylde was watching him closely. 'She would be pleased to have you there and so would I.'

Thanking him for the offer, Gabriel replied that he would certainly think about it and then he left.

He actually spent the night thinking of Adelaide Ashfield. Her smile. Her blue eyes. The quiet lisp in her words. Friar was a threat to her in some way he could not as yet fathom. Gabriel knew that he was. He returned his attention to the notes spread across the table in front of him—maps, drawings and timings—as he searched for a pattern.

Clements was there somewhere in the middle of the puzzle though he had been careful to cover his tracks. His cousin George Friar told others that he had arrived in England a month or so before Hen-rietta had died, on the clipper *Vigilant* travelling between Baltimore and London. But when he had tracked down the passenger list for that particular voyage his name had not been upon it. Why would he lie about such a thing? Had he lied about who he was as well?

Frank Richardson had visited Friar and Clements, too. He had stayed over at the Whitehorse Tavern with John Goode, his cousin.

Four of them now. Gabriel knew there were six, because Henrietta Clements had told him so. She had been so angry she could barely talk when she had come to him at Ravenshill, that much he did remember.

'My husband is here,' she had said simply. 'Right behind me, and I know for certain his political allegiances lie with France and Napoleon's hopes. Take me away to the Americas, Gabriel. I have an aunt who lives there. In Boston. We could be free to begin again...together, for I have money I can access and much in the way of jewellery.' Her arms came around him even as he tried to move away.

Then there was blankness, an empty space of time without memory. He had been trying to fill in the details ever since, but the only true and residing certainty he'd kept was the pain.

The knock at the door was expected, but still he stood to one side of the jamb and called out, 'Who is it?'

'Archie McCrombie, sir.' The reply was firm.

Sliding the latch downwards, Gabriel ushered the small red-haired man inside, the cold air of evening blowing in with him and his coat lifting in the wind.

'Friar is residing at Beaumont Street, where he has spent most of the last week enjoying the charms of Mrs Fitzgerald's girls. I left Ben there to make certain he stays put.'

'Did he meet anyone else?'

'Frank Richardson, my lord. I did not recognise the others who came and went. Someone tailed me as I left, but I shook him off. Tall he was and well dressed. He does not seem to fit in around this side of town. He was armed, too, I would bet my life on the fact.'

'Expecting trouble, then, or about to cause it?'

'Both, I would say, sir. I'd have circled back and tailed him, my lord, if I wasnna meeting you.'

'No, you did well. Give them some rope to hang themselves; we don't just want one fish, we want all six of them.'

'Yes, sir.'

After McCrombie left, Gabriel stood and walked to the window. It was raining outside and grey and the cold enveloped him, his life worn down into a shadow of what it had previously been.

His finances were shaky. He had gone through his accounts again and again, trying to find a way to cut down his spending, but his country estate of Ravenshill was bleeding out money as was his London town house. He wasn't down to the last of his cash yet, as Daniel Wylde had been, but give it a few more years and...

He shook that thought away.

Once he had those associated with Clements he could leave London and retreat to Ravenshill Manor. Then he would sell off the town house. The new trading classes were always on the lookout for an old and aristocratic residence in the right location and he knew it would go quickly. In Essex he would be able to manage at least until his mother was no longer with him. He shook that thought away and swore softly as he remembered back to their conversation at dinner the night before.

'You need to find a wife who would give you children, Gabriel. You would be much happier then.'

The anger that had been so much a part of him since the fire burgeoned. 'I doubt I will ever marry.'

The tight skin on his right thigh underlined all that he now wasn't. No proper women would have him in the state he was in and even courtesans and prostitutes were out of his reach. A no-man's lad. A barren and desolate void.

When his mother reached out to place her hand over his he had felt both her warmth and her age. Her melancholy was getting worse, but he did not mention that as he tried to allay her fears.

'Everything will work out. We will leave London soon and go up to Essex. You can start a garden and read. Perhaps even take up the piano again?'

Tears had welled in the old and opaque eyes. 'I named you for the angel from the Bible, you know, Gabriel, and I was right to, but sometimes now I think there is only sadness left...'

Her words had tapered off and he shook his head to stop her from saying more, the teachings of the ancient shepherd of Hermas coming to mind.

'In regard of faith there are two angels within man. One of Righteousness and one of Iniquity.'

The Angel of Iniquity was a better analogy to describe himself now, Gabriel thought, but refrained from telling her so.

The sum of his life. Wrathful. Bitter. Foolish. Cut off. Even Alan Wolfe, the Director of the British Service, had stated that Gabriel could no longer serve in the same capacity he had done, his profile after the fire too high for a department cloaked in secrecy.

So he had kept on at it largely alone, day after day and week after week. A more personal revenge. Once he had thought the emotion a negative one, but now…?

It was like a drug, creeping through his bones and shattering all that was dull; a questionable integrity, he knew that, but nevertheless his own.

The veneer of social insouciance was becoming harder and harder to maintain, the light and airy manners of a fop overlaying a heavy coat of steel. The lacy shirt cuffs, the carefully tied cravat. A smile where only fury lingered and an ever-increasing solitude.

Adelaide Ashfield's honesty had shaken him, made him think, her directness piercing all that he had hoped to hide and so very easily. But there were things that she was not telling him, either, he could see this was so in the unguarded depths of those blue eyes. And Friar was circling around her, his derogatory evaluation of England's royal family and its Parliament as much of a topic of his every conversation as his need to make a good marriage.

Revolution came from deprivation and loss, and he could not for the life of him work out why George

Friar, a successful Baltimore businessman by his own account, would throw in his lot with the unpopular anti-British sentiments of his cousin. They were blood-related, but they were also wildly different people.

Perhaps it was in the pursuit of a religious fervour he had come with, the whispers of the young prince's depravities rising. America's independence had the same ring of truth to it, there was no doubt about that, a better way of living, a more equitable society and one unhampered by a monarch without scruples.

Conjecture and distrust. This is what his life had come to now, Gabriel thought, for he seldom took people at their face value any more, but looked for the dark blackness of their souls.

Gabriel strained to remember the laughter inside the words of Miss Adelaide Ashfield as he poured himself a drink, hating the way his hands shook when he raised the crystal decanter.

She was the first person he had ever met who seemed true and real and genuine, artifice and dissimulation a thousand miles from her honestly given opinions.

But he did wonder just who the hell had hurt her.

Chapter Five

Adelaide had tried to like Frederick Lovelace, the Earl of Berrick, but in truth he was both boring and vain, two vices that added together led to the third one of shallowness.

'A titled aristocrat no less,' her uncle had proclaimed after noticing Berrick's interest at their last meeting, a lilt in his voice and pride in his step. 'I thought Richard Williams a catch, but here is a man of ten thousand pounds a year, my dear, and a country home that is the envy of all who see it.'

As the earl in question regaled her with myriad facts about horse racing, however, Adelaide struggled to feign an interest.

Eventually he came to the end of his soliloquy and stopped. 'Do you enjoy horses, Miss Ashfield?' he queried, finally mindful of the fact that he had not asked one question that pertained to her as yet.

'No. I generally try to stay well away from them, my lord.' She saw the resulting frown of Lady Harcourt and her uncle as he began to speak.

'My niece rides, of course, though the tutor I employed to teach the finer points found her timid. Perhaps you might take a turn together in Hyde Park if it suited you. I think she simply needs more practice at the sport to become proficient at it.

'Indeed, if you were going there by any chance today, perhaps we could meet, Miss Ashfield? I should be more than willing to help in your equestrian education.'

Her uncle looked pleased and nodded with pride. 'Well, now that you mention it we were intending to take a turn around the park.'

Adelaide did not deign to answer, but her pulse began to race. Please God that her uncle would not promise Berrick her company.

'Perhaps my niece and I could meet you there around five?'

Short of refusing outright Adelaide could say nothing. At least her uncle would be with her, but it was just this sort of ridiculousness that had put her off coming to London right from the beginning.

'I shall be there at five, then. Lord Penbury, Miss Ashfield.' Taking her hand as everyone stood, Berrick bowed across it, his head barely reaching the top of her brow and a growing bald patch clearly visible.

When he was gone her uncle finished the last of the brandy in his glass and turned towards her.

'A well brought-up young man, I think, Adelaide. A man who might suit you well with his wide interests and great fortune. At least we would know it is not your money that he is after for he is well endowed with his own.'

Adelaide listened with horror. 'You promised you would allow me the choice of a husband should I come for the Season, Uncle. I should not wish to be told who is the right one to choose and who is not.'

'That might all be very well, my love, but Frederick Lovelace is a good man from a sterling family and it behoves me as your uncle to offer the advice so that you are aware he'd make a remarkable connection.'

'He may be a good man, Uncle, but he is not the good man for me.'

Alec Ashfield turned and for the first time ever Adelaide saw real anger come into his eyes. 'Then find one, my dear. Find a man who can be all that you need and want and I will give you my blessing.'

Lady Harcourt stood as tension filled the room about them.

'I am sure she will, Alec. It may just take a little time for your niece to realise the honour the Earl of Berrick accords her, but let us hope this meeting you have organised goes somewhere towards the fact.'

Adelaide took her leave, feeling like screaming all the way up to her room on the second floor. She should never have agreed to come to London in the first place, she knew that now. She should have stayed at Sherborne and dug her feet in, refusing to be budged by any argument presented, because this was the result of it all. This coercion and well-meaning forcefulness.

When a tear welled up and fell over one cheek she angrily wiped it away.

She had not always needed to explain things to her old aunts, the fact that she was resigned to a productive spinsterhood simply accepted. An option the same as the one they themselves had taken and nary a second of regret for it, either.

The day suddenly felt heavy and difficult and now there was the further worry of a ride in a few hours in Hyde Park with a suitor who had a lot more hope than she knew was warranted. Could she feign sickness and simply miss it? She shook her head.

No, she would meet the Earl of Berrick with her uncle and tell him herself that she was not interested in marrying him or anybody at all. Hopefully that would be the end of it.

The ride began badly as Lord Berrick took her hand and pressed his lips to her skin, an action so reminiscent of her skirmish with Mr Friar that she found herself snatching her fingers back and standing there speechless. All around her others watched, the eyes of the *ton* upon them.

'I have looked forward to this, Miss Ashfield. I hope you will allow me to help you mount.'

When he placed his hands beneath the stirrup of the horse Adelaide thanked him. At least up on her steed he would be out of touch, so to speak, and she might be able to relax just a little.

She and her uncle had dismounted as soon as they had got inside the gates and now her uncle had elected to stay and wait whilst she took a turn about Rotten Row. This was a tactical manoeuvre, probably, and one that gave Frederick Lovelace some time alone with her.

At least the track was busy. With only a small difficulty she could get around the whole thing without having to converse with him to a great extent save to tell him of her desire to remain unattached.

Adelaide had never been proficient at managing a horse and here amongst many other steeds her stallion seemed nervy and difficult. At Northbridge she seldom rode, preferring instead to walk the short distances between the manor and the village. In London it seemed everybody was an expert, the tooling precise and accomplished.

Taking in a breath, she tried to hide a building fear. She had heard it mentioned more than once that horses could tell if their rider was afraid and acted accordingly. From the prancing of the horse beneath her she was sure he must understand her frame of mind completely. It obviously felt a certain attraction for the filly the Earl of Berrick rode, as it constantly veered to one side to get closer.

Just what she needed, she thought to herself, and, jamming her hand about the reins, made a supreme effort to keep them apart. At that moment when she looked up she stared straight into the laughing molten glance of Lord Wesley.

'Miss Ashfield.' He tipped his hat to her. The animal he rode was huge and black. A mount she imagined one would ride into battle, the arrogant stance of its head marking it out as different from all the others in the park.

Like horse, like owner, she found herself thinking uncharitably, though his presence seemed to have had the effect of making Lord Berrick back off a bit and for that she was glad. Two more turns and she could reasonably call it a day. If she managed one with Lord Wesley then all the better.

'I see you are as proficient at riding as you are at dancing the waltz.'

She could not help but smile. 'You have not yet seen me paint a watercolour or stitch a tapestry. I am even worse at those most necessary of feminine skills.'

When he laughed the sound burrowed down into the marrow of her bones, making her warmer than she had been.

'What are you good at, then?' he asked.

'Healing,' she returned. 'I run a clinic at North-bridge and people come for miles to get my ointments and tinctures. I have a garden, you see, and my aunts taught me many things about—'

She stopped as she saw his surprise and wondered if such skills would be deemed appropriate by the lords and ladies of society.

'Like Asclepius?' he returned and she shook her head.

'Well, I cannot restore the dead to the living as he did, my lord, but then neither do I wish to be smote with Zeus's thunder.'

'It might be argued accepting gold for raising the dead was hardly good form. Someone had to stop it.'

Adelaide was astonished. It was seldom she had met anyone, apart from her aged aunts, with a solid memory for the complicated names and deeds of the Grecian legends. A scholar, then, and a man who hid such learning? Today the sun had brought out the colour in his hair to a variety of shades of light brown, red and gold. When he wiped back the unruly hair on his forehead, she saw that the knuckles on his left hand were bruised and split. From the contretemps with Friar?

Adelaide glanced about to see that Lord Berrick was not too close before she mentioned them. 'I could give you salve for your fingers if you wanted it.'

As an answer to that he merely jammed his hand into his pocket and she pushed back her spectacles with a sigh.

'Why do you wear them?' He did not sound happy.

'The spectacles?' She couldn't quite understand what he meant.

'The glass in them is plain. Poor eyesight normally requires the fashioning of a lens for improved vision.'

She gave back her own question. 'Do you keep hawks, my lord?'

'No. Why?' He shifted on his horse in order to watch her better.

'I think you would hold an affinity with a bird who notices all that is around him even as he pretends nonchalance.'

With a gentlemanly tilt of his head Gabriel Hughes dropped back; a slight tug on the leather and he was gone, Lovelace replacing him.

'Is it not just the most appealing time of day, Miss Ashfield, and might I also say that you ride magnificently.'

As Adelaide swallowed back mirth she also resisted the strong impulse to turn around and look for the enigmatic Earl of Wesley.

Gabriel watched her trot on with the popinjay Lovelace chattering beside her and thought he should simply turn for the gate and leave. But something made him stay. Her uncertainty with the horse, he was to think later, or the unguarded way she had looked at him when she had offered her salve.

The shout came from close by, reverberating as a young man called his friend. Any other day such a sound might not have mattered, but with Adelaide holding her reins so tightly her horse took umbrage and reared. She had no hope at all in managing it.

Berrick simply stepped his horse to the side and watched, uncertain as to what he could do.

Gabriel was off his mount in a second and strode towards her frightened animal, reaching out for the dangling reins as he told Adelaide Ashfield to hold on any way that she could. Frightened blue eyes turned to him, but the message seemed to be getting across as she crouched down on the back of the stallion and grabbed large handfuls of mane in her fists.

Within a moment he had gentled the horse, and when it had settled enough for Gabriel to move around to the side, he reached up to the terrified rider.

'You can let go now. I have you.'

Her fingers seemed frozen and he unfolded her fists before taking her waist and sliding her from the horse. Letting her go as soon as she was on the ground, he was glad someone had come forward to hold the reins.

'You're safe. I promise.'

'Th-thank y-you.' Breathless and shaking, Adelaide found her hair had half fallen from its pins and her hat was missing. The trembling had worsened.

'I...I never l-liked horses and they d-don't like me, either. I sh-should have just walked.'

'And missed an adventure? At least you didn't let the stallion unseat you. Landing on your bottom in the middle of a busy park might be more cause for consternation.'

At that she smiled and brought up the back of her hand to wipe away the tears. She still felt shocked, but his humour was normalising everything and making her feel less panicked.

Her uncle had reached them now, too, and he grasped her arm in a tight hold.

'I saw what happened. Are you hurt?'

'No, I th-think I am f-fine.' Alec Ashfield's attention shifted to Gabriel Hughes.

'Lord Wesley.' Frosty and cold. 'Thank you for your help, but I can manage things from here.'

'Of course, Lord Penbury.'

The chill in the earl's voice was noticeable as he stepped back, leading his horse away as the gathering crowd allowed him a passage out.

She wanted to cry. She did. She wanted to run

after Gabriel Hughes and hold on to his safety and protection. She wanted him to tell her that everything was all right in that particular dry humour of his that made her feel…special.

Lord Berrick took the place vacated by Gabriel Hughes. 'I would have managed your horse, Miss Ashfield, but Wesley had already jumped into the fray. I did not realise that you were so inexperienced or I would never have suggested such an outing and now I am afraid your dress is ruined and your hat is quite flattened. At least your spectacles are not broken and that is something we can be well thankful for…'

Even her uncle watched Lovelace with a sort of disbelief as he babbled on, stopping only as Bertram hurried across.

'My God, Wesley is a hero,' he exclaimed, admiration apparent in every word. 'If he had not dragged your mount to stillness the way he did, Addie, you would have been thrown from its back, and with an animal that size it's a long way down.'

'Quite.' Her uncle's voice was as tight as the expression on Lovelace's face.

'I hope someone thanked him?' Bertram continued on, seemingly unaware of the atmosphere. 'For his shoulder muscles will be sore from the tugging, there is no doubt of that.'

Adelaide smiled. Her cousin was such a dear sometimes despite his gambling and drinking.

'Perhaps we were not quite as effusive as we might have been,' her uncle said quietly. 'I will send a note to Wesley when we get home.'

Home.

The whole episode had left Adelaide exhausted and she was glad when her uncle and cousin took charge of the horses and they headed the short distance towards the town house on Grosvenor Square.

Once she had bathed and dressed and her stomach had settled Adelaide took her large leather bag from the wardrobe and opened the flap.

She seldom went anywhere without all her oils and salves and tinctures. They grounded her and relaxed her in a way nothing else did, and she liked the weight of the mortar and pestle in her hand.

A healing salve was an easy thing to make. Gathering up an amber bottle of herbs infused in oil, she poured out a generous amount. Arnica for bruising and calendula for the abrasions. The smell of comfrey and duckweed made her breathe in, their properties of knitting the skin together and soothing irritation welcomed.

As her small burner flamed she heated beeswax on a very low temperature and added that to her mix. Lavender was placed in last, the smell pungent and masculine.

Choosing a little container of bright-green glass, she poured the salve into it and did the lid up. Around the side Adelaide twisted a thick tie of string and added a stalk of lavender.

Finished.

Taking a sheet of paper from her armoire, she wrapped it, placing a note inside. She had no idea as to where the earl lived, but, calling in her uncle's butler, instructed him with the task of seeing that the parcel reached Lord Gabriel Wesley as quickly as it was able.

The package arrived after a late supper, brought by a minion of the Penbury household who was under strict instructions to place the offering directly into his hands.

'Miss Ashfield says it will spoil otherwise. She said it would need to be used across the next few days to be at its most potent, my lord.'

'Very well.' Gabriel waited till the servant was gone and shut the door behind him. A strong smell of lavender came from the parcel.

Crossing to his desk, he opened the gift and pulled out a small green jar that had been tightly shut, a sprig of the same flower wrapped into the side. A note fluttered from the bottom of the glass, held on by a dob of red wax.

Lord Wesley,

Thank you for your help today in the park. As you were quick to point out I should probably be suffering from bad bruising if you had not saved me.

But it has come to my attention that the same might not be said for you. I sincerely hope that the abrasions on your hand have not been worsened by such a kindness.

This is a healing salve. Place it across your

*damaged skin once at night and then again in
the morning. It would work well on any tender
muscles as well. I am sure you will notice the
difference.*
Yours sincerely
Miss Adelaide Ashfield

Gabriel could not help but smile. His knuckles
were barely wounded compared to all the other hurts
he had suffered. But she had thought of him and acted
upon it; a gesture that was appreciated and unexpected.

Scooping out some of the ointment, he was surprised to feel the coolness of it on his skin. Beneath
the scent of lavender other smells lingered, but he did
not have the expertise to identify them. Comfrey, he
thought. He had smelt that after the fire in some of
the salves applied to his leg and would never forget
it. He wondered if the mixture would ease the tightness of the scarring on his thighs as well and decided
to try it when he went to bed.

He had never really had a gift before, delivered to
him and wrapped in flowers and scent. Oh, he had
given small trinkets to paramours across the years,
but he had not received gifts back and his own family
had seldom bothered with Christmas and birthdays.

Too busy trying to simply survive with a father
who was often angry. When Geoffrey Hughes had
been killed in a tavern brawl in London those left
had breathed a sigh of relief.

Thirteen had been an impressionable age to lose

a parent and whilst he had become difficult, his sister had changed into a wild thing almost overnight.

No wonder his mother had barely coped before slipping into a melancholy that hadn't left her.

The wreck of his family had been allayed a few years later by the warm arms of willing lovers and there had been a long line pleased to allow him succour. But no longer.

Bringing his hand to his nose, Gabriel inhaled deeply; the smell of goodness and healing and Adelaide Ashfield was comforting. He wished she had come herself to deliver the gifts.

Chapter Six

After her fright in the park Uncle Alec and Lady
Harcourt did not press her into any social engage-
ments the next morning. Indeed, they left the day
up to her discretion entirely and when Adelaide
expressed an interest in visiting Lackington, Allen
and Co. at their Temple of the Muses shop in Fins-
bury Square, her uncle readied a carriage to take
her.

Today accompanied only by her maid Adelaide
felt freer than she had done in weeks. The muscles at
the top of her arms hurt a little from her tussle with
the horse yesterday, but all in all the trade-off was
a good one.

With the sky blue above and the air fresh around
her she stopped in front of the facade of the shop
and looked up. A flag waved on top of a large dome
and in the distance she could hear the sound of bells.

Aunt Jean and Aunt Eloise had often spoken of
this place in hushed tones. They had told stories of
the number of books for sale here and of the gener-

osity of Lackington's prices. Adelaide could not wait to see it for herself.

Inside was as prepossessing as it had been without, the rows of books arranged in cyclical order all the way into the ceiling and a good many men and women were browsing what was on offer.

After asking the man at the desk where to find a book on English plant life, she was directed to a less busy part of the building with rows of promising-looking tomes before her.

Milly was delighted when Adelaide assured her it would be most proper for her maid to go on her own search of things to read. She had taught the girl her letters at Northbridge and knew she would enjoy the chance to find her particular favourites.

Forty minutes later and with a large pile of books in her arms Adelaide went searching for somewhere to sit. Turning a corner promising quiet, she came upon the Earl of Wesley reading at one of the private tables.

He did not look at all pleased to see her, a heavy frown marring his forehead, though it did nothing to diminish his beauty.

'Miss Ashfield.'

His reading material seemed to consist mainly of shipping routes and maps, but she did notice a few volumes that looked surprisingly like the botanicals she herself had chosen.

Almost furtively he laid a paper down on top of them. She wondered what he could be doing with a

tome of medical botany by William Woodville outlining diseases of the body and the newest possible
cures.

'I did not expect to see you here, my lord.' Her
glance dropped to the skin on his knuckles. The
wounds appeared to be considerably better than yesterday.

'Because you imagined the gambling halls to
be more to my taste?' He had regained his humour
quickly, but today there was also another emotion
that she had not seen there before.

Wariness. It sat upon his face, ambushing the more
normal indifference.

'I hope the salve I sent you was of some use.'

As he glanced down at his hand he spoke slowly.
'It was. The bruising is almost gone.'

'That will be the arnica, I expect, and the dash of
vinegar. Keep applying the ointment for two more
days each morning and night. It is at its most effec-
tive fresh, but should keep for at least a few months
if you make certain the lid is tight and that it is stored
out of the direct sunlight.'

'You are skilled at what you do, Miss Ashfield.'

'You believed I would not be?'

'I am not truly certain what to believe of you. A
woman of science and healing. A débutante who is
here for the Season and yet eschews the promise of
Holy Matrimony. A lady who fails to see any sort
of a need for women to excel in painting, dancing
or tapestry. But obviously an avid reader of botanicals and the art of medicinal healing. And romance?'

His eyes caught the slender volumes at the bottom of her pile.

But two could play at this game and Adelaide was well up to the task. She squared her jaw. 'And what of you, my lord? Routes of long-distance shipping lines and maps of the English countryside. And botanicals of much the same ilk as mine. Are you ill?'

Amazingly he coloured and looked away.

'No.'

A private worry, then, and one he did not wish to speak of? She had so often seen this reaction in patients and as surprising as it was in him she changed the subject completely.

'Would you be able to find the time to teach me how to ride properly, Lord Wesley?'

His eyes came back to hers, any hint of embarrassment gone. 'Why?'

'I dislike feeling...beaten by anything and you give the impression of knowing what you are doing around a horse.'

His frown deepened. 'Your uncle would allow it? My tuition, I mean.'

'Why should he not?'

'I have a certain reputation that generally worries the relatives of young débutantes.'

'I am not so young.'

He laughed. 'How old is "not young"?'

'Twenty-three.'

He laughed again. 'Believe me when I say that at my age your years look tender.'

'How old are you?'

'Thirty-four. A whole decade of experience ahead of yours.'

'Good.'

'Pardon?'

'I might need that if I am to cope here. Experience in handling others seems a requisite that is useful in the society salons of London.'

'Well, you managed Mr Friar on your own?'

She shook her head. 'No, it was the ill-placed plant holder at his feet that enabled me to vanquish him.'

'Luck is often as important as talent, Miss Ashfield, one learns that quickly.'

'Then I shall claim it was lucky that I met you, my lord; the one man in society with whom I seem to be able to have a reasonable conversation and who holds the same view upon marriage as I do.'

'Let me choose the horse, then.'

The twist in subject made her smile. He was good at putting people off guard. Unsure of what else to say, she nodded.

'Meet me in the park tomorrow at two. It won't be as busy as yesterday was at the later hour.'

'Very well. I shall pay you, of course, for the hire of the small and docile mount I have confidence you will choose for me and for your time.'

He smiled. 'How much?'

'I do not know exactly. What is the going rate?'

'More conversations just like this one, Miss Ashfield. And the chance to get to know you better.'

'Why would you want to?'

He smiled. 'You might be surprised if I answered that honestly.'

For just a moment something passed between them that Adelaide had never felt before, a breathless whirling knowledge of danger and desire. She stepped back, marvelling that, despite her shock, the implacable mask had not changed a whit on his handsome face.

'Perhaps, Lord Wesley, some time in your company may tarnish my desirability in the wifely stakes here. The spectacles do not quite seem to be accomplishing their given task.'

The round curse he used made her turn with her armful of books and head back into the safety that the large numbers of men and women reading provided in the main room.

Damn it. Why did Gabriel Hughes have to be so beautiful? She would have liked it better if his face had been flawed and if she did not see the shadow of vulnerability that he hid so well beneath bravado and indifference. It was a friend she needed here, a confidant who was easy and biddable, one whom she could mould to any form she wanted. But the enigmatic Earl of Wesley was complex, difficult and unknowable, the small scar that ran beneath his ear on the right side only honing his beauty. He was…misleading. Yes, that was the word she wanted. Charm and danger both twisted together in a clever and menacing way. He was also interesting. Not wishing to dissect this thought for another second, she hurried to find her maid.

* * *

Miss Adelaide Ashfield was always running away, always scurrying in the other direction after sending him into a spin with some new and unexpected comment.

She wished to be tarnished? By him? Pain sliced through humour and regret chased hard on the heels of them both. He had not touched her but, oh, how he had wanted to, to feel the smooth softness of skin and the elegance of the line where her throat met the flesh sloping down to her breasts. He stopped still and closed his eyes. Waiting. Hoping. The whisper of her words, the fire in her eyes, her sharp tongue and the girlish romances buried amongst a weighty pile of scientific endeavour.

Contradictions.

Questions.

And nothing at all from his desiccated and useless member. Raising his left hand to his face, he breathed in deeply.

Lavender, arnica, comfrey and vinegar. A surprising combination. There were other things as well that he had no notion of.

'Hell,' he said to himself, Miss Adelaide Ashfield was the human embodiment of her salve. A healer. Brave. Unusual. Captivating. No wonder she had Lovelace and his ilk lapping at her heels.

He should cry off from the riding lessons, he knew he should. If he had any goodness in him he would simply walk out of her life and let her get on with the task of being an innocent and unwilling débutante in

London society. He had nothing to offer her, after all.
More than nothing, he qualified, his body as burnt
out as his custodial mansion.

Yet as one side of his mind dwelled upon the negative the other was already planning where and when
he could organise their first riding lesson.

With irritation he felt the trembling he was now
so often afflicted with. He didn't want her to know
what a wreck he was, that was the problem, because
in her eyes he saw reflected a version of himself that
was still...honourable.

'Hell. Hell. Hell.'

With intent he moved the large map from above
the botanical he had chosen on diseases of the body
and settled down to peruse the index and look for his
own particular malady and its stated cure.

Adelaide brushed out her hair before the mirror.
What did Gabriel Hughes see when he saw her? she
wondered. She was not beautiful in the way some
other women here were, with their blond curls and alabaster skin. She was not dainty or feminine or curvy.

Brown. That was a word she might use to describe
herself. Plain was another. She had not learned the
art of flirting or dancing or conversing with a man
as though everything he said was right and true and
exact. Others here had that knack, she had watched
them. The quiet flick of a fan and the twirling of an
errant curl; the breathless looks that would reel a man
in to produce the long sought-after offer of a hand in
marriage.

Like a game. How often had Eloise or Jean told her of this and underlined the consequences marriage wrought on a woman's independence and pathway in life.

Kenneth Davis, the third-born son of Sir Nigel Davis, a squire on a neighbouring property, had then brought every warning to life. Adelaide shook her head, her eyes in the mirror darkening. She would try not to think of him.

It wasn't running away, she said to herself. No, rather it was protecting her uncle and her cousin and the name of Penbury from a man who had clearly taken her offer of friendship and changed it into something that was different.

She hadn't told a soul other than her aunt Eloise about their exchange, either, preferring instead to sink back into the sanctuary of Northbridge and to the comforting other world of solitude. But sometimes at night when the moon was full and the land was covered in bright shadow she remembered.

She had been sixteen years old when she met Kenneth Davis behind the stables at midnight, creeping from her room with all the delight of one who expected compliments and perhaps a kiss. Small and trifling objects of his affection and regard.

The man who had met her was not the one she had known in the daytime, and when he had pulled at her gown and ripped it to her waist in one single dreadful movement, she was so frozen in shock that she could not even fight back.

Until his teeth bit at her nipples and his free hand

seized the softer flesh beneath her skirt, his touch as unexpected and painful as the one at her breast. When she had tried to scream for help he had placed his hand across her mouth and pressed down hard.

'No more pretending, my sweetling. I have courted you for three whole months in all the small ways, but the real pleasure is here and now, in the dark.' His fingers came between her thighs, sharp and prodding, and the wine on his breath was strong as he swore.

He was drunk.

Drunk and dangerous and different.

In earnest she began to struggle, her knee coming up in the way Bertie had shown her, angled hard and direct to the groin. Kenneth Davis had fallen as if by magic, his mouth open, his breeches grotesquely arranged around his ankles so that the skin of his naked round bottom was pale in the moonlight.

Then she had run, with her tattered bodice, aching breasts and ruin, the stupidity of what she had allowed him beating against her reason. Tears could wait until she had once again gained the safety of her room and locked the door behind her.

Once there she had simply collapsed against the solidness of the wood, her legs like jelly as shock brought on a shaking and she had thoroughly gone to pieces.

She had made a mistake that was monumental and prodigious and far reaching in its consequences. Would Kenneth Davis tell anyone? Was she ravaged? Would she now have to marry a man she hated to the very last fibre of her being? What would her uncle say or her aunts?

This edge of horror was now the truth of her life as the scratches on her right breast throbbed in pain, burning as the night-time faded into dawn.

Aunt Eloise had found her in the morning, cold and stiff, and she had bathed her and dressed her and counselled silence.

'There is no way that you can win a war such as this one, Addie,' she had crooned as she pulled back the blankets and put her to bed. 'This is a truth women of all the ages have known.'

And so nothing had been said and life had regained its patterns and gone on.

In a different way for her, though. Fright filled the cracks of silence and Adelaide made certain that she was never far from her two old aunts. Nightmares replaced dreams, too, and for a good year afterwards she had barely slept.

Then Eloise and Jean had begun to teach her the art of healing, and in the elixirs and tinctures and ointments she had regained a peace long missing and a sense of herself that she had thought was lost.

Aye, in her reflection sometimes she still saw it, that terror and panic, but mostly now it was hidden under calm and manners, only a small ripple of a previous disquiet and seldom on show. Kenneth Davis himself had left summarily on an extended sojourn to Europe. She often wondered if his father had known something of his son's propensity for damage and drunkenness and had exiled him.

Almost eight years ago now, she whispered to herself. A day, a week, a month, a year. She had written down the passage of time as a list in her diaries, counting days and taking comfort from the distance and number as each year marched on. But she had never truly forgotten the horror and her uncle and cousin were the only men she allowed herself ever to be alone with.

But who was she now, she wondered, her eyes meeting the reflection in the silvered glass. Did a lack of trust hold one prisoner for ever, locked into celibacy and destined for spinsterhood?

'Please,' she whispered and then stopped. What was it she was asking for? The curl of hope turned inside darkness, like a frond of some fern in a deep and far-off forest. Nascent. Plump. Moving against shadow. Unfurling against Gabriel Hughes.

Because of his humour and kindness and beauty. His hands around her waist as he had helped her from the horse, his wariness in the library when she had asked him why he was reading a botanical, his lazy drawl as he had taken the pulse at George Friar's neck and commented on his appalling clothing.

She smiled. She would meet him again tomorrow in the park. At two. Her uncle had been surprisingly acquiescent. She had brought riding outfits down from Northbridge and, crossing the room, she opened the cupboard to bring them out across the bed.

Taking the shirt from one, she added it to the jacket of another. Finding a pin of bright red rubies, she placed it across the frothy collar. With her riding skirt this would look well upon her. She wondered if the hat she chose was not too…formal, but added it anyway as she had always liked the dark blue of the velvet.

Her fingers brushed up against the grain, the lush fabric a present from her uncle a year or so before. Her father's brother was a good man and he meant well. He would stay true to his word of allowing her home after the twelve weeks of Season, but just for a moment she wondered what might come to pass in the time left of her London stay. Gabriel Hughes's heartbreaking smile flashed into her memory.

Adelaide Ashfield's hands tightened on the leather reins with such a force that all her knuckles turned white.

'Fear looks like that, Miss Ashfield.' Gabriel pointed to the stiffness in her fingers. 'Demeter will know you tremble through the leather and it'll worry her.' Reaching up, he released the reins. 'Just grip like this and let the leather run over the top. See? Then cup them so that there is space to move.'

'She won't pull away?'

'Try it.'

'Now?'

'I am here beside you. Walk around the pathway and if she becomes fidgety I will stop her.'

She nodded, though Gabriel could see her composure was taking some effort.

'After the other day, riding a horse does not feel as safe as it should.'

'The steed you nearly fell from was largely untrained. Does your uncle have no idea of an animal's temperament or of your ability to manage one?'

'Well, he rides sometimes, but, no, I suppose there is not much need for expertise at Northbridge because we seldom venture out further than the village.'

As the mount began to move she took in a hard breath.

'This isn't the small and docile steed I had imagined you might pick for me, Lord Wesley. Did you get her at Coles?'

'No, she's mine.'

'Oh. No wonder she is so beautiful, then.'

He began to laugh. 'You think I only keep attractive horses in my stable?'

'Well, rumour has it you are a man of good taste… in whatever you try.'

'The titter-tattle of the *ton* in play, no doubt. Wait till you hear what else is said of me. Ahh, but I can see from your face that you have. Bear it in mind that my reputation is one magnified by the interest in it and if I had slept with every woman I am said to have I'd have barely been out of bed. These days I am far more circumspect.'

She looked at him directly then, censure in the water-marked blue. 'Brothels are not more circumspect, my lord, in anyone's language.'

A thread of irritation surfaced. 'The tongues of those with little to recommend them save gossip are seldom still. If you could take it on yourself to disbelieve at least half of what is said of me, the picture might be a truer one.'

'An angel, then? The personification of your name?' Her irony was harsh.

'Hardly that. Were I to proffer an excuse at all it would probably be a lack of paternal guidance. My father was a violent drunk.'

'Well, at least you had one. Mine was killed when I was not yet four years old.'

'*Touché*, Miss Ashfield. Has anyone ever told you that you are beautiful when you are angry?'

The wash of red caught him by surprise. Her blush was intense and unsettling and wide eyes stood out amidst it.

'No, of course not. And they would be lying if they did. I am not beautiful, Lord Wesley, not in the way the *ton* defines beauty and I have no wish to be. Passable is all that I aim for. And interesting,' she added, her top teeth worrying her bottom lip after she had said it.

Despite meaning not to his hand reached out for the arm nearest to him and he laid his fingers across hers. 'If you think I was lying, then you have no knowledge of me at all, Miss Ashfield.'

The park around them dissolved into empty space and without warning a feeling that Gabriel had long since thought dead, rose. It was so unexpected that the world disappeared into whiteness, the dizzying bout of relief making him sway, an unusual heat creeping into the very bones of emotion and wringing out the bitterness.

'God.' The breath was knocked out of his body in shock and confusion.

Adelaide Ashfield was off her horse in a second, a dismount that was as rapid and competent as any he had ever seen.

'Are you well, Lord Wesley?'

He held his fists so tightly curled that they hurt.

'I…am.' Fighting to get the words out, he closed his eyes. Not panic now, but sheer and utter relief. If he could feel like this once, then it stood to reason he could do so again. He swallowed back a thickness and took in air, reaching for the return of that he had imagined never to know again.

'If you describe your symptoms to me, I am more than certain I could find something to help you?'

The laughter in his throat warred with a heady disbelief and that in turn was swallowed by a certain and horrifying realisation.

She had no idea what she was doing to him, this unusual and tall country miss with her ocean-blue eyes and honesty. Already she was digging into the pocket of her skirt to bring forth a twist of powder that was the colour of mud.

'I had this on hand for myself, my lord. Lightheadedness comes from fear, you see, and I imagined I may have had need for it. But you…?'

He shook his head, not wishing for any medicine that might eliminate the effect of warm blood on his masculinity. 'Perhaps we might…postpone this riding…lesson, then, until another day…Miss Ashfield.' Sweat had begun to build above his top lip and temples.

'You are too overheated?' Her face looked aghast.

'Just…breathless.' Each word took effort, and, gesturing to the maid who sat on a bench twenty feet from them, he moved back, the reins of his horses in his hands held as tightly as he had been instructing her not to.

And then he was off his horse, walking, striding towards the park gate and glad that the pathway out of the gardens was clear.

Once through them, he stopped. What the hell had just happened? He wanted to go back and try again, take her hand and see if perhaps the feeling might grow and blossom into the hope of more. A proper erection. The return of his libido. But he couldn't. Cowardice had a certain all-consuming feel to it and if it was an illusion, then…? He shook his head and mounted his horse for home.

Adelaide watched him go, her brow knitted in worry. She hadn't a clue as to what was wrong with Lord Wesley, but the colour had flooded from his face as if sudden pain had consumed him and he had swayed so markedly she had thought he would faint.

If Aunt Eloise and Aunt Jean were here they would have probably known his troubles exactly, but they were long gone.

Milly stood watching him, too, puzzlement on her face. 'Perhaps his lordship is still hurt from the incident with the horse in the park the other day, ma'am, and is not telling us.'

Or he is truly sick, she thought, her worry growing. The botanical she had seen him reading in Lackington's was a sign of something not being right and his symptoms here underlined that fact.

She had enough experience to also know some men loathed discussing any ailment they suffered with a woman, and the knowledge that she was not a trained healer would be a further deterrent. Still, a small sense of sorrow stirred in such a lack of trust.

'Say nothing of this to my uncle, Milly. I am certain once the earl is feeling better we can continue the lessons.'

Chapter Seven

Once home Gabriel helped himself to a stiff brandy and sat down to mull over his afternoon.

He had felt something there in the parts of him that had been numb and dead for a full six months. He could barely believe it. Was he cured? Was this the beginning of a healing he had been so certain was beyond hope?

It had begun the moment he had laid his fingers down across hers and felt an answering tug that had been soft and gentle. Unexpected. Impossibly real. Not the full-blown nakedness of practised courtesans or the come-hither sexual play of a country whore. Just a gentle quiet gesture in the middle of a busy park.

He closed his eyes and breathed in hard.

How was that even possible?

A knock on the door had him standing as his butler announced there was a visitor. Not just any visitor, either, but Mrs Cressida Murray and newly returned from the north. Cressie and he had once been lovers before she had left for Yorkshire and a marriage with a local landowner of some note.

Her face, as she came into the room, was as beautiful as he remembered it to be, though her eyes were somewhat reddened. 'I am sorry to bother you, Wesley, but I had no one else that I could turn to and I need help.'

She removed her coat when he failed to reply and her breasts almost sprang from the very low neckline of a deep red day dress. Then she flung herself into his arms and kissed him full on the lips.

Nothing. He felt nothing. His stomach did not turn with the sickness and his heart failed to pound with the closeness. A new development, this. A further difference in the reactions of his body. Today was one of such constant surprise he could barely keep up.

'It is so very good to see you again, Gabriel.'

Smiling through unease, he extricated himself from her grasp and turned to pour them both a drink. The strong brandy made him feel less edgy.

With the intimacy of Cressida Murray's kiss, and after his encounter with Adelaide Ashfield, he might have expected some warming, but there had been none. Another problem. A further disquiet? One moment hot and the next cold and no middle ground where compromise could result in a cure? Shaking away the thought, he made himself concentrate on what his unexpected visitor was saying.

'I have come because I need a partner for the Whitely ball and I want him to be you.'

'Why?'

'My husband has cheated on me and I have reached the conclusion that if he wants to play at this game then he needs to know I can, too.' Her voice wobbled as she went on. 'I think he needs to know that I am a beautiful woman whom he is lucky to be married to, a woman whom he should not leave alone up in the wilds of Yorkshire whilst he cavorts with others here.'

There was something in her voice that held Gabriel's attention, some quiet and vulnerable honesty. After his shock today he was more in tune with the nuances in others. He waited as she went on.

'I love him. For his good points and his bad, but this...dalliance in London needs to stop. He needs to come home to Yorkshire and give our marriage a chance again.'

Without warning Cressida went to pieces, her tears and sobs filling the room. With trepidation Gabriel moved forward to hold her, till the storm had passed and she had quietened, pleased again when her closeness did not seem to affect him in the slightest. After a good few moments she looked up at him through tear-filled eyes.

'You were always the sort of man that women truly liked, Gabriel, and not only for the way you look. Gavin and I are...having problems and I could not think of anyone else to come to for help without it being all over town come the morning. I need a companion who is attentive and well regarded by the ladies. One who might make my husband jealous without expecting anything in return.'

'So you want me to…?' He stopped, leaving the question in the air.

'Flirt with me at the Whitely ball and dance at least twice with me.'

He began to laugh. 'And will I be called out at dawn by this husband of yours because of it?'

'Oh, if he did do that it would be wonderful, but I wouldn't like you to shoot him or anything.'

Gabriel had to smile at her convoluted reasoning. 'He's a big man, if I recall…'

'But clumsy with it.'

'And he has numerous brothers?'

She nodded. 'Four, but I cannot envisage him ever hurting a soul. Please, Gabriel. You owe me this one favour at least.'

'I do?' He tried to think of why.

'You left me with barely a word. That hurt. A lot. And the one promise you did make before you disappeared was that you were sorry and that if there was anything you could do to make things easier…' She stopped. 'This is the thing you can do to make it easier. I am calling in the favour.'

'I see.'

'Do you? You broke my heart once and Gavin put it back together again. You have no idea of your effect on women and you have never once really been so much in love that you care.'

Her words cut into the quick of truth. Henrietta Clements had said almost the same thing to him and the guilt stung. He couldn't ever make it up to her, but here with Cressida he had the chance of redemption.

'God. I can think of a hundred reasons why this scheme of yours will not work.'

Warm fingers came into the cold of his palm. 'But you will try?'

Adelaide and her uncle and chaperon arrived a lot later at the Whitely ball than they had intended to, Lady Harcourt's brother having visited in the afternoon and staying on until well after dinner.

The theme of the soirée was an underwater one with long strands of shiny green silk hanging from the ceiling around all the four walls of the room. With the lighting dimmed and the chandeliers painted blue the whole place appeared almost unreal. Huge statues of sea gods graced the room; Neptune seated in a shell pulled by seahorses, the goddesses behind with the Tritons and other various nymphs. Fish sculpted from blocks of ice sat on the many scattered tables.

Adelaide had never seen anything remotely like this excess before and even Imelda was speechless as they walked through into the throngs of people.

'Lady Whitely has quite outdone herself this year, I think. Rumour has it that it might be their last big party so we are so lucky to be a part of it. Something to remember with a thrill, I think, my dear. I know I shall.'

The crush tonight was far more noticeable than it had been all Season and it was hard to even move from one side of the room to the other.

'Should you not miss this sort of excitement if you do decide to return to Northbridge, Adelaide?'

Her uncle asked the question, his interest in her answer obvious.

'Indeed, there is something to be said of the scope and wonder of the London soirées. But perhaps after a while a certain indifference might set in.'

Alec laughed and gestured to a passing footman to bring them each a drink.

Adelaide looked around to see whether the Earl of Wesley was in attendance, but she could not see him at all. The room was a large one, but partitions divided it into two and she wondered if he could be further down towards a band she could hear playing. Standing on her toes, she tried to see if she could find him.

'Who are you looking for?' Imelda Harcourt raised her lorgnette. 'Ahhh, there is Berrick, my dear, and he does look well tonight. Why, I do believe he is coming our way. Smile, Adelaide. Men like to see a welcoming face, not a dour one, and you look so much prettier when you are happy.'

If Eloise or Jean could have heard such advice they would have been far from pleasant, but the guileless and earnest way her chaperon expressed such a sentiment made Adelaide smile. Lady Harcourt honestly believed that she was helping, that a woman's role was as an adjunct to a well-connected and wealthy man and that a good marriage made the whole world right.

This was the way of London society. A way to survive and prosper and never let those from the strata below gain a foot up in the world. Solidarity and isolation buoyed by the cohesiveness of the *ton*.

As the Earl of Berrick joined them Adelaide took in breath and made a conscious effort to be at least polite.

She did not see Lord Wesley until almost halfway through the night and any joy that she had from noticing him was snatched away by the beautiful girl beside him, his hand resting lightly on the sway of her back.

She was like a porcelain doll, with blond hair arranged into a cascade of curls, brown eyes that sparkled even from this distance and a dress that mirrored the theme of the evening. Blue-green shots of silk radiated around her and Adelaide gained the impression of a sea creature long hidden and suddenly revealed in exactly the setting she should be.

A large crowd had gathered about them and when the woman's hand crept into the crook of Gabriel Hughes's arm, he laid his own across it in return.

They were so perfectly matched Adelaide could not look away though her heart was thumping in a fashion that she did not like. Almost scared, she thought. Of what?

'Mrs Gavin Murray is back, I see.' Even Imelda for all her short-sightedness had noticed the couple. 'I knew her mother once and what a time she had with that girl, I can tell you.'

'She is very beautiful.'

Imelda nodded. 'Yes, that she is and strong willed with it. It seems the marriage to her Yorkshire beau has come to nothing, then, and she has her talons into the Earl of Wesley once more.'

Her uncle then asked the question Adelaide wanted to.

'Once more?'

'They were an item a few years back and all thought the banns would be called and the deed done. But Lord Wesley went off to the Continent and she disappeared up north and the next thing we knew she had tied the knot with a Mr Gavin Murray. No connection to the Murrays of the *ton*, either, but rich in their own right. Her mother was not pleased, but in the light of the Wesley family fire and its failing fortunes perhaps Cressida made a wise choice...then.'

'The Wesleys had a fire?' Adelaide did not wait for her uncle to ask a further question.

'The family manor of Ravenshill was damaged badly six or so months back and if gossip is to be believed they have not the wherewithal to have it rebuilt. It is why Lord Wesley is here, I suppose. He has finally been brought to the heel of Holy Matrimony by the dire circumstances of an expected financial ruin. Cressida Murray is, however, a poor choice given every other wealthy and unattached woman in the room would probably take him in an instant. Beauty has a certain allure, you understand, but I doubt even with a ring on his finger Gabriel Hughes would have the wherewithal to be faithful.'

Suddenly collecting herself, Imelda Harcourt snapped open her fan. 'His grandfather, Lytton Hughes, was just the same. Every judicious and level-headed girl in court was made half-witted by him and it is happening again. Here.'

A slight stammer led Adelaide to believe the older Hughes patriarch had been important to Imelda somehow.

'The Wesley men are like well-formed rainbows, capturing everyone's notice, but disappearing at the first sign of permanence. Mark my words, Lord Wesley will take what is on offer and then he will leave.'

When Adelaide looked over towards the couple it certainly did seem as though the earl was enjoying himself. He was leading Cressida Murray into a dance now, a waltz, and when he pulled her into his arms there was no space left between them.

Looking away, she was angry with herself for this close observation. Of course a man like Gabriel Hughes would choose a woman of the same ilk: magnificent, resplendent and striking.

Lucy Carrigan chose that moment to come forward and speak and when she saw where Adelaide had been gazing she shook her head.

'They have been the talk of the ball all night because the Earl of Wesley has hardly been a foot from her side. Her husband has just arrived, too, if you can believe it, and yet still she has no shame.'

'Husband. My God.' Adelaide glanced around in consternation. Even given the dubious standards of behaviour amongst the very wealthy of the *ton* she could not imagine this to be...acceptable. 'Where is he?'

'The dark-haired man over there by the pillar with a face of thunder.'

'The man standing in the company of two others all of the same build and colouring?'

Lucy nodded. 'His brothers, and they do not look remotely happy.'

The crush seemed to be the only thing that was saving a skirmish, a hundred bodies between adversaries and a good few moments of pushing.

As Adelaide took in a breath the golden glance of Lord Wesley fell directly upon her before sliding away. No recognition or humour was apparent in his hard and glittering observation. In fact, he looked furious.

Damn it. Adelaide Ashfield was here. Watching him like half of the *ton* was with bated breath and undeniable interest. He had hoped against hope that Adelaide might not have attended tonight but been elsewhere instead.

It was not every day, after all, that a love triangle was played out in such an obvious public space. God, if he had been them he'd probably be looking, too. But for a second the smile on his face faltered. He didn't want Adelaide here watching this and there was no way now he could insist on it being any different.

'My husband is coming over, Gabe.' Cressida whispered this into his ear. 'Remember that no matter what happens you promised me you would not hurt him.'

The stakes rose again, an assurance of non-action

balanced against the safety of those around them and weighed out in the presence of Murray and his two brothers. Nay, three, he amended as the third burly Murray joined the group.

If he had any sense he would leave now, simply turn and make his way out of the room with his tail between his legs and his face intact.

But other things also mattered. His honour. His troth to Cressida and the ignominy that such a cowardly retreat might paint in the eyes of Miss Adelaide Ashfield.

Around them space had opened, an amazing feat in itself given the numbers in the room. A footman dressed as a sea sprite and carrying a well-stocked tray tottered through the emptiness with no inkling of the tension. Gabriel pushed down the need for a drink. If he was to have his teeth knocked out by the jealous fit of a furious husband, he did not want to be holding crystal.

'Gavin.' Cressida's voice was breathless as her unhappy spouse came to a halt in front of them, her hand dropping from Gabriel's arm.

'I have come to take you home.' Murray's tone was anything but friendly.

'To Yorkshire?' Gabriel could hear the hope in Cressida's words, but the dolt of a man seemed to miss it altogether, simply striding forward and laying a heavy blow to his right eye.

At any other time Gabriel would have fought back with ease. He prayed that the brothers might get involved because he hadn't made a troth concerning them and was itching to beat someone up as the full force of pain kicked in.

The second blow was delivered to his mouth and he could taste blood as he went down, the third landing squarely on his temple and blackening his vision.

Cressida, to give her some credit, leant towards him and whispered, 'I am so sorry, Gabriel. If you stay still, he is not a man to kick someone when they are vanquished.' But Gabriel could not have moved if he had tried, the breath gone from him. As she turned to join her husband, Gavin Murray did away with any last shred of humanity and lashed out with his boot, connecting heavily with the soft tissue of Gabriel's back.

Then they left, heads held high as they threaded through the crowd, Cressida tucked within them like a diminutive and valued prize that the Murrays had come to collect.

The green light and the sea creatures swam before him in a dizzying blur, the pain of the blows setting in and making him shake. Then there was a hand on his brow and the soft words of Miss Adelaide Ashfield in his ear.

'You should have fought back, Lord Wesley. There was no reason for you not to.'

Gabriel swallowed and then spat. Blood dripped from his nose and his mouth, the sour tang of copper out of place here amongst luxury and excess.

'Don't stay here, Adelaide. It is too dangerous for you.'

Already he could hear the whispers all around and the hem of her skirt was splattered with red.

'But you are hurt and I can help.'

He shook his head. 'If you stand and leave now, your reputation may not quite be ruined. Please.'

He watched the worry in her eyes turn into anger.

And then she was gone, the blue of her gown disappearing between the legs and skirts of all those within his vision, the floor slippery with his own blood as he sat up, trying not to look at anyone.

Alone.

This is what his life had felt like for so very long. The fury within him vibrated as he made himself stand and walk from the room.

'Why would you even think to interfere, Adelaide? You must have realised what a scandal Wesley had caused and how fitting his punishment was. And now you have placed yourself at risk and at peril, an accessory to the fact of marital disharmony and your dress ruined.'

Her uncle was furious, though Imelda stayed very quiet on the other side of the carriage, her fingers tightly wrapped around the stem of an ancient silver cane.

'Why on earth did you try to help him? You, a débutante, a young woman, a girl of grace and tender years? What possible thought could have been going through your head to imagine you should be the one to do this?'

'No one else was, Uncle.'

Alec laughed at that, but the sound wasn't kind. 'Perhaps, after all, you should not have come to London. Perhaps I should have allowed you to stay at Sherborne and live the sort of life your aunts favoured because now...' he faltered '...because now I do not know what to do.'

Imelda chose that moment to add her twopenn'orth.

'We can wait to see how the land lies in the morning, Penbury. Adelaide's foolish reaction may after all be attributed to a kind heart or an innocent foolishness. There may be some dividend in that.'

'Dividend? Did you see the other girls rush forward? No. They were far too sensible to get themselves embroiled in such a scandal. Lord Wesley is trouble with his wild ways and insolence and good common sense has taught them to keep well clear of a man who ruins everything he touches.'

'He was not the one throwing the punches, Uncle.'

'Because he knew he was in the wrong. God binds a man and a woman together for eternity in marriage and only a dissolute womaniser would want to interfere with that.'

Her uncle looked out the window after this outburst and Adelaide did the same. The lights of London flickered by in myriad colours, the streets almost empty of people as bells somewhere rang out the late hour of two. In the reflection of the glass she could see the stilled outline of Alec and the smaller form of Lady Harcourt. Her own face, too, was mirrored back, her hair tied in an intricate form that had taken her maid, Milly, an hour to secure.

For nothing. For disaster. She wondered what had happened after they had left. Had anyone helped Gabriel Hughes or had he limped off out of the mêlée with a curse? Or not left at all? Had worse things happened? Had the Murrays waited outside for him and beaten him again? Was he now lying somewhere no one could find him? She shook her head against such worries.

The Earl of Wesley had barely looked at her and he had been furious. He'd made no effort at all to protect himself, either in words or in actions, though she knew without any shadow of a doubt that he was nowhere near as civilised as he seemed. Why had he not fought back? Why had he allowed the husband of a woman he must have expected to confront him beat the daylights out of his non-resistance and so very publically? Nothing of it made any sense.

'Lord Berrick will probably withdraw his interest in courting you now.' Her uncle's words broke into the silence. 'And although your fortune is substantial, Adelaide, every family of the *ton* would shy away from a girl who shows such poor judgement in a social situation.'

'I see.'

'No, you don't, my dear.' A thread of cynicism that was unusual for Alec Ashfield could be heard in his words. 'With just a little good sense you could have made a glorious union and now…now they will all be fleeing and you will be left, unattached, unwanted and ill thought of. There is sadness in that which will become more poignant as you age and miss out on all the milestones of your counterparts.'

Adelaide frowned. In his words were the seeds of truth, she thought. Lady Imelda simply stared at her and said nothing.

Cressida Murray sent a note to his town house the next morning, the flourish of ink enquiring after his health and telling him that she would be leaving that day with her husband to go back to Yorkshire and that he was not to contact her again.

Gabriel screwed the paper up and threw it into the fire where the dainty sheet of paper was caught in orange flame and disappeared.

No doubt Gavin Murray had been present when she had written it, but he was glad for the closure. He now owed her nothing. A debt paid in full.

Crossing the room, he looked into the mirror and almost smiled at the face that stared back at him. Hardly recognisable, his left eye swollen closed and his lip split. But it was the bruise that spread from ear to cheek that was the most noticeable, a broken blood vessel that had marked and darkened the surrounding tissue.

Nothing that could not heal though, he thought, as he took Adelaide Ashfield's lavender concoction down from the shelf and layered it thickly over the places that hurt. The ointment had worked like magic on his knuckles and had eased some of the scarring on his thigh. He hoped it would do the same for his face.

He imagined the gossip that must be swirling

around the *ton* this morning after the spectacle last night. God, if he did not have his mother to look after and Ravenshill Manor to rebuild he'd be off on the next sailing to the Americas. Somewhere far and wild and free. Somewhere he could make his own way in a world not bound by propriety and manners and expectations.

A knock on the door had him looking up and Daniel Wylde and Lucien Howard both entered the room.

'Hope you don't mind the intrusion, Gabe. We heard about the altercation last night and came to see if you were still alive.'

'Just.'

The three of them smiled.

'From all accounts you simply allowed Murray to beat the daylights out of you?' The words were phrased as a question and as Gabriel pulled down three glasses and filled them with his best brandy, he nodded.

'I'd given my promise not to retaliate.'

'To Cressida Murray?'

'She loves her husband. I was caught up in the ruse of it.'

'Why?'

'I owed her—'

'Not that much, surely,' Lucien interrupted. 'And what the hell is on your face?'

'A lavender ointment Miss Ashfield made up for me.'

'Miss Adelaide Ashfield from Sherborne? The Penbury niece?'

'The same.'

'I hear she was the only one who tried to help you last night. Her reputation has fallen a little because of it. Seems as if she could well be packed off back to the country by her uncle, ruined by her ill-thought-out kindness.'

'Who told you that?'

'My mother over breakfast.' Lucien's words were quiet.

Daniel Wylde had the temerity to laugh. 'And the countess is always so well informed. Personally, I think Adelaide Ashfield's star may have risen for such actions prove only compassion and tender-heartedness. And bravery. On that score my wife would like for you to come to dinner tomorrow night, Gabriel. At the town house. She has told me that she will not brook a refusal and is down in London only for the week.'

'I am certain the *ton* would frown at her invite if they knew of it.'

'That's why she wants you to come. Amethyst seldom graces any society function. She is of the opinion that anyone who so flagrantly breaks the strict code of manners needs to be encouraged and expects you at eight. Luce is coming, and Francis. He is off to the Americas in a week or so, after the hope of gold and a clue he said you had given him.'

'The chancy pot at the end of a rainbow?'

'Not to St Cartmail.' Lucien's laughter was loud.

'You had better enlighten him, then, Gabe. For if he dies in his quest for gold his demise will be squarely on your head.' Daniel's interjection was measured.

'And if he discovers riches, will it be the same?' Gabriel finished his drink and placed the glass down half-on and half-off the edge of the mahogany table, teetering between safety and peril. 'There is risk in everything. Take that away and life goes, too.'

'The philosophy of jeopardy? Stated like a man with nothing to lose.' Lucien sounded like he was out of patience and Daniel took over.

'Come tomorrow night at eight, then. Bring a bottle or two of this brandy.'

'I doubt Amethyst would want to gaze at my face in this condition. It would probably put her off her food.'

'Nothing much could do that at the moment, Gabe. She is heavily pregnant with our second child and starving.'

'And you have only been married a little under two years.'

'Amethyst wants our brood to meet their grandfather before he dies. If Robert lives for ever, which he looks likely to do despite his heart condition, we will be overrun with progeny. Not that I am complaining.'

And he wasn't, Gabriel thought. Daniel Wylde was a man with a family and a place and a wife who was unusual and interesting. He had not stuck to the rules of the *ton*, but lived outside of them well and happily.

Perhaps he could do the same?

'Could an invite be sent to Miss Adelaide Ashfield as well? I should like to apologise to her for the problems that I have caused her and I doubt the Viscount of Penbury will allow me anywhere near the house now.'

'It can.' In the two words Gabriel heard both humour and question, but he chose to ignore it.

Chapter Eight

An invitation arrived for Adelaide just after lunch, the Wyldes' servant waiting at the front door for an answer.

'The Earl of Montcliffe and his wife have invited you for dinner tomorrow night?' Her uncle was incredulous. 'Have they not heard of the problems at the Whitely ball?'

Imelda broke in. 'Daniel Wylde and his new wife seldom come to anything in London. I hear they spend most of their time in the family seat outside of Barnet, but they are respectable and well thought of. Lady Montcliffe is from trade, of course, though extremely rich in her own right. As I have not heard a bad word about them perhaps we should view this as a chance of…reinstating your niece's reputation in society.'

'She'd need to be chaperoned.'

'Bertram could accompany her. He is an acquaintance of Wylde, after all, and it is well past time to allow him some familial responsibility.'

Adelaide's heart beat faster. Lord Montcliffe was also a friend of Lord Wesley. Had Gabriel Hughes been invited, too? Without Imelda Harcourt there and with her cousin in tow she might be given a greater amount of freedom to speak with him. She waited to see what her uncle might say.

'Very well. As you so rightly argue, Imelda, this might be a way to restore yourself, Adelaide. Pray this time you will remember all your manners and responsibilities to our family name. I will instruct Bertram to return you home by twelve.'

'Thank you, Uncle.' She tried to keep gratitude from her voice and made an effort to avert her eyes lest Alec see the spark of excitement that she knew would be within them and change his mind completely.

Gabriel followed Daniel Wylde as he ushered him into a salon at the front of the house. It was a familiar room. Once a good few years back this had been like a second home to him but then Daniel had been called off to the Peninsular War and Gabriel had met Henrietta.

Amethyst Wylde stood to greet him as he came into the chamber. On the few occasions he had met her Gabriel had found her to be a woman of wit and cleverness who seemed to have little time for the inconsequential chatter and precise manners of the *ton*.

'Lord Wesley, it is good to see you again.' As her eyes ran over his face she did not look away. Rather she observed each injury closely. 'Christine Howard is adamant Gavin Murray is a bully and a cheat. She also swears that his wife would have been much better off under your protection.'

Gabriel smiled. 'I beg to disagree, my lady. Beating him into a pulp would not have solved a thing.'

'So you allowed him to beat you into a pulp instead?'

The anger expressed on his behalf was surprising and he smiled. 'Perhaps I did.'

'Well, then, let us just pray that your sacrifice might count for something. A man who kicks another whilst down and out must have his own set of dubious morals. An uneasy and dangerous fault to live with, I should imagine, for Mrs Cressida Murray.'

Gabriel had the feeling Daniel Wylde was listening carefully, though the way he looked at his wife and took her hand had him glancing away. Solidarity and unity had a certain heat to it. A conversation from an adjoining room suddenly caught his attention.

'Lucien and Francis are here, too, Gabriel as well as Miss Ashfield and her cousin Bertram Ashfield. There will be seven of us altogether because Lucien has brought his sister, Christine.'

Adelaide was in the next salon? So she had come? Sweeping back the length of his unruly hair, Gabriel followed his hosts through the open doors.

She was sitting on the sofa when he saw her, but she stood almost immediately, wide blue eyes through glass taking in the bruising on his cheek in that particular way she had of noticing things.

'Miss Ashfield.'

'Lord Wesley.' Stiff and uncertain. He was careful not to reach out for her hand or make any effort to touch her in such a public domain.

'I hope you thought to use my ointment on your face, my lord?'

Before he could answer Bertram Ashfield spoke. 'Addie is a wizard at the art of healing. Our old and unmarried aunts were the same and she has followed their example.'

Addie. Gabriel turned the name on his tongue— a family nickname that suited her entirely. But her cousin was not yet finished.

'At Sherborne, Adelaide has a clinic that is always full of those interested in her concoctions. I think she could make a fortune if she were to set up a business for the dispensing of medicines.'

'Well, we could certainly do with that.' Francis's interjection made Lucien laugh. When Adelaide looked puzzled, Francis St Cartmail continued on to explain.

'We call ourselves "The Penniless Lords", Miss Ashfield. A half joke at our expense, I know, although Daniel has seen fit to remedy his desperate circumstances and in the nicest way possible.'

Amethyst Wylde took up the cause. 'If I had sisters, I should send them straight into your direction, Francis.' Her eyes alighted on Adelaide. 'You have a fortune, do you not, Miss Ashfield? Perhaps one of these lords might catch your eye?'

Unbelievably Adelaide blushed a bright red, though Amethyst quickly spoke again as if to take attention from her. 'I have a garden at Montcliffe you might be interested in. It has a large variety of different herbs and flowers and you would be most welcome to gather any specimens that caught your fancy. I know if one is passionate about a subject one is always on the lookout for new and different material. My papa is like that. Timber is his love and he can seldom pass a mill without going in to see what is on offer. Daniel's is horses.'

Bertram Ashfield was quick to catch on to the new subject and after a moment the group split and Gabriel stood alone with Adelaide.

'I am glad to see you here, my lord. I expected at least some broken bones.'

'Oh, I have a knack at fending off blows, Miss Ashfield, and surviving them.'

'I have heard it mentioned that you were a champion at the sport of sparring'

'That was some while ago. I have not pursued the activity for years.'

'Still, it must be like horse riding. Once learned, never forgotten.'

He smiled. 'What is it you are trying to say, Adelaide?'

The use of her Christian name seemed to take her by surprise because the same flush from before spread across her cheeks.

'I want to know why you didn't retaliate against Mr Murray in the crowded ballroom?'

'Because I had made a promise not to.'

'A promise to his wife?'

He smiled at her quickness. 'Cressida Murray's husband had been caught cheating. She wanted to encourage him back.'

'By sleeping with you?'

No other woman of his acquaintance would have voiced such a question, but there was something in Adelaide Ashfield that was different. 'Hardly. It was jealousy she was after.'

Blue eyes blazed. 'Asking for such an impossible favour implies more than a passing friendship between you, my lord.'

He looked her directly. 'I hurt her once, badly. Perhaps I deserved it.'

A small frown played about her brow. 'One cannot always be responsible for the feelings of others, sir. Revenge lies in one's own hands, I would hope, and not in the battered face of a former lover caught under an unreasonable promise.'

'You think penance is unreasonable, then, in the repayment of a debt?'

'Her penance or yours?'

Hell. Could mind reading be another of Miss Ashfield's unusual gifts? His temple ached, the burr of voices making it worse, and to top it all off he had the deep-felt impression that she was enjoying this.

Taking stock of his irritation, he changed the topic. 'I have heard that you suffered for your kindness to me at the Whitely ball and I am sorry for it.'

'Well, the Earl of Berrick and the Honourable Richard Williams have turned tail and run. I would not call that suffering. Perhaps it should be me who is thanking you.'

Startled by her honesty, Gabriel laughed. He could barely remember the last time he had done so out of her company.

'You have a fortune, Miss Ashfield. There will be a great number of willing swains behind that lot and of a far better calibre if you just give it time.'

'I hope not. Uncle Alec seems to think my unseemly behaviour at the ball was unforgivable. He is considering packing me off to Sherborne again to live out my days in Dorset in a spinsterly regret.'

'And will you?'

'Regret my lack of a marriage proposal?' She swallowed and Gabriel wondered if she was quite as impervious to her suitors as she made out. Lord, if she was carted off back to Sherborne he'd lose the chance of talking to her again and feeling...something? He dared not risk touching her here, but he wanted to. The ache of desire to discern his body's reaction to her almost undid him.

Her hand lay on the headrest of the chair she stood by, the nails short and tidy, her fingers dainty. A healer's hand. He could see the blue veins through the thin whiteness of her skin. There was a burn on one of her knuckles and it had blistered. From assembling her concoctions, perhaps? He hoped it had not happened when she had made the lavender ointment for him.

A great wave of melancholy kept him rooted to the spot, the emptiness of his life leaving a stillness that was unending. Usually he found some relief in humour, but tonight he could not seem to do that, the truth of all that he wasn't, shocking.

If he were to touch her and feel only indifference, then that was the end of it for him. Excusing himself, he moved away with barely the minimum of manners.

Lucien found him over by the small cabinet that held Daniel's fine brandy. 'You look exhausted, Gabe. Perhaps a holiday in the country at your family seat is in order?'

'Amongst the smouldering ashes of Ravenshill Manor and its roofless walls?' Gabriel returned and Lucien Howard began to laugh wryly.

'I had forgotten about the fire. What the hell happened between us a few years back, Gabe? Why did you just disappear without word or reason? Daniel and I tried to find you before we left for Spain, but you were gone.'

Gone into hell, Gabriel thought, and took a drink, lost in the clutches of Henrietta Clements and the political intrigues of her husband.

What was it Gracian had said in his treatise on worldly wisdom? *'Never open the door to a lesser evil, for other greater ones invariably slink on in.'* One mistake leads to the next and the next until there is no way left to go.

That was how he had felt, still felt even six months after the fire. Once, he might have managed, but now…only guilt was left and a floundering pool of regret.

What had Daniel and Cressida both said of him?

That he was kind. The lie of that made his stomach feel hollow; he was his father's son, a man full of anger and retribution.

The truth of it scalded against honour as he up-ended the brandy.

Adelaide wished she could just go home away from this house and these people and the gaiety of a salon filled with friends. Close friends—a group who were relaxed in each other's company and at ease with the expressing of strong opinion. The Earl of Wesley patently was barely interested in her appearance here.

Her cheeks still scalded her from the earlier blush and she chastised herself. But it was hard to appear as indifferent as she would have liked to when he was standing a few feet away from her with his beautiful face so bruised and broken.

He seemed more reticent tonight, less relaxed, the muscles of his jawbone grinding in a constant motion. She had glanced across at him a moment or so before and caught him watching her, the pale gold gaze pulled away as soon as their eyes met. He was drinking a lot, too.

Tormented. The word came from nowhere, but sat across explanation with a quietly formed ease. If the demons in him were circling even here amongst friends in a cosy London town house, then imagine what they must do at other more lonely times.

Heartsick or soul sick, she wondered, looking at the pulse in his throat. Faster than it should be at rest and his hand trembled as he reached for the brandy bottle. Perhaps he had loved Cressida Murray and was drowning in the sorrow of her betrayal—a wretched public denouncement at that, the bruises on him testament to a sense of honour that was startling.

He'd kept his word. He had not hit back. From the way he looked Adelaide doubted such decency was much of a consolation to him. Indeed, he gave the singular impression that he would like to fling his fist through the hard wall behind him and keep bashing until pain scoured wrath and sanity returned.

She had seen the look Lucien Howard had given Daniel Wylde when he'd joined them at the drinks cabinet.

Be careful, he's suffering and I don't know how the hell to change it.

Adelaide had always been good at reading the nuances, postures and expressions of others.

Lord Wesley's lack of response suggested he'd be here not one moment longer than he needed to be and she was glad that the dinner was to be a formal meal because otherwise she was certain he would have already left. 'Please God, let me be seated next to him,' she whispered beneath her breath, the incantation repeated even as the party were called in to the dining salon, bedecked with candles and small posies of flowers.

Lady Christine Howard took the seat opposite, the smile she offered friendly.

'I am so pleased to be placed near you, Miss Ashfield, as I cannot wait to ask you questions about your prowess in the healing arts. It was always something

I was interested in, but have not really had the chance to further.'

'You would be welcome to come to Northbridge and watch me at work…' The words tailed off as Gabriel Hughes came to take the empty seat next to her under the direction of Amethyst Wylde. He looked plainly wary, eyes cold and distant as he pulled out the chair and allowed a great gap of space between them.

'Lady Christine. Miss Ashfield.' The glass he carried with him was empty and he nodded to the servant behind him to fill it up again.

The skin on his left cheek had been broken by the force of the altercation in the ballroom and Adelaide determined it must hurt a lot for the swelling was still most noticeable.

She glanced away in uncertainty. The earl was plainly not looking for sympathy and neither was he seeking conversation. The silence from him was absolute and solid as he turned to look down the table, three fingers of his left hand beating out a rhythm on the cloth. Marking time. This close she could see that the embossed silver ring he wore was inlaid with a cross of gold. Unusual. Different.

'Do you see many people in your clinic, Miss Ashfield?' Lady Christine leaned forward as she asked the question.

'Many, my lady.'

She knew Gabriel Hughes was listening by the slight tip of his shoulders and the way his hand stilled. 'I have various people from the village who come and buy my potions, though I find just as many want words of reassurance on a particular condition or ailment.'

'Mama is rather depressed with her life at the moment, a result of our failing finances, I think, and Lucien's injuries on the Continent. She now believes we are all fragile and that chaos is crouching around a very close corner. Do you make medicines for those suffering in this way?'

'Indeed I do. My aunt Eloise used to say emotion always has its roots in the unconscious and manifests itself in the body, so I make concoctions to jolt the mind into an alignment with the flesh for those who want to make the change.'

Gabriel Hughes turned at that and addressed her directly, his voice low and a marked crease across his brow. 'Philosophers since Locke have struggled to comprehend the definition and connection of mind and body, Miss Ashfield. Are you implying that you have found the answer?'

A challenge; direct and forceful. Eloise and Jean had been the masters of such discourse and a shiver of anticipation rushed through her. 'I believe every part of our bodies is linked, Lord Wesley, the cerebral and the physical.'

'Is that right? For the life of me and after copious reading I simply fail to see how a mental state can causally interact with the physical body.'

'Belief in one's mind is a powerful force for change, my lord.' Adelaide was mindful that conversations all around the table had ceased in order to listen in to this one. 'And while I agree that the conscious experience is on the one hand the most familiar aspect of our lives and on the other the most mysterious, I also sincerely believe that only together can mind and body form a whole to heal.'

'Any living body?' His glance swept the room to stop at the sight of a bumblebee hovering over by the window's glass. 'Does every living thing employ its own consciousness of being?'

'I for one would not discount it.' Clenching her fingers in her lap, she carried on. 'Religion, law and culture have their hands in moulding our thoughts to be...moderated, but I am not so certain that they should be.'

Daniel Wylde at the head of the table laughed and raised his glass. 'I would like to make a toast to the tenets of free discussion and liberal conjecture. Intelligence is a far underrated attribute and it is always welcome here, Miss Ashfield.'

Amethyst Wylde used the following silence to inject her own observation. 'You would like my papa, Miss Ashfield. He is most interested in these sorts of discussions. His heart is his problem, you see, and his mind refuses to accept the poor prognosis of every doctor he visits. With happiness he has far outlived his naysayers and is that not a triumph for mind over matter?'

'I want it to be true and therefore it is?' Gabriel Hughes's words were flat and yet when she looked at him there was a flash of gold in his eyes that surprised her. Hurt and hope had a certain entreaty to them that was easily recognisable for she had seen the same in so very many of her patients.

Was it for himself that he asked these questions? A malady that was non-physical was the only diagnosis that made sense here. Oh, granted, he had cuts all over his face and hands and bruises probably in the small of his back where the bully Murray had lashed out hard, but she knew there was more to it.

The other day in the park when he had placed his hands across her own she had felt his withdrawal.

Panic. Fright. Disbelief.

The Earl of Wesley had bolted for safety and had been running ever since; even tonight placed next to her in close confinement with no chance of an escape he had been wary, the distinctive echo of a personal battle within that was costing him much.

She wished they might talk again quietly and away from the notice of others. She wished he might inadvertently touch her so that the spark of notice she seemed consumed with might again burn and she could relish the mystery of it.

Aunt Eloise and Aunt Jean would not recognise her here, quivering with the want of a man she hardly knew. Lord Wesley was a rake and a womaniser, an earl who wore his clothes in that particular and precise way of a dandy and one who had admitted to having as much of an issue with commitment as she did.

There would be nothing at all to gain by his company and yet here she was in the quiet lull of other conversations turning to him again.

'The philosophy of mesmerism is gaining in traction as a most useful tool in the healing of the mind. I do have some skill in the area, my lord.'

Hell. Was she suggesting that he place his secrets in her trust? Gabriel could not believe it.

'I think I shall pass up such an offer, Miss Ashfield. Even an enlightened healer such as yourself might have some trouble in knowing what is in my mind.'

She nodded. 'Well, if it is any consolation to you it is also my belief that most people can find the solution in themselves if they are honest.'

'Then that is heartening.' He tried to inject as much lightness in the reply as he could manage, but even to his ears the humour sounded cold.

'Reliving a point of memory sometimes helps, Lord Wesley. It opens the mind to further possibility.'

The flash of fire. The slow burn of skin. Henrietta's last quiet words seared into guilt. Her hands holding something just out of the reach of comprehension.

His stomach turned and he thought for one wild moment that he would be sick all over the table, but as Adelaide smiled at him he regained equilibrium, the warmth of her concern and the goodness in it bringing back a balance. His heart might be thundering in his chest, but he remembered again how to breathe. Around them the chatter of others flowed on unhindered as the food was delivered to the table in a succession of dishes.

Chicken, beef and duck trussed in fruit and heavy sauces and elegantly presented on their silver platters.

He knew she could see him shaking and knew also that he should turn away to try at least to stop her seeing his fear. But he couldn't. Miss Adelaide Ashfield was his lifeline even in the cosy private salon of old friends.

'The food is lovely.' Her words and closeness gave him time to return to the mundane. 'I should not have imagined putting chicken with flowers of nasturtium. My uncle employs a French chef at Sherborne and we are more than used to eating well, but this, well, it is just lovely and I was pleased to get an invitation.'

He made himself smile at her through the haze.

'I am certain you are about as interested in the presentation of food as I am, Miss Ashfield, but I thank you for your effort in distracting me.'

Deep dimples graced both her cheeks and the blue of her eyes was lightened. 'Gratitude suits you, my lord. It makes you look younger.'

At that he laughed and for the first time in a long while felt the tight band of loneliness shift. When the footman came forward with the express purpose of refilling his empty glass he shook him away and took up the jug of lemonade instead.

'I thought Gabriel and Adelaide Ashfield looked good together, Daniel.'

Much later Amethyst Wylde lay curled up against the warmth of her husband and watched the way the moonlight filtered across the strong lines of his shoulders.

'Miss Ashfield was a surprise, I will say that.'

'In what way?' Raising herself on her elbow, Amethyst caught his glance.

'She is clever enough to understand Wesley has secrets and brave enough to try to learn them.'

'She was holding her breath when he looked as though he might very well faint away. I am certain of it.'

Daniel sat up, rearranging the pillows behind him. 'Gabriel thinks the death of Mrs Henrietta Clements was entirely his fault.'

Amethyst heard the worry in his tone. 'He told you this?'

'He has always been complex and I think he has been mixed up somehow in working for the British Service. A few years ago he was easier to read, but now...' His words tailed off.

'Now he hides everything. Like you used to?'

His lips turned upwards.

'He needs a good woman, Daniel, and I think he has just found one. But he does not quite know it yet.'

'Because we men are too...slow to understand exactly what is good for us?' His hand crossed to her cheek and he tipped her head towards him.

'Slow in some ways, but much faster in others.' Amethyst felt his interest quicken as she pressed against him and when he brought her in closer she forgot the conversation completely.

Chapter Nine

Gabriel kept to the shadows as he walked, tucked in against the tall walls of the garden mews. The moon was barely there and for that he was pleased.

A long time ago he had been afraid of the dark, when his father had come home to the family at night screaming and yelling, his fists raised against anyone who might annoy him.

But that was before he had learnt how to use it and make it his own. Now the dark held only freedom and ease. Slipping between the gates, he moved over to one of the downstairs windows.

Friar was inside and talking, for Gabriel could hear the quiet burr of his words. There was a woman present, too, and she did not sound happy.

'No. It cannot be done. He is not a patron of my establishment any more and I have no way to see to it that he might turn up again.'

'You are a force to be reckoned with, Mrs Bryant. Surely there could be some pleasurable persuasions you could use...'

The sound of notes and coins had its own music. A substantial inducement to comply. Her voice was quieter now, but underlined with the sound of cajoling.

'No.' Friar's shout almost made Gabriel jump and he waited—a single curse and then retreating footsteps. Others had come from further within the house, bringing a light with them, the shadows of movement sweeping across the curtains. Then silence.

Gabriel breathed in deeply and held his body against stone. Immobile. Sensing danger before he saw it as three men with a lantern scoured the yard thirty feet away. The woman had left in the midst of an argument. Mrs Bryant. The voice sounded familiar to him, though he could not immediately have placed the name.

Shuffling along to a small door, he brought out his knife and slid the blade between the fastening and timber. He needed to be out of sight before the men were upon him. When the portal opened he simply slipped inside and sank down beneath the level of the glass at the windows. The flare of light hit an opposite wall and then was gone, returning before fading again into the distance.

Safe for this moment at least. The chamber he sat in was a lobby of sorts, small and rectangular, with a number of doors leading from it. Three pairs of boots sat beside him under a heavy oilskin coat. He wondered whose house this was and why they should be meeting here. Friar's rooms were further west in a far less salubrious area of London.

A long sword in its sheath caught his attention for

propped up against the lintel of a door the weapon was patently in the wrong place. He was careful to keep his back against the timber panel as he looked out into the night, glad for black and quiet. He knew he had to get out of here before they came back, but from habit his hands delved into the pockets of the oilskin and came up with a twist of paper. When he heard the returning feet on the wooden floor he left, using the darkness to slip away into shadow and safety.

The note was in French and written on part of a torn map. Alan Wolfe, the head of the British Service, stood beside him as he flattened out the sheet to try to determine exactly what geography it showed.

'Maisy is in the Baie de la Seine. Halfway between Cherbourg and La Havre, the town boasts direct access to the English Channel. We have people in Caen so I will get them up there to look. The writing gives two names: Christian and Le Rougeaud.'

'Napoleon's Marshall, Michel Ney, was named Le Rougeaud for the colour of his hair.' Gabriel frowned. 'Though last I heard he was with Soult in the south of France.'

'Could it be a street, then? Or a description of a place?'

'The name of a boat would make sense, too, bringing things or people to England. Perhaps Christian is the captain?'

And so it went on for an hour or more as they gathered the possibilities of the intelligence and turned it this way and that.

'No one is there at the address you went to last night. The place is spotless and empty.'

'Then they cleaned up.'

'Which indicates they did not want us to know anything. Did they see you?

'No. But I jimmied the door. Perhaps they found it had been tampered with.'

'You are certain it was George Friar?'

'I am. His accent is hard to miss.'

'And the others?'

'English and French. I would recognise the voices if I heard them again. There was also a Mrs Bryant and hers was a familiar voice.' The Temple of Aphrodite came to mind and he made a mental note to go back and check. Trying to remember the words between them, he tipped his head and then went on. 'A brothel owner, perhaps? She said she had an establishment and Friar said something of pleasurable entertainments.'

'I will get someone to look into that.' Wolfe took a pen and wrote the names on some paper before laying them on the table.

'Clements has French ancestry and so does Friar by way of marriage. He is also an American and likely to hate the English. Goode is the son of a squire in Leicester, but he is married to a French woman, Lilliana de la Tour. Frank Richardson has written a treatise on the place of free speech and the rights of men.'

'Henrietta Clements swore there were six of them. Clements. Friar. Goode and his wife and Richardson and Mrs Bryant perhaps?'

'Then we need to find proof of what it is this group is trying to accomplish and we need it soon. I will get more men on to the task and hopefully we will be able to round them all up before too long. You look done in, Gabe, perhaps by the numerous social occasions you are at almost every evening. I have heard it said that Mr George Friar is rather enamoured by Miss Ashfield.'

Wolfe looked at him directly as he said it, but Gabriel, with his years of practice, easily hid emotion. He knew the director had heard of his own involvement with the niece of Penbury, for very little of the everyday happenings of London's society seemed to escape him. Wariness made Gabriel swallow. He didn't want Adelaide mixed up in any of this. He needed all the compartments of his life kept separate.

For years he had built up a reputation that was shallow and dissolute. A dandy and a lover was not on anyone's list of needing to be watched and the rumours of a prowess in sexual conquests had kept him apart from those who would discuss politics, government or anarchy.

Hiding in plain sight was rewarding. A certain smile, some well-chosen words, the cut of his cloth and the tie of his cravat. These were his tools now. Innocuous. Harmless. And ready to listen.

The war against France was not always won on the battlefields of valour, glory and blood. It was also fought well in the quiet comfort of bedchambers and in the presence of whispered secrets and willing bodies suspended in the last thrusts of ecstasy when all the walls were let down.

Daniel had called him kind and so had Cressida. But Gabriel knew that he had not been such for a very long time.

He had lived down to his reputation all of his adult life. *Gabriel Hughes, the Prince of Passion.* He'd heard the name in various places, spoken quiet with a hint of disbelief. Such rumour had helped him squeeze between the cracks of the polite and mannered world and on to the warm mattresses of confession.

A gun killed one man at a time, but words smote many. Anarchy and rebellion had shades of truth and honour, too, but as he passed on the names of those whom his paramours had mentioned, Gabriel could not dwell on that.

Sometimes he wondered though. Sometimes he heard the tales of men who were good and true killed by unnamed others, their blood running into the gutters of martyrdom and innocence. The hidden cost of his subterfuge. Yet still he had not wavered.

Until Henrietta Clements. She was just another mark at first, a way to listen in to the nefarious truths of her husband, but she had been lonely and he had been, too, pneumonia laying him low for many months of winter. With his guard down he had let her in, past the point of simply business. They had met on numerous occasions and by then she was dangerous: to the British Service and to him.

At the time of the fire he had even thought Wolfe had had a hand in it, a way of dealing efficiently with every problem, but he had found out later that Randolph Clements had been camped out in the woods near Ravenshill with a group of his men.

Revenge. Retribution.

The strong emotions left little space for caution and Gabriel had been flung from that life into this one.

No one knew the true cost of his injuries. No one. And he damned well meant to keep it that way.

Lucy Carrigan's small afternoon tea party was finally coming to an end and Adelaide was pleased to see her uncle and her chaperon nearby getting ready to take their leave. The débâcle at the Whitely ball seemed now to be a thing of the past, the rumours of Adelaide's personal fortune cancelling out other perceived flaws. Indeed, despite her uncle and Imelda's misgivings, the gossip and disapproval had quickly dissipated.

She had caught sight of Mr Friar earlier in the day and had managed to keep out of his way since then, but suddenly there he was before them as they were making their way to the door.

'Lord Penbury.' He tipped his head and then straightened. 'I did not realise you were here this afternoon, Miss Ashfield, or I should certainly have come over to give you my regards.'

Resisting the urge to answer, Adelaide stayed quiet, hoping that they might leave their meeting at that. But Mr Friar carried on regardless.

'Well, there was also something that I needed to

relate to you in particular, Miss Ashfield. A friend of mine, Mr Kenneth Davis, has made it known to me that he was a neighbour of yours in Sherborne many years ago and he wished for me to give you his regards if by chance I did see you in my travels.'

Adelaide's world narrowed and then reformed, the spots of fear in her vision threatening to overcome her completely. Was this a warning? The beginnings of blackmail? She pushed her hair back with a shaking hand and tried to smile even as her uncle spoke.

'The world is a small place, is it not, Adelaide? Kenneth Davis and my niece were once great friends until he hared off to parts unknown in search of a fortune.'

'A fortune?' Friar turned the words on his tongue. 'He lives in Baltimore now, Lord Penbury, and is doing more then well.'

'Such a coincidence, is it not, Adelaide?'

As her uncle offered this opinion George Friar laughed. 'Much of his conversation is about the wonderful time he had as a youth here in England. I think he fancied himself in love with your niece, my lord, and after meeting her I can well see why.'

'He was a wild boy, Mr Friar, and rather wayward. The colonies are probably most suited to men such as him.'

'That they are, my lord, but his stories are most amusing. Perhaps you might allow me your company in order to relate them to you, Miss Ashfield.'

George Friar knew what had happened all those years ago and he knew Adelaide knew that he did.

All the horror and fear she felt became entwined in another even more dreadful realisation.

If she refused his suit, for that was obviously what this conversation was about, what might happen next? She could not allow him to see her alone until she could formulate a plan.

The mention of a fortune had caught her uncle's interest, however, and instead of leaving as they were about to he turned with a question in his eyes.

'What is it you do there in Baltimore, Mr Friar?'

'Shipping, my lord. I bring wood from the Americas to England. I also have a large holding on the Jones Falls River in Coles Harbour that I farm, for there are rich pickings to be had if one is willing to work for it and I most certainly am.'

'Indeed. Your family must be proud of your endeavour, then. I always thought my own son should have tried his luck there. Perhaps you might take a turn about the room with Mr Friar, Adelaide. You would probably like to hear about Mr Davis and his new life in the Americas.'

And just like that she was dispatched into the care of Mr George Friar, his hand beneath her arm as he led her around the room.

'I am sorry I did not tell you of my acquaintance with Kenneth Davis at the Harvey ball, Miss Ashfield. I thought it would be nice to get to know you first, to find out for myself if what he said of you could possibly be true. My tripping on that blasted plant put an end to that.'

So he would not mention his own lack of manners? She decided to play along. 'And what was it he has said of me, sir?'

The affable but bumbling tone suddenly changed. 'He said you held one of the richest fortunes in England in your palm, Miss Ashfield, and that if his father had not had him manhandled on to the next boat out of England you would have had to marry him.'

She was pleased that he now showed her his true malice.

'He was wrong in that assumption, Mr Friar. No woman has to do anything she does not wish to simply because of the poor manners of a suitor.'

Her heart was thumping, but she kept her smile in place and was glad to feel her strength returning. Cover a bluff with a bluff; a cardroom strategy that she'd heard from Bertie.

'Society here needs just to hear a rumour of impropriety to believe it to be true, Miss Ashfield. Especially in a woman.' The cold threat in his voice was evident. 'It is dangerous ground that you are treading.'

'You seem to be ignoring the opposing argument that those who tell tales often come under their own scrutiny, Mr Friar. If it is truly a wealthy wife you want from this visit to England, it would pay you to stay out of such quagmires.'

He took a step back, the smile on his face now overwritten with anger. 'My offer to marry you still stands, Miss Ashfield. I believe we could do well together. The beginnings of a dynasty. And if not...' He left the threat unfinished.'

My God, he believed she would simply surrender

to his bullying? Was he mad? 'I will surely think about it, Mr Friar, but for now I need to leave. A headache, you understand.' She brought her hand to her brow and tried to look suitably in pain.

When Friar tipped his head and let her go she knew she had won a short respite at least. Better to let him believe that he was in with a chance than to cut him off completely. Breathing out, she walked towards her uncle, praying all the way that the absolute fury she felt inside would not be showing on her face.

Gabriel fell into a wide leather wingchair at White's and ordered a stiff brandy.

Daniel Wylde sat opposite him, the smoke of a cheroot winding up between them.

'My wife is worried about you, Gabriel. She thinks you are lonely.'

'Lonely for strong wine and shapely women,' he drawled back. The persona he had fostered was so easy to regather in the face of anything personal.

'Lonely in life, were her exact words. She thinks Miss Adelaide Ashfield would suit you nicely as a bride and has bidden me to raise the subject.'

Speechless for once, Gabriel listened.

'She is wealthy and she is comely. But most of all she is clever and real. A woman like that is rare. Amethyst thinks you are half in love with her already.'

'Love is a strong word, Daniel, and one I have had no practice in at all.'

'Love is the only word that takes away loneliness. Perhaps you should think about that.'

Gabriel laughed, but the sound was mirthless. 'Your matchmaking ability leaves much to be desired. Perhaps if you just stop there we'd both be relieved.'

'It's good to be back in your company, Gabe.'

The quiet honesty of the statement floored Gabriel and he remained silent, fighting back the desire to lay down every one of his problems before the scrutiny of an old friend.

Daniel lowered his voice. 'It is also whispered you work for the Service. Undercover?' He allowed this to settle a moment before continuing. 'Battle was wearying in the Peninsular campaign, but it was usually quickly over. You have the looks of a man who has been under fire for a very long time.'

'God. I do not need this.'

'Don't you? I think you need to hear a new perspective. A perspective that includes a life of your own and a liberty unconstrained by the requirements of a country that will be wanting for ever. The army was like that for me in the end. I came out with a bullet in my leg and nightmares and if I didn't know who I was on decommission, then no one else was ever going to have the chance to, either.'

'A brutal ending?'

'True. But my wife saved me.'

The words dropped across hope, flattening it. No woman would ever be able to save him. He was the most renowned lover in all of London town with a string of conquests to his name and yet he could no longer feel anything.

'You have been dallying with the wrong sorts of

women. Cressida Murray was always going to be trouble and so was Henrietta Clements.'

Gesturing to a passing waiter, Gabriel ordered a bottle of fine Scotch.

'Get drunk with me, Daniel, as a friend, and tell me about your horses.'

Chapter Ten

'Are we not besieged by men who are most…unsuitable, Imelda?' Lord Penbury sighed. 'Run over by them like a pack of rats on a sinking ship? Mr George Friar, whom one cannot quite manage the gist of despite his self-proclaimed fortune, and the Honourable Richard Williams, who is afflicted with a dire lack of gumption. This is not taking into account all of the others whom my niece dances with once and then never allows them to enjoy a second turn around the floor.' He stopped, trying to find the words. 'It is so much more exhausting than I had ever imagined it to be, I can tell you that. My daughters were easy to marry off, no fuss, no problems. They came, they found, they married.'

Imelda joined in the one-sided conversation now. 'Your niece inspires strong reactions from men and yet she seems to return none.'

'Well, Lord Berrick at least has offered for Adelaide's hand in marriage.'

'When?'

'Yesterday. He came to see me in the afternoon and on speaking with him I can see Adelaide would have much to gain by looking favourably upon his suit.'

'Have you spoken with her about this?'

'No. I do not wish to have another argument and yet...he is a good man and more than wealthy. He loves her and made much of telling me exactly how he does. He is, I admit, very verbose, but he is more than genuine with it and he has promised to allow Adelaide the space and time to pursue the interests that she holds dear. Her clinic. Her tinctures.'

'Then he sounds most reasonable, though your niece might not recognise it as such. The young have no idea of what their future might hold, in my opinion, Penbury, or of how hard the path of life can be. Perhaps we should help her to make the right choice.'

'How?'

'Oh, there are many ways, my dear, ways that have been used for years and years by the wise chaperons of the young and the foolish. A small push here, a larger one there and, *voilà*, the goal is reached easily.'

'You think Lovelace is a fine choice, then?'

'I do. The best Adelaide could hope for at her age and with her attributes. She is outspoken and her independent nature is not one that most men of the *ton* would find appealing. Besides, I knew Frederick Lovelace's grandmother well and she always spoke highly of him.'

Alec breathed out. Subterfuge was a game he shied

away from normally, but his niece had brought him to his wits' end. Bertram would return home to North-bridge one of these days with a wife of his own and then children to follow and he worried that Adelaide would feel replaced somehow. Lost in the mêlée of a new generation. No. She needed her own life and house and husband, he was damn certain of it. His brother would have said the same had he still been in the land of the living. John would have encouraged his daughter to spread her wings and find what he had had in his own life, a happy, comfortable marriage. He would be far from pleased to see her grown so alone, and whilst Eloise and Jean had been company for each other in their old age, Adelaide would have no one.

'Do what you need to, Imelda, but do it carefully. I should not want my niece to know that she has in any way been pushed into this.'

Lord Berrick was waiting in the drawing room when Adelaide came down that evening having dressed for the McWilliamses' ball. He looked different tonight, happier, and his clothes were stamped with the impression of much thought and coinage. A good-looking man despite his rather dull character.

'Miss Ashfield.' She looked around for her uncle and for Imelda Harcourt, but they were nowhere at all in sight. She could not believe that this would be considered proper to be left alone together according to the strict tenets of the *ton*. Still, his smile was real and he was so very unthreatening she felt herself relax.

'I am honoured to be asked to escort you to the ball tonight, Miss Ashfield.'

This was the first Adelaide had heard of the arrangement, but she stayed quiet.

'I brought your uncle a book I enjoyed and he has just gone to find one that he recommends for me to take home.'

'You read?'

'Anything and everything. I have no taste, only appetite.'

Despite the situation she laughed. 'My oldest cousin, Cynthia, always called me the family bookworm. When I was younger I used to imagine that literally and worry.'

'Well, my dog almost took a bite out of the First Folio of William Shakespeare the other day and it is worth a small fortune.'

'You have dogs?'

'Three of them. All large and unfortunately rather stupid. But I like them.'

Tonight without the whirl of society trapping them she thought the earl seemed nicer and far easier to speak with.

When her uncle returned with Lady Imelda a few moments later, she was sitting next to Lovelace on the sofa, talking of the house that he had grown up in. Lady Harcourt quickly fastened on the topic.

'Oh, Thornbury Manor is a very beautiful place. Your grandmother and I used to walk around the lake there and talk and plan all sorts of wonderful gardens that would enhance it.'

'Did they eventuate?' Adelaide was interested.

'Yes, many of them did,' Imelda replied with a smile, 'and I hope you might one day have the opportunity to see them, too, my dear. There is a white garden down by the lake and pinks and reds and yellows at the front of the house. Are they still there, Lord Berrick?'

'Mother did not have quite the green finger that my grandmama did, Lady Harcourt, but if one looks I am certain the ancestors of those plants might still be rearing their heads come the Season.'

'Family,' Imelda purred. 'How important it is and how vital the connections. Do you not think so, Penbury?'

'Indeed, I do. Without the traditions and the solidarity of kith and kin one would be adrift and alone for ever.'

Adelaide felt the pull of something strange. There were undercurrents she could not understand at play here and she struggled to interpret them.

Berrick smiled wistfully at her, but was all attentiveness. His conversation was not quite as dull as she might have once thought it either, and as the hour wore on she realised she was indeed enjoying herself. Oh, granted, the words were not wit-sharp as they had been at the Wyldes the other evening with Lord Wesley, and when Frederick Lovelace leaned over she was not bothered whether he inadvertently touched her or not. But it was easy and good humoured and for the first time in a while her uncle smiled as though he meant it and looked pleased with her, the genial uncle from Sherborne more apparent.

Family. For all it was and all it wasn't, she enjoyed seeing Uncle Alec happy.

'You have no other siblings, then, Lord Berrick, no cousins?'

He shook his head, the candelabra above catching the gold highlights there. 'None, I am afraid, for my parents were only children in both families. You are lucky, Miss Ashfield, with all your cousins.'

'Well, three of them are a lot older than me and Cynthia and Elizabeth live in the north now. Barbara married a man from Boston and we have not seen her in years. Bertram, at least, resides in London.'

'I should want a large family myself. Sometimes when I was young it was lonely.'

The earl's honesty made her smile. It was rare for a man to admit to such emotion and she lauded him for it, though catching the glance her uncle and chaperon gave each other across the table she stiffened. Knowing. Smug. The horrible thought came that this meeting had more to it than the enjoyment of a simple uncomplicated conversation.

The twelve weeks of the Season that she had promised her uncle were whittling away, yet he had become more and more desperate for her to find a suitor that she held some penchant for. Had he spoken to Lovelace about his hopes? Had he even encouraged the earl?

Berrick himself had no part in it, she was certain. He was a man without the agendas of the more complex males of the *ton*. She almost had to stop herself from leaning over to take his hand and re-assure him when her uncle began to question him more blatantly.

'If you were married, would you live in London or at Thornbury?'

'I like the country, sir,' he answered. 'But I think it would depend on what my wife preferred.'

Her uncle's eyes reflected his appreciation.

'And what of travel? Do you have plans to go abroad?'

'No, sir. I have never wanted to leave the fine green fields of England. I have all that I might need here.'

A further benevolent nod from her uncle.

Imelda remained very quiet, but Adelaide felt her chaperon's gaze pinned upon her.

When her uncle suggested they should start for the McWilliamses' ball, she readily assented. Anything at all to get out of this cosy foursome that was laden with a great dollop of intention and an obvious undercurrent of deceit. She hoped fervently that Mr George Friar would not be attending.

The Earl of Wesley did not ask her to dance, even when Berrick had been called from her side where he had been stuck like glue for most of the night. No, Gabriel Hughes stayed at one end of the salon though sometimes she caught his glance upon her, flat and hard and unreadable. As the music began again Adelaide knew it was a waltz and she looked at Wesley directly.

Come and ask me. Come and hold me close.

The thoughts tumbled forth unbidden and shocking, the force of feeling within surprising even to herself. But Gabriel Hughes simply wandered off towards the top of the room, the tallest man here and the most beautiful, collecting a drink as he did so and never looking back once.

'You look very lovely tonight, my dear.' Imelda's words brought her into the moment. 'I was saying to your uncle how London's society has suited you, made you glow, but never more so than now. Frederick Lovelace looks well tonight, too, do you not think?'

She nodded because her chaperon seemed to expect it.

'He is a man whom many of the other young women here would be pleased to walk out with. Look at Miss Carrigan, for example, she is lit up like a beacon in that waltz with him.'

As she spoke Imelda leaned forward and took her hand. 'The wise choice of a husband is crucial to the certainty of any woman's future happiness, Adelaide. What seems desirable now is often less so when the rosy glow of attraction has lessened.' Her fingers gripped harder. 'And believe me, it will. Pick a man who is rich and biddable would be my advice; one whom you might enjoy the material advantages of, but is happy to allow you to do so. These are two very different things.'

'A man of wealth and weakness, you mean?'

Imelda laughed. 'A woman's strength is all that is

needed in a marriage. The position is too crowded should a man expect to have his say, too.'

Adelaide thought her old aunts would have liked Imelda's sentiments, but for her such an argument spoken out loud was jarring. What of equality and the challenge of each other's minds? Where would discussion and debate be consigned to should a union be so very one-sided?

'My Charles and I were wed for thirty years and nary a cross word between us. Lovelace has a resemblance to my dearly departed husband and should I offer you any advice at all it would be to make certain that he understands your more-than-obvious affection for him.'

At that moment the Earl of Berrick caught her glance between the shoulders of others who stood on the dance floor and smiled. A perfectly sweet smile.

'He has offered for your hand in marriage, you know. Your uncle said I was not to say anything, but these things need to be nurtured in exactly the right setting and, if I might presume to say so, I think that this is it.'

Horror coated humour and then anger cloaked that. This whole evening had been about establishing signposts for the acceptance of a suitable marriage contract. Young women of high-born rank had been tutored extensively in the knowledge of what was owed to the family name and love was not considered an essential element at all. Females here married for security and freedom and wealth and, indeed, who could blame them with the abysmal strictures of manners and formalities attached to innocence.

God, how she suddenly hated the cage she had constructed all of her own making. She should never have agreed to come to London in the first place because the reality of it made her question all she used to believe. Spinsterhood suddenly held as much of a trap as an unhappy union, the length and breadth of aloneness as repulsive as the enforced deceit of an unequal partnership.

Her thoughts fell to Daniel Wylde and his wife, Amethyst. That was what she wanted. The joy of strength in difference and a forged togetherness because of it. Berrick would never give her that.

Her aunt and uncle were plotting a marriage in which she had no say, and Lovelace had already offered his hand. If she did not act now, she might well indeed be married before she knew it and to a most unsuitable groom.

On the pretext of going to speak with Lucy Carrigan, Adelaide left Lady Harcourt and walked further into the room, a vaulted ceiling separating this part of the salon from the next.

She had never thought of herself as particularly brave or desiring of adventure, but tonight everything inside her was different, heightened, alive. Gabriel Hughes stood talking with Lucien Howard, his sister, Christine, next to him, and as Adelaide gave her greeting she was swallowed up into the group with an ease that was both surprising and gratifying.

'I was just saying to my brother how much I enjoyed our evening of discussion the other night, Miss Ashfield, and how we should do it again. Soon.'

'I would like that, Lady Christine.' She did not raise her eyes to Lord Wesley, but felt him there, a solid and startling presence. His shoes were beautifully polished and the cut of his pantaloons a fine one. The damned blush that she seemed cursed with for ever in his presence was beginning to creep into her cheeks.

When Lucien and Christine began to talk to each other of a man they both had just seen, the Earl of Wesley leaned in and spoke quietly.

'Are you well, Miss Ashfield? You seem out of sorts.'

A smile tugged at her lips and she made herself look at him directly, the gold in his gaze questioning. He held the look of a man who did not want to fight any more, wary and drained, but even this did nothing to deter her.

'Would you partner me for the next waltz, my lord?' There it was out, said, blunt and honest.

He was good at hiding things, but still she saw shock on his face and question.

Lost in the consternation of this Adelaide was not cautious with her next words. 'Lord Berrick wants me to marry him.'

It was as if the world around them no longer existed, the people and the noise relegated to a place far away, lost in the ether of what each of them was saying, words under words and the colour of the room stark in only black and white.

Gabriel Hughes stood very still, a grinding muscle in his jaw the only movement visible. 'And what do you want?' he asked finally.

'A home, though it is only recently I have come to realise that a place to be and live is important. My chaperon has been quick to tell me that when Bertie brings a bride to Northbridge I shall be…in the way.'

He turned towards her, using the pillar as a barrier so that they were cut off from the hearing of those around them, but she knew that it would not be many seconds before the world around them impinged again.

'You would be bored to death with Freddy Lovelace in a week.'

'Could we meet privately, then?' She made herself say the words, hating the desperation so obvious within them.

'Pardon?'

'I need to know what it would be like to touch a man who might make my heart beat faster before I settle for one who does not. Your reputation heralds a great proficiency in such matters and I thought perhaps you might…'

'Hell, Adelaide.'

The horror of everything spiralled in her head. She had asked for something so dreadful that even the most dissolute lover in all of London town could not accommodate her.

'I…can't.'

His voice was strangled and rough, the words like

darts as she turned on her heels, hoping he did not see the tears that were threatening to fall as she walked briskly from his side.

Gabriel leaned back against the hardness of cold marble and felt pain pierce his chest. The scent of lemon hung as suspended as his disbelief in her words.

I can't.

I can't touch you.

I can't let you know.

She was going to marry Berrick for a place, for a home, for the desperation of not being tossed out of an estate that had always been her sanctuary.

They would never suit. She was far too clever for Berrick and far too…knowing. Adelaide Ashfield would eat a husband like that up in no time flat and be starving for all the rest of her life, doomed to the ordinary.

She deserved rare and remarkable, astonishing and marvellous. The list of adjectives made him smile, but another feeling twisted, too. Sadness and regret. That he had not met her at another time in his life, earlier, when he was still whole, and good and honourable.

'You look pale, Gabe.' Lucien took up the space that Adelaide had just left, his sister, Christine, chatting to a girl he did not know on his other side. 'And Penbury's niece seems upset.'

'I'm tired, that's all.' He tore his eyes away from following Adelaide's form across the room. She was with her chaperon now and her uncle and they looked to be preparing to leave.

He was glad for it.

'For a débutante Miss Ashfield seems to inspire strong feelings in those around her.' A question lingered in Lucien's eyes. 'Selwyn Carrigan was telling me the other day that George Friar was asking after her.'

'The colonial is a charlatan. I hope she stays well away from him.'

'I am inclined to agree with you, for James Stanhope has just returned from Baltimore and he swears he never heard Friar's name or fortune mentioned even once. Strange, one would think, given the importance he accords himself with his land and business dealings there. But perhaps Friar is more than interested in Miss Ashfield's wealth because his own circumstances are not as rosy as he makes them out to be?'

Gabriel frowned. People lied because they wanted things hidden in order to show themselves in a better light and he'd been long enough in the business of secrets to understand the danger in that.

Could the man hurt Adelaide? He had already tried once at the Harveys' ball. Could he do so again? Marriages happened for the flimsiest of reasons and scandal had been the cause for more than a few of the hastily arranged betrothals in the *ton*.

Gabriel did not want Adelaide Ashfield married off to George Friar under a mistake and dragged off into the wilds of the Americas. He wanted her here, to talk with and laugh with, a woman whose conversation he enjoyed and looked forward to with eagerness. Besides that, Frederick Lovelace's proposal was also something to be considered now.

The arrival at his side of Lucien's sister had him turning.

'I have a good friend who would like to meet you, Gabriel. Miss Smithson is new in from the country and she is most adept at riding.'

Smiling, Gabriel straightened the folds of his high cravat and turned to the short blonde-haired woman behind Christine.

The carriage ride home was slow and laborious. Uncle Alec was quiet in his place by the window, but Frederick Lovelace had not stopped chattering. About the weather and the ball. About the moon and his understanding of space. About the scent that she wore and how it evoked for him a time when he had been young.

Adelaide hoped her uncle or Imelda Harcourt might eventually have told him to be quiet or at least to have filled up some of the space with their own opinions, but they did not, and the dreadful monologue droned on and on uninterrupted until they finally reached the town house.

She refused to allow her mind to turn back to the ballroom and to the last look she had of Gabriel Hughes. All she did was smile, inanely, the muscles at the corner of her mouth frozen into the eternally jovial.

'I can't.'

Everything was wrecked and gone. Hope. Joy. Anticipation. When Frederick Lovelace said goodbye she walked quickly up the stairs.

To her room. At last, where she threw herself upon her bed and cried into her pillow, loud noisy sobs stifled by feathers until the slip was damp and cold.

Then she got up and looked at herself in the mirror, the swollen eyes, the broken dreams, the utter sadness of living.

'This is the bottom,' she said to herself in a firm and even voice. 'This is the worst you will ever feel. I promise. It will never again be this bad.'

Gabriel Hughes did not want her. He could not even rouse himself to touch her.

The quiet sound of her heart breaking into a thousand jagged pieces made her close her eyes and simply stand there. Alone.

The next morning her uncle summoned her to his study.

'Frederick Lovelace, the Earl of Berrick, has done you the honour of offering marriage, Adelaide. He came expressly to ask for your hand and I must say that my advice would be to consider his proposal carefully as it is probably the very best you will ever receive.'

Adelaide shook her head and sat down, feeling her legs could not carry her own weight. 'When I came to London, Uncle, I told you that I did not want to be married off to anyone. Those wishes still stand and nothing you say could persuade me otherwise.'

Her uncle was silent for a moment before he crossed to the desk in his library and pulled out an envelope.

'Read this, child.'

Taking the missive from him, Adelaide was startled to see that the writing was in fact that of her late father's.

'John wrote this six months before he died. Our lawyer had insisted we both redo our wills, you see, and so we sat down together and tried to think of all the things we would want to happen should the unthinkable come to pass. Which it did,' he added and laid a hand across her shoulder.

'Your father expected you to marry and have your own family and was adamant that I as your guardian should be the one to help you choose. He was most concerned, you see, for many young women are made unhappy by unsuitable husbands and he did not wish this to happen to you. He wanted a wealthy, sensible, honourable and settled suitor. A man who could keep you in the style you were accustomed. If you look down the page a little further, you will see a list of the families John hoped you to form an alliance with. The Lovelaces are upon it, about the third name down.'

'My answer is still no.' Her words echoed in the silence of the room.

'Are there others there, then, that could take your fancy?'

'There are not.'

'You haven't come across one suitor in all the weeks of the Season with whom you might imagine a future with?'

She stayed silent.

'Then if that is the case, Adelaide, I have failed your father completely. His line shall be pruned into nothingness and lost into the folds of history, for a family tree depends upon regeneration to flourish. If there had been other siblings your choice might have been less important, but there are not. It is only you.' He poured himself a drink and took a hefty swig of it. 'I take this lack as my failure and know that my brother will be looking down upon me and thinking that I could have done more for you, should have done more for you.'

She shook her head. 'You have been a good and loving man, Uncle Alec, and I have felt at home at Northbridge.'

'Well, I thank you for that, my dear, but such sentiments will not solve this tricky situation. Lord Berrick will be arriving back here after luncheon and I had hoped to have been able to give him the Ashfield family blessing, but I cannot force you into sense. Know at least that I tried to deter you from your poor choice of turning away Frederick Lovelace's most kind proposal.'

The words her father had written swam before her eyes. Her parents had loved her and tried to protect her, guiding her from the grave to see her settled in the way they desired. And with George Friar's malevolence simmering unanswered she knew she was walking on dangerous ground.

'I...just...cannot.' Her reply was bare and quiet, and, standing, she placed her father's letter on the table and let herself out of the silent study, hating the deep lines of hurt on her uncle's brow.

Chapter Eleven

Daniel Wylde came again to visit Gabriel in the early hours of the evening.

'I saw Frederick Lovelace this morning. He hopes to have some news of a wonderful new development in his life, I think was how he phrased it. He then asked me if I knew Miss Adelaide Ashfield from Sherborne.'

Hell. Hell. Hell.

The anger in Gabriel twisted into regret and then reformed again into fury. Would she do it? Would she marry him just for a place in the world?

'Lucien said Miss Ashfield looked more than upset after talking with you at the McWilliamses' ball, Gabriel? Is there some problem between you?'

He shook his head. 'The fault was completely my own. She is blameless.'

'Of what?'

I cannot touch a woman without feeling sick.

He actually imagined he might have said the words

out loud and his heart began to pound so violently he thought he would fall.

'God, what is wrong with you, Gabriel? Are you ill?'

Everywhere. All over. Sick to my very soul.

'It's the damned Service, isn't it? Is Adelaide Ashfield involved somehow in an investigation?'

You never loved me in this life, Gabriel, not like I loved you...

Henrietta's last words before the fire, plaintive, shaking. He still felt her fingers on the pulse at his neck, nails scraping over the bloodline that flowed there, and the world began to fade somehow into a further-away place. It was coming back, his memory, slowly and by small degrees, little pieces of the past fitting into a whole.

'Sit down before you fall down.' Daniel manhandled him into the chair by the window, the moonlight silver across his lap. 'For the life of me, Gabe, I need to understand what the hell is going on with you.

Sitting, he felt better, more able to breathe and think. Betrayal was all mixed up together suddenly, in Henrietta's neediness and Cressida's revenge at the ball. Even the British Service's insistence on a certain persona to confound those in society held the scourge of it. To him as a person, to his life, to his honesty, to the hope of something better and finer and good.

'After the fire...I lost my way.'

'The fire in the Ravenshill chapel? The one that killed Henrietta Clements?'

'I think she wanted to die.'

'God.'

'I can't remember properly, but…' He could not finish.

'Rumour has it you were burned. Badly.'

Looking up, Gabriel tried to find the energy to hide all he had been so very careful with. 'I was. It isn't pretty.'

'That's why you went to the brothels, then, because of the scarring. You didn't want anyone save the prostitutes to see you like that? Barnsley said you'd been at the Temple of Aphrodite and he wondered if you had said anything of it to me. I told him he must be mistaken because you never used to…' He stopped momentarily before going on, a new comprehension in his glance. 'So the body-and-mind discussion of Miss Ashfield's the other night was more personal than you let on?'

'Leave Adelaide Ashfield out of it, Daniel. I mean it.'

'She talked with Christine Howard of mesmerism…'

'I don't want to hear this.'

'…and self-healing. Of reliving the moment when everything changed and moving on with life. Of coming to terms with what has happened to you?'

The heat crawling across his legs and sending the cloth into flame, skin dissolving as other hands had reached him, pulled him to safety, the last of Henrietta Clements's long hair frizzling into black.

She had smiled at him and then cursed him in the

last moments before death. 'There won't be another for you. Only me.'

The sudden realisation floored him. Gabriel could barely move with the truth of what he remembered.

'What is it, Gabe? You look like you have seen a ghost?' Daniel's query came softly.

'I think Henrietta Clements wanted me to die alongside her. The fire was like a pyre...a suttee. If she could not have me here, then maybe in the celestial...?' He left the statement hanging because he no longer had the energy to continue.

'And you didn't remember this until now? God. Perhaps Miss Ashfield's suppositions about speaking of a defining moment holds more power in it than we both gave her credit for. She'll be wasted on Lovelace if she marries him.'

If...

Swallowing, Gabriel pushed back his fear to a place where he could manage it. 'Is there any way, Daniel, that your wife might ask Miss Ashfield to visit your town house again tomorrow afternoon?'

'Because you want to talk with her?'

'Alone if I can.'

'I think that would be a very good idea.'

Adelaide, accompanied by her maid, Milly, climbed the steps of the Montcliffe town house with a feeling of nervous anticipation. The horror of her dreadful conversation with Gabriel Hughes at the McWilliamses' ball had kept her up for nights and she knew she did not look her best.

The last time she had been here he had been, too, but Lord Wesley was nowhere to be seen as she gave Lady Montcliffe her greeting once inside the front door.

'Perhaps your maid could accompany mine and go and find something to eat and drink in the kitchen, Miss Ashfield. That would give us a small opportunity to talk.'

'Of course.' Milly happily got up, leaving her alone with Amethyst Wylde, who shepherded her into a small salon to one side of an opulent hallway.

'I would like to speak honestly with you if I may, Adelaide…might I call you that?'

'Yes.'

'The Earl of Wesley is a particular friend of ours and he is a good man, a strong man, a man who is misunderstood in society, I think. He admires you. I know that for a fact.'

Adelaide hated the flush of red that had crept up into her cheeks.

'He is here today and he has asked to have a private word with you. Is this something that you might consider?'

Adelaide stood, unable to sit longer. The other day she had asked to meet the earl and he had refused. She could not even begin to imagine what he might want to say now, but it could not get any worse than the last meeting, she was sure of it. And he was here, close. She took in a deep breath. 'I would. My uncle expects me to form a union, but a fortune can be a difficult asset in the marriage stakes, Lady Montcliffe.'

'The rich must marry the rich, you mean?' Amethyst Wylde came to stand beside her.

'Exactly, and Lord Berrick has asked for my hand.'

'I had heard this said, but I do not recall the man himself.'

'My uncle prays for an alliance within the *ton*. My father wanted it, too. There was a letter expressing his hopes for a suitor and his family name was mentioned so...' She stopped, unable to go on.

'Strong persuasions, then. As a way of presenting the other side I might tell you that Daniel was almost penniless when I married him and our union has proved a great success. I think a wise woman can find a way to gain exactly what she wants and make it work, and from what I have seen and heard of you, Miss Ashfield, you are more than up to the task. My advice, for what it is worth, is to follow your heart no matter where it takes you. Now if you will excuse me, I shall find Lord Wesley.'

Adelaide stood in the sunlight by the French doors overlooking the garden, the gentle smell of lemons just discernible in the air. For a moment Gabriel faltered, unsure if what he was about to do was a wrong step or a right one, but then he made himself come forward and the noise had her turning.

She did not wear her spectacles today. That was the very first thing he noticed, and because of it her eyes seemed bigger and much more blue.

Other emotions danced there, too, before she could hide them. Fright. Worry. Joy.

'Miss Ashfield.'

'My lord.'

He did not move closer as he shut the door behind him and when a cloud fell across the sun the room darkened markedly. An omen? He prayed not.

'Thank you for meeting me. I guessed I wouldn't be exactly welcomed at the Penbury town house and so I asked Lord and Lady Montcliffe if they might arrange this. The rumour that you have agreed to marry Lovelace has come to my ears, you see, and—' He stopped, biting down on his babble of words. He was seldom nervous, but here he found he was.

Her smile was sad and it came nowhere near to touching her eyes. 'You of all people should know the danger of listening to gossip.

He was surprised by the ache of relief that went through him at her answer. 'So it is false, this proposed union?'

'Oh, parts of tittle-tattle are always true. Lord Berrick did ask me, but I did refuse him.'

'Because you do not love him?'

'Could not love him. There is a difference. One can marry a man whom one admires in the hope that love might follow, but if there is no feeling whatsoever in the first place, I doubt a satisfactory union would result.' Her voice wavered on the last words, the pulse at her throat rapid.

He covered the distance between them and stood just out of touch, watching the secrets he so often saw dancing in the blue of her eyes.

'You told me once that you never wished to marry at all and that you would like to remain a spinster.'

'And I believed that to be true...then.'

'But now?'

'My place in the world is less certain then it once was and Northbridge is not the home I imagined it to be. I thought to come here for twelve weeks and then return unchanged to get on with my old life, but that will not be so easy now.' She smiled. 'I find myself at a crossroads, Lord Wesley, and it is hard to know in which direction to turn.'

It was her bravery, he was to think later, that made him throw off caution and speak.

'Marry me, then, instead.'

Her mouth fell open and she stared at him, her teeth worrying her bottom lip.

'I am not wealthy and I am not safe in the way your uncle would want a husband to be. There are things about me you do not know and that you may never understand, but I promise to protect you. For ever. My family seat is a pile of burned-out ruins and the town house is heavily mortgaged. But your money should stay in your name, separate to anything I own, because in that way you might understand it is not for riches that I ask this question.'

'Why on earth...would you ask me, then?' Her voice was small, barely there.

'I like the way you reason out things and fight for people and heal them. Besides, Berrick and his stupidity would ruin you and George Friar is not to be trusted.'

The clock ticked in one corner, loud as it measured the passing minute, and outside he heard the rumble of a carriage. Small everyday things counterbalanced against the magnitude of his proposal.

'Yes.'

He could not quite for the life of himself fathom for a second exactly what she meant.

'Yes?'

'I will marry you, my lord.'

'Gabriel. My name is Gabriel.'

'I know.'

Neither of them moved, as though in the action the truth of it all might simply disappear, lost in fantasy.

'Hell.'

She laughed at that, a throaty deep sound that filled the emptiness in him. 'I do not think one is supposed to swear after such a moment, my lord.'

Had she truly just consented to what he thought she had? Could it possibly be this easy?

No.

The answer came quickly. She did not know who he was, what he was, the ache in his thigh only underlining more uncertainty.

He should take the words back and leave her to find her own direction for she had told him of her refusal to marry Lovelace. She was sensible, clever and honest and he was dangerous, unstable and impotent.

Impotent.

The word hung in the air around everything he did and said now and yet he had not been candid with her, with a bride who would know from the first moment he touched her that all was not as it ought to be.

Was this marriage proposal simply selfishness because he thought he might be cured by Adelaide Ashfield's touch? Just another worry that he added to the pile of others.

'I wouldn't stop you doing the things you wanted to. I envisage a marriage of equality and independence.'

He needed to put these things on the table to counter all the other negatives. Perhaps in the balance, then, something could be salvaged, some sense of rightness, and Adelaide had always stressed how important autonomy was to her.

But would it be enough when she came to understand all that he might not be able to give her? He waited for her answer.

'My aunts would have liked you, I think, Lord Wesley, and Lady Montcliffe was just counselling me on the fact that a wise woman finds a union allowing her to gain the things that she needs.'

'And are you wise, Adelaide Ashfield?'

'Wise enough to know that the sort of marriage that you speak of is exactly what I do want.'

She did not mention love or lovemaking.

'I also want a man who I can talk to, a husband who understands the power of conversation and debate.'

Even better. Those things he could manage easily. She neither simpered nor flirted as she stated her requirements, rather he had the notion she had not even thought to. Surprising in a woman. He couldn't help but smile, though a knock at the door brought the others in. His allotted minutes were up and Amethyst Wylde was a woman who was careful with the maintenance of a lady's reputation.

'I hope you have had enough time to settle the affairs between you, Gabriel, but Christine Howard has come to call and I thought we could all have some tea.' Her sharp eyes ran across him as she gestured to her maid to bring in refreshments, a worried look beneath her smile and a hint of curiosity.

'Indeed we have, but perhaps champagne might be more in order, for I have asked Miss Ashfield to become my wife.'

'And she has agreed?' Amethyst asked this question, the timbre of her voice rising.

He turned towards Adelaide, hoping she might say something and was pleased when she did.

'I have.' The soft assent brought Lady Christine to her side, though she, too, was looking at him for more explanation.

Digging into humour, he tried to give it to them. 'The luck of the damned can sometimes take a wondrous turn, though in my defence I have made a concerted effort to explain to my would-be bride all that I am not.' Despite his levity the shock was easily seen on their faces. The anger he felt because of this was palpable. He did not deserve Adelaide Ashfield and they knew it. She was everything good, and honourable and right.

It was Christine Howard who broke the silence.

'Well, I think this is wonderful news. Gabriel has always been interesting and kind. I should imagine he will make a sterling husband and at least with your fortune you will be able to rescue his absolute lack of one. That is two down now. Just my brother and Francis to go and all our problems shall be solved.'

Gabriel had forgotten Lucien's sister's penchant to state the truth in a way no one else would have thought to, though her take on the impending union seemed to have broken through the reserve. As the tasks of finding the necessary things for a toast ensued, Gabriel used the moment to have a quiet word with Adelaide. 'I doubt this news can be contained for very much longer, but if you have any regrets you might be wise to voice them now.'

'Do you?' The query was fired back quickly to him.

He smiled because amazingly he knew that he didn't. 'No.'

'Then why should I?'

'Your uncle won't be pleased.'

'I am no longer a young girl foolish enough to imagine that his opinions should shape my life.'

'But you do understand that others' opinions of me might very well do just the same?'

At that she laughed. 'I hope I am made of stronger stuff, my lord. Allowing others to moderate one's private life is not only absurd, but also very dangerous.'

'And yet the reality of such constant disparagement cannot be overstated.' He smiled. 'Even I find it difficult at times.'

'To live down to your reputation, you mean?' The fire in her eyes was as bright as the small flash of a shared humour. 'Are you trying to dissuade me from your offer, my lord?'

He couldn't lie despite knowing that he should. 'I most certainly am not, Miss Ashfield.'

'Good.' The single word held no hesitation within it and as Amethyst walked across to join them, a servant behind came with a silver tray full of long-stemmed crystal glasses and a bottle of champagne. Two moments later Daniel was pouring the newly found tipple.

'I'd like to propose a toast,' he said as he finished topping up the last drink. 'To Gabriel and Adelaide. May their union be as happy as ours has been, Amethyst, and as fruitful.'

Gabriel caught the humour on his friend's face as he finished. A quiet ribbing held a certain look and he knew Daniel would want an explanation of events as soon as they got a moment together.

But for now he tipped up his glass and drank, the first hurdle jumped and a row of others in front of him.

The champagne made her feel a little dizzy and Adelaide knew she would have a headache come the morning, but she could also barely believe what had just happened. Gabriel Hughes, the fourth Earl of Wesley, had just asked her to be his bride. The spectres of Lord Berrick, George Friar and Richard Williams faded into the distance as she looked over at the man opposite her.

His hair was queued today, tied back in a severe style, but the cravat he wore was softer. In the light from the window she saw a small scar crossing his left cheek just below the corner of his eye and it seemed to highlight all the danger and risk associated with him.

Yet she could not care. No other man had ever made her feel the way that he did, with his humour and his menace and his manner of speaking that held her in thrall. Even from this distance she could feel the rise of her body towards his, wanting touch and intimacy and closeness. Wanting all the things that a marriage promised, all the things she had for so long been panic-stricken by.

He was beautiful in a way that had her holding her breath and bringing her fists into her sides, the hope of it all overwhelming and irrefutable. Could it possibly be this easy to finally be happy?

In the midst of all the joy Christine Howard at her side leaned forward to take her hand, squeezing it and smiling.

'I love weddings, Adelaide, and if I say it myself I am very good at knowing what style suits a bride. Amethyst allowed me to help her at her celebration, so if you wish I would be most happy to do the same at yours.'

'I am not…as beautiful as Lady Wylde,' she answered slowly.

'Because you make nothing of yourself. The colours you wear show your skin in a poor light and the style of your hair is old-fashioned and dowdy. But believe me, Adelaide, there is beauty beneath because although you can't see it everyone else who ever speaks about you can.'

'Thank you.'

'You see, there it is, right there. Most women simper at compliments and turn them into something that they are not. Your directness has its own particular allure and Gabriel has been quick to understand this.'

Despite herself Adelaide laughed. 'I would not wish for a big wedding or a very formal one.'

'Amethyst had about four people at hers and she looked unmatched. Perhaps I could show you her dress and we could begin from there. That sort of style would look very well upon you, too.'

Lady Montcliffe had joined them now and she was smiling as she finished her lemonade.

'I cannot wait until I can have a proper drink again,' she said, her hand crossing the roundness of her stomach. 'From your face, Adelaide, I can guess that Christine is regaling you with her ability to transform one into the most beautiful of brides. From personal experience I should grab her offer with both hands for I don't think I shall ever again look as wonderful as I did on my wedding day.'

'Then I do accept, Lady Christine.'

'Just Christine,' she returned and the three of them set to discussing the colour of gowns and the most flattering ways to fashion hair.

Chapter Twelve

The wedding was small and wondrous.

Her uncle had been furious at first with her choice of groom but had, over the days leading up to the service, made a kind of peace with her that she had found endearing. Imelda Harcourt had simply washed her hands of the situation altogether and left London to stay with her sister in Bath.

'You shall rue this decision for every day of your life, you silly girl, for every single dreadful day. Lord Berrick had a fortune whilst your husband-to-be is rumoured to be a whisker away from bankruptcy. Let us hope he does not fritter your money away as well.'

Those had been the last words between them, though Adelaide had returned to her room to find a book left upon her pillow and inscribed in the front page with Lady Harcourt's name. *Letters on the Improvement of the Mind, Addressed to a Young Lady* was a well-used tome, and Lady Harcourt had marked the section on how to make a good marriage. Each paragraph had stressed the importance of wealth, family name and a spotless reputation.

Lord Wesley had stayed away for the most part. Oh, granted, he had made the obligatory call to her uncle, but the visitation had held only awkwardness, the uncomfortable dislike both men had of the other the resounding tone of the meeting.

Alec Ashfield had made it known from the start that he should have much preferred the suit of Frederick Lovelace for his niece and his questions about the financial soundness of the Wesley estate were both embarrassing and disconcerting.

Gabriel Hughes's estate was in trouble and he made no effort at all to disguise the fact. The family seat had all but burned to the ground and the books of the surrounding farmland accounts were in disarray and confusion.

'You have not been tending to the lands of your ancestors, Lord Wesley, but have instead been cavorting with the womenfolk of London town and gaining a reputation that is hardly salubrious.'

Adelaide thought the earl might argue the fact and was surprised when he remained silent.

'You have the reputation of a flagrant womaniser and a spendthrift and that is discounting your penchant for clothing of a certain style and expense. My niece's money shall not be available to you until you can prove you are a stable and faithful husband.'

Privately Adelaide had wondered if her uncle truly had the power to withhold any of her inheritance, for much of it was already in her own accounts. Still, under the interest of concord, she kept quiet and listened.

'I do not covet Miss Ashfield's fortune, sir, and my finances, whilst nowhere near as healthy as your niece's, still hold a certain robustness. I have not been quite as indolent as you might paint me.'

'My niece is not a woman who would welcome infidelity.'

'I am glad of it.'

'Or intemperate spending.'

Gabriel's smile was quiet, giving Adelaide the impression that he was holding back his fury because this was her uncle and he did not wish for disharmony.

'But as she is twenty-three, soon to be twenty-four, and her choice is obviously made, then I should have to honour that preference.'

'Thank you, Lord Penbury.' This time the Earl of Wesley actually sounded as though he meant it, but he had left straight afterwards, beating a hasty retreat for the front door before she had the chance to converse with him privately.

Christine Howard had also arrived each and every day for the past two weeks. The first visit had consisted mostly of draping various fabrics this way and that, but the second had brought a seamstress who had a quick and deft way with the needle.

'Michelle Le Blanc is Paris trained, Adelaide, and she is one of the best there is. Her husband is a tailor with a firm in Regent Street and as that work is sometimes sporadic she is most appreciative of the extra hours.'

And before long a wedding gown had wound its way out of the light blue fabric, an over-cover of blue-and-green embroidery highlighting the flow of the cloth and a veil in the same thin silk attached to her hair with a band of yellow rosebuds.

Adelaide could barely believe she looked quite so...different. Gone was the girl with a poor taste in colour and design to be replaced by a woman who looked...unfamiliar, her hair flowing down her back and around her shoulders in an artful curl.

'I knew blue would suit you with the colour of your eyes, but I had not quite expected...this.' Christine looked almost tearful. 'If Gabriel Hughes is the most admired male in all of London society, then you shall be his equal in the feminine stakes and none shall question his choice of bride when they see you.'

Crossing the room, Adelaide delved into a drawer of her armoire, bringing out a small box that she had wrapped in a golden ribbon. 'This is for you, Christine. For all your help and generosity.'

When Christine Howard lifted the lid from the box she looked up with a frown. 'Oh, I could not accept such a thing from you. It is far too much.'

The rich red ruby brooch was shaped in the form of a starburst, a number of diamonds alluding to the wake of its movement.

'I saw it in a jeweller on Regent Street and thought of you. It cannot be returned.'

'But it must have cost a small fortune...'

'And since I have a very large one I shall not miss

the loss. The man in the shop said it would bring love to the woman who wore it.'

Unexpectedly Christine burst into tears. 'I had love once, but he was killed in Spain. I should not think to ever find the suchlike again.'

Dredging her mind for some words that might help Christine in her loss, Adelaide came up with a line from one of Shakespeare's sonnets,

'"All losses are restored and sorrows end."'

'Do you truly think they can, Adelaide? End, I mean.'

'I do.' Taking the brooch from Christine's shaking fingers, Adelaide pinned it to her bodice. 'And you should, too. There is only so much sadness a person is able to weather in life and you have most certainly had your share. Now it is time for a new direction, a different future. A better one.'

When Adelaide walked up the aisle towards Gabriel Hughes two days later she had no will at all to flee. Lord Wesley was attired in clothes that were almost stark, none of the lace and frills he favoured in society on show, and because of it he looked harder, more distant and larger.

He tipped his head as she joined him, though he did not offer his hand for comfort. The lace and silk of her dress glowed in the light, the full skirt falling in swathes to the floor, the silk almost alive in its movement.

An organ played somewhere close by, the music lilting and sombre. Two large vases of white roses stood to each side of the font. When she breathed in Adelaide could smell the scent of them and it calmed her.

This was the place her parents had been married in and her grandparents before that, the small chapel a reminder of history and permanence.

Her uncle held her elbow firmly and waited until the minister spoke, releasing her into the company of her husband-to-be only after she looked at him and nodded.

'Who gives this woman to be wedded to this man?'

'I do.' Not said in quite the way she might have wished, a flat anger running under the sentiment. For a moment she thought that her uncle would not step away, but then he nodded his head and retreated.

The guests were not numerous, she had seen that as she came in. Her cousin Bertie sat on her side of the chapel with her uncle's older sister. On Gabriel Hughes's side Lucien, Christine, Francis, Amethyst and Daniel Wylde filled the front two rows. Gabriel's mother was there, too, the grey of her hair matching the steely fabric in her gown.

His immediate family was as decimated as hers, Adelaide thought and stood straighter. She usually towered over other men, but with her husband-to-be she almost felt small. Through the gauze of her veil the room was muted, the others further away somehow, just her and Lord Wesley and the quiet voice of the minister as he took them through the vows.

'Do you, Gabriel Stephen Lytton Hughes, take this

woman, Adelaide Elizabeth Ashfield, as your law-fully wedded wife...?'

She had seen his names on the marriage contract, but to hear them said here was different. She knew so little about him: his family, his hopes, his truths, his past.

'I do.'

There was no hesitation in his words, no under-lying uncertainty. He gave his reply quickly as if he wanted the minister to get on with the vows and have them over.

It was some consolation.

The ring he placed on her finger was also a sur-prise. Of a Renaissance design and fashioned in gold, enamel and diamonds, the fragile band fitted per-fectly. She wondered whom it had belonged to, but he did not linger in his touch or meet her gaze as the circle slid into place. His own hands were bare today, save for the ring she had placed there, no sign of the ornate silver-and-gold band he often wore. It was if she were marrying a stranger dressed in dark and sombre clothes, just a touch of fine linen at his sleeves and neck. None of the man in society on show with the frilly embroidered sleeves and the ornately creased cravats. Even his cufflinks were of plain dark onyx, the stone reflecting none of the light that seeped in through stained-glass windows.

His long hair had been fastened at his nape with a leather tie, the deep red and lighter browns dulled under a lotion that held it in place.

'You may now kiss your bride.'

The minister's direction cut through all her thoughts and brought Adelaide back into the moment. But Gabriel Hughes merely shook away the offer and turned. Catching the worried glance of Amethyst Wylde, Adelaide followed him out.

Could this union be a farce, a travesty, a reminder of all she had promised herself never to feel? It was as if at that moment Eloise and Jean stood just behind her and shook their heads in sorrow.

We told you so, but you would not listen.

Even the spectre of Kenneth Davis could be brought forth and imagined, crouched in the corner shadows with his innuendos and evil. She also wondered wildly what George Friar might make of her sudden betrothal when he knew of it and if that would create a further problem. Had she not promised to give him a reply to his proposal, after all?

'Are you well?' Her husband's voice cut across dizziness.

'I am fine, thank you.' The formality of it all was disturbing. They were married, but they barely knew each other. *Marry in haste and repent in leisure*; the words of the ditty turned in her head again and again and again.

Gabriel Hughes's voice cut through her lethargy. 'My mother would like to meet you. She has just returned from staying with her sister in Bath. But be warned she can be…rather distracted, I am afraid.'

The dowager was a small lady, the corners of her lips turned down into deep creases.

'Mama, may I present Lady Wesley. Adelaide, this is my mother, the Dowager Countess Wesley.'

The older lady's hands were cold and she shook slightly, as though a draught cut through the warm room to land only on her, but the squeeze of ancient fingers was unmistakable as the dowager leaned forward.

'I was more than surprised by this marriage, but Gabriel needs a friend and I hope it will be you. If it was, I could die happily as my daughter has been difficult and I never know quite what will happen with her—'

The earl cut his mother off. 'Perhaps we might all go home to the town house now, Mama. I know Mrs Peacock has done herself proud with the wedding breakfast.'

The wedding meal was a large one, six courses and all served on generous trenchers themed with objects pertaining to a wedding, and when Gabriel stood to talk he kept things impersonal as he addressed the small gathering.

'Thank you for coming and enjoying this day along with us and a special thanks to Lord Penbury for allowing me his niece's hand in marriage.'

He turned then, his pale gaze running across her. 'Thank you, too, Lady Wesley, for agreeing to marry me and I hope our union shall be a long and happy one.'

Raising his glass to her, he proposed a toast. 'To Lady Adelaide Wesley.'

At least in strong drink some of the reasons for this marriage might be made less obvious, she thought, as she finished her glass, watching as a servant stepped forward to fill it up again. Her agreement to marry Gabriel Hughes was not quite running away from the worse alternatives presented, but at that moment it felt awfully akin to it.

Lord Wesley had not truly looked at her during the whole ceremony save when he had placed the ring on her finger and even that he managed to execute with only the briefest of contact.

He regretted this marriage, she was sure that he did. Oh, granted, her gown was wonderful, the blue bodice clinging about her waist and hips before flaring out on to a full skirt of colour.

Beneath the silk was a satin petticoat, sleek against the wisp of stockings. Christine Howard had dressed her hair in a style reminiscent of the old Grecian gods, fastening at the back of her head in ringlets and ribbons, a half veil attached on rose buds.

She felt beautiful. She did. But Gabriel Hughes had made no effort at all to touch her, even inadvertently.

No, rather he had spent the whole of the day moving away, creating distance, allowing others to stand between them and barely talking.

Even his mother had observed her in pity as the older woman had retired upstairs earlier and Amethyst Wylde had looked at Adelaide sternly as she had taken her hand on their leaving.

'I hope that your union will be every bit as fulfilling as my own, but if you should ever need an ear to listen or a quiet place to talk you only need to send word.'

But.

The word qualified everything and the deep frown between Lady Montcliffe's eyes saw to the rest.

And then everybody was gone, the busy work of servants the only noise left as her new husband drew her into a small salon to one side of his town house and closed the door.

'I need to talk to you Adelaide. In private.'

Chapter Thirteen

He didn't speak as he stood there, running one hand across the back of his neck as though easing an ache. When the silence lengthened she sought for words herself.

'The flowers in your house are all beautiful.'

Another bunch of white hothouse roses stood on the table to one side of the room.

He glanced across at them and then back at her, clearly having other more important things on his mind. His eyes were so unusual, Adelaide thought, the gold of them traced in darker green around the edges. He had broken his nose at some point in his life, for the bridge of the bone was closer to the skin there, giving his beauty a more menacing air.

'Thank you for marrying me.' His words were quietly said.

'You thought that I wouldn't?'

'I know you have heard many rumours about my past, so...' He didn't finish.

'The ones that elevate you to a lover of some note?'

He laughed unexpectedly and the sound made things easier, less formal. 'Well, perhaps not that one, but there are others.'

'Mr George Friar made certain that I knew of a law case in which a woman of your acquaintance had been killed.'

'I see. And he told you it was my fault?'

'I do not think he likes you so...yes, he did. I have heard other things about you, too. It seems you are a man who inspires gossip.'

'Yet still you married me, knowing this and despite all those who were lining up to court you?'

'Well, that queue had shortened somewhat after the Whitely ball when you were hurt.'

Again he laughed, but she was tired of skirting around their situation.

'My wedding ring fits perfectly.' Looking down at her left hand, she straightened her fingers to where the Renaissance gold glinted in the light. Could this marriage ever be the same?

'It was a family heirloom of my grandmother's. She gave it to me a long time ago and said I was to keep it safe for the wife I would choose. At the time I wasn't sure I wanted a reminder of such permanence, for at seventeen you have such a notion of yourself that everyone else is excluded.'

Adelaide smiled. 'The first time I ever saw you Lucy Carrigan told me that you were the most handsome man in all of society and that the place in which you lived had mirrors on all the walls. To look at yourself from every possible angle, she said, because you were so beautiful.'

'I doubt you would have wanted anything else to do with me if that was the case.'

'Yet there is some truth in what she was saying. Your clothes. Your manners. In society you are a man I barely recognise, but here...?'

The gold of his glance slid away and he turned towards the window.

'I have lived in the shadows for a long time, Adelaide. Now I find myself wishing for something else entirely.'

'The shadows?' She wanted to know what he meant by that word. Brothels? Gambling halls? Drinking parlours?

His eyes lowered and met hers directly. 'I work for the British Service as an Intelligence Officer and have done so since I was eighteen. My life has not all been indolence.'

Adelaide's mouth dropped open. This was the very last thing she thought he might tell her and yet it all made perfect sense: a camouflage to disguise the truth.

'You are allowed to confess to the doing of such a job?'

'I couldn't before, but as you are my wife now...'

'So that was how you were hurt?'

'Pardon?'

'Your left hand is scarred on the top. It has the look of a bullet wound?'

He raised the appendage to survey the damage before frowning and looking away. 'My mission for the British Service was to ferret out information that could be important. Great things that might change the course of history are hard to come by, but tiny clues and small pieces of information glued together can be as valuable.'

His injured hand lay against the window now, fingers splayed out against the glass, parts of his skin almost transparent in the light, though the scars were darker.

'You were on the Continent with Daniel Wylde? In the war on the Peninsula against Napoleon?'

He shook his head. 'There were secrets in London that were far simpler to shake out than those on a battlefield or with force. A woman unhappy in her marriage, a letter that was left unfinished, a drawer that could be unlocked to find the telling remnants of anarchy. With my reputation access was always easy...'

'The persuasive gentle arts?' she returned. 'And you are good at them?'

'Too good,' he whispered back and in those small words she understood with clarity what the subterfuge had cost him. Living in lies, secrets and deceit had had its own price and Gabriel Hughes had paid heavily for it. The darkness beneath his eyes alluded to such a penalty.

'I shouldn't wish for a husband who was...unfaithful even for the cause of King and Country.' She hated the way her voice shook, but she was shocked by his candour and the way he could confess to these sins with barely a backward glance.

'Good, for I do not work for the Service in that capacity any more. After the fire...' He stopped.

'You were too visible? Less able to hide?'

Another truth flickered in the gold and this time it was one she could not quite fathom.

'I have not been a saint, Adelaide, or a man who has made all the right choices. But sometimes the information that I uncovered saved innocent men and women and I am at least glad for that.'

He had not told her the whole story, but for now it was enough.

Mirrors and shadows. Lucy Carrigan's ruminations had had a deal of truth within them, figuratively at least. He lived through each day seeing a version of himself reflected in the eyes of others that was as unreal as it was precarious. His life. For years.

No one had had the chance to know him before he was gone again, lost in the translation of services to the King and spiralling into a desolation that was all encompassing.

He had thought he would never get back again, never sleep again, never smile or marvel at the world or a woman whose mind he could see working even as she stood across from him.

'I married you for salvation, Adelaide.' The words dried in his mouth even as he whispered them.

But she had heard for her eyes widened, bluer than the sea and as clear.

'So in essence you are telling me that your reputation with women stems from business rather than from pleasure?'

'Much of it was a smokescreen. A simple kiss, a few well-chosen words and they were happy.'

'A far more tepid version of the exploits whispered about you in society, my lord?'

Gentle humour crossed into her face as his laughter filled the room, rusty from a lack of use, but there nonetheless. He felt the tension of the last hours begin to unloosen and reform into something else entirely.

He was not the man he had once been, not the man all of London town spoke about as he passed. But the lack of feeling in one part of his body did not exclude his finesse in others and his wife was the most beautiful woman he had ever had the pleasure of knowing.

God, he was stuck in a limbo between want and ability. But he had his hands and head and body still and if he went slowly, following more than just the questionable tenets of lust, who was to know what might happen.

Without his senses trained on jeopardy and deception he could hear the birds singing in the line of trees across the road in the park. He could smell the lemon on Adelaide's skin as well, a soft and lovely scent that came to him as she moved, small wafts of promise.

Life flowed on, after disaster and deceit, after loneliness and dysfunction, after sorrow and guilt.

Tomorrow they would leave for Ravenshill and for the chance at something more, though the shattered remains of the Manor felt synonymous with his own destruction.

He could rebuild. All of it. A better life. A more honest one with a wife whom he admired. But it was up to him to find the way of doing so.

'I hope I will be enough for you.'

God, now why the hell had he said that? It was the lack of being able to touch her, he supposed, and the desperate want that accompanied such a prohibition. If he had been braver he might have simply strode forward and taken her in any way that he could. With his hands and his mouth and teeth if his body would not rise, just to assuage the fury that held him bound and trussed like a slave.

He wanted to see her. He wanted to hold her gently on the generous sofa behind them, late-afternoon sunlight on the velvet, warmth in the room. But already the sweat was building on his brow and the blood pumping in his throat, and if he could not clamp down on the fear then she would know. All of it. His lack. His sins. His guilt. His penance.

'I tried to warn you before of some of the things that I wasn't.' Breathing in hard, he brought his body into check. 'But honesty has its shades, Adelaide. The honesty of a saint? The honesty of a sinner? One person's truth is another's lies, and who has the wit to tell where the lines get crossed or blurred?'

He could see her mind turning as she reached for an answer.

'My old aunt Eloise used to say there are three

things that cannot be hidden: the sun, the moon and the truth.'

'Buddha.'

'Pardon?'

'It is a teaching from the time of the Magadha Empire. Buddha penned it.'

'I did not know that.'

He smiled. 'Perhaps truth is only simple. In the end, there it is. Us. Here. Married.'

Adelaide breathed out, his stillness confusing, but beneath the mask of indifference she could see vulnerability there, too, crossed with an ever-present danger that was so much a part of him.

His hand came forward and he took hers, the fingers warm and strong. She felt him take in a breath, too, as he waited, the frown above his brow deep. The pulse in his throat was fast and his fingers trembled.

Not quite as indifferent as he might make out, then, as the same shock of knowledge she felt each time they touched shimmered between them.

'You are warm.' His words were soft, barely there as his forefinger began to trace a pattern down the side of her right thumb, the circles leading to her palm and then into the hollows at the base of each finger; a slow and calculated message of intent. *This is me. This man. Take me if you dare. I am not perfect and I do not pretend to be.*

Challenge, too, surfaced beneath the deliberate. Did she feel what he did? This violent jolt of connection?

She felt her own breath catch and then hold with a rush of blood and flesh. Each time he stroked the feeling went deeper, linking with other echoes, as her body answered with a will all of its own.

Meeting his eyes, she understood, too, that he knew exactly what it was he was doing, a lesson in loving from the master of the trade; both eloquent and disturbing.

When his head dipped his grip tightened, the arch of his neck exposed as his teeth and tongue joined his fingers. The wetness was hot and then cold, smooth and then rough, the sharp pain of his teeth against utter gentleness. Playing her.

Adelaide shut her eyes and just felt. Him. There. Against her. Close. He took her thumb into his mouth and sucked, lathing hard against the tug of want and need, the heady clench of surprise rushing through her as his arms brought her in.

And then quiet. Peace. The true relief of her body.

She could not move, but stood, curled into his embrace, spent and formless. Her tears were unexpected, falling against the snowy whiteness of his shirt, darkening the linen.

Unbelieving and astonished. Why had she not heard of this before, this perfect splendid gift? Why had not other wives told her of it, time and time again? They should be shouting it from the rooftops and from the bedrooms all over London town. Another darker thought surfaced.

'This is what you spoke of. Before? Your job at the British Service?'

Her words were out, said. She could not take them back or rephrase them even as his reply came quick and flat.

'A woman's body is a temple, Adelaide. Every worshipper should give his thanks in the very best way he can.'

The very best...

He was known everywhere for his prowess and for his mastery. So many people had told her of it. His flair in the bedroom, his talent with the feminine sex.

Yet he stood there as if what had just happened was a mundane, ordinary, everyday occurrence for him. He was not even breathing fast now and his withdrawal was obvious.

'Thank you.' She couldn't dredge any other thing from the shocking truth of it.

And then he was gone. A quick goodnight and gone, a servant dispatched to show her the way up to her room.

She thought it a game, then, a pretence. His insides ached from the intimacy. As he reached the gardens to the back of the town house, he sat abruptly on a stone seat so that he did not fall.

He had managed it, just, managed to keep himself safe in the illusion of distance. His hands went to his pocket and he found a cheroot. It took him three times to flint the match and hold it to the end, so badly did his fingers shake.

God. Breathing deeply, he held the smoke inside,

the tobacco giving an edge to fear and dulling it into something that was bearable.

He had touched her, with an attempt at the sensual and the promise of what had been in him once. A start.

But the truth had a way of striking back no matter how honestly you phrased it and now Adelaide thought him false, a lover that all of London had some knowledge about and one who used his art like a weapon.

When he felt a little steadier he stood and walked out into the oncoming darkness through the gates to lose himself in the dusk, as he always did when he was lonely or worried or the world had turned on its tail once again and left him reeling for the sense of it.

He had felt the spark as he had touched her, as staggering as the last time even though it was hoped for…expected. Closing his eyes, he tried to drag the feeling back, the smell of her, the satin of her skin and honesty.

Adelaide.

His wife.

Oh, the demons circled still and close, bound by regret and guilt and wrongdoing, but for the first time in years he felt himself being pulled back in the right direction, back into life.

He had been so out of step with it for so very long, the nights of sleeplessness leading into long days of haze. But here at this moment, he thought, he could have laid his head down and slept. Before the dawn. At a proper time. Creeping back into normality.

'Please,' he whispered, 'let that be.' He did not

know if it was to God himself or to Adelaide that he addressed his entreaty and as a growing wind caught him up into its coldness he struggled for all that had been lost inside him and all that he hoped to find again.

She had slept badly, though the room she had been allotted was beautiful. Shelves of books graced one whole end of the chamber and the titles had amazed her.

Eclectic was the word that came to mind. The playwrights Félix Lope de Vega and Miguel de Cervantes sat beside lesser-known poets from the same land. Did Gabriel Hughes speak Spanish, Adelaide wondered, given he had the ownership of a great number of books in that language? Looking down to the next shelf, she lifted up a weighty tome containing many maps of France. His initials were penned inside. Under the writing a date was scrawled: 1794.

Sixteen years ago. Her husband had said he was thirty-four years old on one of the first occasions she had met him and this evening he had confessed to being eighteen when he joined the British Service.

Was this book from that time, the dog-eared pages attesting to a good use? Had he travelled there to get to know the lay of the land, the contours of an enemy?

Other books about distant wars lined a further shelf. Below that *The Canterbury Tales* and old medieval stories were stacked and in the next shelf down every book was in French.

His initials were inside these ones, too, and passages were underlined neatly as though a ruler had been used to hold them there. Thin tomes of poetry sat beside more ornate manuscripts depicting the flora and fauna of both France and England. Two or three grimoires of witchcraft and sorcery stood next to them.

Gabriel Hughes was a man of wide tastes, then, and an eclectic general knowledge. No wonder his conversation was as interesting and broad.

His honesty tonight had shocked her, but it was her reaction to his mouth across her fingers that had unsettled her more.

She had wanted him to find other places on her body to caress, too, her mind knowing one thing and her body another. She imagined all the women who had spilled their secrets in the ecstasy of his ministrations, betraying family and spouses for the simple need of touch. My God, she would have done so herself. She would have told him everything had he asked. Her past. Her hopes. Her opinion of their marriage. She had no defence against such expertise and he had not even kissed her or taken her to bed. A blush of desire filled her cheeks and she walked to the mirror to see a woman there she did not recognise, eyes wide with the promise, cheeks flushed in hope.

Honesty.

What had he said of it?

'I think the truth is only simple. Us. Here. Married.'

So simple she could let go of every single truth she believed? Gabriel Hughes had played women false for years now and if the question was whether he'd done so for a greater good or for a lesser one she had no way of knowing.

From the very first second of seeing him she had felt a connection, solid, hard and surprising. It had shocked her with its intensity then and it had grown ever since. Unable to be fought. Absolutely undeniable.

It was why nothing else had felt right ever since: her suitors, her home at Northbridge, her vocation of healing and her acceptance of spinsterhood. She had been thrown into a reality unlike anything she had ever expected, bright against dull, heat against cold, and the truth of it all had led her here. Gasping for breath.

She wiped away the tears that fell across her cheeks in an angry motion. Crying was not a part of it. She needed to understand Gabriel Hughes and allow him to understand her. He had tried to be truthful and she had thrown it back in his face. A lover of repute who could bring any woman he chose to climax, the deceit of it all excused by the intelligence he gathered. Understandable. Even lauded. She knew wars were not always fought on a level playing field and that the compilation of secrets was never going to be tidy, the currency of duplicity having its own payments.

He had not come to her door last night after they had spoken. Neither had he sent word this morning to ask if she would join him for breakfast. Perhaps he, too, was licking his wounds and trying to find a pathway, back to togetherness.

* * *

When she finally got down to the dining room he had eaten and gone. To make the arrangements for the trip up to Ravenshill Manor, his butler had assured her and turned away. She had seen the look of consternation that had crossed his brow, though, and wondered at it.

Servants knew everything. She had discovered that fact years ago when her aunt Josephine had lost yet another baby and the silence of grief filled Northbridge. A stillbirth this one and a boy. With hair the colour of moonbeams and perfectly formed despite his early coming and his lordship sobbing inconsolably, behind his desk in the library. Adelaide had overheard her maid talking to another of the upstairs girls and was surprised by the extent and breadth of their knowledge of events. Like a grapevine entwined on to itself as its runners lengthened and thickened.

The Wesley staff would know that Gabriel and she had slept separately and that they had not sat together for a first breakfast, either. Even Milly, who had come with her from Northbridge, had looked tense as she pulled Adelaide's hair into a chignon with draping curls around her face.

'His lordship went out early, mistress, before the sun even rose and I have heard it said he was not in bed either till late. The maid who does the fire grates said he often did not even come home.'

'Perhaps he has commitments, Milly?'

'Commitments, my lady?' Her eyebrows had shot up into her hairline. 'I would have hoped you were the commitment he honoured.' Laying down the brush, her maid caught her glance in the mirror. 'I am sorry, ma'am. I should ha' held my tongue. He is good to his horses if that is any consolation. Tom, the stable boy, told that to me yesterday.'

Adelaide smiled. In Milly's world a man who was kind to animals could do no wrong at all. She was glad for the information though, for already she had started to worry. If he did not come home night after night, what could she do about it? This was not a love match. Gabriel Hughes had married her out of pity, she thought, or even expedience, her fortune a way to rebuild Ravenshill Manor. She was a salvation, too, a beacon in the darkness he had fallen into.

The problem was that as much as she tried to convince herself her marriage was one of convenience for both of them, other things surfaced to make nonsense of the notion.

The way he had kissed her hand for a start last night, all her senses rising to the surface like water boiling in a pot, the heat and want unstoppable.

The way she saw the sadness in him, too, when he could not quite hide it, his pale gaze lost in other harsher times. Or his ruined right hand when he rested it on his thigh in a way he often did, rubbing it up and down across the fabric of his trousers as though the skin underneath troubled him.

Nay, if she were honest she had wedded Gabriel Hughes because she wanted more. More conversations, more of his smiles, more of the laughter that came quick when she spoke to him of ideas and books

and dreams. She had never felt this before with anyone, a sense of kinship and knowledge, the mystery
of him wrapped in hope. And need, too. Her aunts
had always dismissed that part of a woman, the place
that found magic in intimacy. Granted she had, too,
for a very long while after Kenneth Davis's attack,
but lately some other understanding had budded and
blossomed. She wanted to feel his warmth upon her,
the urgency, the thrill of blood coursing across reason when he touched her.

The new morning lit the patina of the walls in
the breakfast room, the old paint chalked into lighter
squares where paintings had been removed. The gentle stroke of penury, hidden under excess. In society
it was not what you were but what others perceived
you were that was tantamount.

And Lord Gabriel Wesley was the most perfect
example of all. Lost in shadow, but bathed in light.

He needed rescuing. He needed trust. He needed
honesty. And as his wife she was damn well going
to give it to him.

Chapter Fourteen

She had finished her breakfast already. Gabriel saw that as he walked into the dining room and sat to one end of the table, waiting until the servant had brought him his usual plate of eggs and bacon before he spoke.

'I hope you slept well, Adelaide.'

She looked around to check the positioning of his staff before she answered him.

'I have heard that you did not, my lord.'

His fork stopped as he lifted it. 'I seldom sleep for long.' He wondered which servant had leaked out that information. All the stakes heightened again, a wife who might wish to know all the things he'd told no one.

'Do you walk, my lord? Walking helps, I find. In the country I take a long walk every morning and it allows me the time to think.'

'You are full of excellent advice, Lady Wesley. Perhaps I should indeed start.' He wished he could have made that sound a little kinder, but the few hours of slumber he had finally managed were not enough to foster good humour. He needed to arrange the journey up to Ravenshill and his mother had been ill again in the night. Her health was failing, he had known that for a long while, but today of all the days he just did not have the temperament for her constant melancholy and complaints.

He needed to get to Essex with his new wife. He needed space and time to adjust to being married. He could not leave Adelaide floundering in the no-man's land of celibacy for ever without allowing her some honesty at least as to his reasons.

She was looking down now at her empty plate, her hands in her lap and a frown across her brow. Irritation, he thought. Or uncertainty. The bright and quick mind that he admired lost under the weight of their awkward union and he felt guilty and wary over it.

With a considered motion he lay down his eating utensils and stood, swigging down a mouthful of freshly poured tea as he did so.

'Could you come with me to the library, Adelaide? I have things I need to say to you.'

Another flash of concern in blue, though she nodded and did what he asked, following him down the short corridor. He shut the door the instant she was inside and gestured to a seat over by the window.

'I would rather stand, I think, my lord.'

'Very well. Will you have a drink?'

'This early in the morning? No. Thank you.'

'Would you mind if I did?'

She didn't answer that, but her frown told him she very much would mind. Still with the promise of shoring up his own courage he made certain to pour himself a generous brandy and downed much of it in one swallow. The liquor burnt a fiery path back to valour and he was glad for it. He had to stop drinking so much, he knew he did, and at Ravenshill he would make a start.

'I have not slept well since the fire.'

That was honest enough. He had not done anything with any true skill since, but this wasn't the time for that particular confession.

'Have you tried massage?'

The sort of massage the Temple of Aphrodite was famous for? he thought wildly. The type that led to more than just a gentle touch of skin?

'No.'

'My aunt Eloise was an expert. She had a tutor from the East on the subject and people came for miles to have their aches and pains eased.'

Pushing back her sleeve, she laid a finger over a point a little way up from the wrist on her right arm. 'This is *Nei Guan*, a place known to calm the heart and the spirit. With stimulation it can lead to better sleep and is well known, too, for its quelling of anxious thoughts.'

He began to laugh despite trying not to, the guarded tension in his shoulders relaxing with the humour.

'Your aunt taught you this?'

'Indeed, sir, she did.' The words were given back to him without arrogance or pride and the floor beneath him seemed to tilt slowly to one side as he understood what that meant. She was not like any woman he had ever met before, neither boasting nor subservient. She just was. Herself. Different. Unusual. If Adelaide insisted she knew a method of Chinese massage that could put a grown man into the way of sleep, then she probably did.

Finishing his brandy, he placed the glass down on a table beside him.

'I have not the time to try it now, but perhaps at Ravenshill Manor...'

The smile she gave him back made him want to tip caution to the wind and simply tell her everything. But if he did that here in London she might not be willing to journey with him up to Essex and he wanted her to himself and alone with more of a desperation than he could believe.

'We will be departing for the Wesley family seat in a little over two hours as there is word of a storm coming and I don't wish to be caught in it. The house itself has been badly damaged, you see, but has a wing that was left untouched and I sent instructions to the servants yesterday to have it readied.'

'It will just be us...?'

'Yes.'

He saw her take a deep breath before she nodded and, not wanting to have any further argument, Gabriel bowed formally and left the room.

Her husband did not share the carriage, but rode on his large horse beside the conveyance, one of his servants alongside him. Outlined against a leaden-grey sky and with his heavy cloak whipping in the wind, he looked like a figure out of a book: dark, brooding and beautiful.

She'd known he was a good rider back in London, but here on the rough pathways and the undulating hills she saw the true expertise. Horse and man seemed as one flying across the grassy countryside, the sleek pull of muscle and the easy motion of speed.

'I have never seen a gentleman ride like that in me life, ma'am.' Milly beside her leaned forward, watching the earl and smiling. 'If he was unseated...' She left the rest unsaid as Adelaide looked away. She had been enjoying the spectacle until then and wished her maid had not reminded her of the danger.

'It cannot be far to Ravenshill Manor. Lord Wesley said it was only a few hours and we have been travelling all of that, I think.'

'Tom said the drive into the property was lined in oaks. He said in spring the green reminded him of Ireland and of the little folk and that there is not a sight more beautiful in all of the land.'

'The boy in the London stables, you mean? That Tom?'

Milly blushed and made much of finding something in a large reticule she had brought along with her.

Adelaide was astonished. Her maid had been with her for a good number of years and she had seldom seen her embarrassed. But before she could form a question the shout of the driver alerted them to a slowing in motion and turning into a new direction.

'I think we have arrived,' Adelaide said softly as they both looked out.

The oaks were huge and numerous, the green leaves of summer upon them and clouds of blue flowers at their feet. A river wound its way alongside the small roadway, more flowers again along the banks. And then after a full five minutes a wider vista opened and a house came into view against the storm-filled sky.

A ruined house, the remains of its walls rent by fire and left roofless and jagged. Thick carved stone sat at its feet, the only part that had not been taken by flame.

So this was Ravenshill. She had heard the stories of its demise back in London, the magnificence it once had been, reduced to a hollow shell that threatened to bankrupt what was left of the Hughes family funds.

The earl had reined in his black steed now and was walking it in a more sedate fashion to one side of the carriage. What was he thinking, she wondered, as he looked at such damage?

When the carriage stopped and the door opened Gabriel Hughes stood hat in hand, his hair only just tethered by a loosened leather tie.

'Welcome to Ravenshill Manor, Adelaide.'

The stark and dramatic truth of the house this close up was unbelievable, the scent of burning still in the air, but he made no apology for it or explanation.

How had he escaped with his life? was all that she could think. How had anyone managed to get out of this devastation alive?

'If you come with me there is an annex at the back that was not touched. It is a home for now, at least.'

A dozen servants stood in line to one side of the drive, the wind on their faces as they waited.

'If you feel you cannot stay here...'

She stopped him.

'Even as a ruin the place is beautiful.'

For the first time ever he smiled at her without the ghosts of the past in his eyes and the lines that etched each side of his cheeks lessened.

'I always thought so.'

After walking down the row of staff and being presented to each one they made their way around the side of the manor, past the kitchen gardens still surprisingly full of myriad different plants and herbs and into the smaller untouched wing at the back.

It was spartan inside, but the large lobby was open and light.

'We lost much of the furniture and I haven't had the time as yet to replace it.'

The walls were newly painted, she saw as they came into a sitting room, the floors rubbed into shine with a beeswax polish. The furnishings were all of a solid clean line without any excess whatsoever.

A man's room, any small feminine touches completely missing save for a glass vase full of wildflowers that sat on an old desk under the windows.

A pile of books was stacked on another side table, bookmarks of red paper bristling from almost every one. Maps and models of ships completed the tableau. A piano to the far end of the room was surprising.

'Do you play?' she asked and moved towards it. The cover was down and there were initials on the top within a circle of gold and blue.

'Not well.'

GSLH and CEAH. His initials and his sister's, too? She wondered who might have drawn such a thing. A parent, perhaps, the trailing line of darker indigo reaching down into a red heart.

'My grandmother was an artist. The pictures here are all hers.'

Looking around, Adelaide saw that the room held many paintings, of landscapes and houses and in the corner a smaller study framed in gold showed children laughing in the sun.

He caught her glance. 'Charlotte and me, when we were young.'

The two were holding hands, daisies spread about their feet and a large dog beside them.

'The Irish wolfhound's name was Bran. My grandmother enjoyed the exploits of the warrior, Fionn Mac Cunhail. She also thought he would protect us.'

'Protect you from what?' Adelaide's question came unbidden, but there had been something in the tone he used that was not quite right.

'My father was violent sometimes. Bran was trained to growl at noise and one had only to shout to have him bare his teeth in anger.' Unexpectedly he smiled. 'The skeletons in the Wesley family cupboards are numerous and well known. I am surprised no one has enlightened you on more of our shameful excesses.'

'Scandal being the foremost currency of the *ton*?'

He laughed. 'Well, there is a train of thought that implies it is only other people's misfortunes that make the world go around.'

'Unless its your own world? Then I imagine it would be harder. What happened to your sister?'

'She found her solace in bitterness and my mother's sadness propelled her to flight. A dysfunctional family makes you realise that anything that happens from then on can only be better. There is a certain freedom in that when you are young. It allows you the unfettered opportunity to believe in yourself because nobody else does.'

She touched him then. Simply stepped forward and drew her finger down his cheek. The gold in his eyes was brittle and guarded and he stiffened visibly and tried to move back.

Who else had hurt him? she wondered, as her hand fell to his arm.

'I believe in you, Gabriel.'

He nodded and breathed out shakily, his eyes sliding from contact, but he did not break away from her, either. Rather they stood there in the morning light, two people thrust together in an awkward and unusual marriage.

And right now it had to be enough.

They met later in the afternoon in the kitchen gardens of Ravenshill, more careful of each other after the honesty of their last few meetings.

Gabriel had been out for he had the look of a man

new in from exercise, a glow to his cheeks and his jacket over his arm.

'I see that you have taken my advice about walking.'

He laughed. 'You are full of good counsel and the day is a fine one.'

'I had a stroll around the Manor myself. From this direction it looks a little better than at the front.'

He turned to face the structure and breathed out as if even the looking at it was hard. 'Parts of it we may not be able to save, but there are walls that are still structurally sound.'

'Will you rebuild?'

He smiled and the tension seemed to leave the set of his shoulders.

'It will be a long endeavour. I am not certain...'

'We could ask all your friends to come and celebrate starting with a picnic.'

'Here?' From the expression on his face she knew he was not fond of the idea.

'Beginnings are as important as endings, my lord.'

'Gabriel.'

'And the first step is often harder than the last.'

He laughed. 'Little steps. It is what my life has come to these days.'

'You do not think our marriage was a giant leap?'

Again he laughed.

'Let me show you something, Adelaide.'

She followed him down a path behind the house that led through trees and long rows of flowers. A small wooden building sat in a cleared grove.

'Who lives here?'

'I used to.'

'Why?'

'It was a sanctuary.'

Stepping inside, she saw it was bigger than she had thought. A four-poster sat in one corner of the room, heavy brocade curtains hiding it from view. Apart from the bed there were only two chairs placed before the empty grate of a large fireplace.

'I haven't ever brought another person here. You are the first.' The words seemed wrung from him, as if he hadn't wished to say them. 'But then I have not been married before, either.' He smiled.

'Not even close?'

He shook his head. 'Why did you agree to this union, Adelaide? Really?'

A different question from the one she thought he might have asked. 'Perhaps I liked you, too. To talk with.'

The light behind picked up the depths of brown in his hair and the strength of his body, but dulled his features. Like an ancient oil painting etched in shadow.

'Did you ever wonder, Lord Wesley, exactly where your place was in the world, what your purpose was, and your truth?'

'I did once. Now…' He let the thought linger and frowned. As she waited for an answer he dredged one up. 'Now I am not so certain.'

'The house, you mean, with the fire and the burning?'

He moved back. 'Not so much that, exactly. If it is rebuilt, it is and if it's not, then...'

'You wouldn't care?'

'Less so than I had imagined.'

'At least you have a home, though. Mine was sold when my parents died.'

'So you moved in with your uncle in Sherborne?'

'Not immediately. At first my grandmother took me in, but when she passed away I became wary of...'

'Of life, and of trust.'

He finished the thought for her and she nodded, liking that he understood so clearly. 'Are you?'

'Yes.' He did not stop to give his reply a second thought.

After that there was silence and Adelaide had the distinct impression that he wished he had not said so much. But something in her had been released by their honesty and she could not let it just stop there.

'Betrayal can have the same sort of effect, I think.' She spoke carefully, gauging his interest. From the sudden stillness she knew he was listening. 'When I was sixteen I was...attacked.'

He turned to face her directly. 'How?'

His concern was warm and real, no hesitation in it or reluctance. If she stepped forward she would be right within his arms. Safe.

'A boy...I knew...tried to...' The words were harder to say than she might have imagined. She had ceased to blame herself for Kenneth Davis's actions years before, but still... 'He tried...to rape me.'

She was against his body before she knew it, close in, his arms about her and his fingers stroking her hair. She could smell sandalwood and leather upon him, his more normal caution replaced by fury.

'Is he still alive?'

'Yes, but his father sent him abroad afterwards and I did not see him again.'

'And your uncle?'

'Never knew.'

Another expletive, this time softer. 'Who did know?'

'My aunts. They said I needed to…forget it…to get over it…to go on…'

'Tell me his name and I will kill him for you.'

At that she laughed because at the time she had desired nothing more than Kenneth Davis's demise in a horrible and slow way.

'I hated him for a good five or so years and then one day I saw that such a loathing was hurting even more than the scratches and bruises and fright he had left me with. So I forgave him, just like that. There is a power in mercy that allows one the will to live again, I think, a force that nullifies the endless wrath. At least it was so with me.'

She could hear his heartbeat through the thin layer of his shirt, the beat slowing to a more even rhythm. His breathing, too, was deeper as long fingers wound into the hair at her nape, the sun rising over the far-off hills bright today and with more than a hint of the warmth to come.

'I would never hurt you, Adelaide. I hope that you at least believe that.'

'I do.'

His awareness of her this time was tempered by anger. She had been hurt and he could help, the shock of betrayal binding them, like iron filings to a magnet, cleaved together by pain.

His wife was a much better person than he was. After the fire both anger and gall had leached the life from his soul and he had not wanted to offer clemency to anyone.

But here, now, for the first time in six months, he felt he was not made of thin glass ready to shatter and splinter under the pressure of emotion or touch.

He had also not thought of his own impotence for all of the last five moments, the ever-consuming sadness and rage diminished by the quiet trust her confession had allowed him.

He wondered then how she would view any sexual intimacy given the horror of her attack. His celibacy had been forced upon him, but perhaps hers had been, too. He closed his eyes against the measure of terror the sixteen-year-old Adelaide must have felt.

Who had been on her side, hunting out the offender and punishing him? Who had understood her anger and her shame and gone out into the world to diminish it?

Nobody.

She had been as alone as he was with her old

unwise aunts and an uncle who seemed to barely know her.

If he ever had a daughter, he would make certain that she knew exactly who to turn to, he promised that he would. The thought caught him unawares and he stiffened.

A daughter.

God.

He had never wanted a wife until now and here he was conjuring up a whole damned family.

An impotent husband does not a father make.

Uncurling his hands, he stepped back, pasting a smile across regret and hoping Adelaide had not seen it.

He was back to looking furious again, she thought, as he let her go, and her cheeks burnt with the memory of all she had blurted out.

She had not meant to tell anyone, ever, but in the small cottage beside the ruins of his house Gabriel Hughes had looked so damn strong and solid that it had just flowed out, the cork unstopped and years of enforced silence broken.

Making fists of her hands, she tried to find a return to the inconsequential. But it was all so hard.

She liked him.

She did.

She liked every single thing about Gabriel Hughes. His eyes. His body. His voice. His hands. His stillness. His danger. His distance.

He was still hiding things, she knew that, too. She

could see it in his eyes and in his stance and in the way he looked at her sometimes as though the truth lay through a gossamer-thin layer of falsity and he wanted her to know it.

But not just yet.

This was their honeymoon and for now they were skirting around each other, two damaged souls struggling to make sense of things that should never have happened.

Her world had been torn into small chunks of truth that were falling through the air to find a new earthly pattern, locked together before God and the law. Like one of the jigsaws her Aunt Josephine loved, hundreds of pieces, all only waiting to be fitted to form one perfect and complete whole.

Adelaide smiled. She was not perfect and neither was Gabriel Hughes, but together they could be. She at least had to be certain of that. When he turned away to walk out into the sunshine she followed him.

They picked their way towards the Manor, past the ruined walls and blackened timber and then climbing to a higher stand of stone with a platform behind, the pasture studded in clover and daisies.

'This is where I will rebuild at first, out of the wind and with a view across the valley. It will be a smaller house this time, but built on rock.'

'Like the parable in the Bible from Matthew?'

He smiled as though her words held a truth. 'Then the question is, I suppose, am I a wise man or a foolish one?

In answer she simply stamped her feet on the thick bed of stone. The sound travelled around the clearing in an echo.

'It's a beautiful view. Swansdowne, my childhood home, had the same sort of vistas. I remember the river and the trees.' She swept her hand in front of her, indicating the line of oaks along the drive and the lake. 'London holds no real charm against the beauty of the countryside.'

'Amethyst Wylde says the same thing. It's why she seldom ventures down to the city.'

'How did you meet them, the Wyldes, I mean?'

He stooped to pick a sheath of grass and his fingers peeled off the many husks of seed as he spoke. 'Daniel and I were at school together, but it was only later that I got to know him properly. He enjoys horse racing and so did I and we spent a lot of time pitting our skills against each other. He knows horses like the back of his hand.'

'And you?'

'I used to, but it's been a while since I spent a great deal of time upon one.'

'Teach me to ride properly, then, so that I may see the lands of Ravenshill from a horse without being in danger of falling off.'

He was laughing as a shout from behind made him turn. A man whom she did not recognise walked towards them.

'Wesley. I thought it was you.' His smile was wide and generous as Gabriel put out his hand.

'Alexander Watkins, may I introduce you to my

new wife, Lady Adelaide Wesley. Alex is a neighbour and an old friend.'

The newcomer smiled. ''Tis a pleasure, my lady. My property borders this one to the east and my own wife will be more than interested to know I have met you. If you would like to visit, we would be more than pleased for the company.' His eyes swept over the vista of the ruined Manor. 'Will you repair it, Gabe?'

'To start with I will build another house up here.'

'A good choice, then. When you begin it I'll give you a hand. I have some cattle you might like to look at, too. A new breeding programme has given me great rewards and...'

Adelaide turned her face into the sun as they were speaking of farming and profit and new breeds of livestock. There could be windows here facing the valley and wide doors to be able to access the lawn and gardens. To plan and build a home was exciting and hopeful, and something she had not thought she would have wanted to do.

She was taken from her reveries by Alexander Watkins saying goodbye and asking them both to come calling on his wife and himself soon.

'Thank you, that would be lovely.' Adelaide was quick to give him a smile as he left.

'I could help him with his eczema.'

'The red and itchy skin on his cheeks?'

'I will make him up a salve and see how he goes with it. I had another patient once at Northbridge with the same complaint, only worse, and I should like to see if it clears up as quickly and completely as hers did.'

Gabriel Hughes stood before her, the light burnishing his face. All the many stories told of him by the *ton* surged into memory: his finesse, his conquests, his name whispered soft in the halls by those who watched him. A lover of great repute who'd left a trail of broken hearts behind him as he passed.

He was married now, though. To her. The ring on the third finger of his left hand caught the sun. She had seen it in the window of Phillips, the jewellers on Bond Street, and had gone in and bought it, a diamond set in the cut of its gold. Bound to each other through life and death, for better or for worse. For richer or for poorer.

He must have seen her worry for he reached out and took her hand, his skin warm from the sun.

A start. A direction.

She wished he might kiss her, hard and slow and well. But he did not. Rather he tucked her arm into his and led her back to the annex behind the Manor.

Chapter Fifteen

An hour after supper he knocked at the door of the chamber Adelaide was using and waited until she came to open it. She had let her hair down, he saw, and the chestnut of it curled to her waist.

'I thought we might talk.' He smiled, the edges of his eyes creasing in humour.

'Here?' Uncertainty lay in her query.

'It's private.' His glance went to a book left open on the small table near the chair. When she hurried over to close it he caught sight of small neat rows of writing.

A diary and full of the worry he could see so plainly on her face? Once he had written his thoughts and dreams down, too. God, that seemed like for ever ago.

'It is poetry. I am certain that they are dreadful and I have never shown another soul, but…I write them anyway, sometimes two or three a day and then not for months.'

'But today the muse struck?'

'With a vengeance. I imagine I shall burn them all before the week's end, but for now they help.'

'Help make sense of what is between us?'

Her smile dulled. 'Or of what is not, my lord?'

She was braver than any woman he had ever met and much more direct. Under the valour he saw other things, too, fright and concern the most noticeable amongst them. He should tell her all that he was and was not but even the thought made him blanch.

'I had imagined...' She stopped and then began again. 'I had imagined it different...the intimacy of a marriage.'

'What was it you had envisaged?'

The corners of her mouth turned in a smile.

'This,' she answered, bringing her arms around his neck. 'And this,' she added, touching her lips to his before pressing down, the magic of him exploding into every part of her.

She had no idea quite what happened next given her lack of any experience, but she had read numerous romance books from the library and could guess at some of the ramifications of what she was doing.

But he surprised her as he dragged her forward, slanting her mouth to his own and tasting. No restraint in it, either, though there was anger, too, amidst the need as his fingers threaded through her hair. Their breath combined in the closeness and his heart beat like a drum, pounding between them with such a force that she pulled back.

'Adelaide.' Her name before his mouth returned,

his tongue forcing itself in and then she was falling and falling outside of herself and deep into the ache of promise and hope. No boundaries, no notion of where he stopped and she began, a mutual sharing at the well of wonder. Nothing mattered save them here, pressed against each other and asking for whatever they would give, or take. Just lust, the roiling truth of it in the way he deepened the kiss, brokering no refusal and accepting no passive response.

She let him in without holding anything back; he was strong and beautiful, enigmatic and dangerous. All those flavours and more, the sadness in him and the anger were a part of what he showed her, too, as he let her understand just what one could know from a kiss.

And when she thought she might begin to comprehend, he held her still, the shaky sound of her own breath filling the room as he broke the contact.

'I am sorry.' He whispered this as she closed her eyes, the red warm world of sensation lessening, blurred by disbelief.

I am sorry? Sorry because he could not utter the words she might have liked to hear, the forever words, the loving words? Sorry because she could feel the tremble of unease that ran through him as easily as if it were her own?

Adelaide's nails dug into his arms and he knew she wanted more. His heart pounded as noticeably as it always did when he touched her, but his member had not risen. Nay, it lay warm in the crease of his groin, a quiet thing of no mind for all he'd felt as he kissed her.

The anger in him seethed, and the shame, the manners he usually held on to squeezing through the fury. He needed to be away from such failure, to ride against the wind and the rain and the open air until the roiling unfairness of what had happened to him settled and he could cope again.

But he didn't dare to leave her here, alone with her quick mind to pull all the pieces together and make a sense of them. He wanted neither pity nor help. He didn't wish for mesmerising or sympathy, either, hapless words against a condition that was unchangeable.

His mind wanted her, God, it did without a doubt, but his body and flesh had not made the connection. Would they ever?

Tonight she had initiated the play with the flush of sex on her cheeks and the look of wonder in her eyes, as beguiling as hell and as sensual. Six months ago he would have been on her, emptying his seed until well into the night, a shared pleasure, a mutual satisfaction. But he was dead now from the waist down, withered and perished and numb.

Gabriel Hughes. Impotent.

How people would laugh should that come to be known.

By anyone at all.

He set her back from him, making sure that she could stand and was glad that she looked away. He could not answer questions or feign humour. He could barely even manage to speak.

'I shall see you tomorrow, sweetheart.' The endearment rolled off his tongue unmindful and he bowed slightly before leaving the room.

Sweetheart? Was she truly that? Adelaide breathed out. Hard.

If so, why did he not stay to take his ease, and lie beside her? Could he not see that she wanted him to? Should she simply say it to him? *Stay with me. Hold me. Show me what it is to love a woman well.*

Her only experience at a sexual intimacy had been Kenneth Davis's brutal attack on her all those years ago and in the darkness and terror she had no real idea as to what had happened to his body. Gabriel was soft and slow and burning, his hands against her skin as if they wanted to be there, as if she were precious and beautiful and needed.

She still felt the shock of his mouth and the silver flame of light that rose to envelop her, his breath and her breath one, and an age-old knowledge of each other that needed no formal tuition.

She felt quickened somehow, waiting for more, a need that had no beginning or end, but just was.

Her aunts could have told her what this all meant had they still been alive, with all their reading and far-ranging knowledge, but there was no one else to ask. No sisters or cousins. No friends whom she might have confided in, either.

Alone.

She had always been that. Even at Northbridge in the care of her uncle, her fear of venturing out further after Kenneth Davis's attack growing through the years, rather than diminishing. The village girls treated her with respect and her patients with more, but she had never had true friendship until now with Gabriel Hughes. She had told him her deepest secret and enjoyed every single conversation and she had married him for ever.

Before she knew what she was doing she had a thick shawl around her shoulders and, taking a candle, opened the door and followed him.

Gabriel was tired of it all.

He wanted to enjoy his wife in the deepest sense of doing so, with his whole body and his mind. Tonight had left him tense and wound up as tight as any spring. He ached to know how far Adelaide might let him go and if his body naked against her own would respond in the way he had long since forgotten.

'God, please help me.' He whispered this into the smallness of his chamber and crossed to the window.

It was warm and he took off his cravat and unbuttoned his shirt.

He saw her reflection in the glass as she stood behind him, the pale of her face and the candle flickering. He brought the folds of linen together so that at least his chest was not bare. Then he turned.

'Adelaide.'

'Gabriel.' She seldom said his name unbidden and he liked the sound of it from her lips, almost bold.

'I want to be married...properly. I want you to

take me to your bed and help me to understand what it means to be a wife.'

No hidden meanings, no unexplained intentions. So like her to place things down like that. The danger intensified. But she was beside him now and parting the front of his shirt before reaching in.

He waited, feeling the familiar instant spark, but nothing more. Still, the smell of her close and the soft curl of her hair held him captive and when she looked up it was easy to bring her into his arms.

He could pleasure her. He could still do that. A new excitement clung to defeat. His body was not useless. It was well practised and most efficient at eliciting what a woman desired.

Second nature. Understood. An authority and a master at the gentle arts of loving. Even if finally it was not enough, he knew he would try.

'Are you sure?'

She smiled and that was what did it, the happiness in her and the humour. He had never taken a woman to bed he truly liked… That truth left him astonished, but he shook it away and lifted her into his arms.

This time he was careful, careful as he sat her down on his bed and slipped off her shoes, careful as he undid the ties of her bodice so that each loosened thread exposed the soft fabric of a chemise beneath.

He had always relied on sex as a means of communication but here now it was the loving that he could give her. A different approach, softer, quieter, the feel of her skin, the rise of her flesh.

One hand slipped inside the shell of lawn over

her breast, feeling, exploring, his thumb against her nipple, moving quickly and then quicker again. She stiffened and arched and then stayed still, the bud he caressed proud and hard.

Then the fabric lay pooled about her waist, the wide skirt of her gown beneath it, the candles on the mantel throwing her breasts into a mix of shadow and light.

So very beautiful.

And his.

Dipping his head, he used his tongue, trailing a pathway along the side of her throat on to the collarbone and down to the plumpness before covering her nipple, his hands cupping the round and bringing her closer, the sweet taste in him as he shut his eyes.

Always before he had been mindful. Of the armoire nearby. Of the small room off a bedchamber. Of the dangers and secrets of a house waiting to be discovered.

But here, now, he thought of nothing save Adelaide, of her grace and her humour, of her bravery and acquiescence, of the way she made small noises to show him that what he did was beautiful and that she was grateful for it.

A rush of sadness surprised him, the poignancy of all he had missed and all he had ruined there in that one moment of mindfulness, and then another thought that had him reeling.

He loved her.

He loved his wife.

He loved Adelaide beyond reason and comprehension and he had done so since the first moment of meeting her.

She was his for always, with her wit and her wisdom, with her smiles and her goodness and truth.

He couldn't remember ever feeling as if he was not the one in charge, he who had always easily been able to translate the needs of the feminine sex and give them exactly what they wanted.

But now the rules seemed to have changed and instead of distance he was completely involved. Her skin against his own, the touch of flesh, her breath warm where his shirt fell open to bareness. The way her hair tickled his arms as it fell long and dark almost to her waist.

She smelt of lemon, clean and fresh, the heavier perfumes of the *ton* washed away by lightness. He smiled into the scent, wanting it to fill him up with all of the things he hadn't had much pleasure of in the capturing of secrets.

Shaking his head, he laid his mouth against the beating vein in her throat. He had killed people by pressing down on such a spot and hardly a backward glance, another job, a further instruction.

He had not told Adelaide all of it, but sometimes in the heart of lust there also lay the spectre of death— husbands who would betray a nation, brothers with treason in their eyes.

He'd never made love before and been able to relax like this, never had the luxury of time and safety. His glance fell to the scars on his hand, disfigured against the beauty of her.

He would never be perfect, but he could not let Adelaide go. Rising, he caught her chin and covered her mouth with a groan of both ownership and surrender.

This kiss was different, Adelaide thought, intense and deeper, like words that he could not as yet say.

Oh, but how she wanted him, closer, naked, lying with her on a bed of moonlight and showing her exactly what it was she needed.

'Gabriel?'

He glanced up, eyes unguarded, pools of gold and the ends of tawny-and-red curls falling across his face. In London she had thought he looked like a hardened angel, but tonight she could easily see the vulnerability and the sadness clinging to a ragged edge of hope.

'I want you,' she said, then as his hands found the hem of her dress and rose upward she forgot to think at all.

She woke alone, in her own room in her own bed, a sprig of lavender lying across the pillow. She was naked, she knew that even as her fingers went to the place that her husband's had been, the secret warmth beating and a wetness there she had not known before.

No wonder Gabriel Hughes's name was whispered in the way that she had heard it, with reverence and intrigue and plain pure want.

I want you.

She remembered moaning his name again and again as he had taken her to the stars and the moon

and the heavens with his clever fingers and his soothing mouth. And after he had placed one hand across
her stomach and another behind her.

'Can you feel that?' When he had pressed down the
echoes of what had been became stronger, the heel of
his hand low and deep. 'With touch a climax can be
extended. Claim it, Adelaide, for me.'

And she had, rising against his palm and arching as ecstasy beached across her, deeper this time
and longer, wringing the life from any pride she still
had left, the sensation of heat and release making
her float until her body was nothing but feeling and
vibration.

My God, she had barely recognised the woman she
had become. He could have done anything at all to her
and she would have welcomed it, her, the paragon of
spinsterhood and common sense and good manners.

Turning into the pillow, she hid her face, wondering about the smile that tugged at her lips and made
her giggle.

Gabriel Hughes, the fourth Earl of Wesley, was
hers for ever. Nights of lust under moonlight for the
rest of her life. And yet worry blossomed beneath the
realisation. What of him? How had he found his pleasure in what they had done? She had barely touched
him and he had not wanted her to, either. She remembered running her hand up his inner thigh, but he had
captured her fingers and laid them instead upon her
breast, wetting them with his mouth so that the heat
and the cold made her shiver and then understand.

In the opposites one could find fulfilment. He had

been gentle and then rough as his teeth had come where her fingers rested, and the edge of pain had also become the edge of pleasure.

She stilled in order to concentrate on the throb that began to beat with just her thoughts. She wanted him again and again, here and now, in the sunlight and the morning, her legs splayed apart as her fingers sought the flesh swollen from his touch.

Desperate. Had he made her that? With his expertise and his learning. There were no tears at such a thought, but only the beating, dancing delight of anticipation and desire.

Adelaide heard voices as she came down the stairs an hour later and her hands fisted at her sides. In this state of mind she had no want to deal with strangers, though as she listened more carefully she realised it was Lord and Lady Montcliffe.

Would they know? Could they tell? Was there some understanding between married people that she had not known of before, some secret club, some untold confidence? She had hidden the marks Gabriel had left upon her body under a swathe of lace about her neck, but she knew in her eyes and on her face there would be glimmers of all she remembered. She could not even look at her husband as she came into the room, but smiled as Amethyst Wylde took her hand.

'I hope you don't mind our intrusion, Adelaide. Daniel had to come this way to see about a horse and so we chanced it and dropped in for he had some news to share with Gabriel.'

'I am glad you came for it is lovely to see you.' And it was, she thought, for these people were interesting and generous and warm. She included Daniel Wylde in the comment as they sat down again, glad when the men left Amethyst and her to converse alone.

'Christine Howard said I was to give you her love and to say that the lotion you made for her mother seems to be doing the trick.'

'I suppose I should have made some up for Gabriel's mother, too, for she seems most unhappy.'

'Oh, that will be all due to his sister's problems. I have only met Charlotte Hughes briefly and she was a beautiful but bitter woman. It seems the man she had met in Edinburgh was already married according to Lucien's mother and so she is coming back to London.'

Adelaide was glad she was not venturing north to Ravenshill Manor instead. She wanted a few weeks to understand what marriage was about without others staying in the small annex with Gabriel and her.

'Is this the news you said that Daniel brought with him?'

'No. it was something else entirely.' By the brief flare in her eyes Adelaide knew Amethyst did not wish to divulge the matter.

Daniel had also asked her something from the other side of the room and, looking over at him, her eyes collided with pale gold, the humour in them so at odds with the complete embarrassment in her own.

'I'm sorry...?'

Lord Wylde repeated his words.

'I was thinking that married life appears to agree with you, Adelaide, and with Gabriel.'

He was teasing, she knew, but a wash of red covered her face before she could stop it and for one moment she even thought she might burst into tears. My God, what was happening to her? She had always been able to cope with conversations and challenges and yet here she was after one wondrous night unable to find her equilibrium.

Gabriel saved her by standing and drawing attention back to himself. 'Daniel is here to look at a horse at Colton House. I'd heard about the stud, but I have not been up there.'

'Come with us, then. I would value your opinion of the animal, Gabe. We need not be long.'

'Would you like that, Adelaide?' Her husband's full glance was upon her now but it was gentle, giving her the choice of whether they went or not.

'I would. Is Colton far?'

'No. Only forty or so minutes away. There is a tavern nearby, too, that has an excellent luncheon.'

Amethyst looked more than pleased. 'We'll have a short walk together whilst the men look over the livestock. The day is beautiful after all and I have a need for exercise after the carriage ride for my back is hurting me.'

Daniel looked a little concerned. 'The doctor said you were not to overdo things, Amethyst...'

Lady Montcliffe laughed. 'Wait until you are pregnant, Adelaide. My husband has turned into a fussy mother hen who would like to wrap me in cotton wool and keep me from doing anything. Do not worry, my dearest. This child is at least a month away yet. We women know these things.' Her hands lay on the bulge beneath her skirts and her voice was warm—a beautiful Madonna who understood the power of her imminent motherhood very well.

Adelaide chanced a glance at Gabriel and was astonished at the look that lay so visibly in his eyes. Regret. Longing. Or just plain uncertainty. She could not quite decide.

Chapter Sixteen

The stud farm was large but well laid out and as the men went to the stables with the lord of the house, the two women struck out down a pathway overshadowed by weeping willow trees, the lime-green colour of their leaves in the light astonishing.

'I'd heard the gardens here were beautiful, but I did not expect them to be so marvellous,' Amethyst said. 'Lord Herbert has no wife so it must be he who professes an interest in plantings as well as horseflesh.' She laughed. 'He seemed a good man. Perhaps Christine Howard might come with us next time.'

'If you are matchmaking, it seldom works, I hear.' Adelaide gave this advice with a smile.

'Well, do not be certain about that. Papa was the one who chose Daniel for me and that has been most satisfactory. My father was ill, you see, and thought he had not long to live.'

The next quarter of an hour was spent on the story behind such a statement and Adelaide was delighted by Amethyst's honesty. She had heard a little of it whilst in London, but the truth of what had transpired was both funny and poignant.

'So your father is still managing with his heart complaint?'

'Brilliantly. He seldom is in bed and his new wife, bless her, is the sort who refuses to believe he is sick anyway. As his desire is to have as many grandchildren as he has the luck to meet I am doing my best to make his wishes come true.'

'Your other child is only young, isn't she?'

'Sapphire is almost ten months old. She is a beautiful little girl who—'

Amethyst suddenly clutched her side and paled considerably, breathing out with quiet deliberation as she bent over. A stab of worry had Adelaide taking her hand; the pulse at her wrist was racing and she felt clammy though the fingers wrapped tightly about her own.

'Are you all right?' Adelaide knew that she wasn't even as she asked the question.

'I need to…sit…down.' Her voice was breathless and shallow, a gust of wind making her teeth chatter as she collapsed against a small bank.

There was only grass and dirt to sit on and Amethyst Wylde had begun to shake quite badly. From fear and shock, Adelaide thought, her own mind turning over possibilities as to what was wrong and what might happen next.

The gush of water gave her that answer and Amethyst began to cry. 'I can't have the baby now…

I need Daniel...' She stopped speaking as the first contraction came, concentrating on the new pains that racked her.

Oh, my God, Adelaide thought. *She will have the baby here and I am the only one around to help in the delivery.* Her mind could not quite believe what was happening, but she had enough sense not to panic. One of them had to remain calm if this was going to turn out as she hoped and they were too far away from the house for anyone to hear her even if she did cry for help.

No, it was up to her. She was all there was. Without hesitation she stripped off her wide skirt and tucked it about Amethyst's shoulders as both a blanket and a cushion. Amethyst Wylde needed warmth and she needed reassurance and she, Adelaide Ashfield, was damned well going to give it to her. Adelaide Wesley, she amended as she removed her petticoats. She would need cloth to wipe down the baby and to wrap it. The soft, clean lawn was exactly right.

Unexpectedly Amethyst smiled as she saw what was happening.

'I...am...sorry...Adelaide.' Her teeth clattered together as she spoke. 'If you want to leave me and get someone else...'

'There is no time and besides I am more than capable of delivering this baby. You have absolutely nothing to worry about.'

Fright warred with strength inside her but, even though she had never attended a birth, her aunts had always had much to say on the subject. Lifting up

Amethyst's skirts, she placed her hands on the taut belly.

'This is Nature working at its most efficient, you see, and babies that come quickly are usually delivered with ease. Was your first birth quick, too?'

'Yes. It was f-f-fast and furious.' Cold hands tightened across her own. 'Please stay with me, Adelaide. I could not do it alone and I am scared.'

'Of course I am going nowhere. And look, the sun is out. Your baby will be born into a grotto of green and yellow. I think that is a sign of well-being and harmony and just think of the story you will be able to tell your papa.'

Things happened both quickly and slowly after that. Adelaide had no true sense of time as the contractions came closer together and then suddenly the child was in her hands, his eyes opening, a breath and then a lusty cry.

'A little boy,' she told Amethyst, who was trying to raise herself on her elbows to see. 'And he is perfect.'

After checking his mouth and nose and wrapping the baby in the lawn she placed him on Amethyst's chest, making sure the cord was not ruptured and then beginning to massage her stomach.

Five moments later the placenta was delivered and the bleeding stopped completely. For the first time in over an hour Adelaide took a breath that was normal and looked over at her charges.

Both looked peaceful now, the dappled light across them, the tiny hands of the infant pummelling against its mother's flesh as he suckled, dark hair at his nape still wet from birth.

My God, she had done it. She had brought a child into the world and helped his mother. A joy she had not felt before rushed through her as she wiped her hands against the fabric in her bodice and pushed back her loosened hair.

Gabriel found his wife with her hair down, her skirts missing and blood across her face and hands. But it was Daniel's cry that truly alerted him to what had happened as he crouched near his wife and lifted her up to him.

A baby. A birth.

'Adelaide helped me. She did…everything.' Amethyst Wylde had burst straight into tears and was now clinging to her husband. The servant behind was dispatched to the house to bring a dray and quickly.

'I am certain they will both be fine.' Adelaide stood up from where she had sat and Gabriel's arm went to steady her. 'The baby cried immediately and then began to feed, so although it is early I do not think there will be a problem.'

Taking his jacket off, Gabriel laid it around his wife's shoulders, buttoning the garment to the neck. A thin undershift was all that she had on from her waist down and she was shaking violently.

When he had first come into the clearing he thought Adelaide had been hurt badly with the amount of blood around her and the position she sat in, strains of Henrietta Clements coming back and all the death and blood of the Service. He had felt his heart simply stop, the frozen waste of clogging breath. And then the baby had cried.

If he should ever lose Adelaide... If she should die...

His arms tightened across her shoulders as he held her to him.

'I'd never done it before, though I told Amethyst that I had.' She whispered this so that the others would not hear and the earnestness of her confession was heartbreaking.

His wife had not thought to run for help or gone to pieces. No, she had stripped off her own clothes and coped with it all. Even in terror and inexperience, even without the absolute rudiments of anything to help her.

'If one...panics it always...goes wrong, Aunt... Jean said. She said one has to keep...a composure and a peacefulness for the event otherwise a child might be...difficult to deliver...' The trembling had worsened and without thought he lifted her up to him and took her over to a tree where he sat down with it at his back and with her in his lap, trying to give her the warmth and reassurance she needed.

Now that help had arrived she was panicking. In fact, she thoroughly went to pieces in his arms, her sobs ragged and deep, his warrior of the healing arts finally reaching the limit of what could be tolerated.

'It's all right, sweetheart. Everything is all right now.'

And it was, he realised with a great thump of truth.

His wife was in his arms and the world was still going around. That was all he needed. Just Adelaide and her bravery and strength. Just them. Together.

Much later they returned to Ravenshill Manor, Amethyst and Daniel electing to stay on at Colton House with their newly born son and a doctor who had been summoned by Lord Herbert.

Adelaide was exhausted. Gabriel had given her the choice of staying or making for home, but it seemed all she could think of was being somewhere safe, and the annex at the rear of the Manor was where she felt the most secure.

Gabriel dismissed the astonished Milly when they came into her room, telling her he wanted to help his wife himself.

And he did help her, rolling off her stockings and undressing her with an extreme tenderness, and then finding a cloth and ewer to dab at her hands and face.

Finally he placed her into bed, the clean sheets against her skin.

'Please...come in with me...I am...fr-freezing.'

He hesitated momentarily, but then, stripping off his jacket and pants, he joined her. He left on the long linen shirt and held her close, pulling the blankets around her chin.

'Thank God you were with Amethyst...'

But she simply stopped him with her own words.

'No, Gabriel. Thank God I am with you.'

Then she fell promptly asleep.

An amazing statement when he considered her

day, but here after cold and shock and in desperate tiredness he believed her.

He had never had someone true and good on his side before, not like this. Her ring glinted in the light of a single ten-hour candle, but when he laid his warm hand on top of hers it curled about his own, even in sleep.

Safe. She felt safe here at Ravenshill with him in the small annex at the back of the ruined manor. She had not wished to stay at Colton House with all its splendour and luxury, but had elected to return to the place she felt at home in.

His wife.

His saviour.

Usually at this time of night he was prowling the dark watches and the shadows, aware that sleep was very far away and waiting for the dawn.

But here at barely nine o'clock in the evening he was anchored to this bed and wrapped in the long limbs of Adelaide, tethered by something far more enduring than anger, sorrow and shame.

Shutting his eyes, Gabriel said a prayer. For them, for the baby that had been born, for the years he might have with his wife and for the joy that would follow.

And it was only as he fell into slumber Gabriel realised he had not asked God for the miracle of a healing for himself. In fact, he had forgotten about it altogether.

He came awake in the night, the warmth of Adelaide beside him, her hand across his stomach and her leg slung over his thighs. And in the quiet he reached down into her centre as a moth flies to flame, gentle and soft, her body writhing with the touch.

Up into warmth and wetness and the hidden depths of life, he turned her as she opened her thighs and took her across him, almost real, the bud of her arousal harnessed against his thumb as he quickened his rhythm.

He felt her come, the beaching waves of release, rigid and then loose and quiet. When he pressed in again straight afterwards she cried out, but he covered her mouth with his own and brought her to the flurry of a second climax, this one clenching hard over him and making her shake with the intensity of it.

Like birth, he thought.

Like the beginning.

Lifting his fingers to his mouth, he tasted her sweetness.

She was lost in love, shivering now with delight instead of fear as she reached all the places he wanted to show her and then held her whilst she recovered.

The candle burned low and the moon had waned, the dawn not far off, she thought, for already the eastern sky had lightened through the crack in the curtains. She cuddled in, her hand inadvertently touching the twisted skin at his thigh as she did so.

When he stiffened she knew why he had left his shirt on. He didn't want her to see this or to know it. When his hand came down over hers though she simply pushed him away and continued to explore through touch. A burn, she surmised, for nothing else could have left a mark quite like this one. The fire in the chapel at Ravenshill.

'Did it hurt?'

She felt him smile into her hair.

'Yes.'

'Who tended you?'

'The Wesley physician.'

'Did he use honey?'

'I don't think so.'

'Lavender oil, then, or diluted vinegar?'

He shook his head. 'He wrapped the leg in wet bandages and changed them frequently for a very long time.'

'And is the pain still there?'

'Sometimes.'

'I will make you something for it, then, to relax the tightness. Is it on your stomach as well?'

She went to reach up further, but he stopped her by capturing her palm and bringing it to his lips where he kissed each finger.

'Clever hands. Healing hands, hands that have brought a child who was not meant to have arrived so soon safely into this world. Daniel will never be able to thank you enough. I think he will be your servant for life.'

She giggled, imagining the lofty and austere Lord Montcliffe in such a role. 'I would rather his friendship.

'Well, I am sure that you will have that.'

She liked the laughter in his words and the way his fingers traced circles across the bare skin on her back.

'Would you like to have children, Gabriel?'

All movement stopped and his breathing became shallow.

'Our children, I mean,' she added as he did not say anything. 'An heir for the Wesley title and lands?'

She made herself carry on. 'I do not know a lot about what happens between a man and a woman in bed, but I do imagine it is something like the farmyard and there has to be a contact between us that is…more intimate.'

He still did not answer though his heart raced hard in his chest. She could feel it through the linen.

'If you would like to do this thing, I would be happy to do it with you.'

His swear word took her by surprise as he rolled away from their embrace and sat up on the bed. His profile against the new dawn looked wary and tired, a man fighting more demons than he might ever name.

'Is it some illness that stops you?'

He stood at that and pulled down his shirt, reaching for the candle and blowing it out. The smoke curled into the grey light, a small puff of blackness and then gone.

Like her husband.

Without another word he had disappeared through the door frame and shut it behind him.

She did not see Gabriel until well into the next day when she spied him on horseback on one of the hills a good distance from the house. She knew him from the easy style he had of riding, fluid and graceful, and because the horse was the same one that he had ridden beside the carriage on the journey up from London.

Walking purposefully down to the stables, she thought to intercept him and indeed as she came down the pathway he was cantering in from the other direction, a groom coming to take the steed into the stables proper.

And leaving them to face each other.

'You ride well.' It was the only thing she could even think to say that did not include a question.

He smiled and hit his whip against his jodhpurs, a cloud of dust rising as he did so.

'Practice makes perfect.'

She was at a loss as to how to reply. He had had a lot of practice in the bedroom and yet...

It was as though he could see what she was thinking. 'We need to talk, Adelaide, but not here. If you could meet me in the blue salon in, say...an hour?'

He sounded so serious her heart began to beat quicker, a new dread coming from nowhere. Would he tell her that this marriage was a mistake or that he never wanted children? A hundred other possibilities crossed her mind, all fleeing as he stepped forward and placed one warm hand across hers.

'It is my problem, Adelaide. Not yours.' And with that he walked back into the stable to see about his horse.

He watched the clock on the wall slow in its minutes as it turned towards eleven. He had to be honest with her, he had to tell her who he was now, a man ruined from circumstance and foolishness, a broken man who should never have married her.

'God, help me.' The words echoed in the room and in his stomach, hollow and sick, scared and lonely. This was the truth of him. This man.

He swore again beneath his breath when he heard her coming, light footsteps on the parquet floor. Could he do it? Would he do it? How was one to sacrifice heaven for hell and barely a backward glance?

'Thank you for coming.' She was here now and he crossed to close the door behind her, standing against it for a moment in indecision, weighing up his strength.

'You thought I would not?' The nervously asked question helped somewhat as did the shake in her fingers as she wiped back a curl that had fallen across her cheek.

He wanted to step forward and hold her, make her understand all that he was inside even amongst the shattered fragments. But it was not fair to do so. He had to give her the facts to make her own decision about their marriage without coercion. Without feeling. Cold. Hard. Honest.

I am impotent.

Say it, his body chided, but his mind refused.

He hated the way he was breathing fast and the sickness was again back, sweeping over him so that he could barely take in air.

He sat down hard on the chair behind him and held his head spinning with the horror of everything. For one moment he thought he might even cry in front of her like a baby.

And then she was beside him, her hand across his brow and at his wrist, feeling for the signs of sickness, he thought, trying to determine what to do.

Fix me up. Make me better. Make me the man I once was with your potions and your kindness. Make me whole again.

These words turned in his mind. Foolish hopes that would never come to pass.

'I might be able to help you, Gabriel, if you could only tell me what's wrong.'

He shook his head. 'No one can help me.' He hated the self-pity he could hear in his words, but could not take them back.

And then because she had seen him at his very worst, a man with nothing left to lose save his final pride, he simply blurted it out.

'I cannot make love any more because I am impotent. The accident took that part from me, the burns, the fire. I cannot father children. I cannot be a husband. I should have told you, of course I should have before you married me, but I wanted...'

He stopped and swallowed. 'I love you, Adelaide, and I wanted you to love me back.'

Adelaide could not believe the words he said. Not the ones on impotency and the fire and burns, but the other ones; the ones of love and wanting.

'I love you, too, Gabriel. With all my heart and

soul. I loved you from the first moment of meeting you, the very first in the small arbour at the Bradford ball when you warned me about your reputation.'

Placing her hands on either side of his face, she knelt down beside him and looked into his eyes, a darker bruised gold today, though a flare of hope was there, too, amongst the anguish and disbelief.

'The physical things you speak of are only one side of a union. What of trust and love and closeness? A marriage is about friendship and honesty and laughter. I have all of that with you. And more...' She smiled. 'When you take me to bed I cannot remember anything at all save the way you make me feel. If that is our life, then I am more than happy with it, though I should like to be able to pleasure you, too. You could teach me.'

He stood at that and brought her into his arms, the scent of soap and linen filling in the cold of the room. He had washed and shaved since she had seen him last, the hair at his nape still damp, spots of water darkening the loosely tied cravat he wore at his neck.

Beautiful. More beautiful than she had ever seen him with the edge of vulnerability staining his eyes and deepening the lines in his cheeks.

Not a boy but a man, honed by tragedy, seasoned by fire.

'And the promise of children, Adelaide? What of this loss?'

'We shall enjoy the offspring of your friends.

Already there are two little Wyldes whom we can shower with our love. Your friends will have others.'

She felt him smile rather than saw it, felt him relax and meld into the shape of her, exhausted by his truths.

'I don't deserve you.'

'Why?'

'Because you did not know who I once was and that is unfair. All you have now is the wreck of me.'

'And what of me, Gabriel? Did you know the girl who used to laugh more, enjoy life more? The one who was not scared of strangers and men and the midnight dark? That girl was lost, too, with Kenneth Davis's attack, gone in a second, replaced by a new woman. But you know me as I am now, lessened, less trusting, more uncertain. I hope it is enough.'

'Enough?'

'Marriage is just that, don't you think? Change and challenge and chance. The people we are now will be different from the ones we will be in ten years or twenty. Or fifty when we are old and grey and wrinkled. But will we love each other less because of life marking us, moulding us, strengthening us? Like steel in a forge, stronger in adversity and more tempered. Less breakable because of the hardships and of the joy.'

'I love you, sweetheart. I love you so much that it hurts, here.' He placed one of her hands across his heart and she could feel the thump of it, neither as fast as it had been, nor as heavy. She was glad for the fact even as sadness crouched close, for him and for her and for the things they would not have together, but also for all he had just given her. Love. Truth. Himself.

And then just like that his touch changed back into the magic, drawing a line down her neck and on to the flesh above her bodice in the way only he was able to.

'You are so beautiful,' he whispered, his lips grazing the place where his fingers had been, down and down on to the rise of her breast. She felt his tongue there, too, the dampness and the heat, and then a heavy suckling, hollowed and echoing. Sounds of her heartbeat and her breath and then his and an answering call somewhere lower. *Take me*, it cried, *and make me yours*. And he did then, with his hands and a swift sharpness that had her arching backwards, the heavy beat of blood and want coursing through her. Her fingers were now in his hair, pulling him in, making him hers.

'I love you.' Softly said and formless. He took her loving and stretched it around desire and appetite before changing it again to the white-hot heat of knowledge.

When he was finished and she simply stood there watching him, spent, he took her hand and laid it across his nipple.

'Here,' he instructed, 'like this,' he added, shepherding her fingers and pinching in a certain spot between forefinger and thumb.

She understood what he was doing. In the ashes of honesty a new phoenix was rising, a different one, a finer one. Together they could make this marriage the best it could be. She licked the tips of her fingers as he had done with her and set to work.

When the bud hardened she was pleased and when his breathing ran into quickness she was even more so.

And then she laid her mouth on his and found the taste of him with her tongue, slanting across wetness, taking the breath from them both, the power he allowed her now more exciting than anything she had ever known.

This was what it was like to truly love someone without reservation or embarrassment. Threading her fingers around his neck, she brought him down with her on to the thick burgundy rug.

'I will never stop loving you, Gabriel. Ever.'

'And I will make certain that you do not,' he whispered back.

They barely left Gabriel's bedchamber the next day and the one after that as they discovered things about each other by talking through the hours.

'I think Henrietta Clements meant to take me with her when she died because I did not love her enough.' It was late afternoon and they were sitting near the window, wrapped in each other's arms in the large leather wingchair.

'Was it she who set the fire, do you think?' Adelaide's question came quietly and just like that the last piece of the puzzle clicked into place. The candle. The flame. The chapel curtain dust-dry with age.

'Yes,' he said, the last vestige of doubt falling away. 'It was she. I remember now.'

He'd gone to meet her because she had sent him a message. She had the names of those her husband was associating with, the men and women who might bring down a kingdom at worst or a government at best.

He had not wanted to go, he knew that, because already there was a glint of madness in her eyes that worried him.

She had pulled a gun on him as he arrived and made him stand still, there by the marbled font, under the ruined body of Christ. Her hands had been shaking so much he thought the weapon might have gone off without her even meaning to shoot him.

'Place your right hand on the Bible, Gabriel.'

He had done so, waiting for his chance to disarm her.

'Swear you will love me for ever, in God's name. I want to hear you say it now and mean it.'

He'd swallowed and hesitated. He wasn't a man unable to use a lie for his own means even in a house of God, but there was something else at play here, something hidden and desperate.

'Say it.'

As one hand had covered her belly in that certain protective gesture he suddenly understood.

'You are with child?'

She had nodded, the gun lowering, but not forgotten.

'Is it mine?'

Please, God, let it not be. If you ever do anything at all for me, my lord, please do not let this child be mine.

She shook her head and relief flooded through him. 'But it's not my husband's, either. George Friar, my husband's cousin, took me against my will and I could not stop him.'

She was crying. Loudly. 'I think he would kill Randolph if he had the chance, too. Take me away with you, Gabriel, because you are the only one who has ever been truly kind to me. Say you love me and we can be free.'

And when he could not the candle was in her hand and then it was within the old curtain dividing the font from the chapel proper.

The horror must have shown on his face as the flame took, for she suddenly and simply stepped back into it, fire racing up her wide skirts and into her loosened hair.

He had tried to save her, tried to find the woman under the heat and bring her out, but the smoke had billowed, death tracing their skin with its blackness, the last echo of reason as he reached for the water in the font and poured it across them.

'It was a month before I remembered anything again,' he said softly as Adelaide's hands traced the ravages of fire upon his thigh. 'For a time I thought it was me who had killed her and then bits came back.' Guilt made his voice hoarse. 'We both betrayed each other, I think, her in love and me for the love of secrets. She was a means to an end and I deserved all that I have now.' He sat up straighter and frowned. 'But she gave me the names and I remember them now. George Friar is the one who killed Randolph Clements, the one we want.'

'We?'

'The Service. When Daniel was here he brought me a letter from Alan Wolfe that said Henrietta's husband had been murdered. They found his body in a tavern near Oxford. Odds are it was Friar's work for he has left his lodgings and disappeared.'

'To go where?'

'That's what I plan to find out.'

'I met him at an afternoon soirée in London just before we were married and he insinuated he knew about Kenneth Davis and the way he had attacked me. He wanted me to go with him as his wife back to the Americas, though it was my fortune he had his eye on. There is a side to him that he does not show often, a darker side.'

'Is Davis in England, then?' Gabriel tried to keep the fury from his tone.

'No.'

God, could Friar come back here, then, to Ravenshill Manor where it had all started? Was he after some sort of twisted vengeance with Adelaide as the bait? He held his wife closer and kissed her hair, but the darkening sky outside looked more threatening than it had done before and the lack of manpower at Ravenshill needed redressing.

He did not want to worry her with this, but he needed to be ready just in case. Standing, he stretched, trying to look nonchalant, but he should have realised that Adelaide's mind was turning as fast as his own.

'Would he come here, do you think? Would he be after you next because of Henrietta Clements?'

He smiled. God, this is what it was to be married. You forgot about yourself and thought of the other person. The stakes heightened and a new fear rose. If anything ever happened to Adelaide he would not survive. He knew that with a certainty that took the breath from him.

'We will be safe, sweetheart, I swear it.'

Gabriel sat at the window that night and looked across the land of Ravenshill before him. Bathed in the oncoming dusk he could see as far as the Barron Hills in one direction and the Scott River in the other. His land. Wesley land; land that had been in the family for generations and generations, wrought in pain and protected in blood.

He felt safe here, he thought, because he knew the lie of it, the hidden places and the valleys, the streams and the meadows. Oh, granted, Henrietta had surprised him once in the chapel with her madness and her delusions, but he was not the same man that he had been then. Now he had a purpose to live for, a reason for laying down his life and protecting his family.

Adelaide. They might never have children, but they would always have each other. His mind wandered to clever dark-haired little girls with smiles like their mother, but he shook the thought away. Even given his love for his wife his libido had not awakened. He swore beneath his breath, but softly, for Adelaide was asleep behind him, curled up in repose, and he did not wish to wake her.

'Come on, you bastard,' he whispered and his fingers curled around the barrel of his gun. 'Show yourself to me so that we can meet honestly and finish this.'

But nothing moved as the sky lightened and the dawn broke pink over the lush green landscape that was Ravenshill.

Chapter Seventeen

Daniel, Amethyst and baby Robert Wylde came to the Manor the next morning, stopping in on their way back to Montcliffe.

'Amethyst was fretting at Colton House and she wanted to be home, but we needed to tell you again, Adelaide, of how much we will always be in your debt. If there is ever any favour you wish from us...' Daniel Wylde stopped and shook his head. 'You would only need to ask and it shall be yours.'

'I would like your friendship,' she said and gave Amethyst a hug before taking the baby. He was small and beautiful with rosebud lips and a shock of dark hair. As unfocused blue eyes watched her own she smiled.

'He is Robert after my father,' Amethyst explained, her fingers stroking the downy head. When Adelaide looked up and saw her husband's eyes on her holding little Robert she also saw what no one else ever would.

Loss.

It was scrawled across the gold with a flaring damage. Fleeting and then hidden.

Did he think it mattered so very much to her? Did he imagine he was less of a man only because he could not father a child? Crossing the room, she laid the baby in his arms, liking the way his bigness cradled the fragility. Their circle of progeny might be broken, but others could be formed. Others like this child, one small hand winding its way around her husband's finger. Adelaide knew enough of life to understand the beauty of compromise.

'We shall always be here for you, little one,' she said softly. 'In good times and in bad.'

'Speaking of bad,' Daniel suddenly said, 'have you heard any more from the Service about Clements's death, Gabe?'

'I'm certain it was George Friar who killed him. Clement's cousin,' he clarified as Daniel looked puzzled. 'He was the one who stood to inherit any money. Friar told Adelaide he needed cash to inject into a Baltimore project, and with Henrietta dead there was only Randolph in the way.'

'But wouldn't others suspect him?'

'He set himself up an alibi with those who he'd been in cahoots with, men whose interest in politics did not quite reach to the shedding of blood for it. Friar undoubtedly was the one who did that and he chose his accomplices well.'

'Do you have proof?'

'Only the memory of Henrietta's last words. She

told me about Friar before she threw herself into the flames, but I had not remembered it until yesterday.'

'A timely recollection, then. How dangerous is he, do you think?'

Gabriel ignored Daniel Wylde's question and posed one of his own. 'When you go back to Mont-cliffe, would you take my wife with you?'

'No.' Now Adelaide understood. 'I am going no-where without you, Gabriel. We could both leave and then Lucien and Francis could help you, too.'

'Daniel will bring them back once he has seen you safe. Please, Adelaide. I can't think of you and Friar both and I am well able to look after myself here.'

Adelaide thought wildly. She could not ask Daniel to stay and assist Gabriel because he would want to be sure to shepherd his wife and baby to safety. And there would be a gap of hours that Gabriel would be all alone. She thought of the servants and knew they would be some help, but against a trained killer...?

'You would return to Ravenshill immediately?' This question she asked of Daniel.

'I would.'

'Then I will do as you ask, Gabriel.' She thought that her heart might just break there in that room with the jagged thought of leaving.

'Gabriel is the happiest I have ever seen him look,' Amethyst said as the carriage swept through the im-pressive lands of Ravenshill. 'Daniel says we should take to the game of matchmaking with more alacrity as we are undoubtedly successful at it.'

'Where is your husband?' Laughing, Adelaide glanced outside to see if she could see Lord Montcliffe on the horse he had mounted as they left the house.

'He's scouting ahead probably. Just to be certain that it is safe and that all...'

Her words died on the sharp crack of a bullet and then a second and third one. Any hope that there was a hunter nearby died with the slowing of the coach.

'My God, where is Daniel?' Amethyst Wylde's panicked voice rose above the silence and she tucked baby Robert into his tiny bed on the floor and draped her skirts across him.

Protection.

Adelaide saw the look of it in her eyes even as she swallowed back her own fright.

The carriage door opened a few seconds later and George Friar stood there, a different man from the way he had looked in London with a bloodied bandage around his hand and in clothes like those worn by the countryside peasants.

'Get out.' The gun he had was pointed straight at her and without thought she did as she was told, shutting the door behind her once she was through it and hoping it was only she that he was after.

Please, God, do not let the baby cry, she thought as she walked away with Friar towards his horse. *And please do not let Daniel ride over that ridge unarmed.*

So focused on trying to keep the Wyldes safe she had forgotten about her own well-being, and when Friar brought his hand up and slapped her with all the force he could muster, she fell at his feet. Would he kill her here before she had the chance to fight back? Dizziness made her feel sick.

'Get up.' His mouth was a hard slash as he hailed her to the horse. 'That is for slapping me at the ball and this is from Kenneth Davis.' This time he punched her in the stomach, a hard indifferent fist that jammed the air from her windpipe and made her shake violently.

'Now keep quiet and you might live awhile longer. It's your husband I want. He killed Henrietta and he needs to pay for it.'

'No. She...killed...herself...'

'Liar.'

He hit her again across the cheek before hauling her up on the horse. Adelaide knew it would only be a matter of hours before Gabriel came to find her and she prayed to God that the mad and dangerous George Friar had not killed the Earl of Montcliffe.

Red-hot anger filled Gabriel's head, anger that would not help anything.

The bastard had his wife. He had dragged her off out of the carriage and hit her. Hard. Amethyst had said so.

Daniel lay on the sofa with a bullet through his side, the kneeling apothecary trying to staunch the bleeding.

'Friar caught me...as I came through a glade...of trees. Knocked me clean off my horse and...out cold.'

'I found him after I had left the carriage. Our driver is dead and so is the other guard.' Tears trailed down Amethyst's cheeks and the grime of the day stained her clothes. Baby Robert had been taken upstairs, the housekeeper and two maids seeing to his every need.

'So he took the track through the river?' Gabriel asked again, already selecting guns and a knife from a cabinet in the corner.

It would be getting dark in a few hours. He had to find Adelaide before nightfall or else... Shades of what had happened to Henrietta Clements came to mind, but Gabriel pushed those away and barked out instructions to the few male servants he had kept on at Ravenshill after the fire.

'Lock the doors after I go and don't let anyone in, unless you can see it is me.' He shoved a gun into the hands of his elderly butler and gave another to the footman. 'Cover the house from each direction. If you see anything move, shoot first and ask questions later.'

Daniel had lost consciousness again now, his face pale and drawn.

'Can you fix him?' This was barked at Andrew McAuley, the local apothecary.

'Yes. It is a surface wound. The bullet passed through the muscle on both sides, which explains the bleeding, but it is already stopping. But he mustn't be moved for a good few hours until the blood sets.'

'Very well. Amethyst, find some blankets from upstairs and make him warm. Get the housekeeper to make you a hot drink as well. You are shaking.'

And with that he left, the house behind him and the greying dusk in front.

Friar had gone to the old homestead near the quarry, he thought, as he mounted his horse brought to him by one of the stablehands.

'I heard about your wife, sir, and I hope you find her soon. The building near the slopes of scree could be where he has taken her if the other lady was correct in her directions.'

'My thoughts exactly. I want you to go up to the house and get the butler to give you a gun. If I am not back by the morning, tell Lord Montcliffe to organise a search party and send for the constabulary. Go and find Alex Watkins, too, and make certain he is armed.'

'Very well, my lord,' the other answered, holding the reins as he mounted and then handing them to him. 'Good luck, sir.'

Then Ravenshill was behind him as was the growing, swirling wind. He'd have to be careful with that. If Friar's horse smelt his one...?

He left that thought alone and thundered onwards.

Adelaide was tied to a tree, the bindings at her neck cutting off breath so that she had to sit up and tip her head backwards slightly just to gain air.

Don't panic, she thought, as she watched George Friar. *Don't move, either.* He had split her lip as he had hauled her from the horse and she had a pounding headache from where he had knocked her unconscious with the back of his heavy knife in order to tie her down.

She was expendable now. Gabriel would come and it did not matter if she lived or died. Friar had made that point eminently plain.

'Do anything to annoy me and you are dead.'

The wind blew in steadily, a low and keening cry as it hit the tall pines and whistled through them. The sound of her heart kept the rhythm of the wind, too, thump, thump, thump, in her ears heavy and hard.

She felt sick and began to shake. If she vomited, she would be dead, the oxygen she took nearly too minimal to allow life even as it was. She swallowed back the bile as well as she was able and thought of Gabriel.

If he came straight through the path, that would be the end of it, but this was his land and he would know the traps. She prayed Amethyst had thought to see which direction Friar had struck out in as spots of white began to dance in her eyes, heat rising like flame across her.

A slow death. Unnoticed. Degree by degree. She could not even whimper for fear that Friar would kill her. Heavy dread gathered across pure hate and the waste of everything spread over that.

To only just find happiness and then to lose it. She had finally understood what it was to be loved without reservation, without limits and now to have it snatched from her. No, she could not allow it.

Sitting up straighter, she tried to find the little air still left to her and clamped down upon her shaking.

'Please,' she whispered. 'Please.'

* * *

His wife was dead. He could see the whiteness
across her face and the blood at her lip and eyes and
head. The ropes had killed her, tightened by fear as
a collar about her neck and from this distance he
could see no movement and no breath. Her hands
lay crooked at her sides like wooden marionettes in
the Marais in Paris, abandoned after a puppet show.

Nothing mattered any more save to kill Friar. He
came from the trees at the side with a guttural scream
and fell upon the man before he had the chance to
lift his gun.

One slice with his knife and another to the stomach; let him bleed out everywhere, his guts spilling
on to the ground beneath him. A fitting end.

And then he was at the side of Adelaide, cutting
the ties, loosening the ropes and laying her on the
ground. Amazingly she took in breath, a huge gulp
of air that changed her pallor from white to red in a
matter of seconds and allowed her to lift one hand
to his face, fingers shaking as she grasped his hair.

'You are…here. I prayed to God…that you would
come, but…'

He simply lifted her, away from the cottage, away
from the stinking, bleeding body of Friar, away from
the ropes and the reminder of what had been. She was
recovering quite rapidly, her arms gripping his and
her voice stronger. He thanked the Lord for it.

'I love you, Gabriel. I knew you would come for me.'

When he sat her against the wall at the back of the

house he began to laugh, the shock of escape perhaps, and the luck of it.

God. They were both alive and safe. She still lived and breathed and was. Alive.

The feeling of power hit him like a heavy blow right into the groin, taking the deadness and replacing it with pure and unadulterated lust. Vital. Quickened. Energetic. Any humour fled.

'I want you.' The words were out before he knew it.

'I want you, too, to forget,' she returned, reaching up and he lifted her skirts as she opened her legs. The blood beat through him out of control and frantic. If he wasn't within her he would die, it was that simple.

Not just want, either, but need, and not just need, but desperation.

When she bit into his shoulder to hurry him on, he moved her thighs over him and sank in, as far as he could go, claiming her as his own.

'Mine,' he cried as he felt the giving.

Her breath caught as the barrier of her virginity fell away and he stopped, dead still, giving her the time she might need to accommodate him, both their hearts beating in unison and desire. Her nails dug into his skin, keeping him close.

He rode her with the thought of possession, pressed in tight with the understanding that they could both be saved by it and survive with the oneness and the relief. Almost seven months of grief and loss flowed now into elation and when she shouted out and arched he went with her willingly, the spill of his seed deep in her womb as her muscles clenched and held him still.

Life and lifeless lay on each side of the same coin, happy and sad separated by a thread. This was the little death the French spoke of, the place where nothing else mattered save sensation, the suspension of energy whilst time stopped and each separate beat of two hearts lay perfectly merged, blended and united.

He turned her head and kissed her in the same hard way, deep and rough, and she kissed him back, without reserve or restraint, giving as good as taking.

This was not the time for a fragile tryst or a tentative trust. His body shook with the want of her and he felt himself harden again.

'I love you. I love you more than life itself and if I lost you…'

She placed a finger on his top lip.

'There are no ifs, Gabriel. I will never leave you.'

She smiled as she drew him back in, guiding him to the slickness of her centre. This time his ardour was quieter and more tempered, fierceness buffered and held in check. The wrath was gone, but the wonderment still lived on, her warmth and her tightness. The bruising around her neck was already turning black and the cut on her head had begun to bleed. But he could not stop and tend to her just yet, the shake of fear still in him, the fright of loss unquenched. He felt the crescendo before it even came, cutting into him like a hot knife across butter, the relief of it making him shout her name again and again in pure and honest gratitude. The noise of the pines above snatched the sound away.

Afterwards Gabriel took her in his lap and wrapped her with his cloak so that they were enfolded in the darkness and the quiet. The moon had risen, the light of it spilling through the trees and across them both.

Unreal and shadowed.

'You are no longer impotent?' There was humour in her whisper and he drew his hands through his hair.

'Rage has cured me, I think, and fear. When I first saw you I thought you were dead and then I was in you, scrambling for life and love and for ever.'

In the moonlight he saw her smile. 'I think all those rumours about your prowess might very well be true. But from now your expertise is only for my benefit.'

When he laughed the sound travelled through the glade and then echoed back, the small joy bouncing and reverberating against the trees. Like music.

It was his life now. Complete. Adelaide had brought him that. Acceptance. Resurrection. Absolution.

He looked upwards into the heavens and thanked God for bringing her to him, through the darkness of his life and into the light.

They arrived back at Ravenshill at midnight to find Daniel Wylde had been put to bed and that the bleeding on his side had stopped hours ago. Amethyst came to meet them at the doorway and when she saw Adelaide she took her into her arms.

'Thank God you are safe. Thank God we are all safe. Your housekeeper made us take your room, Gabriel, but I can always move Daniel...'

'No. We will sleep in the cottage at the back.'

'You are sure? Did you see your neighbour—Alexander Watkins, I think he said was his name? He came looking for you.'

'Yes. He helped me clean up...things and then went to get the constabulary. That's why we have been so long.'

A cry from Robert had Amethyst turning.

'We shall have to talk in the morning.' She smiled at both of them and then went back into the annex, leaving Gabriel and Adelaide to gather a few things and then make their way outside.

The world seemed softer tonight, more gentle after the terrible day, and Gabriel was glad for it.

Once in the cottage he made certain the lock on the door was secure and then lit a few of the candles he had brought over from the annex. Taking off their clothes, they jumped beneath the heavy eiderdown and settled against the cushioned bedhead.

'I think George Friar actually loved Henrietta Clements, despite all that she said of him, Gabriel. He repeated over and over that he wanted you to feel the anguish he knew in losing her. He still thought it was you who had killed her despite everything that was decided by the courts. He said you had paid them off.'

'But she threw herself into the fire after lighting it.'

'I told him that, too, but...' She stopped.

'He did not believe it.'

'Friar said her husband had never loved her properly, either. But he didn't kill him. Friar said John Goode had done that himself because of money Randolph Clements had taken, money that was supposed to go to the coffers of France.'

'A hive of iniquity, then, with no one trusting the other?'

'These were the sort of people you stopped, weren't they? The ones who would cause havoc on society out of madness and hate if they were just left? It must have been horrible to be amongst them and to pretend.'

He frowned. 'I did not always have to pretend, Adelaide.'

'I know. Tonight... I could tell you had...done that before.'

'Espionage has the same rules of war. Kill or be killed.' He took her hand, his fingers threading though her own, holding on. 'It was not always easy and it wasn't always right.'

'Can you stop, then...working for the Service, I mean?'

'I almost have. I will send the names to Alan Wolfe tomorrow and they will be rounded up and questioned. There is enough proof of foul play to put them in jail, I think, and that will be the end of it.'

'And then we can live here at Ravenshill and farm and rebuild and...' She stopped and blushed as his eyes looked closely at her face.

'Is this sore?' Her lip was swollen and there was another bruise on her cheek. In the candlelight he could see so much more than he had been able to outside the cottage and his anger against George Friar returned.

'I hope I did not hurt you when...'

She finished the sentence. 'When you made love to me as if I was the only woman left in the world.'

'The only one I love, at least. As you know, I thought you were dead when I saw you in the clearing tied to the tree and I wondered if I could ever live again. It is a rare thing to have your life held in the hand of another and not want it different, I think. To belong to someone, I mean, for ever, and be the happier for it.'

'My old aunts used to say that independence was the key to a good life and for a long time I believed them. Until you. Until you smiled at me and asked me questions at the Bradford ball with your golden eyes and your quick-witted words. You smelt like woodsmoke and leather and I thought I had never had another conversation like it.'

'I should have touched you then and there and felt the magic. I should have taken the chance and grabbed your hand and kissed you and carted you off to Gretna Green. Instead, I watched you dance a waltz with the Earl of Berrick and he held you much too close.'

'Close like this?'

She wrapped her arms about his neck and pulled him down into the nest of duck feathers.

This time she wanted to be the one in control, the one to set the pace and the tone. Her mouth closed over his nipple and she took him hard, like he had taken her against the wall of the abandoned building, unyielding and fierce in the dark.

Biting the skin across the plane of his stomach, she went lower and saw the damage that he had not wanted her to see, the swathe of burned skin across his upper-right thigh and groin.

She knew he waited to see just what she might say for his breath stopped and his fingers clenched the softness of the cotton sheets beneath, the wedding ring he wore catching the candlelight.

With care she traced the ruin with her tongue, along this ridge of damage and then down to the next. Always coming closer to the hard shaft that lay amidst a bush of light-brown hair, only a small burn marking the smoothness.

And then he was inside her, the taste of him salty and masculine, sweet and known. So easy to make him hers, she thought, the rise of him sure and quick now. The power of what he allowed her boiled in her blood, too, a shared joy, a further intimacy that held no words, but only feeling. Then the thickening, as the tempo changed to a reaching, surging ache of trust.

Gabriel. Her angel delivered from Heaven.

'I love you.' Whispered on the edge of tears, her voice quiet with feeling. He had killed a man to protect her and then banished her demons with his own body. Only strength in it and an undeniable honesty, because in the gift he gave her she had lost all fear.

He lifted her upwards and took her mouth into his own, other flavours, further discoveries. Abandoned and open she accepted him in and she writhed with the beauty of it and the truth. She was no longer only herself. He was of her, inside, curling around constant loneliness and ancient shame. There were no rules here, no inhibitions, no places the ache of knowledge could not touch as love accompanied the sensual.

'I love you, Gabriel. Till for ever.'

'Make a child with me, then. Here and now. Let this be the moment of his conception, in this bed with the moon outside and Ravenshill safe. But this time together and in gentleness. This time only with love.'

'Yes.' She felt tears fill her eyes, not of sadness but of joy. She felt his hardness and her own answering push. She felt the starch of cotton beneath them and the cool of the night on their skin. She smelt the wax of a candle and heard the call of an owl, far away in the lines of trees that ran behind the high ground where a house could be rebuilt.

Home. Here. With Gabriel.

And then as he came within her and his fingers found that place that only he could know, she closed her eyes and simply was.

* * * * *

LET'S TALK

Romance

For exclusive extracts, competitions and special offers, find us online:

f MillsandBoon

𝕏 @MillsandBoon

⬚ @MillsandBoonUK

♪ @MillsandBoonUK

Get in touch on 01413 063 232

MILLS & BOON

THE HEART OF ROMANCE

A ROMANCE FOR EVERY READER

MODERN

Prepare to be swept off your feet by sophisticated, sexy and seductive heroes, in some of the world's most glamourous and romantic locations, where power and passion collide.

HISTORICAL

Escape with historical heroes from time gone by. Whether your passion is for wicked Regency Rakes, muscled Vikings or rugged Highlanders, awaken the romance of the past.

MEDICAL

Set your pulse racing with dedicated, delectable doctors in the high-pressure world of medicine, where emotions run high and passion, comfort and love are the best medicine.

True Love

Celebrate true love with tender stories of heartfelt romance, from the rush of falling in love to the joy a new baby can bring, and a focus on the emotional heart of a relationship.

Desire

Indulge in secrets and scandal, intense drama and sizzling hot action with heroes who have it all: wealth, status, good looks…everything but the right woman.

HEROES

The excitement of a gripping thriller, with intense romance at its heart. Resourceful, true-to-life women and strong, fearless men face danger and desire - a killer combination!

To see which titles are coming soon, please visit

millsandboon.co.uk/nextmonth